An Alternative History of Britain

An Alternative History of Britain

The Hundred Years War

Timothy Venning

Pen & Sword
MILITARY

First published in Great Britain in 2013 by
Pen & Sword Military
an imprint of
Pen & Sword Books Ltd
47 Church Street
Barnsley
South Yorkshire
S70 2AS

Copyright © Timothy Venning 2013

ISBN 978-1-78159-126-0

Typeset in 11pt Ehrhardt by
Mac Style, Beverley, E. Yorkshire

Printed and bound in the UK by CPI Group (UK) Ltd, Croydon, CR0 4YY

Pen & Sword Books Ltd incorporates the Imprints of Pen & Sword Aviation,
Pen & Sword Family History, Pen & Sword Maritime, Pen & Sword Military,
Pen & Sword Discovery, Wharncliffe Local History, Wharncliffe True Crime,
Wharncliffe Transport, Pen & Sword Select, Pen & Sword Military Classics,
Leo Cooper, The Praetorian Press, Remember When, Seaforth Publishing
and Frontline Publishing.

For a complete list of Pen & Sword titles please contact
PEN & SWORD BOOKS LIMITED
47 Church Street, Barnsley, South Yorkshire, S70 2AS, England
E-mail: enquiries@pen-and-sword.co.uk
Website: www.pen-and-sword.co.uk

Contents

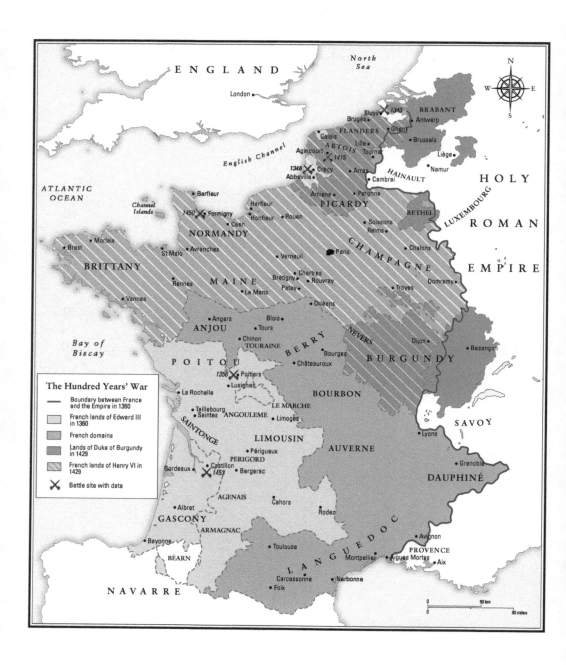

ENGLAND

North
Sea

London

ATLANTIC
OCEAN

Channel
Islands

Bay of
Biscay

Barfleur
Harfleur
Honfleur
Rouen
Caen
NORMANDY
Morlaix
Brest
St Malo
Avranches
BRITTANY
Rennes
MAINE
Vannes
Le Mans

Sluys
1340
BRABANT
Bruges
Antwerp
Calais
FLANDERS
Ghent
Lille
Brussels
Agincourt
ARTOIS
Tournai
1415
Liège
Crécy
Arras
HAINAULT
Namur
1346
Abbeville
Cambrai
HOLY
Amiens
Péronne
PICARDY
ROMAN
RETHEL
LUXEMBOURG
1450
Formigny
Soissons
Reims
Verneuil
Chalons
EMPIRE
Paris
CHAMPAGNE
Chartres
Brétigny
Rouvray
Patay
Troyes
Domremy
Le Mans

Angers
Blois
Tours
ANJOU
Chinon
TOURAINE
BERRY
NEVERS
Dijon
Besançon
Bourges
BURGUNDY
Châteauroux
POITOU
1356
Poitiers
Lusignan
BOURBON
La Rochelle
Taillebourg
LE MARCHE
SAINTONGE
Saintes
ANGOULEME
Limoges
SAVOY
LIMOUSIN
AUVERNE
Lyons
Périgueux
PERIGORD
Castillon
Bordeaux
1453
Bergerac
Grenoble
DAUPHINÉ
AGENAIS
Cahors
Rodez
Albret
GASCONY
ARMAGNAC
Avignon
Bayonne
Toulouse
PROVENCE
Montpellier
Aigues Mortes
Aix
BÉARN
LANGUEDOC
Carcassonne
Narbonne
NAVARRE
Foix

English Channel

The Hundred Years' War

— Boundary between France
   and the Empire in 1360
▢ French lands of Edward III
   in 1360
▢ French domains
▢ Lands of Duke of Burgundy
   in 1429
▢ French lands of Henry VI in
   1429
✕ Battle site with date

N
W E
S

0   50 km
0   50 miles

Introduction

The so-called 'Hundred Years' War' is one of the dimly-remembered stock clichés of nine hundred years of fraught Anglo-French relations. In the popular memory there is a long tradition of mutual antagonism between the nations on either side of the Channel, from the Battle of Hastings in 1066 to Anglo-French disagreement over European centralism. In the case of conflict the British usually win, as shown by Crécy, Agincourt, Trafalgar, and Waterloo – with London place names such as Nelson's Column a constant reminder. In this tabloid-fuelled myth, it seems appropriate that the two kingdoms fought for over a hundred years, from 1337 to 1453 – though in fact this is a myth and there were long truces, in particular in Richard II's and Henry IV's reigns. Even under militant Edward III there were truces in 1350–5 and 1360–9, and the wars (rather than war) were most active in short bursts in the mid-late 1340s and 1350s, the 1370s, and finally in the struggle launched by Henry V from 1415.

One of the underlying reasons for conflict was the English kings' possession of lands in France, the remains in the Duchy of Aquitaine of the so-called 'Angevin empire' of Henry II and Richard I, which was mostly overrun in 1203–4. Under the treaty of 1259 this remained part of France so the English king, as its lord, was his neighbour's vassal like the other holders of French 'feudal' fiefs – as those English kings who had been dukes of Normandy in 1066–1204 were the French king's vassals too. This produced inevitable grounds for tension – how could one king be the loyal vassal of his potential enemy? – and continual grounds for problems, with legal excuses for confiscation in case of a conflict. If Philip Augustus of France had reconquered Aquitaine as well as Normandy or Anjou, or the 1259 treaty between Louis IX and Henry III had made the latter fully sovereign in Aquitaine, would there have been less warfare? In the complex mid-medieval world of a pan-European, French-speaking culture of which the English kings and nobility were part, the post-1066 English kings were, in fact, dukes of Normandy who had gained England by conquest. Their politico-cultural orientation was French. The vagaries of the Norman dynasty's succession had seen England and Normandy pass to the son of Henry I's daughter, Matilda's by Count Geoffrey of Anjou, Henry II – Count of Anjou (and buried in Anjou, at Fontevrault, not in England) and overlord of Brittany. Henry added his wife Eleanor's Aquitaine to this huge melange of polities – and was more powerful in France than its king, his overlord. The so-called 'Plantagenet' dynasty – the name was a personal sobriquet of Count Geoffrey, only revived as a surname by the House of York in the mid-fifteenth century – was as much French as English, and until the mid-fourteenth century rarely spoke English. Abandoning its European role after losing Normandy/Anjou in 1204 to concentrate on conquering the British Isles was never a likely option, with a succession of foreign wives an additional incentive.

The marriage of Edward II to Isabella of France in 1308 and their son Edward III's resultant claim to the French throne after her three brothers died without surviving sons (1316–28) was the seeming reason for the post-1337 English wars in France. But the situation was more complicated than the matter of 'honour' and 'justice' to pursue his legal claim that Edward's propagandists portrayed. For a start, the 'Salic Law' ban on a female inheriting or transmitting a claim to France was not actually stated in 1328, and only appears later in the century – though its being part of the reason for the French courts' choice of heir in 1328 is logical. Edward did not pursue his claim until 'usurper' Philip VI had assisted his enemies in Scotland and seemed to be threatening to encircle him – and both Philip's aid to Scotland and confiscation of Aquitaine followed normal precedent for times of Anglo-French tension (e.g. 1294). Edward was perfectly willing to give up his claim if the price was right – once his demands for a restoration of his ancestors' lands in France had been granted (1360). But – like French legal threats to their English royal 'vassals' in 1154–1337 – it remained a latent political weapon ready for re-use.

If Charles V of France had not been able or willing to obstruct the English king's demands (as Dauphin) in 1358–60 or showed bad faith in implementing them after 1367, would a war have resumed? What if the distinctly war-averse Richard II, who reached a comprehensive Anglo-French settlement in 1396 despite nobles' objections, had not lost the throne to his aggressive and insecure cousins of the House of Lancaster in 1399? Or England had been weakened by his replacement Henry IV's overthrow in 1400, 1403, or 1405? There would have been no Henry V invading France to re-start an attempt to build an English 'empire' in 1415 in these cases.

Arguably, Henry would have done better to concentrate his limited resources on re-occupying and fortifying a defensible redoubt in Normandy than claiming the French crown and over-stretching his army. But would taking the French Crown have ever been practical military politics for this ruthless opportunist but for the – unpre-meditated? – murder of Duke John of Burgundy by the French 'royalists' at Montereau in 1419? This drove his son Philip to throw the huge weight of Burgundian resources onto Henry's side – and when he changed sides again in 1435 the English suffered disaster. If Henry had not died aged 35, could he have conquered France in the 1420s – or at least forced the war into a lengthy stalemate?

Was Joan of Arc's appearance in 1429 epoch-making, or the sort of reverse that the over-stretched English would have received anyway? And once French fortunes revived, could the English have extricated themselves by abandoning all except a defensible Normandy? Was the humiliating cost of accepting military reality unacceptable to English policy-makers, 'bogged down' but too proud to give up? Was the 'unworldly pacifist' (an exaggeration) Henry VI more realistic than his aggressive uncles, or was he undermined by his fiscal incompetence and poor choice of generals? And did Charles VII of France 'double-cross' Henry in the mid-1440s truce by his hard-line doggedness in trying to retake all the English conquests?

Chapter One

Edward III – and Edward 'IV', the 'Black Prince'

Luck or shrewd judgement? Edward III, the 'Black Prince', and the comparative English triumphs of 1338–60. What was 'inevitable' and what was down to chance?

The claim to France: could it have been made in 1328 not 1338? And was the outbreak of conflict Edward's fault or Philip's?

Despite the English victory at Crécy in August 1346 and conquest of Calais in 1347, the practical achievements of the English expeditionary forces by 1355 were limited. Edward III had secured a stunning and unexpected victory against a confident and numerically superior force from the largest state in western Europe in 1346, showing that a new military power had arrived on the scene. The dominance of French knightly chivalry on the battlefield and of the (comparatively) centralized French state in providing finance, men and supplies for war had been 'givens' of the early fourteenth century international power-system, particularly since the reign of the ruthless Philip IV (1285–1314). France, the largest and most efficient state in western Europe and ruled by a line of competent adult male rulers except in 1316, had even secured a compliant papacy based near its territory at Avignon, with a succession of French or French-allied popes from 1309. (King John I had acceded at birth in 1316 and died within days.) England seemed to be a marginal, minor 'power' with the defeat of the unimpressive, luckless Edward II by the Scots in 1314 and his overthrow (by his French wife, Isabella) in 1326–7 adding to its poor reputation.

Despite Edward III's impressive military debut in the 1330s against Scotland, his claim to the throne of France was not expected to succeed against the incumbent Philip VI (1328–50). Not least was the reason that France was over twice the size of England and as of 1328 the English kings only held the central core of Aquitaine, the province of Guienne surrounding Bordeaux – as a French royal vassal – plus minor and indefensible Ponthieu in Artois. The population of the French king's dominions was around twenty million and of Edward III's around five million, and if fully used the French king's potential army could be up to 60,000 men strong. (The 'general call-up' in France, the '*arrière-ban*', was, however, not applicable to all provinces and some important ones were exempt; in practice its alternative of paying a fine rather than fighting was often resorted to and the money used to hire mercenaries.) Nor were the French nobility or populace likely to look with favour on a foreign contender for their throne, as we can already discern a degree of basic 'national' rivalry between the English and the French in this period even though the English elite was French in its culture as it had been since 1066. Edward III spoke French as his primary language, as had his royal ancestors, although he seems to have been able to speak English too; French was the international language of 'high culture' and chivalry. (The first primarily English-speaking king of England was either Edward or his grandson, Richard II – ironically born in France.)

The choice of Count Philip of Valois, the late King Charles IV's cousin and nearest male heir, as the new king of France after Charles died on 1 February 1328 was not universally accepted. (The decision had to wait until it was clear that Charles' pregnant widow would not give birth to a son.) There were nearer heirs in the female line, from Charles' sister and his brother Louis X's daughter, and it was arguable if the legal/customary ban on female inheritance, the so-called 'Salic Law', applied to transmitting a claim via a woman to a male. If it did not, either Charles' sister Isabella's son Edward III of England or his late brother Louis X's daughter Jeanne, Queen of Navarre's heirs were eligible. Edward was closest to Charles IV by blood, but Jeanne's family – from 1332 her son Charles 'the Bad' – were genealogically senior; Jeanne's line had been passed over when Louis X and his infant son John I died in 1316. Edward duly made a claim on France, though not at the time of the succession-dispute in 1328 as then he was only fifteen and the insecure regency government of his mother and her paramour Roger Mortimer had other priorities. In that context, the 'Hundred Years' War' could have broken out in 1328 not 1338 if it had not been for the English rebellion in 1326 when Edward and his mother, Isabella, invaded to depose his father, Edward II; due to this England was not in a state to pursue the claim to France in 1328.

The dynamic and warlike Isabella, the so-called 'She-Wolf of France', has received a very bad press from her own time to the present, partly through conventional observers' indignation that a queen could flout normal 'mores' by flagrantly invading England with her lover to depose her husband (and led troops in person) and partly from the belief that she was behind her husband's subsequent murder. (One theory, championed recently by Ian Mortimer, claims that Edward II was not murdered but was allowed to flee to the Continent in disguise.[1]) Whether she was a murderess or not, the point is that Isabella was quite capable of organizing and even leading an army to secure her son's claim to France in 1328 if she had not been otherwise preoccupied, heading a shaky regency with her unpopular and ruthless paramour, Roger Mortimer. If her marriage had not broken down (due to her husband's involvement with the Despenser family and possibly his homosexuality) England might have attacked France in the late 1320s, provided that the exhausting and humiliating loss of the Scottish 'War of Independence' was successfully negotiated first. The power-crazed and acquisitive Despensers were unlikely to have encouraged a war had they still been in power in the late 1320s as Edward II's chief advisers, given that if either Isabella or a royal kinsman (Earl Henry of Lancaster? Earl Edmund of Kent?) led an English army to success they could then turn it on the Despenser regime. Similarly, Edward II was not enthusiastic about waging war in person, and had had a humiliating experience at Bannockburn in 1314 – although he was prepared to fight hard 'in extremis' for his own preservation, as he did in confronting Earl Thomas of Lancaster in 1322. But an English government that had avoided the polarization of high politics in 1322–6 might have risked a French venture, at least if there was a threat to their possession of Guienne, which was possible from an over-confident new French king hostile to Isabella such as Philip VI. The centralizing French Crown had tried to confiscate Guienne before (1294) and the fact that as of 1259 the English King was the former's vassal was a problem easy to exploit.

Edward III's formal claim (in 1338) only occurred once Philip VI had repeatedly shown his ill-will towards his rival, who he seems to have consistently under-valued. The young and highly energetic English King was the type of ruler to seek to revive his grandfather Edward I's successes against France as a 'morale-booster' for the monarchy's reputation after the loss of Scotland, but as of 1333–8 he was already engaged in war in the latter country so he was not free to look for a target. The death of the ailing Robert Bruce in 1329 left his 5-year-old son David II as king and left the Scots without an adult ruler, and so Edward sought to restore the enforced vassalage of Scotland, which he had had to abandon in the Anglo-Scottish treaty of 1328, by installing a vassal-king to replace David.

The physical reconquest of Scotland as an integral part of England was impossible so that part of Edward I's international strategy had to be abandoned; instead Edward III reverted to his grandfather's strategic plan of 1292–6 by restoring the Balliol dynasty, under Edward Balliol, as his vassals. The King did not, however, act rashly; a private expedition by a party of pro-Balliol barons expelled from Scotland by the Bruces, the 'Disinherited', to restore Edward Balliol and regain their 'just rights' in 1332–3 saw surprising success with a victory over the Bruces' army at Dupplin Moor and the capture of Perth. This initial success showed that the Scots army was less dangerous than it had been under Robert Bruce – his nephew the Earl of Moray and his lieutenant, Sir James Douglas, had both died recently – and so Edward could intervene himself safely in 1333 to aid the 'Disinherited' against a Bruce fight-back. This led to a major victory at Halidon Hill near Berwick, the conquest of most of the Lowlands, and the flight of David II to France, but the Balliol regime soon met serious resistance and throughout the mid-1330s Edward III was undertaking regular expeditions to Scotland to back them up. It was then that Philip VI of France not only gave David sanctuary but sent troops to aid him (1335) and allowed damaging raids by French warships on southern English ports, principally Portsmouth (the usual embarkation-point for English expeditions to France).

Even if assisting David II was in the French strategic tradition of trying to weaken England by propping up its northern enemy, the so-called 'Auld Alliance', Philip had less excuse for claiming that Edward's ceremony of homage to him for Guienne in 1331 had been defective and was thus legally invalid.[2] The implication of that was that he could confiscate the duchy whenever he wished. Philip also required Edward to surrender the refugee French dissident noble Robert d'Artois, and specifically declared in 1336 that any peace was impossible so long as he was in England[3] – the sort of minor issue that could be overlooked with goodwill. Thus, although David II's refusal to abdicate his claim to Scotland for Edward Bruce's lifetime then succeed him stymied the 1335–6 papal attempts to solve the Scots crisis,[4] Philip, not Edward, was the main obstacle to a settlement. The papacy, keen for Edward and Philip to use their armies for a crusade in Asia Minor instead to back up the 1334 naval attack on Smyrna, was endeavouring to sort out the Anglo-French tension throughout this period and had he been willing Philip (a man with pretensions as an international crusading leader and with dynastic interests in the Byzantine Empire) could have diverted his energies to the Crusade as a devoted son of the Church. There was no 'foolhardy' and 'unrealistic' attempt by a young and inexperienced English king to conquer a kingdom with vastly superior resources; rather, Edward was driven to respond to repeated French provocations in 1331–7.

This culminated with Philip's announcement of the confiscation of Guienne and the title of Duke of Aquitaine in May 1337.[5] Did the insecure new ruler, Philip, feel he ought to emulate his renowned great-uncle Philip IV's confiscation of 1294 and miscalculate the reaction? Notably Edward and his senior noble commanders gained useful military experience in Scotland – giving him confidence to tackle Philip? – and he pursued similar tactics there to his later ones in France, leaving time-consuming sieges alone for 'razzia' marches.

Personalizing the issue of Anglo-French conflict, contemporary literature claimed that Count Robert of Artois (who had opposed Philip's claim in 1328) provoked Edward to swear to invade France and seize his 'rights' at a banquet (the 'Vow of the Heron') by taunting him over his cowardice.[6] This is far too simplistic, though it probably suited Edward for it to be thought that he was a chivalrous hero-king like King Arthur who undertook solemn vows at ceremonial occasions and was too honourable to back down. The formal English claim was as much a diplomatic weapon as an idealistic, non-negotiable decision to claim Edward's legal inheritance. By making himself the rightful king of France he enabled potential French or French-allied defectors, such as the leadership of Flanders and Brabant, to 'save face' by transferring their allegiance from one ('usurper') king of France to his rival rather than breaching their oaths of loyalty. At the time of his claim, he was doing his best – in person – to rally the rulers of the Low Countries and northern Germany to his cause, aided by the fact that his wife, Philippa, was sister of local Count William of Hainault (who inopportunely died). Given the size and resources of France compared with England, Edward – like all predecessors waging war on France from the time of Richard I – needed a coalition of European allies to even the odds, provide men and money, and attack France on a second front. This was bound to rely on Flanders, an autonomist county restive under French control since the crushing of past revolts, and the 'Holy Roman' emperor of the German kingdoms and principalities. Given the pro-French stance of Count Louis of Flanders (to be killed at Crécy in 1346), any English attempt to secure money and troops from the region was likely to be resisted by him and to draw in King Philip too. In financial terms, important Flemish towns such as Ghent, Antwerp, and Bruges were vital sources of loans for the impecunious Edward who visited them in person with his entourage. In military terms, the Flemish ports were also a potential source of invasion-threat to England – a major factor as late as 1940. Hence Edward's initial concentration on securing reliable allies in Flanders and his expedition there in 1339–40, leading to his first crushing victory over the French (at sea, the battle of Sluys). In Germany, Edward made a prestigious and munificent pilgrimage to the shrine of the 'Three Kings' (the 'Magi') at Cologne and secured a grant of the title of 'Vicar of the Holy Roman Empire' from the Emperor, Lewis of Bavaria;[7] this obliged Lewis' vassals to support him in war as their sovereign's trusted lieutenant.

The most that can be said about Edward's 'aggression' in claiming France in 1337–8 is that he 'jumped the gun' by naming himself king of France in documents while papal mediators were still trying to arrange peace;[8] but chances of the latter were minimal given Philip's equally provocative confiscation of Aquitaine.

Under the show of being an honourable paragon of chivalry keen on his just rights, Edward was to be prepared to abandon his claim if the alternative offers were substantial enough. Indeed, when he first made the claim verbally in 1337 he postponed making a public statement of it by issuing letters patent or a heraldic coat of arms containing the title – allegedly to satisfy appeals by the alarmed Pope. The formal claim, in writing and a heraldic 'device', was only made in 1340 – from Flanders on French territory, and thus probably at the request of the local lords to secure their support for him as their rightful king. It was to be retracted in 1360, and modern historians are more convinced than earlier interpreters that for all Edward's bold claims about it being a matter of 'honour' to pursue it to victory he was quite prepared to reconsider it as practical politics and was less naïve than appears. By making such a show of his devotion to the claim he put up the price for surrendering. Arguably, practical politics rather than points of law or honour were also involved in the French courts' rejection of Edward's claims – the 'Salic Law' ban was not cited by them in 1328 and they could hardly deny powerful local candidate Philip's claims on behalf of a foreigner. Did Edward in reality understand this, but use it as a weapon after Philip aided Scotland?[9]

The first war: from 1338 to 1350

Conquering France – or even recovering the English kings' ancestral domains of Normandy, Maine, Anjou and Aquitaine – would not be easy or a short process, not least due to the number of walled towns to take and the limited effectiveness of (primitive) artillery. Maine and Anjou, moreover, were the personal fiefs of the House of Valois, which now held the French throne so giving them up would seem a mark of ignominy for Philip VI. There was also the minor but psychologically important problem of which kingdom was to be named first in documents – as king of both England and France, Edward would insult his English countrymen if he named France first but it was the larger and more prestigious of the two kingdoms. In the end he named England first on documents intended for an English administrative use and audience, and France first on those to be sent to the Continent. (He could not dodge the issue this way in his official heraldic arms and thus put the French royal arms in the more important, upper left-hand 'quarter' of the 'device'.[10]) The size of France and easy defensibility of walled towns presented a more serious problem.

Current 'bombards' – primitive cannons – could fire stones at city walls at a slow rate and produce breaches for attackers to use, but were not yet decisive and were cumbersome to cart around; their first decisive role in a siege was over a century ahead (arguably at Constantinople in 1453). The English king could not afford to take a great number of them with his army anyway, and most sieges had to rely on starving out the defenders or disaffection within the walls. Concentrated work on undermining the walls by sappers and mounting a quick attack was, however, possible, but only on special occasions when a major force was present and speed was the priority. It was also difficult if a town was surrounded by marshes; mining was impossible, and siege-towers would sink in the mud – as at Calais in 1346–7. The English tactic of avoiding slow, piecemeal sieges but staging impressive marches across large areas of country had already been seen in Scotland, where Edward had marched right up the north-east coast in 1336 rather than concentrating on securing all the castles to his rear first.[11] As later in France, this and calculated devastation was intended to terrify local nobles into submission but at most secured ephemeral success in terms of areas controlled.

Arguably, Edward was more of a gambler than Edward I in avoiding long sieges – though he also kept his nerve during setbacks. The financial 'crash' of the Florentine banking-houses of Bardi and Peruzzi, who were funding his war with huge loans, in 1343 failed to curtail his expensive invasion-plans – though it now appears that he did not owe nearly as much as the Italian chronicler Villani alleged (£13,000 not £225,000?) nor bring the banks down by refusing to pay his debts.

There is also the question of the 1341–5 civil war over the Breton succession to consider. This led to a 'proxy war' between France and England on behalf of their rival claimants, the late Duke John's niece Jeanne (and her husband Charles of Blois, Philip's nephew) and his half-brother John of Montfort. Ironically, in declaring a female able to inherit Brittany the Paris *'parlement'* contradicted the 'Salic Law' 'ban' that Philip used to justify his inheritance of France – though technically Breton, not French law was cited. Jeanne and Charles' loyalty to Philip was what counted in Paris, and Montfort was believed to be about to transfer his fealty to Edward. Granting him Brittany could lead to him opening its ports to an English invasion-fleet en route to Guienne or Normandy. Philip tried to arrest him, so he fled and called on Edward to back his claim; the English duly invaded Brittany. This gave Edward and his captains, e.g. the Earl of Salisbury and Sir Walter Manny, invaluable experience of fighting the French on French soil – perhaps making victory in Normandy in 1346 easier. Without this war, would the current Anglo-French truce of Esplechin have held for longer? But Philip was unlikely to have allowed the potential defector Montfort to take over Brittany. If Duke John had not died in 1341, however, this would have postponed the clash, and denied Edward a 'rehearsal' for his Norman war.

It has been argued that Edward initiated a 'military revolution' in England, both in his systematic and well-organized provision of a suitably-sized, trained, and equipped army (from 'captains' commissioned to raise a fixed contingent) and in his adaptation of the tactic of archery to inflict devastating showers of arrows on his opponents in a concentrated barrage.[12] This, as seen at Halidon Hill against the Scots in 1333, would destroy a packed mass of infantry or cavalry provided that they did not have the chance to overrun the archers first. The new English tactics relied on a barrage of missiles to destroy a numerically superior force, not mere weight of numbers on foot or horseback – a contest that the English were unlikely to win against any major French army. The army that he led to Normandy in 1346 was substantially smaller than the overall French army, and met its king's 'active' troops in the field outnumbered by around three to one – the English army had around 13–14,000 men, with the French (over 30,000) relying heavily on 6–7000 Genoese mercenaries. The southern army of the French king, under his son Duke John of Normandy (later King John II), was luckily absent attacking Aiguillon in Aquitaine and did not arrive in time; it was intended to hurry north and trap Edward south of the Seine but he slipped across the river at Poissy and headed north to Ponthieu, chased by Philip's army. Philip again lost the chance of trapping Edward as the English forded the Somme unexpectedly, but eventually caught him up at Crécy. Edward was able to inflict a devastating defeat on the French at Crécy with disproportionate losses – the French casualties included eleven princes (led by the King of Bohemia, Duke of Lorraine, and Counts of Alençon and Flanders), one archbishop, eight senior lords, and eighty bannerets, plus 1,542 knights and esquires in the area by the English 'front line' alone. The French 'secret weapon', the Genoese crossbowmen, could not fire as fast as the English longbowmen and were massacred in a hail of arrows, which cut through their protective clothing. Unable to attack from several sides at once due to the terrain, the French had to resort to a frontal charge and 'push and shove' tactics, and were (just) held to a standstill and slowly driven back.[13]

The English army was clearly more 'professional' and better-led as well as a more coherent and experienced body; the French relied on a mixture of contingents from their allies, larger in number but unused to fighting together and reliant on one basic tactic of charging the opposition and riding it down or hacking their way through. The French tactic might have worked at Crécy, had the disciplined English not stood firm and the nature of the site prevented the larger French army from attacking from several sides at once. The Prince of Wales, in his first battle, was hard-pressed and was knocked off his feet in the melee, a sign of how dangerous the French 'push' forward was – hence the famous exchange when his father, Edward III, was asked if he should send in the reserves to rescue his son and he replied 'Let the boy win his spurs'. In the event, the French were halted and ground down by superior fighting power, and the brave but futile charge and death of the blind King John of Bohemia, Philip VI's close ally, seemed to sum up the French attitude to war.[14]

With the French army forced to pull back in disarray, the English were able to go on and besiege Calais unhindered, starving it out and commencing a 210-year occupation. Notably, Edward chose not to head for Paris despite the road lying open. The impressive walled city of around 100,000 inhabitants was very unlikely to surrender and it was too far up the River Seine for an easy siege due to the long supply route to the river mouth. Philip failed to use his army to relieve Calais during the winter of 1346–7, though he did arrive in the vicinity and rescue or a battle was expected in the town, possibly due to fear of another battle like at Crécy. French naval relief-efforts were defeated, and the garrison eventually had to surrender; the well-publicised (and exaggerated for show?) fury of the King at the stubborn defence hints that he realized he could have had to give up the blockade.[15]

The outbreak of the 'Black Death', destroying the manpower of both sides and making the war a lower priority, then aided the successful arguments for a truce, although 'proxy' fighting over the Duchy of Brittany continued.[16] The rout of the French's Castilian allies at sea off Winchelsea in August 1350, though less decisive than as played up by English propaganda, helped to prevent the Castilians from using their potent fleet to disrupt English links to Guienne or even a Castilian invasion of that province.

The Castilian naval 'carracks' were larger than English ships, and thus could either ram them successfully in close combat or fire missiles down onto the decks; their intervention was to be feared and was a disaster for England after 1370. Indeed, in the battle off Winchelsea Edward's own flagship was rammed and nearly sank, which it would have done had its damaged side not been jammed against that of its attacker; Edward and his men had to leap aboard the Castilian ship and take it for their own safety. The King came close to drowning, and was – as usual – lucky in battle.[17] But the possibility of a Franco-Castilian alliance in 1350 was a result of two unexpected setbacks for Edward and could not have been anticipated – first his daughter Joan, en route to marry King Alfonso XI of Castile and secure an alliance, died of the 'Black Death' and then Alfonso died of it too, at the siege of Gibraltar.

Had events gone according to plan England and Castile would have been allies through the 1350s – and possibly Alfonso, born in 1310, would have been securely still on the throne in 1366–7 when in real life England had to intervene in Castile and so waste time and resources there. In the long run, did the crucial deaths of Joan and Alfonso undermine the English war-effort sixteen years later?

The war in France, stage two: from 1355. How the war was nearly avoided

The so-called 'Hundred Years War' fully resumed in 1355 at the end of the agreed truce, but this was far from inevitable; indeed, the peace-negotiations of 1354-5 seemed likely to be successful. The terms agreed by Edward's and John II's secret negotiators at Guisnes early in 1354 anticipated the settlement of 1360, in that Edward was to receive an enlarged Aquitaine (including the Limousin and Poitou) and parts of the lower Loire basin but not Normandy. Also, Edward made no quibble at this point over renouncing his claim on the French throne.[18] The sudden French willingness for a deal was probably due to the domestic security problem raised by Charles of Navarre, who (with his equally unsavoury brother Philip) had murdered the 'Constable' of France in a private dispute early in 1354 and then sought English aid for his subsequent rebellion. Edward sent Duke Henry of Lancaster to arrange an alliance, with Charles' need for his aid meaning that he could insist that the latter should accept his rival, Edward, as king of France; they would divide up the country between them. Had this worked Edward would have had a substantial 'native' French faction backing him out of mutual hatred of the 'usurper' Valois King of France, anticipating the English-Burgundian alliance of 1420–35. He might even have gained Paris, though Duke Charles was less likely than the early fifteenth century Dukes of Burgundy to accept a bloc of English territory in France, including Normandy (where he had lands himself). Unfortunately, Charles received a better offer, with full pardon, from King John and blandly switched back to his side, humiliating 'middle-man' Lancaster.[19] But the threat of revolt from Charles continued to worry King John, and the result was the Anglo-French secret talks and tentative agreement at Guisnes. The papacy, hoping to end the war and enrol the two kings for a Crusade against the Ottoman Turks (who entered Europe at Gallipoli in 1354), organized 'follow-up' talks at Avignon at Christmas 1354, but it became clear that the French were not serious and John had had second thoughts. Lancaster's embassy left Avignon, and the preparations for war resumed – but it is clear that it was John, who had regained confidence in his military power, not Edward who was at fault.[20] As in 1335, Edward was not the principal culprit in the collapse of peace-talks.

The resumed war in 1355 seemed to be headed for the 'long haul' for the English, with the assumption that Edward's proposals at Guisnes represented his basic aims with Normandy less vital than Aquitaine. Whether Edward seriously hoped to secure recognition of his rights to the kingdom of France or just to use this as a 'bargaining chip' to gain a vastly larger share of Aquitaine (and/or Normandy) by treaty, his practical gains so far were small. Military victories were impressive psychologically and gained him a reputation and possibly more international allies, but they did not substitute for territory. If the main French army evaded battle and relied on their walled towns to hold him up, his expeditions were reduced to impressive and unchallenged marches across wide areas of country, which he could burn, loot and demoralize but not achieve anything tangible – as seen by Edward's expedition to Paris in 1359–60 and his sons' 'razzias' across central France in 1355 and 1356 (the Prince of Wales) and 1373 (John of Gaunt). They were backed up by increasing numbers of '*chevauchées*' led by lesser captains, starting with the Duke of Lancaster and then turning to practically independent 'free companies' led by men such as Sir Robert Knollys. These involved deliberate application of terror and destruction or seizure of valuable French resources by burning, pillaging, and assorted atrocities, and soon spiralled into burgeoning 'free enterprise' brigandage out of control of the King of England. These campaigns served to demoralize the French government by destroying its property and food-supplies, thus reducing the amount of men and supplies available to the French armies and the amount of money that the King could raise in taxes to pay his troops. They showed that the King could not defend his people, a substantial point in an era of chivalric values – but the attackers often achieved little either and lost men to disease, exhaustion and ambushes en route.

This post-1355 tactic of 'hit-and-run' raiding and psychological demoralization by terror was in contrast to the systematic conquest of Normandy, town by town, which Henry V was to launch in 1417 when he, like Edward III, had defeated the French army in the field (Crécy/Agincourt) and taken a major port to use as a base for invasion (Calais/Harfleur). Edward chose not to return to Normandy and overrun its remaining towns, a time-consuming and costly business, but to keep his armies mobile and secure conquests by forced concession from the French government – probably arising from another major military victory. But in any case he had very limited support from local French nobles, e.g. Sir Godfrey de Harcourt, so mass-desertions were unlikely – though to encourage this factor he deliberately refrained from plundering the land around towns that he hoped would surrender of their own free will, such as Rheims in 1359.[21]

A war of sieges was a slow business – and Edward's main gain of 1346 in Normandy, Caen, was due to luck as his men were able to follow retreating troops from the garrison into the town and prevent them from shutting the gates.[22] It is also probable that the 'showy' and restless Edward, who had a taste for display and great 'set-pieces' such as his numerous chivalric feasts and the pardoning of the 'Six Burghers of Calais', did not have the patience for many long sieges that Henry V did. His alleged impulsiveness may have been exaggerated, but he was significantly willing to risk his life in unnecessary personal combat as when in 1350 he joined his knights to intercept a party of French warriors sneaking into Calais for a hand-to-hand encounter.[23]

This piece of vainglorious risk, like the King indulging in personal combat on a Castilian ship off Winchelsea as his flagship was rammed, was in the tradition of kingly 'knight-errantry' by Edward's ideal, King Arthur as interpreted by twelfth and thirteenth century writers. It helped to 'bond' him with his nobles and win the admiration of his men – like Caesar and Alexander, he 'fought in the front rank'. But there was always a personal risk in such actions. Like Henry V, he was quite capable of using terror and atrocities as a political weapon and clearly understood psychological warfare – the whole tactic of '*chevauchées*' was based on this. But although his blackmail of the French elite into surrendering by destroying their financial-military resources and humiliating their sovereign was not enough to gain him the throne in 1359–60, it succeeded in securing a generous offer of all Aquitaine and Poitou without him having to spend time, money, and troops in garrisons in Normandy as Henry did after 1417. To that extent it worked – and unlike Henry he made a point of being seen to be merciful, with his carefully-staged rage at the 'Burghers of Calais' being ameliorated by an appeal from his wife. A proper king was supposed to be wrathful to his enemies but also open to generosity, and to know when to be chivalrous to his opponents. In this respect, Edward understood 'man-management' far better than his father, Edward II, and grandson Richard II, who both resorted to executions and secret murders of opponents – and lost their thrones as their elites turned on them. As of April 1356 it was John II who seemed to be a rash and untrustworthy ruler alienating his elite, with his sudden personal arrest of Charles of Navarre and some of the latter's aides at Rouen Castle and execution of the latter without trial for the murder of the 'Constable of France'. There was an obscure plot involving Navarre to put John's son Dauphin Charles on the throne at Christmas 1355 – a 'first' for the dynasty, which argues for considerable noble discontent. If it had succeeded, would the English have faced a French army in 1356 backed by Navarre but boycotted by John' s loyalists?

The new war saw the Prince of Wales' despatch to Aquitaine in 1355 and his deliberately provocative 'razzia' into central-western France in summer 1356, which was to lead to King John II leading a major army to intercept him. In the event, the clash was a second overwhelming victory for the English; the overwhelming French numbers[24] served to disadvantage them, and John and many of his nobles were captured. The battle of Poitiers on 19 September 1356 served to secure the 'Black Prince's heroic reputation, show that the English now seemed to be invincible, and shatter the morale of the humiliated French elite. King John, never an impressive leader or a shrewd statesman, was removed from the French command as he was deported to captivity in England. The 'regency' government of his eldest son, Charles, was put under severe pressure to which social unrest added, and virtual anarchy in Paris and across France followed in 1357–8. The disorganized peasant 'Jacquerie' with its overtones of 'class war' against oppressive landlords was supplemented by the seizure of Paris by a faction of 'reformist' citizens led by Étienne Marcel, reducing the Dauphin to a cipher until he could regain control. The breakdown in French government and military paralysis seemed to justify the English tactics and present the current French government as disastrous, and in 1359–60 Edward could march across France to the gates of Rheims and Paris. When the cities failed to fall he opened the negotiations that were to secure him most of Aquitaine at the Treaty of Bretigny. This advantageous English position would have been impossible but for the crushing triumph at Poitiers, which started the unravelling of the French government.

But it should be remembered that this 'narrative' can be put forward as a result of the English winning at Poitiers, and that was by no means a foregone conclusion. As of 18 September 1356 the 'Black Prince's' expedition, moving back from its point of furthest penetration into French territory towards Angoulême and then Bordeaux, had been unexpectedly intercepted by a larger French army, which their scouts had not expected to find.[25] Indeed, he had been intending his march north-east from Guienne to Anjou (another ancestral English dominion) in early September to lead to a rendezvous with the other English expedition under his cousin Duke Henry of Lancaster, operating southwards from Normandy. Instead, the waiting French forces at Tours avoided battle (which could have led to defeat and the fall of that city with its crucial Loire bridge) and stayed inside the city until King John approached with a large army down the Loire from Orléans to rescue them. The 'Black Prince' had to move back south to avoid being trapped, abandoning the main purpose of his campaign, and even then John's army managed to intercept him – hardly a triumphant campaign that had gone according to plan. Instead of having Lancaster's army to support him as planned, he was seriously outnumbered when John cut across his line of retreat.[26] The startled Prince was willing to open talks for a truce, as suggested by the would-be mediating Cardinal of Perigord, although this enabled more French troops to arrive overnight on the 18th–19th to reinforce their King.[27] When he moved off on the 19th, it appears that he was not determined on battle and merely had this as an option if the circumstances proved hopeful; if possible the English would evade the French, or only clash briefly in passing, and would march on towards safety.[28] In the event, the confident French precipitated a battle. Moreover, the initial French plan, showing full awareness of the English use of archers to destroy their ranks, was to use their limited cavalry force to ride down the archers and so destroy the English 'secret weapon'. Instead, the two French cavalry commanders – the Count of Clermont and Marshal D'Andrehem – ignored orders and succumbed to temptation to ride at the English vanguard and rearguard respectively as they found the English army on the march. The English vanguard, under the Earl of Warwick, was unable to use its archers to shoot down the French horses as the latter were well-protected from in front, but another contingent of archers across the river were able to shoot the horses from behind. In the case of the Earl of Salisbury's rearguard, the French under Clermont 'bunched up' to ride through a gap in a hedge and a body of English archers within range used this chance to pick them off; Clermont was killed.

The French cavalry were thus nullified, and the first 'wave' of French dismounted knights – who were supposed to charge the main body of the English once the archers had been dealt with – moved forward to the attack without waiting to find out what had happened. This grouping, led by the King's heir, the Dauphin Charles, was probably about the same size as the waiting English, and was certainly not large enough to overwhelm them. Joined by Warwick's men and protected by a network of barricades, the English held the attackers back, and once the latter retreated exhausted the Dauphin was escorted out of the 'danger zone' to keep him safe (which would have looked like retreat to watching French troops).

The second 'wave', led by the Duke of Orléans, failed to move forward as planned when it could have posed a serious threat to the exhausted English, who instead had time to rest and collect spent arrows for re-use. The Prince sent one of his best commanders, the Captal de Buch, and a small cavalry force to sweep round the French army and appear to its rear, thus causing fear of encirclement though at first some of the English thought he was abandoning the battle – which could have caused them to flee instead. Then the Prince ordered a general advance towards the French royal banner, the 'Oriflamme', to the blast of trumpets; these unexpected moves left the French on the defensive. Still outnumbering the English but not acting coherently or showing any initiative, they appear to have been driven downhill off their current position by Noailles wood towards the river and systematically broken up. The English military elite concentrated on smashing in the French King's bodyguard, and the latter struggle ended with King John and his son Philip held prisoner. According to the English, 2,446 French men-at-arms were killed; around 80 senior nobles were killed including the 'Constable' and 'Marshal' of France (the two senior military figures) and Geoffrey de Charny, owner of the 'Shroud of Turin'. Some 1,974 captives were taken including one king, three royal dukes, thirteen counts, five viscounts and twenty-one bannerets. [29]

The victory was total – but, as seen above, it owed a great deal to French miscalculation and poor command and until the actual battle it had been the English who had had the worse results from the 1356 campaign. On those occasions when the French royal army prudently avoided battle, as John did when Edward III marched into Artois from Calais in autumn 1355, the English could burn and loot but achieved nothing practical. As a result of the greatly improved English position after Poitiers, the subsequent peace-talks of spring-summer 1357 included an offer by the papal mediators for full restoration of all Edward III's ancestors' lands – that is, Normandy, Anjou, Maine, and all Aquitaine.[30] Perhaps surprisingly, he still insisted that the formal negotiations should discuss his claim to the French throne instead of taking this chance to secure vast territories with many walled towns and cities that he could hardly take by storm. He may have reckoned that the shaky government of the Dauphin's in Paris were not yet sincere and were stalling for time, but accepting the proposal would put the onus on them and earn them papal disapproval if they failed to deliver. As it was, the interim terms agreed in May 1358 – leaving the issue of the French Crown for later – required the French to pay a ransom of four million florins for King John, with 600,000 florins to be paid before his release, plus restoration of all Aquitaine and Ponthieu.[31] The Dauphin's government then failed to hand over the first instalment on time, and rejected King John's desperate agreement in the 'Second Treaty of London' to hand over Normandy and the overlordship of Brittany as well – which would have given the English control of all the French coast from Calais to Bayonne and ended French naval raids on the English coast.[32] Possibly John realized that his ruined country might well not be able to pay the ransom money and he hoped to fend Edward off with enough lands to persuade him to overlook this – in which case John was too confident of the Dauphin's acquiescence. The surrender of Normandy was not that disastrous for France at the time, given that it was a stronghold of their King's rival Charles of Navarre (as Count of Evreux) and was riven by civil war between the two factions – but the Dauphin and his Estates-General were clearly confident of holding on to it somehow. Given the recent turmoil in Paris itself in 1358 and the possibility of more, their ability to hold their nerve in spring 1359 and not agree to any terms King John suggested was surprising. This precipitated renewed war, and may indicate that Edward was correct to distrust that the French 'regency' in Paris would obey their King's wishes and capitulate – thus his refusal to surrender his claims yet was logical.

But when he marched on Rheims in 1359 – to force the issue of his claim by securing the site of French royal coronations and having himself crowned – he was unable to take the city, which held out against his blockade.[33] He had to move on to ravage the 'Isle de France' and Burgundy to obtain supplies, attack Paris to try to secure the capital and/or force the Dauphin out of the city to fight (neither occurred), and was eventually forced to reopen negotiations. In the resultant Treaty of Bretigny, he had to waive his demand for the French Crown – which he could have done at far less cost in 1358 – in return for all Aquitaine and Ponthieu. He also failed to secure Normandy or Anjou/Maine either, and reduced King John's ransom from four to three million florins.[34] The settlement was thus poorer than he would have achieved in 1358–9 had the Dauphin and Estates-General backed up their King's proposals. Edward's failure to secure either the French Crown (by a '*coup de main*') with Rheims or force the French capital to surrender in winter 1359/spring 1360 was partly due to factors beyond his control; at the siege of Paris a freak hailstorm ravaged his camp,[35] a circumstance that he could not have anticipated. But it must be asked if he seriously thought that his army could secure victory in this campaign, at least by inducing mass-desertion by the leading citizens of Rheims and Paris to save themselves from starvation or (less likely) the sack of their cities. Or did he expect his physical presence in the region at the head of an army to lead to mass-defections by the war-weary French nobility? The indications are that he was over-confident, especially that Jean de Craon, Archbishop of Rheims and a distant relative, would lead his city to abandon the French royal cause during the blockade of Rheims.[36] Possibly he was unable to accept that 'nationalist' resentment of himself as an Englishman would be a potent factor in keeping up resistance, or that the lengthening list of English atrocities would stiffen resistance not induce 'sensible' surrender.

The successful defensive stance of the city authorities at both Rheims and Paris was critical to Edward's failure, and for this the Dauphin must take principal credit; his determination to resist the English was vital both in 1358–60 and again when he resumed the war in 1369–70.[37] Had the Dauphin been captured at Poitiers with his father and brothers in September 1356, France would have been left leaderless and the administration would have been likely to fall to a military coup by the royal family's would-be supplanter, Charles 'the Bad', King of Navarre. This direct descendant of Philip IV in the female line had been barred from the throne by current French legal interpretation of the 'Salic Law' in 1328, as Edward had been, but was eager to seize it and in 1356–60 did his best to use his lands in Normandy as a base for overthrowing the Dauphinist regime. Had the Dauphin been captured at Poitiers, would he have seized Paris? Or could he have secured Paris by his shaky alliance with the 'Marcel' faction's regime in 1358, and used his leadership of a large faction of the northern French nobility against the insurgent 'Jacquerie' to achieve military victory against the Dauphin? The latter, fleeing the Paris insurgents to Meaux, was able to rebuild his forces and later regain the capital – but what if Charles or the Marcel faction had managed to capture him instead? Charles' weak claim to the throne would have meant that even if he was in control of Paris and claiming to be king of France he would have had to negotiate a more one-sided treaty with Edward, probably giving him all of Normandy, Maine, and Anjou – or possibly only the latter two if he (a local landholder) was strong enough to hold onto Normandy himself. But he was unlikely to have been willing to give up his own claim to France on Edward's behalf in 1359–60, unless indignant loyalists of the captive French King and royal dukes seized Paris from him and he needed Edward's support to regain the capital.

The years after 1360: an unexpected successor to England. The effects of the decline and early death of the 'Black Prince' long-term on Richard II

The psychological investigation of figures from past centuries is a problematic venture, not least due to the nature of the evidence. Richard's deposition in 1399 left him, like Edward II, with no sympathetic contemporary chroniclers. But there was probably some connection between his (over?-)dependence on figures such as de Vere in the mid-1380s and the early death of his father, Prince Edward (known to John Leland in the 1530s but not in his lifetime as the 'Black Prince'),[38] at the age of 46 in 1376. The latter, the greatest military figure of his era in sharp contrast to his son (whose promotion of peace with France must have led to infuriated veteran aristocrats making unfavourable comparisons), was set to succeed his father, Edward III, and was indeed often referred to in contemporary chronicles as 'Edward the Fourth'. Indeed, Richard 'of Bordeaux' was not even the younger Edward's first son at his birth in January 1367; his older brother died in 1371. But Edward, Prince of Wales and Duke of Aquitaine, suffered a sharp decline in health from the time of his expedition to Castile to restore the evicted King Peter 'the Cruel' in 1367. Seriously ill for the first time in years of hard campaigning during his Spanish expedition – probably as part of an epidemic of dysentery and malaria – his condition returned and his rule in Aquitaine became less active in the next two to three years. The contemporary accounts of the 'bloody flux' probably indicate chronic dysentery,[39] though it is possible that there was an underlying medical weakness that this exacerbated as his nephew Henry IV also suffered serious medical deterioration in his early forties. Logically, he may have picked up some infection on his expedition to Castile in 1367, as his health had given no concern previous to this time.

Whatever the cause, Prince Edward was mostly sedentary in Bordeaux rather than touring the rebellious frontier lordships to overawe the turbulent barons. This may have emboldened them to risk seeking the arbitration of the traditional overlord of Aquitaine, the King of France (now Charles V), in disputes with the Prince – in defiance of the terms of the Treaty of Bretigny, which had granted Aquitaine in full sovereignty to Edward III. The alleged arrogance and harshness of the Prince as lord of Aquitaine[40] may also have been exacerbated by his poor health and so hastened the appeals of disaffected nobles to Charles, though these claims may only be French propaganda. The residence of a vigorous English royal viceroy in Bordeaux was a novelty for Aquitaine, which had largely been neglected by the Crown since the loss of Normandy in 1204; the equally vigorous Simon de Montfort had met similar resistance as governor in the 1250s.[41]

Aquitaine, a large and decentralized dukedom with many powerful local lordships, had always been turbulent with the great vassals furthest from Bordeaux particularly restive; the Lusignan dynasty had defied Richard I as Duke in the 1170s. The French kings from Louis VII (r. 1137–80) onwards meddled in it to encourage revolt, as the ultimate legal overlord of Aquitaine and the hereditary enemies of the English kings.

Whether or not encouraged by Edward's ill-health, Charles V chose to make an issue of English 'breaches' of the terms of Bretigny (e.g. not removing all the mercenary 'Free Companies' from France), instead of just continuing with a technical refusal to recognize Aquitaine's independence as Edward III had refused to end his claim to the French throne. The French backed the rebels and received their homage in defiance of the Prince's rights, the Prince was summoned to his 'overlord' Charles V's court and refused, and war resumed.

In 1370 the Prince, in sharp contrast to his earlier vigour, had to travel to the siege of rebel-seized Limoges in a litter – though the subsequent sack and massacre might have been carried out at any point in his career as a warning to other rebels.[42] The brutality was no worse than that used by the English army as it crossed France on its 'chevauchées' in the 1350s and 1370s – intimidation as a substitute for permanent occupation. The following new year he returned to England as an invalid, never campaigning again, and was too weak even to travel immediately from Plymouth up to London after the voyage. He played no role in politics as his father too became an invalid in the early 1370s, the political 'lead' passing to his next surviving brother, John of Gaunt, and lived in retirement in the Home Counties. By the time of the vital Parliament meeting early in 1376 he was too ill to do more than attend the opening session, and he died shortly afterwards.[43] His father outlived him by a year, and Richard succeeded to the throne at the age of ten.

If the 'Black Prince' had been able to operate in politics and war from c.1370 – would it have made a difference to perceived English decline?
Henry III had lived to 65, Edward I to 68, and Edward III to 64, and in normal circumstances Prince Edward (born in 1330) could have been expected to live into the 1380s and probably the 1390s. Among his brothers, John lived to 59 and Edmund to 61. A reasonably long reign by 'Edward IV' from June 1377 would have had major effects on the later reign of his younger son, who would not have succeeded with a quarrelsome and ineffective regency council in 1377, and the sense of 'drift' in English domestic and foreign policy in the 1370s would have been less had the ageing Edward III had an active heir on hand. The Prince of Wales, like John of Gaunt, who was the effective head of the government in the King's last years, would have faced difficulties in running policy in c.1372–7, with the war going badly and France and Castile now allied to threaten seaborne links to Bordeaux.

The Prince, like John, would have had to rely on good relations with the reputedly venal royal mistress Alice Perrers (and tolerance of her grasping court allies such as Lord Latimer) to secure access to the King, a major source of complaint against John's governance. Tolerating Alice's clique would probably have been more difficult for him, as punctiliously honourable, than for the more pragmatic John who had his own mistress,

Katherine Swynford, and a growing brood of illegitimate children (the Beauforts). John was also accused of excessive and provocative public spending, particularly on his palatial residence at the Savoy, which was to be sacked in the 1381 revolt.[44] His elder brother, by contrast, lived quietly in his manor houses near London (Kennington and Berkhamsted) without ostentation – partly due to his ill-health.

John made no effort to curtail the appointments and acquisitive habits of Alice's associates at court, and seems to have gone beyond good-natured acquiescence in his father's relationship to a pragmatic alliance of convenience with the Perrers faction. Even though Edward III seems to have been mildly senile and thus resistant to any attempt to prise him away from his lover (or to annoy her by refusing her requests), John's tolerance helped to pave the way for the angry public reaction of the 'political nation' in Parliament in 1376. When the Parliamentary criticism extended to his own governance and dignity, he reacted violently to the 'insult' – as seen by the treatment of 'Speaker' De La Mare. His inability to control his wrath in public was also seen when he threatened to drag Bishop Courtenay of London out of court by his beard for daring to prosecute John's 'client' John Wycliffe for heresy.[45] Edward III had a hasty temper but was perceived as being capable of having second thoughts and controlling himself in public, as with the incident of the representatives of surrendering Calais in 1347. He had once threatened Archbishop Stratford with violence, but prudently forgave him.

The position of the Prince of Wales in the confrontations of 1376 was crucial as head of the 'reversionary interest' and a man who his father trusted. In real life, constrained by his poor health, he made his support known for the 'purge' of Alice's supporters by the 'Good Parliament' in 1376 and his political clients were involved in that. Had he been fit enough to intervene then or earlier, he had the prestige to challenge John in court politics – and in front of the King. Had he been in full health, if his loyalty to his mother's memory and his rash temper led him to argue for her dismissal this would have aroused his doting father's distrust. John's problems in c.1371–7 were exacerbated by the fact that he was not the heir to the throne; hostile rumours emerged that he had an ulterior motive for his gaining political power, namely that he aimed to usurp the Crown from his nephew Richard when the Prince of Wales died.[46]

This lack of legitimacy and fear of his aims also affected John's position as leader of the regency council after June 1377, making his position less secure than that of an adult new king, 'Edward IV'. The failings in co-ordination of the new regime must have played a part in the sense of 'drift' in the Anglo-French war from 1377 to 1381, when it was complained that over £250,000 was spent on campaigning to little effect.[47]

This discontent in turn added to the malaise that preceded the 'Peasants' Revolt', when it appears that the leadership of the latter could co-ordinate a series of assemblies of angry minor landholders (farmers as much as labourers) across south-east England with no fear of government discovery and 'police' action by the gentry on Council orders to disperse them. Even as a dying man in 1376 Edward was able and willing to lend his support to popular discontent about the state of the government, venal court favourites in particular; John, however, seems to have been taken by surprise by the extent of public rancour both then and in 1381. Contemporary chroniclers blamed the laziness of the nobility as well as lack of leadership for the failures in the war,[48] but the main problem was probably a lack of forceful co-ordination – a sharp contrast to the actions of a vigorous King (and later the Prince of Wales) from the late 1330s to c.1369.

Although John was a capable administrator with military experience, he was no substitute for the absence of a king. His authority was never as complete as that of the sovereign, with rivals among the nobility willing to plot against him, and he became increasingly unpopular – as seen by the criticism of his nominees to office in the 'Good Parliament' in 1376 and the London and Kentish crowds' sack of Savoy Palace in 1381. Unlike Edward III and Prince Edward, John's religious affiliations were suspect to the Church; he personally escorted the accused 'heretic' John Wycliffe to his trial by Bishop Courtenay in 1377.[49] John was potentially at odds with the more forceful and militarily capable of his surviving brothers, Thomas, Earl of Buckingham (later the Duke of Gloucester), so there was no unity within the leaderless royal family.

The position of Lionel, Duke of Clarence – and of his heirs. Would there have been a a major alteration to the dynamics of the late fourteenth century royal kindred had he lived?
It should be noted that another early death also aided the instability among the senior royals in the 1370s. Edward III's second surviving son Lionel, Duke of Clarence – another notable military figure like his elder brother, though more known for jousting success than for warfare – died at the age of 30 in 1368. He died as a result of illness while journeying to Italy for his second marriage (to the daughter of the Duke of Milan).[50] As Edward's next son after the 'Black Prince', he not John would have been effective regent in the 1370s had he been alive; he would have had a claim on the throne as an alternative to Richard when his elder brother died in 1376, as an adult of 38 not a boy of 9. It is unlikely that his father would have set Richard aside to avoid a disruptive regency, as by this date strict patrilinear succession was the norm but there were no definitive legal rules. A new-born infant, John I,

had been allowed to succeed to France when his father, Louis X, died in 1316 in preference to his uncle Philip V (who was only made regent, not king, for the short time from Louis' death to his widow giving birth). But in England itself, Richard I's youngest brother, John, had been able to claim the throne in 1199 ahead of his deceased elder brother Geoffrey's teenage son Arthur so Edward III could have used that precedent to set Richard aside; Richard had not been born in England (neither had Arthur) and a legal case could be made out that his parents had not been legally married given the ambiguities surrounding his mother, Joan's, first two marriages. Even if Lionel was unlikely to have been named as heir in 1376, he had the right to be regent/'guardian' of the next king on the precedent of Earl Henry of Lancaster, nearest uncle and thus 'guardian' to the young Edward III in 1327–8.

Lionel left only a daughter, Philippa (died 1380), whose Mortimer descendants' rights to the throne were the subject of endless argument in succeeding decades. They were senior to John of Gaunt, Lionel's next brother, and his family; but could a female (Philippa) inherit or transmit a claim to the throne to her male heirs? The much-disputed supposed 'Salic Law' in force in France had excluded the rights of Edward III's mother, Isabella, as sister of the late kings Philip III and Charles IV, in favour of their male-descended cousin Philip of Valois in 1328; but Edward had claimed France as Isabella's son, arguing that the throne could pass via if not to a female. In England, Edward I had allowed succession for females – his daughters – and their descendants, in preference to his brother Edmund of Lancaster, at a time when he had no son in the 1270s.[51] (The fact that Edward I had named Lancaster as his next heir was used by Henry IV in his claim on the throne in 1399; it was mistakenly assumed by some people that Lancaster was really Edward's older brother.) Edward III made John of Gaunt not Philippa the next heir after Richard II in 1376, in a private document that not many nobles may have known about and which Richard II may have destroyed;[52] Henry could not produce it in 1399. Richard II preferred to regard Philippa's son Roger Mortimer as his heir rather than John, ruling in this vein to Parliament in 1385,[53] but Roger died in 1398 as Lord Lieutenant of Ireland and thereafter his son Edmund (born 1391) had the disadvantage of being under-age and so a potentially weak ruler. An adult Roger would have stood a better chance of opposing Henry's claim in 1399 than his son's partisans did, though if he had still been in office as governor of Ireland he would not have been in England to act. Had he been alive, he was likely to have ended up stranded in Ireland in September 1399 as Henry 'usurped' his throne though with a plausible right to call on French help for an invasion of England. He would have been a more formidable foe for

Henry than his teenage son was to be in the 1400s – and in any case Henry had physical possession of Edmund, who was carefully kept under lock and key (and was abducted by plotters in 1405). Lionel could even have provided a male heir by his second, Milanese, marriage after 1368 and so cut the House of Lancaster out of the succession; any son of his would have been named by Edward III in 1376 in the line of succession as ahead of John and his family.

The conduct of the renewed war in France
All this would have been absent under an active King Edward IV from 1377, a man who had been as effective a civil and military leader as his father and indeed had been accused of being too overbearing by his vassals in Aquitaine in the late 1360s. It is unlikely that the Prince of Wales' continuance as a vigorous leader after the Nájera campaign of 1367 would have much affected the breakdown of relations with Charles V, given that appeals to the King of France by plotting English vassals in Aquitaine (whether spontaneous or co-ordinated with the authorities in Paris) were not unique to the circumstances of the Prince's decline in health. Charles V was gaining in confidence to challenge England anyway, as shown by his refusal to end claims of overlordship over Aquitaine or make an effort to finish paying the ransom his late father John II had owed the Prince from 1356. He had been a 'hard-line' anti-English politician ever since his regency regime had refused to confirm John's treaty settlements with Edward III in 1358 – though at the time he had had a militant Estates-General to appease so this firm line then was not definitively 'his' policy. But Charles V might have been more hesitant about a military challenge had the Prince been more active after 1367, at least about taking him on in open battle. (Given the terrain of western France, Charles' main need was to avoid another disastrous confrontation in flat Poitou – guerrilla war in the Massif Central or the wooded valleys of the Garonne and Lot on its western fringes was easier.) He would be expected by his countrymen to show his mettle by intervening if revolt broke out within Aquitaine – as was likely anyway, given long-term attitudes to strict English rule. Turbulent nobles had been defying Richard I as duke in the 1170s, and lords such as the Lusignans had played England off against France for centuries. The hundreds of Aquitanian appeals to Charles as overlord in 1368–9 could not all have been co-ordinated from Paris to take advantage of the Prince's health and arrange a *casus belli*; it was a sign of genuine local resentment. The strict, tax-based nature of royal rule in Aquitaine did not suddenly become harsher due to the Prince's poor health or even to his costly intervention in the civil wars in neighbouring Castile (allied to France and a potential threat, as seen from its naval clash with England in 1350).

The Prince's first major tax-demands of Aquitaine were made in 1364; his ally King Peter 'the Cruel' of Castile was evicted by his pro-French half-brother, Henry of Trastámara, and fled to Aquitaine for aid in 1366. The most that can be said of the Prince's financial demands is that if he had acquired more loot in Castile and Peter had paid his debts they might have been lesser in the late 1360s – and possibly postponed a showdown.

The 'run-up' to resumption of the war in 1369. Was the failure of the settlement inevitable? The Prince's fault? Or due to personal ill-will by Charles V and the early death of John II?
The most obvious factor that would have improved matters between England and France would have been if King John II, Charles' father, had not died in April 1364 – when he was only 45. An ineffective ruler whose reputation and morale had never recovered from his capture by the Prince of Wales at the battle of Poitiers in 1356, John had been politically eclipsed by his eldest son while in captivity in England awaiting his ransom in 1357–61. It was Charles who had had to face the collapse of the French governmental structure in the face of a populist rising against royal authority in Paris led by Étienne Marcel (in which his ministers were killed in front of him by rebels), the armed defiance of the Valois dynasty by its challenger Charles of Navarre in Normandy, a peasant revolt (the 'Jacquerie') in the plague-hit countryside, and inability for the government to raise all the King's ransom in 1357–61. The extra burden the ransom – eventually set at £500,000 for all the Poitiers captives – had placed on a tax-raising system short of taxpayers after the 'Black Death' had been catastrophic and demands that the public pay full taxes (partly to compensate the King's ministers and feudal vassals for having to ransom him) had led to armed resistance. The resultant fury of the northern French peasantry against the 'oppressive' nobles led to what amounted to a 'class war' in 1358; the main insurgent army was put down by Charles of Navarre rather than the Dauphin. In the circumstances it was an achievement to have raised as much as the Dauphin Charles' regime did in meeting the first instalment of £100,000 and securing John's release.

The failure to pay the rest of the promised sum led King John, who had promised that the outstanding payment would be met when he was released in an interim agreement, to keep his word and return to captivity in London where he soon died. Quite apart from his punctilious sense of honour, it is probable that his decision – which amounted to abdicating power as the money was unlikely to be found quickly – showed that he had abandoned any attempt to restore his shattered government and believed that his son could manage it better. Fulfilling his pledge to return to captivity headed off a resumption of the war, though the indications are that Edward III was not as belligerent as he had been the last time that France had failed to fulfil its King's promises. The refusal of the Dauphin's regime to accept the captive King's agreement to hand over Normandy and Anjou as well as Aquitaine in full sovereignty (the 'Second Treaty of London') had led to Edward invading France again in 1359; this time there was no military response, possibly due to the unwelcome return of the plague in 1362–3. Edward's best and most trusted general among his own generation, Duke Henry of Lancaster (father-in-law of the King's third son John of Gaunt), had died in 1361 and in 1362–6 the King sent his second son, Lionel, with a substantial force to Ireland to reassert English power there; France was not a priority.

Had John lived after April 1364, either in power in Paris or as a nominal king resident in London, his personal good relationship with Edward would have been a factor in favour of continuing the peace of Bretigny. The Dauphin was, however, implacably anti-English and was capable of defying his father's orders if John was living in London, as he had done in refusing to ratify the 'Second Treaty of London'. At the time (1358–9) he had judged correctly that even if Edward invaded France again the advantage would lie with the defence; siege-gunnery had not developed adequately to batter down strong walls so Edward had failed to take either Rheims or Paris and had had to come to terms at Bretigny in April 1360. He would have been capable of the same defiance of England if John had still been nominal king, arguing that his captive father was unable to act independently so he (Charles) should behave as a regent with full powers.

The physical state of war-ravaged and plague-hit France meant that it was unlikely to pay up the full ransom, so Edward III would have been well advised to magnanimously renounce it to preserve peace and send John home to resume power from his Anglophobe son. But that still left the problem that the Treaty of Bretigny required the cession of Aquitaine and Calais (and Ponthieu in Artois) to England in full sovereignty, conceding which would cost France prestige rather than money. John was prepared to do this, but Charles refused and failed to carry out this part of the Treaty when he became king in April. This was a less excusable breach of the Treaty than the question of the ransom, and shows that – as in 1358–9 – he was the main obstacle to a settlement lasting and once he was king he would be seeking an opportunity to resume conflict.

The only way that England could have put greater pressure on the government in Paris to co-operate would have been if the proposed cession of Normandy had been carried out, which would have given Edward military bases within striking distance of Paris. Edward had sought this major military gain in 1358 from his captive only to see the Dauphin (and the representative estates) ignore it; the combination of resistance from the shattered French government and the higher social classes' representatives means that it was unlikely that John could ever have forced this concession on his vassals. A temporary concession – resisted on the ground by the local nobles and unable to be carried out? – could have been possible had Edward had a major military success in the 1359–60 campaign, such as the capture of Rheims or Paris. Both cities would have had to be starved out as the English army lacked the artillery to batter down the walls – and in the event a disastrous hailstorm during the siege of Paris broke down Edward's tents and flooded his camp, ruining the siege (March 1360). The other circumstance that could have enabled Edward to enforce his terms easier would have been if the control of Paris in 1358–9 had passed to his sporadic and unreliable ally, Charles of Navarre, rather than to the Dauphin. The latter was a helpless puppet of the insurgent city bourgeoisie under Marcel for some weeks in early 1358, but was able to escape to Compiègne and raise an army. The subsequent uneasy alliance between Marcel's regime and Navarre's aristocratic army soon broke down, with Navarre's English mercenaries being resisted and Marcel being lynched (May 1358). The Dauphin then secured the capital. A victory for Navarre in securing Paris would have weakened the Dauphin and given Edward more room to manoeuvre in his 1359 invasion, but anti-English feeling was strong enough to encourage the French government to go back on any concession of full sovereignty in Aquitaine or Normandy later. A greater English success in 1360 need not have led to a long-lasting peace – particularly once Charles V assumed the throne.

The Prince was accused of holding an extravagant court at Bordeaux, far more expensive than usual, by contemporaries.[54] Did this put too much of a burden on the magnates of Aquitaine and stimulate resistance to him?[55] The cost does not appear to have been unduly high, at around £30,000 per annum, and expense was natural for a man of his character seeking to impress his nobles – if also a source of grumbling at his autocratic behaviour. It can be guessed that the Prince's purpose was the same as that of his extravagant father, who hosted sumptuous gatherings of the nobility in 'Arthurian' mode at Windsor – they were seeking to present themselves as the focus of chivalric loyalty and bring their elite together under their supervision, which in large and laxly-run post-1360 Aquitaine was a desirable objective. The English King had not had a close relative as his personal representative there for a century, or been there since Edward I's residence in Bordeaux in 1287 (when he received the era's first Chinese ambassador). The Prince was thus using his money for a political aim, and possibly there would have been no complaints had the flow of loot to fund the court (as in 1355–6) not dried up.

Personal quarrels by the Prince with senior nobles were also blamed for discontent by the contemporary chivalric historian Froissart, with the Prince's arrogance and cupidity as factors;[56] he appears to have been unaccustomed to the need to conciliate the notoriously 'touchy' and usually poorly-controlled Gascon nobility. Given the size of their fiefs, they had large bodies of retainers available to use against their sovereign lord – and had not been ruled firmly from London through the early-mid fourteenth century as the kings of England concentrated their efforts elsewhere. The phenomenon of haughty and autonomist border lords resisting their duke and turning to a scheming French king as their ultimate overlord was not new either – the house of Lusignan in Poitou had played the Angevins off against the French monarchy from the 1160s to the 1240s. (In an era of a nobility proud of its genealogical links, it should be noted that the Prince was a local as much as an 'alien Englishman' by blood – his grandmother Isabella was French, his great-grandmother Queen Eleanor was Castilian, and another ancestor was King John's Queen, Isabella of Angouleme.) Ironically, the recent extension of the borders of Aquitaine in 1360 was a problem for the Prince's government, although it technically added to his military power and income and took both away from France. These extra eastern areas of his authority in Quercy and Rouergue had not been under control from either Bordeaux or Paris for generations and their lords were accustomed to autonomy, not officials (often foreign-born Englishmen under Edward's rule) demanding taxes and asserting dormant legal rights.

The Prince and Castile: a war too far that led to excessive financial demands on Aquitaine? Or was France the aggressor and the English loss of Castile luck not incompetence?

Short of money or not, Edward certainly found the attack on Castile to restore Peter in 1367 convenient from a financial point of view, with his client making extravagant offers of recompense, which he turned out to be unable to meet. Peter was accused of bribing the Prince and his advisers to secure support;[57] but in reality the Prince could not afford to risk a French client, Peter's half-brother Henry of Trastámara, on the Castilian throne and restoring the Castilian naval aid to France, which Peter had halted. The Prince had fought beside his father in the naval battle off Winchelsea against a Castilian fleet in 1350, and was aware of its potential to aid France. The terms of Trastámara's 1366 alliance with France entailed him entering the Anglo-French conflict on France's side, which was bound to invite an English reaction, and removing him was essential. The mention of the Anglo-French war resuming indeed implies that Charles V and his general Du Guesclin were already thinking ahead to this probability. It was, however, unfortunate that the Prince made bold, unsupported claims of the lucrative expectations of success in order to lure semi-independent Aquitaine nobles into joining the Castilian campaign. Instead they received little money and in 1368 the Prince made new demands of them in taxes. The contemporary chronicler Froissart played up this as a reason for the nobles' anger – though it was conceivably no more than an excuse.[58] But this demand might not have occurred had Peter repaid his patron for his aid in full, and it is quite possible that the devious Peter exaggerated his own ability to coerce money out of his country in order to lure the Prince into assisting him.

The Prince's 1368 request for extra taxes was at a lower rate than earlier demands (a 20d not 24d rate), but for a period of five years not one.[59] It thus represented encroachment on traditional 'rights', and was further evidence of a desire for centralization, systematization and order by a vigorous new resident governor (of royal blood so socially superior to and able to demand obedience of the highest-ranking nobles). King Peter of Castile, who he had now restored, was never able to assert full control of his subjects despite precautionary executions of captured rebels after Nájera – or, more importantly for the future of Aquitaine, to pay off the vast debts he owed to the Prince. The latter appears to have received about an eighth of the money he was owed for the 1367 campaign – an expedition that had cost around the entire annual revenue of Aquitaine.[60] He occupied part of Castile (Vizcaya) as surety for the money, but it was still not paid. Exasperated, the Prince sent envoys to Peter's long-term foe King Peter IV of Aragon (principal backer of the 1366–7 rebels) and a secret protocol was drawn up providing for the division of Castile between Aragon and the Prince's ally, Charles 'the Bad' of Navarre; had this been implemented it would have avoided the real-life result of Trastámara retaking Castile with Aragonese help and aiding France.

In 1369 Peter was murdered by his rival and Aquitaine faced a renewed threat from the south. Ironically, the most successful French general of the new war in the 1370s, the 'Fabian' Breton tactician Bertrand du Guesclin who carefully avoided frontal battle, had fought for Trastámara at Nájera – and been captured and ransomed. Had he been killed Charles V would have been deprived of his most successful commander, though the tactics he employed to avoid a suicidal battle with the invincible English archers were already in evidence in France before he took control of their armies and had frustrated Edward III in his march on Paris in 1359–60. Charles, as Dauphin, had refused battle then, so du Guesclin's tactics were merely in line with his master's long-term strategy – which Charles had logically learnt as a survivor of his father's disastrous frontal attack on the English army at Poitiers in September 1356. But Charles had also a long history of stubborn ill-will towards the English, as seen by his refusal to ratify the 'humiliating' Second Treaty of London proposed by his captive father to Edward III in 1358. Even before the Castilian crisis in 1366–7 he was negotiating with King Peter IV of Aragon for an Aragonese expedition across the Pyrenees to overrun Aquitaine in return for part of Navarre[61] – he could be expected to take any opportunity to undermine the Prince's control of the region.

The Prince's ill-health and lack of massive 1356-style 'razzias' after 1367 did not determine greater French confidence in tactics towards his duchy. Charles V could not have known when he took up the cause of Aquitaine rebels in 1369–70 that Edward's decline was permanent, or that his brothers would not be able to substitute for him adequately in damaging attacks on France. Charles and du Guesclin continued to evade battle as they had done earlier, with the tactic of wearing down the English armies not emerging now but since 1359. There were two still major devastating raids across France in the Prince's absence, by John of Gaunt in 1373 and by Thomas of Buckingham in 1380; they failed to entice the French into battle and had no time to spare in lengthy sieges so they achieved little, which the Prince would also have faced had he been in command. Even his father, Edward III, had had little success in a march of this nature when he could not bring the enemy to battle or take a major town, as seen in 1359 with the advance on Paris. The differences under the Prince's command would probably have been a more forceful reaction to the 'nibbling' French attacks on the periphery of Aquitaine and withdrawal of allegiance by emboldened border lords from 1370, with a regular series of royal campaigns to regain lost castles and towns and deter potential rebels. Without the Castilian entanglement there would have been less of an immediate financial problem for his military campaigns, but once war broke out any large-scale campaign was likely to lead to demands for higher taxes. The English aim was clearly to make the local war in southern France self-supporting, not dependant on English subsidies. As with the attitude of George III's government to America in the 1760s, forcing the overseas territory to assist in paying for its defence was eminently just and sensible; and the clearly irritated Prince must have thought the resisting nobles ungrateful and in need of a lesson.

What if the Prince had not fallen ill, possibly due to avoiding the hazards of a campaign in the uplands of Castile? (Nájera had been fought in April, not the summer, but he had stayed in Castile for several more months as Peter failed to pay his debts.) His continued vigour should have put off local lords and town leadership who risked English revenge by coming over to the French side, though the strongest affronted lords – e.g. Armagnac and d'Albret – might have risked a challenge due to their large retinues of tenants and strong castles. In one of these cases the Prince did have right on his side in his demands, Armagnac having taken out a loan to pay a ransom and the Prince asking for it to be repaid; but d'Albret had reason to complain that he was owed instalments of what was meant to be an annual pension from the government even if this was in effect 'hush money' for him to stay loyal.

Another complainant, the Count of Foix, came from a traditionally autonomist dynasty with international pretensions who were as disloyal to the Valois kings as they were to the English. But possibly if King Peter had paid his debts to the Prince on time or the latter had had adequate loot from his campaign to distribute to his lords the financial 'screws' in Aquitaine would not have been tightened in 1368–70. And it was bad luck – or worse? – for the Prince that Armagnac's refusal to allow him to levy his taxes on Armagnac land coincided with the latter's nephew becoming engaged to Marguerite de Bourbon, a relative by marriage of Charles V. Armagnac was able to have a cast-iron excuse to travel to Paris for the wedding, where he was doubtless encouraged to defy the Prince by King Charles. His nephew, d'Albret, did homage to Charles for his lands, saving the duties he owed to Edward III (but not to the Prince); Armagnac lodged an appeal that the Prince's taxes were illegal with the '*parlement*' of Paris; and a few weeks later, in June 1368, he and his allies agreed with Charles that neither would sign any agreement with the Prince without each other's consent.[62] This was clearly a plot to undermine the Prince's rights over his lords and if necessary push it to the point of war.

The Prince would hardly have been challenged in open battle if he had remained active given his reputation for victories, but a successful 'razzia' around rebellious border-areas could not keep his army in the field indefinitely if there was rising resistance to paying taxes. Unable to hire local troops due to his inability to pay them after King Peter evaded his debts and defied by more lords in a 'snowball effect', he would have been reduced to depending on his English retinue and the troops they had brought from England. The French King would have been able to stir up ill-will as the ultimate legal authority, and let his captains launch attacks on isolated border towns and castles far from Bordeaux; there was no useful geographical 'frontier' to garrison but a patchwork of lordships stretched across mountainous and lowland countryside. A major loss of a region such as Poitou (in real life in 1372) would have been reversed temporarily as it was well within campaigning reach of Bordeaux (as the Prince had proved in 1356). The vital assistance of the Castilian navy to France – as at La Rochelle in 1372 – would have been halted if the Prince had bought off Trastámara's ally Aragon in 1367–8, preventing him from overthrowing Peter (except by luck), or had crossed the Pyrenees again in retaliation to fight Trastámara.

The Prince's ability to raise as large an army to do this as he had done in 1367 must be questioned, given that his known financial troubles would make him a less viable paymaster to local nobles and to the roaming companies of English mercenaries that were plaguing southern France. Even in 1366–7 many of the latter had preferred to fight for Trastámara and Aragon, with greed outweighing patriotism.

The Prince had already evicted Trastámara in 1367 and thus knew the local territory for campaigning. Although his candidate as the new king – Peter – was dead as of March 1369 Peter's daughter Constance was married to John of Gaunt. John used this second marriage to claim the throne of Castile and wasted part of the 1380s trying to take it from Trastámara's son John I. The Prince of Wales could thus have sought to ward off the Castilian naval threat after Trastámara killed Peter by replacing him with John – most probably if the Castilians had won their real-life naval victory at la Rochelle in 1372. The prospect of Castile interrupting the English naval supplies to Aquitaine would have made it vital to stop this. The relationship between Edward and his brother was at times uneasy in the mid-1370s, with their domestic English 'affinities' at odds over the governance of England; but once John had married Peter's daughter and heiress in 1372 he was the obvious candidate for the Castilian throne. His younger brother Edmund married her younger sister and had the next claim, but he was an inferior political and military leader who had little impact on English affairs in the later fourteenth century and Edward is less likely to have assessed him as a man capable of holding onto the turbulent crown of Castile. If the Prince had managed to replace Henry of Trastámara with a friendly king of Castile in the early 1370s, this raises the issue of how Castile would have reacted to the death of the last legitimate male of the Portuguese dynasty, King Ferdinand, in 1383. In real life the marriage of Ferdinand's sister Beatrice to King John I of Castile led John to attempt to take over Portugal on her behalf, being evicted by a nationalist revolt under John of Avis (Ferdinand's illegitimate half-brother) in 1385. The removal of the Trastámara dynasty from Castile would have prevented this crisis.

Effects of the mid-1370s crisis

French successes would have been much reduced, at least until Edward III's declining health brought the Prince back to England – probably in 1376. Had they lacked Castilian support, the French would have found it more difficult to launch the massive, morale-sapping raids on the Isle of Wight and Sussex (Rye and Winchelsea) in 1377, which added to English perceptions of disaster at the end of Edward III's reign.[63] (A 'hit-and-run' attack was, however, possible, as on Southampton in 1338.) At the least,

England would have been unlikely to lose a substantial number of its ships – and thus its ability to intercept or punish raiders – at the Earl of Arundel's naval defeat off La Rochelle in 1372.[64]

With Castile able to assist France, the latter had freedom to attack across the Channel from 1372 onwards and made the most of this in 'hit-and-run' raids. These had, of course, occurred before, as with the attack on Southampton in 1338, and were often committed not by royal orders but by private initiative from the inhabitants of the French Channel ports in Normandy and Brittany. (Both England and France relied on impressed private shipping from their major ports to provide fleets – hence the importance of the English 'Cinque Ports'.) The victims of the French raids were as much long-term commercial rivals 'targeted' to repay old grudges as 'military targets' of a state-sanctioned attack; in 1377 the main English victims were the newest 'Cinque Ports', Rye and Winchelsea. The practical results were limited – wooden houses could be rebuilt and new inhabitants brought in to repopulate sacked towns, though a massacre such as that at Winchelsea hampered the towns' manning of their fleets for years. But there was a major effect on morale and a perception that the King's government was not defending its subjects; the previous humiliation of the English state and its king by unhampered raiders had been by Robert Bruce's descents on the north-east in Edward II's reign (the 1320s).

Notably the 'regency' for Richard II after June 1377 did not take the initiative in restoring security along the Channel coasts; we owe the impressive late fourteenth century fortifications of Bodiam Castle in East Sussex to the continuing insecurity along its Rother valley (inland from Rye) in the early-mid 1380s. The Ricardian government licensed a local landowner with military experience in France, Sir Edward Dalyngrigge, to build Bodiam as a centre of local defence;[65] it was not prepared to attack Normandy in reprisal as Edward III had done after the Southampton attack of 1338. The government that gave the licence to Dalyngrigge in 1385 was led by Richard's controversial favourite Robert de Vere, who was soon to be removed by the insurgent nobles and commons; it was criticized for its lack of warlike intentions towards France. A far more vigorous response could have been expected from a regime led by the military veteran 'Black Prince' – if he had not been fit or willing to fight, his brothers John (shortly to invade Castile) and Thomas were.

The conflict in Aquitaine and/or another attack on Castile in the mid-1370s would have demanded the Prince's presence there for as long as possible, and thus meant that the perceived weakness and corruption of the royal government in England under Gaunt's leadership still led to the popular discontent shown in Parliament in 1376. The Prince was believed to sympathize with the protesters at the time, and in real life regarded the crisis as serious enough to have himself brought by litter from Berkhamsted to London to attend.[66] Once he was dead, the 'opposition' sought the support of his widow Joan. Had he returned to England earlier and been active in government his closeness to his father could have led to him persuading the latter to dismiss some controversial and corrupt figures such as Latimer (though probably not the royal mistress Alice Perrers). The priorities of the Prince's rule in Aquitaine make this less likely than him only returning after the domestic crisis had come to a head, probably at the end of the campaigning season in 1376 and too late to affect events in the Parliament. There were, however, connections between the leaders of the latter and his own 'affinity' of clients,[67] so had he been physically able to intervene in politics he would have been aware of what was planned against the political allies of his brother John. Once he was back in England, he would have had the right as heir to take charge of the government once he deemed his father incapable and the political and military power to face down any resistance to his dismissals of court 'embezzlers' by John – who would logically have replaced him in Aquitaine. Certainly none of the ministers removed at Parliament's demands would have been able to creep back to office later, or John to have retaliated by victimizing the leadership of the 'opposition' under Speaker De la Mare.

As king from June 1377, Edward IV could have been expected to co-ordinate the war more effectively than the regency government did. There would have still been shortages of men and money, though a vigorous king would have been able to chivvy more of the nobility into raising troops or funds for large-scale expeditions than John was able to do. The opportunities offered by the French-Castilian attack on the English ally Charles 'the Bad' of Navarre would have led to a more large-scale expedition to save Navarre from conquest in 1378–9, and more effective use of Cherbourg (which Charles handed over to England in 1378) as a base for devastating raids across Normandy. The tactic Edward III had used of conquering Calais in 1347 to serve as a base for forays on the French mainland would have been repeated from Cherbourg, though it is dubious if the English 'war-machine' and morale in the late 1370s were strong enough to sustain any long-term attempt to conquer more of Normandy. As with Caen in 1346 and 1417, this would have entailed long and costly sieges – though the death of Charles V in 1380 would have deprived the French of their most effective leader and thrown them onto the resources of the 12-year-old Charles VI's feuding uncles as leaders. The French attempt to confiscate Brittany in 1378–9 would have led to an even larger English expedition to back up the evicted Duke John in regaining his duchy, which would then have become a base for English raids into Normandy and Anjou.

The only drawback to this policy would have been the vast cost of such garrisons, apparent in real life in the late 1370s and worse if more coastal towns had been held and/or a larger force committed to Brittany. According to Chancellor Scrope in 1380, Calais cost £44,000 per annum and Cherbourg £5,500;[68] Brest (the English base in Brittany) would have cost around the same as the latter, as would any port seized in Normandy. Buckingham's sizeable expedition across Northern France in 1380 could be presumed to be smaller than the cost of a royal 'razzia' launched by the new king, 'Edward IV'; the financial demand of £160,000 that Treasurer Archbishop Sudbury made of the autumn 1380 Parliament would not have been much smaller for Edward's plans. (It has been suggested by Nigel Saul that the sum included secret subsidies for John's new ally Portugal and/or his intended attack on Castile;[69] if Edward had deposed Henry of Trastámara in c.1373 he might still have had to prop up John or another candidate as king of Castile.) That sort of expenditure could have required the launch of a major new tax-initiative to raise funds as in real life, and the 'Poll Taxes' of 1377 and 1379 were increased in 1380–1. A different council – nominated by Edward, not John – and a different Treasurer from the politically unsophisticated Sudbury might have amended this third 'Poll Tax' to ensure that it was graded according to means to pay, as in 1377 not at a 'flat rate', or not raised at the level of three groats per person (thrice that used earlier). Perception of unfairness can increase resistance – as in 1990.

It is unclear how much the resulting unrest, evidently from its widespread and simultaneous nature co-ordinated, was owed to the willingness of tax-protesters and others to take advantage of a royal minority. The lack of a strong king or regent ready to put down protests was, however, a spur to action, as with the disturbances in France in 1357–8 (when Prince Edward had King John II captive) and with England in the 1450s. Under an active adult king popular discontent could still be channelled into support for an ambitious, politically sophisticated magnate excluded from influence at court – as when Thomas of Lancaster organized defiance of Edward II in 1322 and when Edward IV faced the Neville-backed East Midlands risings in 1469–70. Even a known ruthless 'strong man' king could be defied, as Edward I had faced as heir from Earl Gilbert of Gloucester in 1268–9 and as king from nobles opposed to the French war in the early 1290s. 'Evil ministers' could be a target for discontent if the king was believed to be innocent of misrule, or at least used as an excuse by magnates excluded from court as a way to stage a coup against their rivals as when Gaveston's and the Despensers' enemies sought to force their removal on Edward II. John of Gaunt was vulnerable to this charge as a focus for assault on the current government in 1377–81, as an ambitious royal uncle of dubious loyalty and had a bad 'track record' in his alliance with Alice Perrers' associates in 1371–6. This element of criticism of the regency regime in 1381 would have been unavailable for would-be rebels had 'Edward IV' been an adult king.

1381: was the revolt conceivable if there had been an adult king?
The 'Black Prince' was as known for ruthlessness as his father, as seen at Limoges, though the belief of anti-government activists in Parliament in 1376 that he was on their 'side' against John indicates that he was regarded as amenable to listening to appeals against injustice as a good lord should be. There were claims again in the real-life rising of 1381 that Richard was on his subjects' side and their problems lay with the corrupt and oppressive gentry and nobility, as seen in the popular rallying-cry for King and Commons. Many of the rebels who marched on London and hunted down ministers (the Archbishop was dragged out of the Tower and beheaded) and Fleming 'aliens' may have believed that they were doing the King's will, even if their leaders had invented this as a means of persuading these loyal subjects into rebellion. This was a common phenomenon seen in lower-class risings against an entrenched elite as late as the French and Russian peasant revolutions, with the populace persuaded that the King or Czar had no idea of the misdeeds of his ministers and would back the rebels when he discovered the truth. Famously, when the Kentish leader Wat Tyler was publicly killed by Lord Mayor Walworth at a confrontation in Richard's presence the King was able to ride over to the massive crowd of armed rebels and call on them to follow him, which they did, averting a probable massacre of his escort.[70] Richard was an unknown quantity to the populace in 1381 so it was easier to make up claims that he sympathized with the rebels than it would have been to do so for an adult king and experienced war-leader. But the record that the 'Black Prince' had as a good lord who listened to his vassals would have made it possible that angry men marching on London with agrarian/economic grievances (or opposing high war-taxes) c.1381 would have believed that their king would listen to their grievances, as he had done as prince in 1376.

The scale and co-ordination of the 1381 revolt across the south-east is impressive, and the government was clearly taken by surprise. Would this have been the case under 'Edward IV', even as a sick man attuned to the popular mood in real-life 1376? The whole point of the impressively co-ordinated war-preparations of England for Continental expeditions under Edward III was that local nobles and gentry commanders received the King's orders to collect and arm a certain number of men and take them to a named rendezvous by a certain date, prepared to campaign for a stated amount of time. This required regular and smooth communications between the King's chancery in London and the provinces – and this system should extend to the local 'county elite' being able to warn the government if there was any unrest. King 'Edward IV', who had campaigned with the land's nobles and gentry since 1346 and been a 'regular' at assemblies at court (e.g. for the Garter feasts), would have known many of them personally; he could logically have been expected to call on them for information and help in a revolt by the lower orders. The regency of real-life 1381 seems to have been taken by surprise.

Of course, given his martial interests and determination to defend his rights 1381 might have seen him exploiting the recent death of his foe Charles V to campaign in France, and thus not be present in London to be aware of the popular mood. He could have raised an extortionate tax to pay for this campaign and then sailed to Aquitaine leaving John of Gaunt as regent to face the resultant surge of discontent. But there is less probability that thousands would have been willing to risk a revolt against 'Edward IV', who lacked John's unpopularity, even had an extortonate war-tax (a poll-tax?) been risked by a more astute government under his leadership. There had been close co-ordination between sovereign and provincial leadership in each county to organize recruiting and supplies for each campaign abroad under Edward III until the early 1370s. (An impressive muster had been held as late as 1373, only to be prevented from setting sail by consistently adverse winds.) 'Edward IV' would have continued this co-ordination across the country to maximize his army for campaigns after 1377, with better success than Buckingham (born 1355) as he was far more experienced and was personally known – and was respected by – the entire nobility from thirty years of warfare. The importance of personal relationships and a reputation for 'no nonsense' in such an era (of rudimentary and indirect government) needs to be remembered. The King would have been tipped off about trouble at an early stage by the local leaders of society, even if they could not stop the co-ordinated attacks on manorial courts (apparently aimed at destroying legal and financial records) and the 'armies' of rebels assembled in defiance of the local nobles' retainers.

Had a rising occurred and Edward been in England, the royal response would have been as vigorous and uncompromising as Henry VII's was to the massed march of the Cornishmen on London in 1497. An adult and sane king able to co-ordinate a response and sure of obedience from his nobility (unlike Henry VI in the Cade revolt of 1450) would not have lost control of London, and would have had armed royal guards and Londoners ready to block London Bridge and keep the rebels south of the Thames. The disaffected within the city were able to admit the advancing attackers in real-life 1381 and 1450, but an adult king present at Westminster or the Tower with armed support was less likely to be defied even had more rebels from Essex marched on the capital from the north-east. He would then have been able to assemble enough armed retainers of noblemen from outside the affected area in a few weeks to take on and defeat the rebels, possibly at Blackheath.

If King 'Edward IV' was subsequently forced to spend more time in London due to domestic discontent at the cost of the war, either John or Buckingham would have been the probable commanders of the English forces. Certainly, the presence of an effective and experienced co-ordinator of the English war-effort from 1377 would have given England the advantage over France and made Charles V (a survivor and captive of the new King's victory at Poitiers in 1356) even more cautious about open warfare. Even if 'Edward IV' had been unable to take many major towns in Normandy in expeditions after 1378/9, and higher taxation had fed domestic discontent, the deaths of Charles V and du Guesclin would have reduced French effectiveness and the war at best turned into a stalemate. It is very unlikely that the French would have been in a position to contemplate invading a weakened and faction-ridden England by 1385–6 as in real life, even if the new English king had proved as unable to bring the war to a successful end as his father had in 1359–60. Crucially, it is probable that despite the diversion of effort to Normandy and Brittany the English government could have sent an effective force to Flanders in 1382 to assist the Ghent revolt against the new French regime and oppose the French military response. Flanders (with the Scheldt estuary ports) had been the centre of English strategy to neutralize the danger from French fleets in 'Edward IV's' boyhood, hence the battle of Sluys in 1340. The King would have made more of an effort than the preoccupied Ricardian government did to intervene as Charles VI's uncle Duke Philip of Burgundy crushed Flemish independence and secured Flanders for himself and Brabant for his brother. In real life, only a small force of around 2–3,000 men was sent under Bishop Despenser without experienced military commanders, disguised as a 'crusade' to evict the French supporters of the Pope (Clement VII) in Avignon.[71] (The English recognized his rival in Rome, Urban.) This petered out in 1383 as a large French army intervened. It should be pointed out that the acquisition of the heiress of Flanders for Duke Philip – the root of the crisis – had been foreseen by Edward III, who had intended her to be married to his fourth son, Edmund, instead. This eventuality had been prevented by a papal ruling by Pope Urban that they were within the prohibited degrees of consanguinity[72] – a not unusual problem for the inter-related royal houses of Europe, and usually circumvented by Church permission. The presence of the papal court in southern France at Avignon made it more susceptible to French pressure, but it is possible that a greater English success in the campaign and treaty of 1360 could have involved the French government having to persuade the Pope to allow the marriage. In that case, Flanders would have been under an Anglophile regime in the 1380s and 1390s and England would have been able to use its troops to attack Paris from the north-east – as the French had faced previously in 1214 and 1302.

At the worst, if an anti-tax rising in England had unluckily coincided with the Ghent crisis – leading to the defeat of the Flemings as in real life – England would have been unable to assist the immediate request for aid in June 1382. But Edward would have replied with a major invasion later in 1382 or in 1383, and Charles VI would have been unable to intervene in force had the French been threatened at home by extra English 'bastions' along its northern coast. Flanders would have been preserved as an English ally and the consolidation of the Low Countries as a possession of the House of Burgundy prevented, at least until the English were next distracted by internal crisis.

Chapter Two

Richard II

Richard II's reign: what if he had not succeeded as a ten-year-old?
Would he have avoided disaster in 1387 or 1399?

A tyrant king, or subsequent blackening of his reputation? The
confrontation between Richard and Henry in 1398–9

Any consideration of Richard II's character and its connection to his
downfall in 1399 is under a disadvantage from the sources. History is
written by the winners, and nobody in the late mediaeval period was
more careful in that regard than his replacement, Henry of Bolingbroke. The
current monastic chronicles were all called in to be examined after his
seizure of power in September 1399, which was a clear sign to their writers
that any accounts sympathetic to Richard would have to be heavily edited to
satisfy Henry's agents. The documents that resulted, whether altered or not,
make it clear that Richard was universally regarded as an untrustworthy,
unstable, tyrannical despot and Henry's accession was regarded with public
relief.[1] This is not to say that such a view was the invention of chroniclers
eager to satisfy Henry as to their loyalties. The facts speak for themselves –
though the extent of dissatisfaction with Richard may have been played up
after he lost power, and a 'backlash' against Henry's expensive government
alone cannot explain the extent of 'Ricardian' plots after 1399. The blatantly
'political' execution of the Earl of Arundel, the suspicious death of Duke
Thomas of Gloucester in 1397, and the banishments of Henry of
Bolingbroke and Thomas Mowbray in 1398 are ample evidence that Richard
indulged in personal revenge for past humiliations as Edward II had done –
and both suffered similar fates later.

Henry's invasion of September 1399 was a desperate gamble following his
disinheritance from his father's legacy, the vast and profitable Duchy of
Lancaster – a far more serious blow to his standing and financial prospects
than his ten-year exile from England in 1398. His relationship with Richard,
his contemporary, had been fraught for years with modern historians

suggesting an element of jealousy on the unmilitary Richard's part for his heroic cousin, a first-class participant in tournaments and other favourite sports of the warlike nobility who – like Richard's father but not him – shared his lifestyle and standards. (It is not clear which of them was the elder; Ian Mortimer thinks it was Richard.) Back in 1381 Richard, aged fourteen, had failed to provide for the adequate manning of the gates of the Tower of London, refuge of the Court from the rampant 'mob rule' in London, as he rode out to confront the rebel army of the 'Peasants Revolt'. In his absence at a meeting with Wat Tyler a determined crowd had broken into the Tower, let in by the guards, and dragged out the Archbishop of Canterbury and Chancellor, Simon Sudbury (originator of the hated 'poll tax'). He and the Treasurer had then been executed on Tower Hill; Prince Henry, as son of the equally hated Duke John of Lancaster, had been among the helpless Court refugees who the lynch mob had considered killing and eventually spared. This may have given him a grudge against or contempt for the self-centred Richard, who had left him to his fate.

More certainly, Henry's participation in the successful revolt of a bloc of alienated magnates (the 'Lords Appellant') against Richard's favourites and ministers in 1387 exposed him to the King's subsequent desire for revenge. Earl of Derby at the time and without any obvious political grudges apart from Richard's enmity towards his father, his participation was probably sought by the more senior 'Appellants' as the representative of his father (absent in Spain attempting to conquer Castile). John was arguably Richard's heir, as his oldest surviving paternal uncle, although Richard had declared to Parliament in November 1385 (after the first threats had been made to depose him) that he regarded his heir as the under-age Roger Mortimer, whose mother's father had been John's late elder brother Lionel. This logically gave Henry (and John if he had been in England at the time of the 'Appellant' revolt) reason to back any attempt to rein in Richard by his magnates – the latter should use a sympathetic Parliament to reaffirm that John and Henry were the rightful heirs.

Henry could bring in his and his father's substantial 'affinity' of tenants and retainers to fight in the rebel army; he thus helped to destroy an army being brought by royal 'favourite' Robert de Vere to rescue Richard at Radcot Bridge in December 1387. It is noticeable that Henry had not joined the initial rebel rally at Waltham Cross in November to demand that the royal 'favourites' be put on trial by Parliament. He was at court in London when the rebel leadership arrived to put their requirements to Richard and only joined the rebels as de Vere assembled his army in Cheshire (where Richard was earl) to oppose them. Had de Vere been captured by the 'Appellants' or fled abroad earlier, the confrontation would not have occurred; but Henry would still have had to choose which side to join, at the latest when the rebels' Parliament assembled. He might not have joined the coalition and earned Richard's enmity without the royal decision to raise troops and fight – which was probably due to the King's desire not to repeat his humiliation of autumn 1386 when he had refused to stay in London to meet a hostile Parliament (which was being used by his uncle Thomas and other peers to impeach his favourites) but been told it would go ahead whether he was there or not. In autumn 1386 Richard's decision to 'go on strike' and refuse to legalize his enemies' moves to prosecute his friends had not halted them; their representatives had implied that Parliament not the King had the final say in the matter and had impeached the accused. (Notably, once he regained control Richard sought to obtain a legal judgement from the leading judges that this was illegal.) Thus in autumn 1387 he realized that he could not just refuse to co-operate with Thomas and his allies, and instead he firstly attempted to have Arundel arrested at his fortified base, Reigate Castle, to scotch the rebellion and when that failed he resorted to his Cheshire tenantry. Richard's naming of the rival (Mortimer) line of his father's elder brother Lionel as his heirs threatened Henry's chances of kingship and may have been decisive. Henry's participation may thus have been a defensive move, aimed at securing a recognition of his and his father's rights as heirs by the rebel-controlled 'Merciless Parliament' and heading off the threat that it would instead back his uncle Thomas, the new Duke of Gloucester, John's younger brother and a senior 'Appellant'.

Was the danger of Thomas securing the heirship or the throne in late 1387 serious? In strict genealogical terms Thomas' right to the Crown was dubious, given that the last time a younger brother had been preferred to a (deceased) elder brother's son had been in 1199. If Richard had been deposed in 1387 Henry's father, John, was the next adult male of the royal family, followed by his younger brother Edmund of Langley – Thomas was the youngest of the three brothers. But John was not in England at the time and Edmund had little political experience or support, so if the forceful Thomas had rallied a 'claque' of his clients in Parliament to propose himself as king he might have succeeded (and then faced a civil war from John and Henry?). It is only the chronicle of Whalley Abbey, however, that states that after the 'Appellants' took control of London Thomas and Henry quarrelled over who was to be the next king and Richard was temporarily 'suspended' from exercising his power.

Defensive move or not, Henry's part in the coup placed him with the other rebels as an object of revenge for Richard as he reasserted his power in punishing the rebel leadership in 1397–8. He was initially exempted from the list of past 'rebels' accused of treason by Richard's loyalists in the 1397

Parliament amidst an apparent promise of safety,[2] but this is not decisive proof that Richard was then prepared to exempt him from punishment. His past pardon had been revoked and his fellow-commander at Radcot Bridge, Sir Thomas Mortimer, accused of treason in killing the King's men there. The King was even prepared to alienate his intended heir, his cousin Roger Mortimer, by ordering him to arrest his uncle Sir Thomas 'or else'. It is possible that Richard turned against Roger at this point, as one source claims that as of 1398 the King regarded either Henry or Edmund of York's son Edward as his probable successor, not the Mortimers. Roger did not get a dukedom like other close aides. Given Richard's subsequent turning on Henry and lack of explicitly naming Roger's son Edmund as heir in 1398–9, would York's – adult – son have been named heir if Richard had needed to name one after Henry's exile?[3]

Henry's subsequent confrontation with Richard in 1398 followed a dramatic meeting on the road near Brentford with his fellow-'Appellant' Thomas Mowbray, Earl of Hereford (and soon to be Duke of Norfolk), who claimed that they were about to be singled out for punishment too and that Richard's arch-loyalists, led by his nephew Thomas Holland, had plotted to murder Henry and his father. Richard had supposedly backed this plot but pulled out. There was also the question of Mowbray's part in the murder of the arrested Duke of Gloucester while in his care at Calais in 1397 – again, he had acted at Richard's behest. Richard had apparently ordered Mowbray, as Captain of Calais (where Gloucester had been sent on his arrest) to kill him in August, weeks before he died; Mowbray failed to do so and the King sent out some 'heavies' from his Chamber with a second order in early September to ensure that he obeyed. This time Mowbray's servant John Hall and some others removed Gloucester from his cell in the town's castle to an inn and smothered him with a feather-bed, or so Hall claimed to Henry's Parliament in 1399. The intention was to forestall the legal necessity that if Gloucester was accused of treason by Parliament he would have to appear to answer the charges. As a peer, he faced trial by his fellow-lords, some of whom had acted with him in 1387–8, and the Lord Steward of England (the presiding officer) would be his own brother John of Gaunt. Would he be able to persuade them to refuse a death-sentence, or at least reveal embarrassing details about their past defiance of their King? Accordingly, Gloucester was liquidated before this scenario could occur – and the incident apparently played on Mowbray's conscience. The possibility of a 'show trial' of the King's enemies getting out of hand was a real one; the accused Earl of Arundel, another 'Appellant', tried to argue at his trial that he had been pardoned for his misdemeanours by the King in person (twice) at a time when Richard was of age and at least once when not under restraint so acting of his own free will. In reply, the no doubt embarrassed John of Gaunt retorted that the pardons had been revoked and tried to 'shut down' the discussion, with Arundel still arguing that he was no traitor. The Earl was hastily condemned and executed. Gloucester could have been expected to put up an equally strong resistance, from a better position as the King's uncle.

Did Gloucester's secret murder provide the final spark to the crisis of 1398? Public execution for an allegedly dangerous royal relative 'framed' for treason was more normal, as for Thomas of Lancaster in 1322 and Edmund, Earl of Kent in 1330. (In Kent's case, like Lancaster's, it had been counter-productive for the person behind the execution – Roger Mortimer.) It led to a series of charges and denials, mutual accusations of treasonous slander between Mowbray and Henry, and the reputed plan by the panicking Mowbray to waylay and murder John of Gaunt (who Henry had told about Mowbray's revelations) en route to Parliament. Mowbray would have done better to call on Henry and Gaunt for help against the King. It ended with the King's decision to call Henry and Mowbray to take part in a judicial 'trial by combat' by a 'Court of Chivalry' at Coventry in September 1398. At the last moment, the combat was called off – with Henry the better duellist so expected to win and thus be able to show that Mowbray was guilty (and that the King was guilty by association). Henry was banished for ten years and Mowbray for life.[4]

Once Mowbray had blurted out the truth about the King's patronage of the murder-plot against Gloucester, Henry had little option but to pursue it, with backing down unlikely to save him from revenge from a terrified Richard; and Mowbray had to try to prove his innocence or face humiliation, unthinkable for a senior aristocrat. The whole crisis had been caused by Mowbray's unexpected decision to approach Henry with his worries, a sign that he was afraid that the King was planning to move against him – though he had in a sense asked for trouble by failing to show his loyalty by publicly denouncing the anti-Ricardian legislation of the 'Merciless Parliament' along with other regime stalwarts. Clearly Mowbray panicked, and the King's unsavoury reputation for brooding malevolence and holding grudges drove him to seek Henry's support. The execution of Arundel, death sentence (revoked as a sign of Richard's alleged graciousness) to the 'Appellant' ally Lord Cobham, and grovelling confession and exile for life of the Earl of Warwick thus backfired on the King in late 1397 – as someone more realistic than Richard could have expected. But it should not be assumed that Henry would have been safe but for Mowbray admitting the extent of Richard's treachery and the killing of Gloucester to the possible next victim. This period in 1397–8 also saw Richard reversing the legal judgement of treason against the royal 'favourites' of Edward II, the Despensers, for using military force to defeat and seize the rebel Earl Thomas of Lancaster – Henry's maternal ancestor, from whom the Lancaster estates had descended to his mother, Blanche – in 1322. The successful rebellion of 1326 had seen Lancaster's attainder for treason reversed, his estates confirmed to his heirs, and the Despensers condemned instead. But reversing this would mean that the Dukedom of Lancaster and its estates could be confiscated from John, or later from his heir Henry, as heirs of a traitor. This intention was part of Mowbray's warning to Henry[5] – and even if the 'trial by combat' crisis had not occurred Richard's judicial action would have placed Henry's future under permanent threat. The possibility of a confrontation between them was thus high in any case, with Richard as the aggressor. The Despenser verdict's reversal showed that the King was at the least considering seizing the Lancaster inheritance, logically when John died, before the 'Henry vs Mowbray' confrontation gave him his opportunity for revenge. The incident on the road to Brentford and Henry's reaction, however, possibly caused an impatient Richard to 'jump the gun' rather than wait a year or two.

When Henry was first exiled after the dramatic aborted 'trial by battle' against Mowbray at Coventry all contemporaries knew this to be a punishment for a political crime – his part in the successful revolt of the 'Lords Appellant' against Richard in 1387–8. But he still had his estates and titles and the prospect of succeeding his father, Duke John, as the greatest magnate in the kingdom after the King – and if the Crown was to be inherited by male rather than female descent John and Henry were the childless Richard's heirs. Crucially, Richard's second wife, Isabella of France, was a girl of seven when they married in 1396 – the King would not have children for years. It has been suggested that both Henry and John expected him to be recalled in a few years, and he had a past predilection for travel (including a pilgrimage to Jerusalem) and overseas military service, which he could resume as a lordly knight-errant. Depriving him of his right to the dukedom would impoverish and humiliate him and make him dependent on others' charity, quite apart from it being of dubious legality. Nor would it improve his treatment by and hospitality from foreign rulers nervous of incurring Richard's enmity; a shorter exile was less unusual or demeaning. Accordingly he launched a sudden invasion of England while Richard was overseas in Ireland in July 1399, with a small group of his friends and clients and no support from his host in exile, Charles VI of France – Richard's father-in-law so with no interest in removing him. It seems that he deceived Charles as to his intentions, and at best had a small foreign contingent from Brittany.

The final decision to invade may have been due to Henry being encouraged by the deposed and exiled ex-Archbishop Thomas Arundel (Fitzalan) of York, who joined him in France shortly beforehand; Arundel's brother the Earl of Arundel had been executed in 1397 as another 1387–8 rebel and was being hailed as a martyr. Arguably, then, Richard's dismissal and exile of the Archbishop in September 1398 was a major blunder, in providing Henry with his most ruthless supporter (a man who would go on to initiate burnings for heresy under Henry as king) and welcome Church support. Arundel had lent his ecclesiastical sanction to the 'Appellants' in 1387–8 and been their choice for Lord Chancellor, in which rank Richard had been forced to retain him for years; the King had clearly been awaiting his chance for revenge and was to denounce him in personal letters after his condemnation. The Archbishop's prosecution by Parliament was technically at the request of the Commons, as supported by Speaker Sir John Bushy, but this was clearly a 'put-up job' directed by the King.[6]

1399 was not the first such invasion of England by an unjustly disgraced member of the immediate royal family, as Edward II's estranged wife, Isabella, and eldest son, Edward, had invaded (successfully) with help from Hainault and German mercenaries in 1326. But they had had far greater military assistance from abroad; the Queen (sister of her backer the King of France) had been treated with public vindictiveness by her husband and his allies the Despensers, and the Prince had been his father's undisputed heir. Their army has been estimated at anything from 500 to 2,700, with the Hainault contingent professional mercenaries; Henry had at most a couple of score, mostly English exiles.[7] Isabella's invasion seems to have been greeted with considerable public enthusiasm and a flood of recruits, especially magnates alienated by the iron grip of the Despensers on patronage. Most of Henry's flood of recruits in England – probably into the thousands, but not the 30,000 one source said – came once he had established himself in Yorkshire and been joined by the leading local magnate, Henry Percy Earl of Northumberland. Until that crucial reassurance that he would not be overwhelmed, his military position had been precarious; he could not even land at his first choice of site, Kingston-upon-Hull, due to local resistance.[8]

Nor was Henry's revolt that of the accepted heir, unlike Isabella's which had the King's eldest son among its nominal leadership. Henry's position as heir was more equivocal despite his popularity as a 'star' of tournaments and 'crusader' to Prussia, given that Richard had indicated the rival Mortimer claimants as his probable successors.[9] Henry's claim rested on his being the direct, male heir of Edward III's third surviving son, John of Gaunt; Edmund Mortimer was the heir by female descent of the second surviving son, Lionel of Clarence, and was also one more generation removed from the King as his great-grandson not grandson. The female descent would count as a bar to the throne in France, as shown by Isabella's being barred from transmitting her French royal claim to her son Edward III in 1328. It is arguable what the position was in England.[10] On a practical level, Edmund was underage and the nobles did not want another regency after the troubles of Richard's regency in 1377–81. Once Henry claimed the throne, therefore, it opened up the question of him being a usurper – and he was careful not to raise it until he had Richard in his hands and all resistance had ended.

Richard had weakened his position by going back on the terms of Henry's original exile with minimal explanation. If the King's cousin and a potential royal duke could be deprived of his rights by royal fiat, was anyone's title or lands safe from Richard? Henry could use this to present Richard's arbitrary action as a threat to all landowners. Indeed he carefully claimed to be returning to regain his estates (for which he had legal grounds) rather than to depose Richard; the usual legal excuse for rebellion of 'rescuing the King from his evil counsellors' could be deployed with a faction controlling office as in 1264, 1309, 1322, and 1326. It had been used against Richard himself by the 'Lords Appellant' in 1387–8. Given the structure of the kingdom's military machine – no 'standing army', and men being recruited for each campaign by their lords under royal licences – the reaction of the landed nobility was vital to both Henry and Richard. The precedent of 1326 would have suggested what was likely to happen if Henry won. Even senior political actors, the peers who had the estates and households available to deploy their retainers to stop Henry, would have realized that if he succeeded Richard was likely to be deposed like Edward II had been. The King had been spared such a fate in the 1387–8 rebellion (though his uncle the Duke of Gloucester may have suggested deposition)[11] and had subsequently killed or exiled all the leaders of the revolt. This had not been done by strictly legal means either – Gloucester had been sent out of the public view to Calais and apparently smothered by Richard's 'heavies', possibly supervised by Thomas Mowbray, later Duke of Norfolk (Henry's fellow-exile after their aborted judicial combat at Coventry in 1398). Backing Henry was likely to make him king, with failure meaning the full penalties for treason from an increasingly vindictive Richard – though the Percies were later to claim that they had only supported Henry because they believed his public oath not to take the throne.[12]

But the question of whether Henry's allies expected him to take the throne obscures the very weak military position that he was in as he landed with a few hundred men, though he gained support as he marched south from Yorkshire to confront the royal government. Richard had taken a large army to Ireland, led by his own trusted bodyguard of Cheshire archers, but there were many magnates available to rally to his cause. One crucial issue is why the position of the government was so weak as well – and why the regency failed to react but passively awaited Henry's arrival, retreating west to the Bristol area. If only a few senior magnates – led by the Percies under the Earl of Northumberland and his son, 'Hotspur', and brother the Earl of Worcester – really supported Henry's landing, why did not more people rally to Richard's regent, his uncle Edmund, Duke of York? Or to Richard himself as he belatedly returned from Ireland? The striking lack of resistance to Henry cannot be written off as simply fear.

Why did York himself, the next heir to Richard if the exiled Henry was excluded and the young Edmund Mortimer's claim disavowed, not endeavour to halt Henry's advance? He had every reason to oppose his nephew's invasion, with the succession to Richard in prospect if Henry was debarred from the throne by reason of his exile – as Richard may have already hinted.[13] He apparently knew Henry was at sea with hostile intent, though not where he was heading as he expected an invasion of the south or south-west. (Isabella had landed in Suffolk in 1326.) But he remained supine at Bristol until Henry arrived and then came to terms with him. He was a timid character with little military experience and in his late fifties, but he had other nobles to rely on. Richard had murdered his brother Gloucester, dishonoured his brother John of Gaunt by invalidating his will, and was relying on men who were accused of being 'low-born' adventurers not the usual high nobility – did this encourage him not to act? This apparently outweighed the fact that his own son and heir, Edward of Aumale, was one of Richard's abruptly-elevated new peers, the 'duketti'. Either he was aware he would have no support against Henry or he believed Henry had justice on his side. The speedy collapse of Richard's rule in 1399, as with the similar desertion of Edward II in 1326, shows that it was not just propaganda by the victors that they had popular opinion and at least the tacit support of most magnates on their side. Henry may genuinely have had enthusiasts flocking to his cause; the size of his army by the time he reached Bristol was clearly much greater than it had been when he landed in Yorkshire.[14] By contrast, when the similarly exiled Edward IV landed (at the same site, Ravenspur) in 1471 his army remained small until his unstable brother George, Duke of Clarence, abandoned the usurping regime to join him at Coventry. He claimed only to be returning to secure his estates as Duke of York, to which he had unquestionable legal rights, not the more dubious title of king. His position was thus similar to Henry's – though support may have been deterred by the superior military reputation of the foe he faced, Warwick 'the Kingmaker'.[15]

Great store was set by legality in senior political and Church circles in the world of fourteenth century courts, with important scholars arguing out the legal and moral justifications of increased powers for kingship. Richard defied the legal norms by refusing to pass on the massive Lancaster inheritance from John of Gaunt to Henry in February 1399, despite his promises to John – though it is possible that he was seeking to negotiate better terms with Henry for granting it, not denying it permanently, and Henry hid this detail to make himself seem the wronged party.[16] In legal terms, the Despenser judgement's reversal implied that John's wife's ancestors might have had no legal right to the Lancaster title and lands, and so Richard seizing them was technically legal and he could – and would? – grant them out again later as a personal favour. But if this was Richard's intention, he should have sent messages to Henry to assure him of this instead of – sadistically? – leaving him in limbo at the royal mercy. If Richard was thus engaged in blackmail rather than outright illegality, he did so incompetently and caused a reaction that he was not expecting. In any case, it was clear that he could not be trusted to keep to an agreement.

The use of the King's large new Cheshire bodyguard to intimidate Parliament, his overhaul of the judiciary to promote his right to arbitrary decisions, the punishment of the leaders of the successful attack on the King's 'party' in 1387–8, and the promotion of 'low-born' royal friends to senior noble rank in 1397–9 may have been less feared or resented across the political 'nation' than Henry later alleged. The point of the massive creation of peers on 29 September 1397 was not so much to ennoble 'low-born' royal toadies as to entrench Richard's closest allies in leading roles within the peerage, supplied with lands forfeited from the ruined 'Appellants'. Most of the creations were of existing peers or heirs of ancient blood with higher rank, e.g. Henry of Bolingbroke, Thomas Mowbray, Thomas Percy (Earl of Worcester), the Duke of York's son Edward of Aumale, John Holland (Richard's nephew), John's brother Thomas Holland, and Thomas Despenser. The most controversial of them, royal chamberlain and ex-captain of Cherbourg, Sir William Scrope, was the only 'self-made' courtier ennobled, and he was the eldest son of former Chancellor Lord Scrope. Sir John Beaufort, only recently made Earl of Somerset and now made Marquis of Dorset, was also elevated suspiciously fast but was the eldest illegitimate son of John of Gaunt and so of the royal blood. But it is clear that Richard had embarked on an unusually intensive programme of promoting royal power, which the new pomp and dignity of his appearances in state at court complemented.[17] His attack on the right of the judiciary to declare the law autonomous from royal reinterpretation and persecution of defiant judges shows that he had a concept of '*L'etat c'est moi*' if not incipient megalomania.[18] At the least, it indicates an obsession to put himself beyond the reach of legal control by his nobles, reacting to their use of Parliament to restrain him by going against his wishes to exile his favourites in 1386. It is notable that any judges who expressed reservations about carrying out his wishes met royal fury, not reluctant acceptance of their independence of thought – Richard could not contemplate any defiance. In terms of international academic and constitutional law he may have been influenced by contemporary writers who built up the concept of the supreme secular sovereign, the 'emperor', as opposed to the all-too-fallible and divided papacy; his first wife, Anne, had been sister of the Holy Roman emperor-elect, King Wenceslas IV of Bohemia. (Wenceslas was to end up deposed too.)

But this autocratic theory was not practical politics in England, where the magnates' consent was essential. Did Richard make the same mistake of assuming that his magnates would obey his demands and accept his theorists' elevation of the royal office in all circumstances that Charles I did? Defenders of his reputation against Henry's propagandists may argue that he was seeking to build up the royal power – and the King's ability to act for the country's benefit – as a principled idealist and an opponent of defiant magnates, hoping to end the run of successful revolts against royal authority. In his letters after the 1397–8 'purge' to his fellow-sovereigns, Duke Albert of Holland and Emperor Manuel Paleologus of the Byzantine Empire, he stressed that he had suppressed his factious and untrustworthy nobles to restore peace to his nation for his lifetime.[19] He may well have believed this. But the personal is rarely separable from the theoretical in Late Medieval politics, and his vengeful actions towards his past coercers were those of spite as much as of principle. The private murder of Gloucester, in particular, avoided any necessity of an embarrassing public trial – although he was a controversial figure and did not deserve much sympathy given his crude threats to Richard in 1387–8 and his insistence on the execution of Richard's tutor, Sir Simon Burley. Revealingly, at Arundel's trial his alleged verbal insistence in 1387 to the King that Burley be killed was dragged up by Richard[20] – was this seen as his worst crime? The arbitrary extension of the terms of exile imposed on Henry of Bolingbroke and Thomas Mowbray in 1398–9 was also blatantly unjust and deceitful. It is clear that it was the arbitrary nature of Richard's decisions that helped to unnerve his enemies and stimulate the decision to remove him. If he wished to reverse a solemn legal promise without explanation he did so, as when he ignored his 1394 pardon of the Earl of Arundel (not forced out of him like the 1388 pardons of the 'Appellants') and executed him in 1397.

Richard's choice of victims was an evident reaction to his powerlessness in 1388 as a faction of rebellious magnates, led by his uncle Gloucester, ruthlessly executed or exiled his friends and reputedly threatened him with deposition. Much has been made of the psychological implications of this humiliation on the young King, and his desire for revenge and need to promote an image of power and majesty thereafter. It is notable that his choices for court influence and senior office in the mid-1380s (led by Robert de Vere and Michael de la Pole), as in 1397–9, excluded most landed magnates from families who were traditionally important at court – and both occasions led to a violent reaction from those affected. (This was not, however, limited to Richard's reign; armed revolt against an unpopular faction of promotion-monopolizing courtiers faced Henry III and Edward II.) Those men of noble birth who were honoured with titles in 1397–9 were criticized as the 'duketti', unjustly over-promoted cadets; the grant of a dukedom to Richard's nephew Edward of Aumale, Earl of Surrey, was swiftly reversed by Henry in 1399 and led to the recipient revolting. It is clear that Richard preferred to rely on men of his own creation, both within and from outside the nobility – and that his emotional instability did not commence after the humiliations of 1388, as he had already been reliably believed to have considered murdering his uncle John of Gaunt in a bizarre incident earlier (see below).

Even at the time, some writers stressed the King's lack of wisdom and reliance on a coterie of 'unworthy' and resented advisers, with some hints being made about the sexual implications of his excessive fondness for and lavishing of honours on certain supporters.[21] An insecure need for emotional 'dependence' on trusted figures is as likely as an explanation as suppressed homosexuality, which Henry of Bolingbroke or his ruthless allies such as Archbishop Arundel (deprived of his see and his brother executed by Richard) would have been capable of exploiting in 1399 – as the more clearly homosexual Edward II's deposers did in 1326 – if feasible. It should be remembered that, unlike his father and grandfather, Richard had been brought up until the age of ten away from court in the household of his ailing father, mostly at Berkhamsted well away from London – he did not know his elite contemporaries on easy terms as a boy, as Edward III and the 'Black Prince' did. His isolation, firstly away from London and then in the unique role of king where deference was required to him, plausibly increased if not caused his 'distancing' from the great nobles and a corresponding reliance on a small coterie of friends. Nor were women absent from his court. It seems that he was quick to turn on friends who seemed to betray him, and reluctant to forgive; Thomas Mowbray had been one of his intimates in the early 1380s but was never to regain this status after he joined the 'Appellants' in 1387–8. This indicates emotional insecurity rather than homosexuality, and Richard is less easily accused of the latter than Edward II. Richard's reliance on his mother's kin, the Hollands (descendants of her first marriage), can be paralleled with Henry III's dependence on his mother, Isabella's, Poitevin relatives and his French wife Eleanor's family. In all cases, the King trusted his personal dependants rather than the independently-landed aristocratic barons. And Henry III, like Richard with Henry of Bolingbroke, was turned on by a relative who he had elevated to honours but who could not trust him – Simon de Montfort, his brother-in-law.

There is an undeniable fact that time and again Richard is said to have either thought up or encouraged others' plots to murder his relatives. The most frequent victim of these ideas, from 1385 right through to late 1398, was his uncle John, who was supposed by his enemies to be aiming at the throne during Richard's minority. Richard had been planning to kill him in a surprise attack at Sheen in 1385, when he was only eighteen, and when John heard he apparently turned up at Court by surprise with a large entourage, ordered the King's guards away, and confronted him with the charge. Henry, as John's heir, may have feared being poisoned in the late 1390s as he purchased a stone said to give protection.[22] When Richard decided to dispose of his youngest uncle, Gloucester, most violent and implacable of the 'Appellants' who had destroyed his power and killed his advisers in 1388, he did not give him any trial but had him sent away to Calais and smothered in an inn by his retainers. He was then said to have planned to murder John (and Henry?) before the Shrewsbury Parliament of January 1398, in panic at what they would do after the Duke of Norfolk had confessed to them about killing Gloucester on Richard's orders.[23] As early as 1394, it was said that the King had had a hand in a mysterious Cheshire revolt aimed at seizing and killing Henry and his father; the rebel leader Thomas Thwaite was arrested but allowed to escape.[24] Even allowing for post-1399 Henrician propaganda, Richard was clearly mercurial, totally untrustworthy, and ready to resort to violence as a first not a last resort as early as 1385–6.

In medical terms, it is quite possible that there was a manic streak of emotional instability in the Plantagenet dynasty and that Richard was the latest manifestation of this trait. In the twelfth century there had been stories about the supernatural origins of the savage temper of the 'Devil's Brood' and their father Henry II, namely the elusive Countess Melusine who allegedly flew out through a church window rather than have to celebrate Mass.[25] Henry and his youngest son, John, were notorious for their explosive tempers, supposedly leading to them rolling around the floor in uncontrollable rages. Both had made unwise outbursts in the heat of the moment, Henry asking who would rid him of Thomas Becket and John killing his nephew Arthur with his own hands.[26] Simular violent outbursts were reliably reported of Edward I, who once tore out his son's hair and on another occasion threw a daughter's coronet in a fire.[27] A reaction to his father's violence marked Edward II, in his case involving unwise emotional dependence on controversial figures and possible homosexuality. Although less affected by his dominant father as John died when he was nine, Henry III was as dependant on a small number of unpopular advisers – and as stubbornly attached to them despite the political risks – as Edward II, in his case his Poitevin kin. Edward III and his eldest son (the perpetrator of a bloodbath at Limoges in 1370) both made harsh decisions like John in the 'field', though Edward III was talked out of killing the emissaries from Calais in 1347. John, by contrast, cold-bloodedly executed a number of Welsh hostages after his vassal Llywelyn ap Iorweth of Gwynedd revolted and probably starved Matilda de Braose and her son to death. Richard II, a son of a strong father like his great-grandfather Edward II, bore notable emotional similarities to the latter; and Henry III, son of the ferocious John, was regarded as equally untrustworthy. This alternation between energetic men of violence and 'weak', dependant men cannot be explained away as a result of the pressure of office on medieval sovereigns, as these distinctive character-traits were not common to other royal families. Was this history of emotional instability in the family a hereditary trait?

What if Richard II's reign had commenced later... ?

Given normal health and longevity, 'Edward IV' could have been expected to live into the 1390s. This would have had a major impact on his son Richard's reign, not only from Edward's dynamism and qualities of leadership producing a more favourable position in the French wars through the 1380s. Aggressive and acquisitive younger nobles seeking military success, such as Buckingham/Gloucester and Earl Thomas of Arundel, would have been in the ascendant among the King's younger captains and not driven by resentment of a 'pacifist', pro-peace policy at Court. The lack of French campaigns and the drive towards a truce in the early to mid-1380s may or may not have been the primary responsibility of Richard's new Chancellor, Michael de la Pole (from a successful merchant dynasty), who was to be dismissed and indicted by the 'Wonderful Parliament' in 1386. Even if the teenage Richard was not the main organizer of this policy at the time, he clearly approved of it and promoted its enthusiasts; and in the early 1390s he returned to it once he was free of the constraints imposed on him by the 'Appellants'. The continued rule of a group of 'pro-war' noblemen as close allies of a sympathetic king under 'Edward IV' would have meant that the militant Thomas was among the King's confidants, not excluded from influence, and so he would not have been building up the grievances that led him to rally the 'Appellants' to overthrow Richard's ministers in 1388.

Whether 'Edward IV' would have passed on the role of military leader in later French campaigns to Thomas, Duke of Gloucester or to the Earl of Arundel and been physically in decline by the mid-1380s, the English failure to defeat the French would have made an eventual truce attractive to both noble rivals of the 'war party' and in Parliament. Nor was the continuation of war popular within France, which despite its real-life improved military position in the early 1380s had anti-war outbreaks among the rural populace affected by English raiding. Exhaustion would have led to a renewal of the stalemate of 1360, possibly around 1384 to 1387.

Whether or not the effects of excessive campaigning hastened 'Edward IV's' early death in the 1380s, Richard could probably be expected to be king some time in his twenties. His unmilitary character, and love of the latest international 'luxury culture', make it possible that his relationship with his hot-tempered and militaristic father might resemble that of Edward II as a young man with his father Edward I, with Richard similarly showing excessive partiality for and lavishing gifts and office on an unpopular Court 'outsider'. In Edward II's case the recipient was a charismatic but sharp-tongued Gascon squire, Piers Gaveston, who mocked the nobles and infuriated the elderly Edward I, who exiled him; he was only recalled once Edward II was king. His prominent place at the coronation, an earldom normally kept for royal relatives (Cornwall), and a semi-royal bride flaunted his power over the new king, and he was forcibly exiled after an aristocratic coup; his second recall led to his being hunted down and killed in 1312. In Richard's case in the mid-1380s the recipient of the young King's affection and excessive patronage was Robert de Vere. De Vere, made Duke of Ireland and regarded like Gaveston as an unworthy monopolizer of royal patronage, was at least English not Gascon, and a 'respectable' titled aristocrat. But like Gaveston he was removed from office and England as soon as his enemies seized control of political power (1387/8), though he was of more acceptable birth than Gaveston (a cadet of a titled family) and was not accused of homosexuality. De Vere was the focus of Parliamentary hostility in 1386 and 'Appellant' hostility in 1387, even if his unpopular Lord Chancellorship and surprise elevation to a dukedom were a useful 'peg' on which to hang general magnate hostility to the King's choice of ministers.

Had 'Edward IV' lived through the 1380s this crisis would not have taken place, with the 'pro-war' nobility being in the political ascendant under a king whose whole career had centred on war against the French. The financial exhaustion and military frustration of the sort of war that Edward could be expected to pursue might in due course have led to a truce, with more practical and financially realistic men such as de la Pole taking a role in government. (All Edward's senior contemporaries and close friends, such as

Chandos, Manny, and Knollys, were dead by this point.) But the younger and militarily inexperienced de Vere could have expected no power at Court or endowments with land and offices until Richard was king, although the judicial proponents of the royal prerogative (e.g. Tresilian) who the 'Appellants' attacked might have been called on by a frustrated King Edward to give legal backing to increased royal powers over raising finance. The focus of the 'Appellant' punishment of the judges in 1387 was their legal decisions in favour of royal power and against Parliamentary oversight of royal exercise of power – but if a war-weary Parliament in the 1380s had refused to fund more royal warfare King Edward could have been equally keen to rein in Parliament as Richard was. An experienced and charismatic handler of the senior nobility and personally adept at their favourite sports (such as the hunt and tournaments), Edward would never have alienated a substantial group of nobles as Richard did during the mid-1380s, even had he been constrained into peace by lack of money or ill-health and 'pacifist' ministers gained influence. And with him as king, his son Richard would have been free of his real-life political 'mistakes' of factional rule pre-1386.

Was a magnate rising against Richard II possible c.1399 even if there had not been a previous crisis in 1387–8?
Richard would not have had the opportunity to be threatened by questions about his emotional stability and competence – as indicated by odd episodes such as the apparent plot by his close friends to murder John of Gaunt with his backing early in 1385.[28] Assuming that he would have come to the throne around the late 1380s to mid-1390s, he would have been free of the 'trauma' and insults to his dignity inflicted by his humiliation in 1387–8 and the desire for vengeance on the relatives and nobles who had murdered or exiled his close advisers. But his character and interests would still have been at odds with the 'war party' who would have favoured a return to conflict with France, and the personal attitudes and financial needs of men like Gloucester, Arundel, Thomas Beauchamp (Earl of Warwick), and Richard's cousin Henry of Bolingbroke (Earl of Derby) impelled them into opposition to continued peace and its proponents. An event such as Richard's treaty with Charles VI and marriage to the latter's daughter in 1396 would still have brought matters to a head, with the possibility of a military confrontation between 'favourite'-dominated king and magnates as in 1308, 1312, 1322, and 1326. Had Richard's acquisitive friend Robert de Vere still been alive (he died in 1392 in exile), he could have been the focus of enmity now rather than in 1387. But the resulting crisis would not have been made worse by Richard's memories of the executions of 1388, although it is possible that the harsh and vindictive Gloucester in particular might have resorted to

executions of royal allies and so stoked up Richard's resentment. (The chroniclers of the 1387–8 crisis put the main blame for the killings then on him and Arundel, with Henry of Bolingbroke attempting to mediate.)

It should not be assumed that Richard's unacceptably autocratic behaviour in 1397–9 – and the insecurity caused by his executions – was merely a reaction to the events of 1388–9, and would not have existed but for the Appellants' violent intimidation. He had already behaved similarly in 1385 when his personal clique were involved in his potentially violent confrontation with John of Gaunt. Robert de Vere seems to have been a prime mover in this harebrained plot, but the essential point is that Richard was prepared to listen to him not ignore the idea. Fearing murder and retaliating with intimidation, John had felt obliged to enter the King's presence with an armed escort at the height of that crisis (as the Appellants did in 1387), in this case at usefully isolated Sheen not the Tower. Parliament had attacked the King's resented ministers such as de Vere in 1386 as the Appellants' tame MPs did in 1388. The legal assertion of royal autocracy from compliant judges such as Tresilian had been apparent in the mid-1380s as well as in 1397–9.[29] Nor was the Appellants' intimidation of Richard possible only because John was absent in Castile in 1388–9, as John had used similar tactics (though he had left the King's advisers alone) in 1385–6;[30] he was as likely as Gloucester's allies to react with force to royal policy that threatened him. A violent man, he had threatened Bishop Courtenay with physical assault in front of witnesses for trying his protégé John Wyclif; the young King possibly feared deposition or murder by his ambitious uncle. An armed appearance by militant 'excluded' magnates in a king's presence as intimidation was not unprecedented, as it had been used by de Montfort's party to constrain the untrustworthy Henry III in 1258 and 1264 (the latter involving battle as in 1387) and several times against Edward II. So was constraint by a magnate council appointed by the King's critics, which had been used by the de Montfort party and by the anti-Edward II 'Lords Ordainers'. This use of a council appointed against the King's wishes was imposed on Richard in 1386 after de Vere's dismissal as Lord Chancellor. The tactic of intimidating the King by murdering his 'favourite' so he could not be recalled from exile had been used against Edward II's first intimate, Piers Gaveston, in 1312, and the main culprit (Thomas of Lancaster) was duly executed by the King a decade later. Perhaps Richard's uncle Thomas, Duke of Gloucester, should have remembered that when he had Richard's allies executed in 1388.

If John had been in England at the time that the Appellants rose, with his son Henry amongst them, they would have had to take account of his possible reaction but could still have gone ahead – the major difference would have been that Gloucester would have had no hope of gaining the Crown and thus the real-life autumn 1387 talk of Richard's deposition in his favour would have been unlikely. A cabal of leading aristocrats constraining the King for 'unwise' advisers and policies in the 1390s should then have led to a reassertion of royal power and retaliatory arrests and executions, as in real life were carried out in 1397–9 in reply to events in 1387–8; the timetable would have been different from what happened in real life.

The deposition of Richard II, 1399: the events leading up to Richard's deposition

Richard staged a major reassertion of royal power in 1397–9, following his humiliations in 1387–8 when he had had to submit to the superior force of the coalition of 'Lords Appellant' and allow the execution of his closest supporters. Having arrested and probably murdered the leader of the 1387–8 revolt, his youngest uncle Thomas, Duke of Gloucester, he proceeded to take advantage of the quarrel between Henry of Bolingbroke and Thomas Mowbray to require them to fight a rare judicial duel at Coventry in 1398. Instead of allowing the duel to proceed he cancelled it when they were already horsed and about to fight, and announced that they were both exiled. This quarrel, which aided Richard's plans, indeed, hinged on the allegation that Richard was planning revenge on them despite all his solemn promises to forgive them for their earlier actions – which they clearly thought only too likely. (Thomas was alleged to have personally killed Gloucester on the King's behalf and later to have been part of an aborted plan to murder John of Gaunt and Henry in February 1398, so Richard had reasons to discredit and silence him.) Henry was banished for ten years, later extended, and Thomas for life.

The Earl of Warwick was arrested and exiled to the Isle of Man for his actions in the earlier revolt, the Earl of Arundel executed, and the latter's brother deposed as Archbishop of Canterbury. Warwick's panic-stricken grovelling at his trial[31] bears a resemblance to a Stalinist 'show-trial', and must have worried other potential victims of royal revenge. Arundel, by contrast, argued with his judges about his earlier pardon still being valid. Popular reaction was shown by rumours that Arundel's head had been miraculously reunited with his body, i.e. that he was a saintly victim of unjust royal murder like Thomas of Lancaster in 1322.[32] Parliament was intimidated by the King's large bodyguard of Cheshire archers into passing whatever legislation Richard desired, and the King seemed to be invincible. It was now made treason to coerce the sovereign, all past 'controlling' councils such as that of 1310 and 1388–9 were roundly condemned, and all new peers and office-holders had to swear to approve and uphold Richard's recent legal reforms. He attempted to make it treason to reverse the actions of this Parliament, a misunderstanding of the powers available to him to restrict his successors which the Chief Justice had to point out, and was supposed to be intending to reverse the posthumous pardon of Lancaster (under which his lands had passed down through his family to John of Gaunt, who could be stripped of the Duchy of Lancaster without it.) His methods undoubtedly caused disquiet, particularly the implication that nobody who had acted against his authority in the past was safe from a long-meditated vengeance, and people made comparisons with the behaviour of Edward II in 1322 – with the unspoken reminder of what had happened to Edward.[33] There was no one monopolizer of royal patronage like the widely loathed 'favourite' of the 1320s, Hugh Despenser, and Richard had a bloc of loyal peers loaded with new titles – led by his Holland half-brother and nephew.

The lynching of his 'low-born' ministers Bushey and Bagot in 1399 suggests that they were widely unpopular, and not only with the nobility as 'arrivistes' – even if the executions at Cirencester were led by Henry's agents who may have paid the locals to show enthusiasm for an act of justice on the 'tyrant's favourites.[34] But the King's desire to stress his legal rights and achieve constitutional verification of 'autocracy' suggests that Richard, isolated in a hierarchical Court where flattery not plain speaking was the order of the day, mistook the image of power for its reality. His father and grandfather had never made that mistake, governing more by the consent of their senior nobles than by legal theory; they had also led the aristocracy in traditional – military – pursuits, acting as the personal focus of a chivalric ethos in competitive sports (e.g. the tournament). The image of King Arthur by which Edward III set such store – and which he replicated in the Order of the Garter – was as grandiose and magnificent as anything dreamed up by Richard in his Court, but it was of a king who led his nobles by personal example and shared their knightly ethos. Edward III began his effective reign by personally leading a band of young nobles to arrest his mother's lover, Roger Mortimer, at Nottingham Castle in October 1330, centred his creation of new peerages (and the Garter knighthoods) on these comrades, and ventured his person in individual combat. His actions were rash at times, as in his ambush of a party of French knights seeking to sneak into newly-conquered Calais (they could have been overwhelmed at once but he preferred a challenge to equal combat) and in the naval battle off Winchelsea (his ship sank).[35] Foolish or not in terms of the danger, it acted as a bond with his peers – and the well-known aversion of the unmilitary Richard to warfare was a psychological barrier between him and the men he would need to back up his authority whatever legal decrees he issued. The 'manly' chivalric warriors Edward I and III had faced major magnate dissent from their policies, in 1294 and 1340, so a confrontation between autocratic king and critics was possible even with a wiser and more 'military' king – but it was only the 'unmilitary' Henry III, Edward II, and Richard II who came off worst in these confrontations. Arguably, it was lack of respect or trust for the sovereign by the King's senior nobles that added a crucial element to their being willing and able to constrain him.

The revolution of 1399: how unlikely was it that it would take place? Richard's absence – Henry's luck

The invasion – or rather, small expedition – that Henry mounted against Richard in 1399 depended on a number of factors. First, Richard's departure for Ireland – his second such expedition there, to a land previously unvisited by its English suzerains since John (also a double visitor) in 1210. Military expeditions to enforce the King's rule in person over the 'Celtic fringe' outside England were not unusual, but were more usually land-based ones to Scotland – most recently Edward III's in 1336. Edward and his grandfather Edward I had both enforced their direct or indirect rule of Scotland in person with huge and impressive expeditions, and Edward I had memorably died at Burgh-by-Sands on the Solway Firth as he travelled north in a litter to seek a final showdown with the returned 'usurper' Robert Bruce in July 1307. Edward III had marched as far as Lochindorb in Moray to back up his protégé and vassal Edward Balliol against Bruce loyalists, with only temporary effect. Expeditions to France were more common for overseas ventures; despite their limited 'direct rule' of the Anglicized 'Pale' around Dublin and indirect overlordship of larger areas, neither Edward I nor Edward III had seen fit to lead expeditions to Ireland to 'show the flag' and increase their territory. The military situation there under Edward I was much more secure than that facing later fourteenth century rulers, as 'Longshanks' inherited the strong thirteenth century Anglo-Irish baronial control of much of the country and his feudal vassals ruled as far west as Connacht. But in the 1310s a 'nationalist' (ethnic and cultural) revival by previously evicted or subdued Irish tribal rulers drove out the Anglo-Norman settler barons and their allies from much of central, northern and western Ireland, aided by Robert Bruce via a Scottish expedition under his brother Edward as 'King of Ireland' (which Robert assisted himself in person in 1316). This was halted by the English, but as of the 1370s their king only directly ruled the 'Pale' in Midhe and Leinster and had nominal authority over those allied Anglo-Norman barons who had survived further west, e.g. the Fitzgeralds and Butlers of Munster, plus a few 'friendly' Irish dynastic rulers nearer to Dublin.

Edward III notably did not think of fighting to restore his ancestors' position in Ireland as he did in Scotland, though by the time his Scottish wars were winding down in the late 1330s he was heavily embroiled with the Bruces' French patron Philip VI. He probably regarded the absence of 'modern' castles and walled towns, knightly aristocrats reading chivalric romances and involved in pan-European feudal chivalric culture, and use of armoured cavalry or sieges in warfare as showing that Ireland was an uncivilized place unworthy of his attentions. Instead, Edward betrothed his second (surviving) son Lionel to the heiress of the Earls of Ulster – a key baronial dynasty previously married into the Bruces – as a baby in 1342.[36] Lionel was clearly intended to take over the earldom and use Ulster as a base for serving as his father's viceroy once he was adult. When Edward finally bothered to consider improving the English King's position in the island in 1361–2 – after peace had been signed with France – he despatched Lionel there as 'King's Lieutenant' with a medium-sized army, but military results were mixed;[37] both Anglo-Irish and Irish lords were likely to submit temporarily to greater military force but revolt or ignore royal policies once the threat was abated. Garrisoning castles to contain them was expensive and time-consuming, and the scattered and usually small garrisons were difficult to hold without continual reinforcement; reliance on a loyal local magnate was much easier. Lionel's wife Elizabeth de Burgh died in 1363; he went off to Italy in pursuit of a prestigious second match with the Visconti and died, and in due course his daughter Philippa was married off into the Mortimer family so these experienced Welsh Border barons could act as the King's Irish lieutenants. Unfortunately, her husband Edmund Mortimer soon died (1381); their son Roger was chosen by Richard II as the new Lord Lieutenant in 1392, aged eighteen, i.e. as early as was practicable.[38] Richard had previously bestowed the governorship, for life, with an unprecedented Marquessate, on his favourite Robert de Vere in 1385 – 'contracting out' the problem to a loyal family connection as Edward III had done, but not to one with any lands in (and thus a call on local loyalty from) Ireland. The de Vere grant was greeted with hostility in both England and Ireland, and was cancelled at the favourite's fall.[39] Richard then led an expedition there in person in 1394, claiming to the Duke of Burgundy in a letter that the purpose was to punish rebels and restore good government and justice.[40] His interest was commendable after a century and a half of royal neglect, though the recent shock death of his first wife, Anne of Bohemia, probably meant he was anxious to find distraction away from London.[41] The expedition, of around 7–8000 men, had clear military superiority over the ill-armed Irish 'kerns' of the local tribal Irish dynasts and duly achieved the submission of Art MacMurrough, principal 'rebel' lord of Leinster, and of the leading

O'Neills of Ulster.[42] By the end of his expedition in early 1395 he had obtained the submission of all the Irish dynasts within reach of his military power in south-east Ireland, and wrote that his intention was to show politic mercy to the 'rebel Irish' (i.e. those lords of non-English descent traditionally subject to his ancestors), alienated by past misgovernment, to coax them away from alliance with the 'wild Irish' (i.e. those never subject to English rule).[43] Treating the Anglo-Irish barons, descendants of the twelfth to thirteenth century settlers (some of them semi-Hibernicised in culture), and the ethnically Irish lords as equal parts of the 'lordship of Ireland' showed political sense. It helped to cut costs by avoiding endless warfare for the bankrupt government in Dublin, though of course it also played to Richard's desire to extend his own rule; and Richard's itineraries show that he generally spent more time outside southern England than most thirteenth and fourteenth century kings so he was interested in his outlying dominions.

Arguably, the 'British' dimension of his rule meant more to him than to any king since Edward I – and the literary fabulations of 'Arthurian' enthusiasts since Geoffrey of Monmouth had built up a picture of the King of England as a sort of 'emperor' within the British Isles, which no doubt appealed to Richard. Thus, in summer 1399 he returned to Ireland rather than resting on his laurels after his crushing of the 'Appellants' – and left his kingdom open for Henry to invade. The surprise expedition may have been planned even before John of Gaunt died in February 1399, and new disputes between Art MacMurrough and the Dublin government in 1397–8 had built up to the point of open warfare. (The bad faith was mostly on the English side).[44] Richard had removed his cousin Roger Mortimer as Lord Lieutenant, replacing him with his nephew and favourite Edward of Aumale (Duke of Surrey), on 26 July 1398. Surrey was required to take homages from his Irish vassals, but not to send these men on to England to repeat their vows to the King as was usual – which suggests that Richard was already intending to come to Dublin to receive them there.[45] In June 1399 Richard arrived at Waterford to lead his second expedition against MacMurrough, but this time could not corner him into surrendering. The news of Henry's landing in England then caused the expedition to be abandoned. The dispute between MacMurrough and the Dublin government in 1397–8 thus served as the main reason for Richard to return to Ireland – so without it would Richard have left his kingdom? Given his restlessness and his interest in Ireland, it is conceivable that he would have gone anyway, albeit possibly waiting until 1400 or 1401 to see how Edward of Aumale fared as Lord Lieutenant and if he needed royal military support. The O'Neills as well as the MacMurroughs were restive,[46] and ambitious Richard could have sought to restore the politico-military strength of his probable heir Edmund Mortimer (Roger's son and Lionel's great-grandson) as Earl of Ulster by seizing land from the O'Neills.

Even once Richard had left for Ireland, Henry's expedition to England was not certain. The news of the expedition was sent by Richard to his father-in-law, Charles VI of France, in late May 1399,[47] and presumably Henry then planned his invasion. But Charles offered him no support, and so he had to rely on French and English private initiatives; the current chief minister at the French Court was Charles' uncle Duke Philip of Burgundy who relied on Richard's goodwill for English trade with his Netherlands dominions and so opposed Henry's plans. Henry had also failed to secure a marital alliance with Philip's brother, the Duke of Berri, probably due to Philip's intervention,[48] and possibly sought aid from the autonomous French vassal Duchy of Brittany (according to Froissart);[49] he was later to marry into that dynasty. To put Philip and other Ricardian allies off the scent, he pretended that his journey to Boulogne for embarkation was the first step in a pilgrimage; his English allies then sent ships to Boulogne to pick up his small force and take them to England. But Philip apparently got wind of what was afoot and sent orders to the port authorities of Boulogne not to admit any English ships.[50] Henry managed to evade this, embarked his men, and sailed – but if Philip had succeeded he would have been stranded.

The revolution of 1399: popular? Supported under false pretences?

It is debatable to what extent Henry had active support as he returned in 1399, as opposed to leading aristocrats being unwilling to oppose an experienced and tough campaigner – a veteran of the brutal Teutonic Knights' wars against the Lithuanians who had legal right on his side as long as he claimed to be pursuing his duchy not the Crown. The latter claim was not made until he had Richard in his power, as his Percy allies later complained. Once he had landed in Yorkshire at the end of June, he apparently swore that he had only returned to secure his legal rights to the Duchy of Lancaster.[51] The location of his oath (or oaths) was not clear – Bridlington, Knaresborogh, or Doncaster? – though he may have sworn more than one. He was supposed to have sworn either not to claim the Crown at all or to hand it over to the 'worthiest' candidate – the latter, of course, could mean himself if his peers judged him worthy, and the 'election' by Parliament when Richard abdicated on 30 September could be judged as meeting that condition. He also swore not to levy the oppressive taxation that Richard had done, which he more definitely violated under the needs of war in 1401 with resultant riots.[52] It is possible that some magnates who joined him either expected Richard to be placed under restraint, as he had been in 1387–8 only now permanently, or to be removed in favour of his chosen heir, Edmund Mortimer.[53] The problem of restraining a monarch with a council given special legal powers was of the resultant reaction when the King recovered his freedom of action – as shown by Edward II's recall of the banished Gaveston and his and Richard's hunting down of the nobles who had led their humiliation. The question had hamstrung Simon de Montfort's rule in 1264–5 as he could not claim that Henry III was insane or senile, and arguably had helped to rally support to the escaped Prince Edward to challenge him in battle as a power-hungry 'usurper'. We know that Henry was to establish a dynasty that lasted for sixty-one years in September 1399, but contemporaries did not have foresight; it may have seemed to Henry (or to his Percy allies as they accepted his claim to the throne) that if he only became 'regent' he would end up like Simon de Montfort did in 1265.

Given that Edmund Mortimer was aged eight, if he was put on the throne there would be a long regency. Henry was the rightful claimant to that as the nearest male kin, being son of the next of Edward III's sons to Edmund's ancestor. The previous personal 'governorship' of an under-age new king, Edward III, had gone to his nearest male kinsman, Earl Henry of Lancaster, while the boy's mother, Isabella, had been effective regent (assisted by her lover Roger Mortimer). Richard's 'regent' while he was overseas in Ireland, his surviving uncle Edmund, Duke of York, was incapable of – or unwilling to? – organize resistance and remained inert in the south-west as Henry marched southwards. Whether or not this apparently sluggish and 'apolitical' elderly prince decided it was not worth risking execution by defying his nephew Henry's advance, his inaction was decisive. It is even possible that the fact that Richard had made him regent gave him hopes of securing the succession, the role of regent normally going to the male heir – though the 'rightful' heir as Richard saw him, Edmund Mortimer, was too young to be regent in 1399 so a substitute had been needed. The next choice of regent after Edmund of York, his son the new Duke of Surrey (Edward of Aumale), had been sent to Ireland in 1398 and so was unavailable. If Edmund of York had any hopes of the throne in 1399, helped by Henry's avoidance of claiming the Crown when he landed, these were to be disappointed. The climactic assembly of the lords spiritual and temporal at Westminster Hall on 30 September did see the claims to the throne of York and his sons, Edward of Aumale and Richard of Cambridge, formally raised – but only after the King's abdication had been announced and Henry had made his claim first. According to French witness Jean Creton (more reliable than a Henrician partisan) the lords did not speak up for York and his family, and acclaimed Henry instead; it would have been a brave man to stand out against the clear intention of the assembly with the current Archbishop of

York (Scrope) and the soon-to-be-restored ex-Archbishop of Canterbury (Arundel) flanking Henry to show Church support for him.[54] (It is more to the point that Edmund Mortimer's name was not mentioned.) It is possible that the York family's hopes and their thwarting led to the equivocal attitude of Edward of Aumale to Henry IV's regime – though Edward had other reasons to revolt as Henry had required him to hand back the Dukedom of Surrey, which Richard had given him. Edward joined the plot to murder Henry and his sons at New Year 1400, only to swiftly change his mind and inform the King who thus escaped assassination. He was never charged, and may even have acted as a 'double agent' once he had decided to change sides.

It is clear that nobody else hurried to fill the vacancy in raising troops for the absent King in July 1399. The contemporary sources which all approved of Henry's invasion cannot be entirely trusted, given that the new King prudently called them in for examination afterwards so any unfavourable references to himself or poor assessments of his support would have been 'edited out' then. But the fact remains that Henry was not opposed by a large number of magnates hastening to rally to the Duke of York, even granted that he had the formidable Percies on his side, which would deter resistance. The elderly York was not a military figure, and both the Earl of Northumberland and his son 'Hotspur' were veterans of decades of fierce fighting against the Scots and had a force of ruthless Borders fighters who it would be folly to resist. Richard was unlikely to have been deserted so comprehensively in September 1399 if he had not violated custom/law by confiscating the Lancaster inheritance (or possibly just the revenues rather than the actual title) from Henry on the death of his father.

It remains possible that Richard *was* willing to negotiate with Henry about an earlier recall, using his confiscation of the duchy's revenues to blackmail him into accepting whatever offer he made, and that Henry chose to pre-empt him. The fact that Henry called in all the monastic chronicles of the realm for examination – and implicitly for punishment of anyone who wrote a version unfriendly to his cause – once he had taken the Crown shows that he recognized the importance of controlling information on the precise truth of what he and Richard intended in 1399. Hence, presenting Richard's action as harshly as possible aided his own cause. But it does not mean that he was 'covering up' an unpopular invasion to overthrow a well-loved monarch. The crucial reason for Henry' needing to 'spin' on the events of September 1399 was surely that he had deposed the King, not constrained him, with the Percies claiming (at least in retrospect) that Henry fooled them into thinking the latter was intended. The situation was not like that of 1327 when the reigning king had also been deposed, as then he had been removed in favour of his undoubted heir, his eldest son – in 1399 it was a moot point if Richard's legal successor was Henry, as son of his uncle John, or if it should have been the eldest (Mortimer) descendant of John's elder brother Lionel of Clarence. Richard had nominated the Mortimer claimant as his heir. Mortimer's aunt was married to Northumberland's son 'Hotspur' so the Percies had a reason to back the Mortimer claim, but this does not mean that their indignation was feigned.

Richard's illusion of security in 1399. Was he doomed whether he was in England or Ireland when Henry landed? Comparisons with the situation of Edward II in 1326

Richard gave Henry the opportunity to land in England without a major challenge by taking his army off to Ireland in summer 1399 and leaving only his elderly and ineffective uncle Edmund, Duke of York, as regent. Once he had confiscated the Lancastrian inheritance, there was already a danger that Henry and the allied fellow-exiles (e.g. the Fitzalans) in France would invade. But with the French King as Richard's ally and father-in-law they would have minimal aid thence and would have to rely on mustering rebels within England, rather than a Continental army such as invaders Queen Isabella and Roger Mortimer had used in 1326. If Richard was out of the country, there was less incentive for powerful nobles who could muster retainers for Richard or Henry to remain loyal and more motive to risk aiding the rebels. Richard, isolated at court amidst his flatterers like Edward II in 1326, does not seem to have realised the alienation caused by his high-handed and dubiously legal activities in 1397–9, or the fact that his striking against successive opponents without warning (and use of an army of Cheshire archers to intimidate Parliament and the judiciary) meant that prominent subjects might well fear that they were next. The evidence of the chronicles indicates that neither York, in command in England and heading to the south-west to link up with Richard's return once he heard that Henry had landed, nor Richard's loyal lords in the Marches – e.g. the Despensers who held the Gloucester lands in Glamorgan – were able to muster troops to defend Richard's cause before or after Richard had landed. York, indeed, backed away from his initial 'stand' at Oxford in central England to retreat towards the Severn valley, indicating that he was unsure of having enough men to confront Henry – and of not wanting to do so anyway? It is a moot point if he would have felt more confident had Richard been quicker to return, and had Richard done so via the Severn estuary to land nearer York's new position at Berkeley Castle. The King's lack of Welsh support as he landed in Pembrokeshire was also notable. According to Adam of Usk, a local, he sent the Earl of Gloucester to raise his tenantry in the latter's (de Clare) lands in Glamorgan but there was a poor response.[55] In effect, both the majority of tenants-in-chief and their juniors seem to have been disillusioned enough – and once Henry had landed confident enough – to refuse the King aid.

If Richard had been in England not Ireland he could still have faced these desertions, as Edward II did in 1326, or an ambiguous response and a lack of adherents such as Richard III faced in 1485. From the time of Edward II, the precedent had existed of senior subjects daring to desert a challenged, unpopular king who relied on a small clique of dubious and over-promoted court favourites. (There had been major desertions from John to Louis of France in 1215–16, the invader gaining control of most of the south-east, but this revolt had failed.) The extent of disaffection with Richard in 1399 is the crucial point, though it has been obscured by the fact that Henry had the monastic chronicles – which were not official state-sponsored writings – censored in 1400. This has enabled Richard's modern sympathizers to claim that they cannot be trusted on their account of events and the popular mood. However, there was some literary disaffection to the Ricardian acts of 1397–9 before Henry's landing, which he could not have influenced, e.g. John Gower's *O Deus Immense* (which claimed that the people were suffering due to Richard's incompetence and recklessness) and the anonymous *Richard the Redeless*. There was one anonymous attack on the King's low-born ministers for misleading him, naming specifically Bushy, Bagot, and Green who were to be lynched in 1399. The monastic chronicler Thomas Walsingham, abbot of St Albans, had abandoned his early enthusiasm for Richard by the mid-1390s, reversing early dedications of his works to the King and claiming that his 1380s 'favourite' Robert de Vere had won the King over by black magic or homosexual practices.[56] These works cannot be put down to seeking Henry's goodwill. There was also one minor local rising against misgovernment at Bampton in Oxfordshire in 1398, though nothing on the scale of 1381.

It was the magnates, who had control of armed retinues that could support or abandon the King in his hour of need, which mattered more than the populace, as shown by the massive army that five senior magnates had put together to intimidate Richard and destroy his own army in 1387–8. In that respect Richard had carefully neutralized the centres of disaffection – albeit superficially, with his dominance secured by fear not consent. The local 'power-blocs' of his enemies had been broken up by land-grants to reliable nobles in 1397, such as giving the Earl of Warwick's lands in the Severn valley to the Despensers and in Warwickshire to the Earl of Huntingdon (now Duke of Surrey) and giving the Earl of Arundel's lands in Surrey to the new Duke and lands in Shropshire to the (Percy) Earl of Worcester. The confiscation of the Lancaster lands on Duke John's death in February 1399 secured the north-west, with Richard seemingly obsessed with the legal issue of reversing the 'insult' to royal power implicit in allowing this inheritance to descend from a 'traitor' (Earl Thomas, executed 1322). The grants of lands and titles in 1397–8 had enfeoffed a group of loyal courtiers centred around the King's half-brother, the Duke of Exeter, and nephew Kent/Surrey, although it had included men who were to desert to Henry in 1399 such as the Percies (now controlling the north-east and part of the Welsh Marches) and Beauforts. Richard had raised his own loyal Earldom of Chester, recruiting ground for his bodyguard of archers, to a County Palatine to match the Duchy of Lancaster – and with the latter his from February 1399 he controlled the entire north-west. The new Duke of Surrey controlled Kent and Surrey, and Exeter the south-west.[57]

In addition, an unprecedented number of political loyalists had been carefully placed in sheriffdoms so that the principal source of local power was under control, and the 1397 Parliament had been assiduously 'packed' and had been forced to meet under the watchful eyes of the King's Cheshire bodyguard to terrorize opposition.[58] As far as the structure of government went, Richard was in full control and had been able to pass all sorts of new laws reinforcing royal political power and the duty of his subjects to obey him in all matters, compelling all would-be peers and office-holders to swear oaths to uphold the new laws. It is notable that Richard was obsessed with legal requirements, whereas the equally insecure new regime of Edward III after 1330 had relied on the King securing control by a personal relationship with and leadership of his senior nobles. The power of the Crown had been rocked as badly in 1326–30 as in 1386–9, but Edward III sought different solutions – and died in his bed after a fifty-year reign.

The comprehensive nature of the 'revolution' of 1397, which went beyond the physical elimination or political neutralisation of all who had humiliated the King in 1387–8 into legal enshrinement of the royal supremacy, showed that Richard intended to enforce his concept of royal power on the constitution as well as safeguarding himself from his enemies. In that respect it went further than Edward II's equally determined efforts to restore royal power after 1322, which had similarly concentrated land and power in the hands of a small clique. Richard's government in 1397–9 was not dominated by one land-hungry minister, his effective viceroy in a large area of the kingdom, to the extent that Edward's had been by the 'Younger' Despenser in 1322–6 – and although his 'low-born' trio of ministers, Bushy, Bagot, and Green, were executed in 1399 like Despenser was in 1326 the main noble beneficiaries of royal landed bounty escaped the new government's vengeance apart from having to renounce their new titles and some land. (The executions of 1400 followed the first plot to reinstate Richard.) But the physical control of the country, and indeed the requirement to swear oaths to the 'new order', did not mean that the King could be sure of his magnates' loyalty. Indeed, if anything his intense legalistic concentration on royal power and his insistence on oath-taking and deference – and his reliance on his bodyguards – were signs of his insecurity. He probably attempted to enforce his new power like this precisely because he feared a repeat of 1388, which explains his determination to make examples of Henry and of Mowbray/Nottingham and seize their lands too in 1398–9. The constant harping on in his propaganda in 1397–9 about the misdeeds that his victims had committed in 1388[59] shows his obsession with these events, going beyond anger at the infringement of royal authority to personal trauma and vengeance. As with Edward II's executions and land-seizures in 1322–6, or with Richard III carrying out exemplary executions and flooding southern English sheriffdoms with loyal northerners in 1483, the terrorization of opposition could only bring about short-term security. In both cases the magnates were liable to desert the King – at least not to hurry to aid him – once a challenger invaded. It was worse if the King was personally an unmilitary figure who could not act as his own general and rally an army, and in this respect Richard II was more like Edward II than Richard III.

It was also notable that Richard placed great emphasis on the visible signs of royal power, such as the anointing oil. This was normally kept locked up in the treasury of Westminster Abbey but was now carried about by him on his travels (and taken to Ireland in 1399); after his deposition the Abbot was quick to regain it and assert his rights as its keeper.[60] The King also seems to have promoted the mystical powers of the mysterious 'holy oil' for the rite of anointing, which was now either found or re-discovered after being brought to England in Edward II's reign. (The link with another over-confident authoritarian king was significant.) It was supposed to have been passed on from heavenly hands to St Thomas Becket during his exile in France in the 1160s, being designated for the coronation of English kings, and been kept abroad until the 1320s. On its arrival Edward II had wanted to use it but his council had vetoed the idea; it was now 're-discovered' with Richard being enthusiastic to use it but the Church insisting that it could only be administered at a coronation. He made do with carrying a phial of it around his neck as a holy charm, e.g. on his Irish trip – and the first king to use it at his coronation was thus his usurping cousin Henry IV, who found its extra holy sanction invaluable for his new regime.[61] The precedent for the idea of this holy oil 'sent from Heaven' was that which was used at the coronations of the kings of France, and which was said to have been brought from Heaven by a dove for the anointing of their first Christian king, Clovis, in 481. Whether or not this inspired a direct copy by Ricardian propagandists, it was first used to legitimize the extra powers and prestige of an English kingship above human control in the 1390s. Richard also played up his rights to control the 'coronation church' at Westminster, as an English equivalent of the French site at Rheims, and his iconography of close royal patronage by the national Saints can be seen in the famous 'Wilton Diptych' commissioned in the 1380s or 1390s. (The saints featured were the royal holy men Edward 'the Confessor' and St Edmund, plus John the Baptist who had anointed Christ.)[62] The impression given is of a king keen to promote his otherworldly blessing and his freedom from earthly control, with a clear element of wishful thinking that was to receive a rude shock in 1399.

What if Richard had been in England as Henry landed?

The magnates would not fight for Hugh Despenser in 1326, and there is no sign that Richard could have relied on a competent and popular commander to save him in 1399 had he been in England at the time. The Dukes of Exeter and Surrey and his uncle York's son Aumale, his closest male relatives of military age, lacked experience and the Percies were to desert him. The best hope he would have had is that his presence in England would have made Henry more cautious about landing, although it is unlikely given Richard's recent miscalculations that the King would have offered him good enough terms for an early end to his exile or the handover of his Duchy's revenues in 1399–1400 to head off an invasion indefinitely. More likely Richard's over-confidence would have kept Henry exiled, and enough encouraging letters from disaffected magnates promising to abandon the King would have led Henry to gamble on an invasion within a year or two. Henry needed to act to keep his own entourage in exile together, or he would have lost his 'bargaining-counters' as his men drifted away and he ended up a powerless dependant of some charitable ruler.

If Richard had been in the south-east or the east Midlands touring his dominions as usual for a royal summer, or had the sense to be poised at a strategic castle ready to meet the invader and ready to send out orders to his tenants-in-chief the moment he heard the rebel had landed like the much more martial Richard III did in 1485, he could have faced an unwillingness to muster. Like Henry Tudor did in 1485, the challenger could have landed in a distant part of the kingdom protected by distance and poor roads and advanced on the King without a major noble standing in his way. In 1471, when the deposed Edward IV copied Henry's tactics in 1399, the kingdom's military master Warwick was in central England awaiting attack but the local magnates in Yorkshire – including Warwick's brother, the Marquis of Montagu – chose not to stand in the invader's way and let him advance into the Midlands. This fate could have occurred to Richard had he been in southern England at the time of Henry's landing. If Richard had been in the east Midlands and close to the potentially disloyal Percies so that they were less likely to desert him, Henry was less likely to have risked nearby Yorkshire – but he could have landed in the south instead and advanced on London as the invading Yorkists were to do in 1460. Richard had had a major legal dispute with the city in recent years, and its civic leaders may thus have been willing to stand aside if a rebel force advanced claiming that they were acting in the name of Henry's legal rights. They had already abandoned Edward II, and lynched his minister Bishop Stapledon, in 1326.

Given Richard's over-confidence about carrying out all his divisive acts of retaliation in 1397–9 and lack of military experience, he was likely to have reacted as sluggishly to the threat of Henry as Edward II had to his Queen in 1326 and been similarly deserted to his surprise. His obsession with legal acts to bolster the royal authority and oaths of loyalty shows that he relied on the law more than the practicality of winning support, and his small circle of advisers and ordered, deferential court cut him off from realistic assessment of his magnates' reliability. In such an atmosphere at court as that of 1399, it would be a rash adviser who gave the King unwelcome news. The crucial factor in Henry's initial success was that the only local military challenge he faced as he arrived in Yorkshire, the Percies, stood back from aiding their sovereign and professed themselves satisfied that Henry – only claiming the Duchy of Lancaster as yet – had right on his side. The fact that Henry did not immediately claim the Crown added to this factor, as it could be argued by waverers (like the Duke of York?) that Henry had a legal right to reclaim his duchy.

The question of who would replace Richard – who could not be expected to take constraint pacifically after the revenge he had recently taken for the humiliation of 1387–8 – could be left aside for later. If the story that Henry swore to restrict taxation while he was rallying support in Yorkshire is true, his supporters understood by this that he would be in a position to grant or abolish taxes – but he could do that as 'governor'/regent for Edmund Mortimer as well as in the role of king. Unless Richard, in England, had responded to Henry's arrival with a determined march to the scene of conflict that could have persuaded waverers like the Percies to stand by him, he faced overthrow even if he had been in his heartland around London as Henry landed unless he had a capable military commander. It is uncertain if one of his Holland relatives or another beneficiary of his recent rash of peerage-creations would have had the personal support of enough major nobles to keep a royal army together as it advanced on Henry's force. Richard – like the similarly-abandoned John and Edward II – had been vindictively punishing his personal enemies among the nobility and could be expected to continue this. Arundel's execution, Gloucester's murder, and Warwick's imprisonment were no more a guarantee that the nobility were effectively intimidated than had been Edward II's killings in 1322.

The Ricardian collapse: but what if Richard had fled and not surrendered?

Richard delayed his sailing home from Ireland for a crucial two weeks or so, while his position in England collapsed as the unhindered Henry crossed the Midlands. The Duke of York, unable to raise an army around Gloucester and Bristol, gave up and came to terms with him at Berkeley Castle on 27 July. (The choice of that site by York was probably a deliberate echo of the fact that the last king to be deposed, Edward II, had been imprisoned there – a hint to Henry that he accepted the likelihood of history repeating itself.) The leading 'Ricardian' ministers were seized and executed as Bristol, the main port in the west of England and key to the south-west, defected, and tenants in the Welsh Marches failed to muster for the King. By the time Richard returned directly to Pembrokeshire on c.14 July – and landed in an isolated part of Wales, far from the centres of power in England – Henry had already gained control of most of England. The King advanced east to reach Whitland on 29 July and Carmarthen on the 31st, and according to the monastic chronicler Thomas Walsingham was initially looking forward to fighting Henry.[63]

But lack of local support condemned him to abandon a direct march against Henry's positions around Bristol, probably bolstered by news of the fall of that port. Instead, he made a slow advance north through difficult country along the Welsh coast to attempt to link up with remaining loyalists in the north under the third Earl of Salisbury (an ex-ally of Wycliffe). According to the Dieulacres Abbey chronicler he abandoned his army to travel with only fifteen companions[64] (including Gloucester and Edward of Aumale), possibly for speed or else through fear of betrayal. When his steward, the Earl of Worcester (brother of the Earl of Northumberland), found that he had gone he realized that the King would lose his throne. He broke his rod of office as was done when a monarch died, and tearfully suggested that the bemused royal army disperse. One writer who was with Salisbury claims that Richard disguised himself as a priest, suggesting that fear of arrest was his main motive. But he was out of touch with his continually deteriorating position within England, and ended up trapped with Salisbury at Conwy Castle as the superior Percy army blocked his route and Henry arrived at Chester to join them. Arriving at Conwy around 15 August, he agreed to open negotiations, although his first envoys (his Holland half-brother Exeter and nephew Edward) were arrested on arrival at Chester.[65] As of this point, he had an inferior army to Henry's – Salisbury had suffered desertions too, so fighting was not an option. But he still had the ability to flee before or after Northumberland and ex-Archbishop Arundel arrived with Henry's terms (probably on 12 August). He may well have been tricked into surrendering with a false promise that he would preserve his throne, whether or not the Percies were being honest later in assuring that Henry had told them that Richard would not be deposed so they had negotiated with Richard in good faith at the time. Whether Henry was being honest at the time in his oath is impossible to know, as Richard's deposition followed the captive King making threats to have his revenge later. But Henry would have known from experience that Richard was untrustworthy before that, and he showed a slippery ability to dodge accusations on an excuse when he later claimed he had not had Richard killed. He protested that Richard had gone on 'hunger strike' at Pontefract Castle, but few seem to have believed him.[66] Technically Richard's captor, Sir Piers Exton, had been responsible if Richard had been starved to death, but Henry showed no eagerness to hold him accountable for exceeding orders.

Northumberland and Arundel apparently swore to Richard that he would preserve his dignities, and the claim by pro-Henrician sources that the King offered to abdicate at this point has been 'rubbished' by modern analysts. The more neutral sources, e.g. the French eye-witness Jean Creton, claim that Northumberland merely required Richard to accept a Parliament presided over by Henry plus the trials of five leading supporters, including the Dukes of Surrey (Thomas Holland) and Exeter and the Earl of Salisbury. The Earl also swore that Henry did not intend any deceit[67] – though as Parliament had required Edward II to abdicate in similar circumstances in 1327 it was obvious that Richard could be deposed later by this means. Richard duly emerged from Conwy Castle to accompany Northumberland to a meeting over dinner at Rhuddlan east of the river. Only when he was away from the walls did an armed Percy contingent emerge from a nearby valley and take him captive. Confined at Flint Castle, he was said to have realized that he was doomed when he saw Henry's army approaching the walls.[68] Given his failure to carry out his promises of permanent amnesty for actions carried out by his critics when he had been in their power in 1388–9, it was naïve of him to think that he would be given a second chance to go back on his word. At best he would probably be reduced to a powerless figurehead for far longer this time – presumably either by a 'Lord Ordainer'-style committee of peers or even a regent such as Henry. This may have been what Northumberland expected to happen, if he was sincere. In any event, it was disastrous that Richard was reported to have boasted (in another 'mood-swing'?) that he would not consider himself bound by any promises that he gave to Henry, who would be punished later.[69] This is known to the chroniclers, so it is apparent that Henry was told about it and made the most of it on his arrival at the London Parliament to urge the other peers to depose the unreliable King. Henry, unlike Queen Isabella with her husband Edward II in 1326, had his victim brought to London to abdicate publicly – so that a larger group of nobles could witness the act (and it could be done quicker) than had been possible with Edward II being kept at Kenilworth Castle while Parliament met?

Once Richard had found his route to England blocked, he would have been wiser to flee with what few retainers he had left – on a ship if he could find one in Conwy or Caernarfon, either back to Ireland or to France. Seeking their self-preservation in the new order and with no confidence in Richard as an experienced general who could defeat Henry, his remaining captains in Ireland would probably have started to desert as soon as Lancastrian representatives landed in the country and the less-well-armed Irish tribal chiefs would have been more loyal but less useful in military terms. Richard would have had to retreat to France, or just possibly Scotland, to preserve himself from capture. At best, winter storms preventing a Lancastrian fleet from sailing to Ireland and a strong showing by pro-Ricardian Irish magnates in Dublin could have kept Richard in control of Ireland until a French force arrived in spring 1400 and the threat of a French attack on Kent kept Henry IV in London. If Richard still held Dublin his father-in-law Charles VI of France would have had a good reason to aid him to keep the active and warlike Henry preoccupied. The French were still allied to the former enemies of the 'Black Prince' and John of Gaunt, the Trastámara dynasty of Castile, which had a large fleet active in the Channel; this could be deployed to protect Richard in Dublin from a Lancastrian attack.

Chapter Three

Henry IV

The challenge to Henry IV, 1399–1405

What if a viable rival had been at large – if Richard had escaped to Ireland and then France? Wales – a Ricardian link to a national revolt

If Richard had fled and been deposed in his absence, he would not have been available to sign his abdication so Henry's position would have been less secure. But a refugee Richard would have been unlikely to have secured any immediate aid from the faction-ridden French court, which had its own domestic priorities. At best Charles VI, currently (1400) though not always mentally stable and not a military leader, would have taken some time to accept the reality of Richard's permanent loss of power and come to terms with his militarily experienced – and dangerous as an enemy – successor. At best, the Welsh rebellion of late 1400 would have belatedly encouraged Charles to meddle on Richard's behalf and keep the potentially hostile, militarily experienced Henry from re-launching the war of the 1370s in France. In general, the Welsh revolt added an unwelcome extra dimension to the resistance to Henry, one that presented a contrast with the situation of the new regime in 1327 when no revolt had occurred despite the deposed Edward II's links with Wales. (Born in Caernarfon, he sought sanctuary in South Wales after losing control of England and was captured near Neath.) Underlying discontent at English political control, land-seizures, cultural humiliation, and a form of administrative/judicial 'apartheid' had been present ever since the 1280s, but the actual outbreak in September 1400 was immediately due to a personal dispute between Owain Glyndwr and his local rival, Lord Grey of Ruthin – a strong Henrican. The latter implied that Glyndwr could expect no redress for his legal disputes with Grey at the new King's law courts and might well be judicially prosecuted, but staging a 'national' revolt was an unexpected and risky move.

It should be pointed out that the notion of defying the current government by force was not uncommon in England or Wales in the turbulent medieval era. Nor did all revolts in the turbulent area where the Glyndwr rebellion broke out amount to a 'nationalist' uprising; Anglo-Norman border lords had been as willing as men of Welsh royal blood to defy the King and/or an unfriendly government in London. The Marshal Earls of Pembroke, sons of the late regent William Marshal, had defied the young Henry III's ministers in the 1220s; Gilbert de Clare, the 'Red Earl' of Glamorgan, had defied the elderly Henry and his heir Edward (I) in the late 1260s. Taking up arms against the government and your local enemies (sometimes with the two perceived to be allies) was regular practice; Glyndwr's action against Lord Grey of Ruthin and his patron Henry IV was not that unusual. The grievances of local Welshmen against discriminatory English law added fuel to the flames, as Glyndwr's descent made him able to use an appeal to national feeling. But had the rebellion been halted quickly, would it have merited more than a footnote in history? Would it have had quite so much support had Richard II not had a close relationship with the men of his Earldom of Chester, within reach of the seat of rebellion in eastern Powys? Or if Henry IV had not had to concentrate on the threat from Scotland in 1400 and so been unable to bring his full force to bear on the rebellion quickly?

Inability to put down revolts quickly was inevitable, given the lack of a standing army or close supervision of the gentry and magnates – and their possession of 'private armies' of servants and tenants. Armed defiance of the English government and its local officials was nothing new to local lords in the remote Welsh borders, particularly English 'Marcher' ones with their own armed affinities. Individuals or groups of more powerful and obstreperous peers had been plotting against the King since the 1075 revolt of the Earl of Hereford, and judicial orders were sometimes difficult to enforce. A frequent response of the Crown was to rely on one particular local magnate – usually in favour at court – as a 'viceroy', as with the younger Despenser in South Wales in 1320–6 and with the chosen nominees of the Yorkist kings (William Herbert in 1461–8 and the Duke of Buckingham in 1483). In 1485–95 Henry VII was to rely on his uncle Jasper Tudor, Earl of Pembroke and a leading actor in the region back in the late 1450s to mid 1460s. This resulted in fears by their rivals that the court favourites' enemies would not secure justice from a biased king and his courts – a reason for Glyndwr's action. At the worst, dispossessed lords with a grievance could retreat into the hills and live as bandits until they were caught or pardoned – as famously done by the legendary outlaw Fulk FitzWarin around 1200. This defiance was more common among English than Welsh landowners –

and Glyndwr had indeed been educated at the Inns of Court in London and at one time lived at court. He was acting within an English Marcher tradition, and his defiance of anticipated punishment by his court-affiliated foe was thus nothing new. It was his dynastic claims and his declaration of a national movement for independence that brought an extra danger to the revolt – though even so he could have been militarily neutralized quickly by luck or a 'tip-off' in autumn 1400. Alternatively, the government could have kept control of the major castles and reduced him to a minor irritant – as seemed likely in 1400–02. His revolt would then have had no more than a mention in the history books, alongside all the other abortive plots for a revolt since 1284. Edward I had kept control of a restive Wales by securing a network of well-garrisoned strongpoints, which could hold out until he had time to bring a relief-force, as in the major revolt of 1294–5 (which was led by princely pretenders as in 1400–12).

Was Glyndwr's success aided by lack of a viable loyalist leadership?
It should also be noted that as of the anti-English troubles in 1294–5 the revolt in the south had been contained by the long-established Marcher lordship of Glamorgan, held by the de Clare dynasty. In the early 1400s there was no English 'strongman' in this area to help Henry IV hold back Glyndwr as the Glamorgan lands had been ruled by the pro-Ricardian Thomas Despenser, Earl of Gloucester, who was killed in the January 1400 rising against Henry. (His widow, Constance, daughter of Edmund Duke of York, was later to betray Henry by trying to take her ward, the King's rival Edmund Mortimer, to South Wales to join the Glyndwr revolt in 1405.) John of Gaunt, Lord of Ogmore as well as Duke of Lancaster, had died in February 1399 and thus his lands in central South Wales were under the control of the King's agents in 1399 after being confiscated from Henry; on Henry's return he was their nominal lord but had little local experience. (He had been resident in the region earlier at times; his eldest son was born at Monmouth.) The central Marches lands of the Mortimers were also now owned by an unreliable and under-age lord, the aforementioned Edmund Mortimer. In the north-central region, the lands of Clun and Oswestry had been seized by the King on the execution of their hereditary lord, the Earl of Arundel, in 1397; Gower and Chepstow had been confiscated on the exile of their lord, Thomas Mowbray, in 1398, and his son (restored by Henry) was young and inexperienced. Thus as of 1400–05 Henry could not rely on a vigorous and local adult male lord in crucial Marcher lordships to head an army and hold Glyndwr at bay. (Mortimer's uncle Sir Edmund was defeated and captured by Glyndwr, then defected to him.) Did this give the rebels an unusual advantage – and what if Henry had been able to rely on capable and

locally-accepted Marcher lords in these regions? Would the revolt have been contained far more easily if, for example, Thomas Mowbray had not died in exile but had been reconciled to Henry and had his lands returned?

The fact that Glyndwr, had been a junior retainer in Richard's court and was to be interested in various 'Ricardian' pretenders as well as in Welsh independence[1] suggests that if Richard had been alive and in France he might have acted in his name. The catalyst for revolt would still have been Glyndwr's personal confrontation with his pro-Henry local rival, Lord Grey of Ruthin, a beneficiary of the 1399 revolt. The latter was expected to secure royal backing from the new King for his predominance in north-east Wales politics, plus immunity for any legal or illegal measures he took to punish his enemies; Glyndwr's revolt was thus partly self-preservation, in the manner of an outlawed Marcher lord such as Fulk FitzWarin (victimized by King John) or the resistance of Roger Mortimer and his family to the over-powerful Despensers in South Wales in the early to mid 1320s. Without the new threat of ruin at the hand of Lord Grey, it is possible that he would not have risked all on a revolt – at least until he was sure of French military assistance. The latter had been planned to embarrass Edward III with a Welsh revolt in 1376; the last of the direct male line, Owain 'Lawgoch', descendant of Rhodri the brother Llywelyn 'the Last', had been serving as a French officer and planning a French-backed invasion when he was assassinated by English agents.[2] Despite his claims to hereditary leadership of and loyalty from the local residents in Powys as a descendant of its ancient Princes, Glyndwr had no such dynastic claims to the Welsh heartland of Gwynedd except by remote female descent. Indeed, his Powys links would normally have been a drawback to seeking support in Gwynedd – his male ancestors had been rivals of the two Llywelyns of Gwynedd. The same applies to his remoter links to the Dyfed dynasty.

Ironically, the nearest heirs to Gwynedd were the Mortimer family, Henry IV's dynastic rivals, through the female line from Gwladys, the daughter of Llywelyn 'the Great'; Glyndwr's foe, prisoner, and eventual ally Sir Edmund Mortimer had more hereditary rights to Gwynedd than he did. (The Mortimer claim to Gwynedd was later to be used to boost support for their descendant Edward IV in 1461.) Possibly his marriage to Glyndwr's daughter after he defected implied a 'deal' that he would be Glyndwr's successor, but this was never stated. The literary tradition of travelling bards and the Welsh gentry's use of resident household poets – both harking back to the glories of old before the Conquest – gave a distinct advantage to a dynastic claimant to any Welsh principality. Prophecies of the nation's restoration of independence and the importance of genealogy all acted in Glyndwr's favour. Indeed, before 1400 he had already been the subject of six prophetic poems looking forward to his future role as a national rallying-point – a sign of either (or both) bards' appreciation of his potential or his actively seeking this role. After 1400 he was to use the language of ancient Welsh historic-literary tradition to boost his claims to legitimacy, writing to Robert III of Scotland that they were both descendants of Brutus (legendary founder of the ancient British royal line in Geoffrey of Monmouth's book).[3] The 'Tripartite Indenture' plan to divide England between him, Edmund Mortimer, and the Earl of Northumberland in 1405 saw him use the terminology of a seventh century prophecy about the restoration of the ancient Welsh realm of Cadwallon in Britain in delineating his intended boundary on the River Trent.[4]

1400 was a particularly dangerous time for a revolt to break out, quite apart from the situation in England. It is important to note that there was a vacuum of leadership in the English Marcher lordships – there was no loyal and experienced great magnate available to rally his tenants to the Crown. Had there been, the local Welsh gentry would have had to think twice before backing Glyndwr against a militarily superior local army. The non-local henchmen to whom Richard had given confiscated Marcher lordships (e.g. his nephew the Duke of Surrey) had been killed or evicted in 1399–1400,[5] and their successors had had no time to assert their authority. Nor did the government have many loyal major Welsh magnates of equal dynastic legitimacy with large armed followings to call on to counter-balance Glyndwr. The obvious candidates for this role, the Lords Charlton of Powys (direct heirs in male descent of the senior royal line there), were too Anglicized. The Crown had kept most of Gwynedd and Ceredigion in its hands since the Conquest in 1277/83, as the appanage of the Prince of Wales – and Henry's son the new prince was only thirteen or fourteen in 1400. The leaders of the Church in North Wales, the bishops of Bangor and St Asaph, soon defected to Glyndwr who could promise the restoration of ecclesiastical independence from the arch-diocese of Canterbury (and secured the backing of the Pope at Avignon, foe of the rival Pope in Rome who backed Henry).[6] Like Robert Bruce in Scotland in the 1310s with his Church lieutenant William Lamberton, Glyndwr thus had both local Church and papal support – the latter more readily granted than it had been to 'murderer' Bruce – plus an explicit 'national' mandate from an assembly of the people.

Glyndwr's self-proclamation as 'Prince of Wales' on 16 September 1400 was of uncertain dynastic legitimacy in a country with a nobility and gentry obsessed with their lineage, as the title had previously only been held by the line of Gwynedd (Llywelyn 'Fawr' and Llywelyn ap Gruffydd.) He did have the crucial blood-link to past princes, though not of Gwynedd, and could call on sympathetic bards to claim that he was the destined fulfiller of prophecy who would restore the Welsh kingdom of Britain lost in the seventh century. His title could be propounded in terms of popular acclamation by the oppressed nation, though this was unusual. There was no enthusiastic mass-revolt in Glyndwr's favour in autumn 1400, despite current tensions; only a few hundred men rose in the area around his estates and they were swiftly defeated in open battle by Sir Hugh Burnell. This did not halt a guerrilla war and Henry's quick march to Caernarfon could not lure the rebels out of the mountains, but it was only after the vengeful English Parliament of winter 1400–01 enacted new anti-Welsh legislation that the revolt spread. It then gathered momentum as a mixture of domestic and international distractions kept Henry from another campaign until later in 1401 and no major army could be sent due to the popular resistance in England to his 'betrayal' over promises of lower taxation. His next campaign was equally fruitless as the Welsh army melted into the hills, as was the far larger triple attack of 1402 (when heavy rain affected morale and led to stories of the 'magician' Glyndwr controlling the elements).[7] As seen by the failure of superior numbers and weaponry to hold down a rebellious mountainous countryside even in the 2000s (e.g. Afghanistan), a guerrilla army could retreat out of reach of the invaders and wait for them to go home before tackling the remaining garrisons. In the case of the Welsh revolt, therefore, even a better-funded and larger royal invasion in late 1400 or 1401 would have achieved little in the long term unless Henry could hold down the rebellious areas with adequate garrisons and a mobile 'field-force' able to outmatch any force the rebels could bring into the field. Superior numbers, systematic ravaging to destroy enemy morale and supplies, and war-weariness might then assist him in winning a long war. This combination could be achieved by his eldest son, Prince Henry, after the end of domestic English distractions and the threats from France and Scotland in 1405–6, at which point the tide was to turn against Glyndwr. The English also had a virtual monopoly of artillery, meaning that they could batter down rebel towns' and castles' walls and the Welsh could not; and neither Charles VI of France (who sent troops in 1405) nor the Scots government countered this.

As of 1400–02 keeping the rebellion within limits would have required a major military concentration year after year, without distractions elsewhere; this was not an option for the beleaguered new King. The situation was not similar to those of 1277, 1283, and 1294–5 when Edward I had been able to concentrate his military resources on a successful military defeat of the North Welsh. Quite apart from the lack of distractions elsewhere then, the English had been fighting Gwynedd alone; they had been aided by the passivity of the remaining princes of divided Powys, who had been bought off by and were in fear of Edward. Lacking the ability to bring overwhelming force to bear as Edward had done, Henry was only able to mount brief invasions and in between this was reliant on his lieutenants (led by the Marcher lords) maintaining local military superiority. Instead, Sir Edmund Mortimer (uncle of his superseded rival claimant to England in 1399) was defeated and captured by Glyndwr at Pilleth in June 1402 and the King was distracted by the Percy rebellion in summer 1403. Potential rebels were thus emboldened to join the winning rebel cause through 1402–5, and the rebellion spread into Deheubarth to the south-west (to which Glyndwr also had a – distant – hereditary claim).[8] It should be remembered that in fifteenth century terms it was not an option for Henry to have negotiated with Glyndwr and bought him off with lands and titles – his declaration of himself as prince was a direct act of open treason to which any king had to respond firmly. Unlike the rebellious Gwynedd princes in the late thirteenth century, Glyndwr could not claim to be an independent sovereign who had been illegally forced into temporary submission by military might; he was legally unquestionably a usurper by English law. That question of 'usurpation' had not prevented the defeated English government accepting 'usurper' Robert Bruce's independence in 1328, with the 'rebel' having explicit national backing from his people as shown in the Declaration of Arbroath[9] (an inspiration for Glyndwr's use of a national Parliament at Machynlleth to back him?) But Bruce had at least been a legitimate and direct heir to the previous Scots royal line, as grandson of one of the contenders for the throne judged by Edward I in 1292. He had been crowned according to national tradition, and his country's annexation by Edward I was of dubious legality; Wales had less of a history as a unified and legally accepted concept. Nor did Henry have the political power in London in 1400–01 to block the anti-Welsh legislation passed by Parliament and head off discontent, as he needed its co-operation to raise taxes and circumvent his promises of a lighter tax-burden.

Had Richard been alive and in exile, it is likely that Glyndwr's demands of him in any alliance would have been the same as those he made of the Percies in 1403 and the Mortimer-Percy plot in 1405. Once Glyndwr had proclaimed himself prince – at the start of his revolt – this would have had to be recognized. The possibility also exists that had Richard been definitively known to be alive the loyalists in his main area of military support, Cheshire, would have been quicker to revolt before 1403 and thus could have risen to aid Glyndwr once he proved that he could hold the King's army at bay (in 1401). Had the ex-King been able to retreat safely to Ireland in September 1399, secure the control of Dublin, and rally the local Irish lords, he might also have been able to maintain a military position there into late 1400 had French aid arrived before Henry's troops – and in that case Anglo-Irish barons or Irish lords would have been able to send support to Glyndwr.

The extent of Henry's problems – even with his predecessor killed. Extra difficulties from prophecy as well as hostile neighbours
The number of challenges to Henry as early as New Year 1400, however, show that his usurpation was controversial and that he received far from unanimous noble support. Despite his generosity towards the 'duketti', the junior nobles who Richard had lavished with lands and titles in 1397–9, he had had to force them to give up a significant part of their gains, thus producing a pro-Ricardian 'party' ready to attempt a coup. If Richard had been at large in France in 1400 his adherents would have had even more reason to strike at Henry than they did when Richard was in prison at Pontefract and could be killed before they secured his person. Richard's nephews and their allies planned in real life to slaughter Henry and his sons en masse over the Christmas holidays at Windsor and then restore Richard to the throne, though their victims were tipped off at the last minute and fled.[10] If they had succeeded and Richard had only been across the Channel they could then have seized London, disposed of Archbishop Arundel and the Beauforts as the remaining Lancastrian stalwarts, and invited Richard back. The leaders of the new regime would then have been Edward of Aumale and the Holland family, and some major clash with the sidelined Percies could have been expected; presumably Richard would have been expected to name Edward as his heir. (If Richard had been a captive as in real life and not been rescued first, would the Percies have used Richard as a hostage to ensure a continuation of their grants from Henry?) If the plot had failed but Richard been rescued or already in exile, Richard would still have been at large. As such the assorted anti-Henry plotters from then on could have acted in his name as the legitimate king rather than on behalf of the untried and largely unknown 'legitimist' candidate, Edmund Mortimer; they would not have had the problem of real-life 1400–05 plotters that Henry held their claimant prisoner.

It is noticeable that the plotters thought it better to rise in Richard's name than in that of the less politically controversial Edmund, who they could plausibly claim had been denied his rights by the treacherous Henry. Indeed, they even had the first of a number of pretenders who looked like Richard – Richard Maudelyn – to hand to impersonate him in rallying support.[11] There was also a network of friars apparently spreading rumours of Richard's survival through 1400–02, with arrests following; they were aided by the 'Prophecy of the Six Kings' (dated around 1312?) that a king of

England identifiable as Richard II would lose his throne to a ravening 'wolf' and then recover it.[12] These prophecies had a habit of being self-fulfilling as people fitted past events into their terms and expected the outstanding parts of them to be carried out. In more prosaic terms, people of some education could argue that Henry's government was illegal. One arrested Franciscan friar in June 1402 (Roger Frisby) was bold enough to tell the King to his face that it had been illegal to force Richard to abdicate against his will.[13] Edward II too had resigned his crown 'freely' while in custody, telling an assembly of magnates at Kenilworth that it was of his own free will, and there had been no widespread revulsion in his favour. But Richard had only addressed a smaller gathering of the 'opposition' faction among the nobility, in the Tower of London,[14] and this news had then been relayed to a larger assembly at Westminster; he was not so widely believed. Even with Richard declared dead his name served as a rallying-point in a way that Edward II's had not done after the latter's survival had been mooted in 1329–30 with reports that he had been seen living quietly at Corfe Castle in Dorset, leading to his half-brother the Earl of Kent endeavouring to investigate and being arrested and executed for it. (The story may have been invented by the government to lure Kent into committing treason.)

But despite Richard's misrule his name could be used repeatedly for inspiration for a revolt, which Edward II's had not been. One difference was undoubtedly that Edward, unlike Richard, had been replaced by the undoubted heir; Henry's position was more dubious. Indeed, the capture of Henry's rival Edmund Mortimer's eponymous uncle by Glyndwr at Pilleth led to the latter changing sides and creating the potential for a Mortimer-Welsh-French alliance. The French could supply the manpower and funds for any major revolt after 1402; by contrast, in 1327 the new government was headed by the French King's sister Isabella. Nor had the Scots government been meddling with English pretenders after 1327; Robert Bruce's preferred course of action had been to use the new regime's military weakness to extort recognition of Scotland's independence (as achieved in 1328). After 1400, by contrast, one of the most durable 'Richard II' pretenders, the 'Mammet', took refuge at the Scots court. It was crucial in this instance that the elderly King Robert III, in his sixties and crippled by a leg-injury, was a reclusive depressive (self-proclaimed 'the most miserable of men')[15] who spent most of his time out of politics at Dundonald Castle. His brother and effective regent the Duke of Albany, the 'Governor', was not interested in risky aid to Glyndwr and had been warned off by an English march on Edinburgh in 1400. The more vigorous and warlike Prince David, Robert's elder son and heir, was at odds with Albany in 1400–02; he lost out in a power-struggle, and was locked up at Falkland Castle and mysteriously starved to death (probably at Albany's orders). The next heir after David was the much younger Prince James, born in 1394, who was sent to France in 1406 (to get him away from murder by Albany?) but was captured en route by English sailors off Scarborough and handed over to Henry IV.[16] There was thus no possibility once Prince David was dead of vigorous Scots aid to the Welsh. But if he not Albany had been in charge of the Scots government in 1402–6 Henry could have faced another serious military opponent.

Edmund Mortimer, descendant of Edward III's second son, Lionel, in the female line, was the genealogically senior claimant to the throne after Richard but lacked experience or an established magnate clientage. If his father, Roger, a former lieutenant of Ireland, had not died in 1398 he would have been a more viable threat. Crucially, Mortimer was only nine in 1400 so there would be disputes over who would govern in his name if he was the contender; the way in which York's son and heir Edward was reliably suspected of plotting on Mortimer's behalf in 1404–5 suggests that he saw himself as the intended regent. (His legal claim would rest on being the nearest adult male Plantagenet, and son of Richard's chosen regent in 1399.) The Percies, probably dubious of the wisdom of trusting a restored Richard to keep his terms about an amnesty for them for their actions in 1399 and so far less likely to revolt in 1403 on Richard's behalf than on Edmund Mortimer's, might still have quarrelled with Henry. In the event, they were supposed to have been annoyed at him demanding control of and the ransoms for top-ranking Scots prisoners captured at Homildon Hill in 1402. In addition, Henry had handed the justiciarship of North Wales over from Northumberland's son Henry 'Hotspur' Percy to Prince Henry in spring 1402 – a not unreasonable precaution given that 'Hotspur' was brother-in-law to the recently-defected Sir Edmund Mortimer. He had refused to reimburse 'Hotspur' for his financial outlay on war against the Scots and Welsh – which he could not do anyway due to popular resistance to new taxes – and had shared out offices on the Scots Marches between the Percies and their local rivals, the Nevilles. One story even had it that Henry had punched 'Hotspur' in a violent quarrel at court.[17] The Percies' decision to revolt apparently took Henry by surprise as he was en route north for the latest North Wales campaign, with the news that 'Hotspur' was raising the men of Cheshire against not for him sending him off in haste to join his son Prince Henry at Shrewsbury. Hearing the news at Lichfield, he was luckily as close to Shrewsbury as 'Hotspur' was and was able to arrive first; when his foe reached the town he found the gates shut (20 July 1403). The catalyst for the Earl of Northumberland – Henry's long-term ally – to join his rebel son may well have been Henry's refusal (or inability) to pay up funds he had promised for the Earl's imminent campaign to take Ormiston Castle in

Scotland. A final – possibly threatening – and unanswered letter from Earl to King urging immediate payment preceded his revolt.[18] Once 'Hotspur' had decided to revolt the Earl was in a difficult position of being likely to be suspected of collusion in any case; his son's defeat would inevitably mean the forfeiture of his lands and offices and a major blow to the dynasty. The Earl accordingly joined in the revolt, but Henry was at this point closer than him to Shrewsbury so the King could link up with his son in time.

The Welsh revolt, the Percies, the French, and the 1403 campaign. Did timing aid Henry IV? What if Prince Henry had been killed at Shrewsbury?

If Richard had been alive and in exile, or his 'heir' Edmund Mortimer been available away from Henry's control, the 'rightful king' would have been a probable ally for Owain (under French auspices?). In the event, Owain had to make do with Edmund's uncle Sir Edmund Mortimer, a Henrician captain who he captured at his first major victory at Pilleth in 1402 and who went over to his side. Marrying Owain's daughter, Sir Edmund acted as the 'agent' of the Mortimer family claim of his nephew to England in allying with Owain – who in return was recognized as Prince of Wales. The eventual Mortimer-Owain-Percy 'Tripartite Indenture' of 1405 divided Henry's domains among them, with Owain ruling as far east as the Severn and the Trent. This, an enhanced Wales in full sovereignty, was clearly Owain's aim. He would not have been negotiating an alliance with a surviving, exiled Richard or a refugee Edmund Mortimer (junior) without the right to independence as part of the treaty.

Genealogically Owain had little claim to Gwynedd, being in the direct male line of the royal house of Powys. His declaration of himself as Prince was more of an 'election' by popular acclaim, as had been Henry's by Parliament in 1399. He was aided by the extinction of the (side-) descendants of Llywelyn 'the Last' with the murder of Llywelyn's brother Rhodri's descendant Owain 'Lawgoch' in France in If Owain, backed by France as a challenger to Edward III in Wales in the 1370s but stabbed by an English agent before he could invade, had not been killed or had left sons the French would have been likely to use this opportunity to distract the warlike Henry by backing the line of Gwynedd. But would Glyndwr, the leader 'in situ' with his tenants as the core of the rebel force, meekly stand aside for the legitimate contender and restrict his claim to Powys?

What if Glyndwr had been acting as an ally of the exiled Richard, as sponsored by the French? There is no indication of any strong feeling for Richard in Wales, as opposed to neighbouring Cheshire, and the King attracted no enthusiasm as he crossed the country en route from Pembroke to Caernarfon in autumn 1399. Owain's former service at Richard's court might imply a personal link and willingness to fight for him, but this would have been less important to his Welsh adherents than their demands for legal independence. The Welsh Parliament at Machynlleth would have been a likely chance for the local lords to demand permanent and irreversible legal recognition of their 'national' rights, so that a restored Richard could not go back on his promises. As a former Prince of Wales himself and a ruler keen on expanding his Celtic dominions (as shown by his nearly unprecedented royal visits to Ireland) Richard would have found that difficult, but he had abandoned his French claims in the interests of peace in 1396 so he was capable of flexibility in ending family claims. He would have had to accept an alliance on these terms; the French, as in real life in 1405, would then supply Glyndwr with troops. The same would have applied to Edmund Mortimer (junior), if he as well as his uncle had been in Glyndwr's hands in 1401–5. As far as France is concerned, there is a clear line in policy from their use of Owain 'Lawgoch' in the 1370s to their use of Glyndwr in the 1400s – and to their use of Henry Tudor, also given French troops to invade a hostile England in 1485.

The 'triple alliance' between Percies, Welsh, and Mortimer partisans of March 1405 looked forward to a division of England between the three allies. Its potential was somewhat spoilt by Mortimer being safely in royal hands – though he had temporarily escaped a few weeks earlier. Given the need to muster a viable military challenge to the English royal army, the 'input' of French troops was vital and about 10,000 seem to have landed in Pembrokeshire that summer.[19] Having taken the town of Haverfordwest, they marched as far as Herefordshire – the first French incursion into England since 1216 – without achieving much. But this attack was too late in one respect – it would have had far greater impact in 1403. It occurred once the Percies' northern 'power-base' had already been wrested from them as a result of their defeat at Shrewsbury by the King in July 1403, and Northumberland's part in the plan consisted of revolting from his remaining lands (graciously returned to him by Henry in 1404 in return for grovelling for mercy) without his confiscated wardenship. It was thus problematic; he would have been far more formidable had he still been in office as a trusted royal servant, but in 1405 the loyal Earl Ralph Neville of Westmoreland had his offices and troops. He had the support of Archbishop Scrope, who added the Church's prestige to denunciations of Henry as a tyrannical usurper who had broken his pledges on lower taxes and nailed up rebel manifestoes on York church doors. But Ralph Neville defeated Scrope and the army of his ally Lord Nottingham (the late Thomas Mowbray's son) at Shipham Moor by luring the two commanders to talks with a pretence of sympathy and telling their men falsely that agreement had been reached so they could go home. Scrope and Nottingham were arrested and later executed by Henry, and Northumberland (crucially absent from the Shipham incident) had to flee to Scotland as his castles of Alnwick and Warkworth were attacked. (For the first time, cannons were used to encourage the garrisons to surrender.) After this, Northumberland was a landless 'broken reed' and his arrival in Wales in 1406 to help Glyndwr was of little use; his only use was as a rebel envoy to France, in which capacity he persuaded Charles VI to hurry up his expeditionary force. Moving on to Flanders in search of men and then back to Scotland, he was largely ignored by the regent, the Duke of Albany, and the latter's good relations with England thereafter make it likely that he was seen as an embarrassment. The double-dealing regent may have colluded in the English capture of his nephew Prince James, soon to be king, in spring 1406 and certainly benefited from the boy-king's prolonged absence in English hands. The state of affairs in Scotland made Northumberland's capacity to invade his home county marginal, and in 1407–8 he was to be lured into a desperate invasion and end up killed.[20]

But what if the 'Triple Alliance' of Glyndwr, Mortimer and Percy had been arranged earlier, when the Percies still held their lands? And the French had sent troops to back it up? And would Richard's presence abroad have stimulated his father-in-law, Charles VI (or the mentally unstable Charles' powerful uncle Philip of Burgundy or brother Louis of Orléans) to act more quickly? Something similar could have been set up in 1402/3 on an exiled Richard's behalf, assuming that Richard had the energy and determination to try to regain his throne and would thus have been encouraging French military support. It is hopeful that the loss of his throne might have stimulated Richard – after a period of depression, as he possibly showed after his deposition in real life at Pontefract[21] – into showing some of the bravery he had revealed as a 14-year-old in 1381. He had been an energetic traveller in the late 1390s and had campaigned twice in Ireland, albeit not fighting in person as his father and grandfather had done. (It is questionable if he ever fought in tournaments either; he possibly participated at one in 1390, but this is uncertain.[22])

Richard was possibly a more potent rallying-point for rebellion missing rather than alive and in command. His past conduct as king would have made him a more controversial figure for the Percies to back in 1403, as in real life they could claim to regret aiding in his deposition – and excuse it as a trick by Henry – without having to face the possibility that a vengeful Richard would later break his promise of pardon and murder them as he had done the Duke of Gloucester in 1397. But a triumphant conquest of North Wales by Glyndwr as Henry's weather-battered army retreated in 1401 would have opened the way for Ricardian loyalists in Cheshire to rise in his support in 1402 or 1403, even if fewer English nobles joined that revolt.

The battle of Shrewsbury

An army of Cheshire rebels and Glyndwr's Welshmen would have provided a strong challenge to Prince Henry and the King at Shrewsbury in July 1403. Even with Richard dead, this had not stopped prolonged rumours in 1402–3 of his survival and truculent declarations by the new King's enemies that what mattered was to remove the usurper, whether or not Richard would be the beneficiary. The absence of Richard or a plausible pretender from the Welsh or Percy armies was less important in their defeat than their failure to unite or to secure Shrewsbury. The original intention of 'Hotspur' had been to take Prince Henry hostage, with or without dispersing his (smaller) army, though even if he had reached Shrewsbury first the Prince could have fled east to join his father. As it was, the King was at Higham Ferrers on 12 July 1403 and Nottingham on the 16th, en route to join the supposedly loyal Earl of Northumberland for the summer's Scottish border campaign and unaware that 'Hotspur', raising troops at Chester, intended to attack the Prince of Wales at Shrewsbury not join the planned campaign. He apparently heard rumours of the treacherous intentions of 'Hotspur' that evening, as he wrote to his council in London ordering the ports to be closed and then left southwards at speed next morning; on the 16th he reached Lichfield. His original intention was to halt to raise the local Midlands levies before joining his son at Shrewsbury, but on the 17th he heard that 'Hotspur', at Sandiway about thirty-eight miles from Shrewsbury, was heading for that town and he left for it later that day with what men he had at hand. The King and 'Hotspur' were about the same distance from Shrewsbury, but Henry's 'advance guard' arrived before the Percy troops did; on the 20th 'Hotspur' arrived to find the gates shut and the King's men in the town with the Prince. He retreated, and Henry himself probably arrived a little later – though details are confused. In any case, the King was able to have intelligence of the planned rebel attack in time to counteract it; what if he had been taken by surprise, as Edward IV was to be in similar circumstances in 1470?

The absence of Glyndwr from the rebel army was important, whether it was due to bad liaison with 'Hotspur' or a deliberate decision to avoid the battle.[23] Without him the two Percies ('Hotspur' and his uncle the Earl of Worcester, without Northumberland) seem by the credible account of John Capgrave to have had around 14,000 men; this matches the 14,000 ascribed to the King by the monastic chronicler Thomas Walsingham. The claims of up to 80,000 rebels by the foreign writer Jean de Wauvrin and 60,000 by the

Dieulacres Abbey chronicle are unlikely; Thomas Capgrave's 14,000 is more logical for a force made up of Percy tenantry and Cheshire (and North Wales?) volunteers. The battle on 21 July seems to have been fairly close-fought; Thomas Walsingham says both sides had 14,000. Crucially, the Percies only had around 1,000 Cheshire archers and could not destroy the royal troops with a hail of arrows as the victors had done at Crécy.[24] Even so, the combination of rebel archers and the employment by 'Hotspur' of his Scottish captive from 1402, the military veteran Earl of Douglas, led to the initial defeat of Henry's vanguard, which had to charge up an incline into a hail of arrows and could not use cavalry because of the enemy's position in a beanfield full of tangled plants. De Wauvrin and Walsingham agree that the royalists suffered heavy casualties, and the vanguard's commander (the Earl of Stafford) was killed. The rest managed the crucial task of holding out until the Cheshire archers had run out of arrows, but then Douglas and the Percy infantry smashed into them and drove them back; Walsingham says that 4,000 royalists fled back down the hill. This could easily turn into a rout if panic spread, and it enabled the Cheshire archers to run across the battlefield to collect their spent arrows – an echo of how the archers of the 'Black Prince' had managed to collect their arrows for a second volley at Poitiers. The King then led the rest of his men into the battle and ordered Prince Henry to launch a flank attack, leading to a second head-on clash. 'Hotspur' sought to decide the outcome by a 'suicide attack' as his remaining men started to fall back against superior numbers, in the manner of Richard III at Bosworth – he led around thirty knights in an assault on the area around the royal standard, aiming to kill the King, and Henry (like Henry Tudor at Bosworth) had his standard-bearer cut down. But 'Hotspur', like Richard III, failed to catch his target whose bodyguards cut him down instead. The royal victory was far from certain, in a battle described by de Wauvrin as the bloodiest in England since 1066. It took hours of hard combat for the royal army to prevail and the chronicles of Walsingham and de Wauvrin agree on its ferocity.[25] A larger rebel force could well have succeeded, and the impetus of the rebel charge after Stafford's vanguard was routed could have driven the King's men into flight if they had been under a less disciplined and effective commander. Or 'Hotspur', like Richard III, could have turned the tide of battle by killing the enemy commander – a less likely result as Henry obeyed the Earl of Dunbar's advice to pull back and let his henchmen deal with the attack.

If 'Hotspur' and Glyndwr had managed to reach the town before the King did they could have defeated the outnumbered Prince. But even without the Welsh contingent the rebels could have defeated their opponents. There is also the possibility that Prince Henry could have been killed in the battle, as in real life he suffered an arrow-wound in the face that would have been fatal had it hit him a few inches to one side.[26] In that case, the news of his death would have been dangerous to his army's morale even had the King been there to rally them and had he been in sole command it would probably have caused them to flee. The Percies would have been left in control of the Northern Marches. Had Richard been alive and in exile they would have been able to proclaim him as king and await his arrival or else march on London themselves. Had Richard been unavailable the young Edmund Mortimer was the likeliest beneficiary, with 'Hotspur' married to his aunt and in a position to act as 'king-maker'. Henry IV, if defeated but still alive after escaping the battle or else arriving too late to save his son, would have faced a disintegrating army and been lucky to have time to muster a second one in the south-east before the feared 'Hotspur' and his Border veterans arrived in London. Like Edward IV when faced with a huge Neville army closing in on him in the east Midlands in 1470, he would have been prudent to flee overseas. Prince Henry, if still alive and in possession of an army, would have been likeliest to abandon London for a retreat to his Welsh border strongholds.

The nearest factual parallel to the advance of a large army of veteran northern fighters, already victorious in one battle with the enemy commander dead, on London is that of Queen Margaret's advance on London early in 1461 after the killing of the Duke of York at Wakefield. On that occasion there was panic and no significant resistance, though luckily the Earl of March (Edward IV) arrived from the Welsh Marches in time to induce Margaret to withdraw. Henry IV would have been likeliest to flee abroad, as the loss of his and Prince Henry's armies at Shrewsbury would have given a decisive advantage to the Percies and Glyndwr and the French could be expected to take advantage to land troops in Kent to assist them.

Had Henry IV won at Shrewsbury but his eldest son been killed, he had three other sons to take the Prince's place and the eldest, Thomas (born in 1388), would have succeeded as Prince of Wales but been too young to be an effective commander for several years. In real life Thomas got on better with his father than Prince Henry did in 1410–13, possibly as the King did not see him as a threat to his crown, and he was trusted with a military expedition to France in 1412. A rasher commander than Henry, he was killed at Baugé in 1421 after taking on a larger French force during a raid into Maine. Thomas backed his father's more cautious policy towards intervention in France, rallying to him not to the Prince in the confrontations that developed over governing in 1410–12 (out of ambition or principle?).[27] It cannot be taken as certain that 'King Thomas' from 1413 would have been willing to invade France in the same manner as Henry V did in 1415. Henry IV used Thomas in a limited intervention to back up one of the rival faction-leaders at the French court, Duke John of Burgundy (in control of Paris by 1412), against the 'Armagnac' partisans of the Dukes of Orléans. Had Thomas been king from March 1413 and thus able to decide the extent of intervention in France, he may have been equally willing to use the French civil war to regain Normandy if practicable – as Edward III had considered doing in the 1340s. The way in which Henry V allowed himself to be trapped by the vastly superior French army en route to Calais in October 1415 shows that Thomas, guilty of rash tactics in the 1421 campaign when he was killed, was not alone in over-confidence about the superiority of English arms. But even if Thomas had taken on the conquest of Normandy piecemeal like Henry did in 1417–19, events would have taken a different turn from real life. He was married by then, unlike Henry, so he could not have married Charles VI's daughter Catherine as part of the subsequent peace-treaty in 1420 and used this as a means to supplant his brother-in-law Charles (VII) as the heir to France. Catherine was the key to France, as her surviving brother, Charles, could be written off as illegitimate and the succession routed through her, so she would still have been needed for a Plantagenet prince – presumably Thomas' unmarried next brother, John (Duke of Bedford). In that case Bedford, not Thomas, may have been set up as the next king of France, and the two crowns kept divided.

That eventuality would have made it easier to agree a settlement with France as the Valois cause revived after 1429 – it would have been the English King's brother, not the King himself, who was at risk of 'loss of face' by having to abandon his claim to France. Events cast a long shadow, and if it had been Bedford who was the Plantagenet king of France as Catherine's husband in 1422 he would not have been marrying Jacquetta of Luxembourg in 1433/4. Would this mean that Edward IV's queen, Elizabeth Woodville (Jacquetta's daughter by her next marriage), would never be born as her mother never came to England?

The 1405 campaign and Edmund Mortimer's planned escape
Even if the 1403 revolt had failed, the French-Welsh alliance could have led to the 1405 campaign seeing French ships landing not only their troops but exiles in south-west Wales and an advance towards the West Midlands on Richard's or Edmund Mortimer's behalf. There were still stories circulating in real life 1404 that Richard was still alive and (probably) in Scotland, when he had been dead for four years – in June the abbot of Revesby Abbey, Lincolnshire, preached a sermon saying that 10,000 Englishmen believed the ex-king to be alive.[28] (The continual involvement of churchmen of all ranks, from an archbishop down to ordinary friars, in Ricardian plots

possibly indicates principled anger at the 'illegal' deposition of an anointed king.) Another, unrealistic plot was launched to organize a rising in Essex – within reach of a French fleet – by the Countess of Oxford, mother of Richard II's late favourite (and a cousin of the Percies) and presumably bearing personal grudges against the King dating back to the 1386–8 coups.[29] More seriously, the 'moderate' senior French court leader, Duke Philip of Burgundy, died, leaving power with his more anti-Henrician nephew Louis of Orléans. All this indicates widespread dislike of the current regime, which could have been worse had Richard been definitely known to be alive and available to lead a revolt. The so-called 'Mammet', the pretender in Scotland, was apparently aided by the machinations of the unsavoury Ricardian 'hard man' William Serle, a Royal Chamber valet who had led the murder of the Duke of Gloucester on his master's orders in 1397. He was captured and executed in 1404, after confessing that he had forged letters with Richard's personal seal from Scotland to make the 'Mammet' seem more plausible a pretender.[30] But the plot continued.

The plot to arrange the escape of Edmund Mortimer and his brother from 'protective custody' at Windsor Castle in February 1405 meant that there would be a pretender available to take the throne in the event of success, albeit one too young to fight in person. Luckily for Henry, when the boys' governess, Lady Despenser, secured duplicates to the castle keys and fled with them on horseback (13 February) Henry was quickly informed. His half-brother John Beaufort then led the pursuit. A gallop west along the main road for South Wales ended with the royal posse catching the escapees up in a wood near Cheltenham; their rescuers were overpowered or killed, and they were taken back to Windsor.[31] Had the boys had a few more hours' leeway they would have reached Glyndwr's rebel area and their uncle Sir Edmund Mortimer, who was shortly to agree a division of England between the young Edmund, Northumberland, and Glyndwr. The agreement may have been planned in anticipation of the boys' arrival to act as a focus for the rebel campaign, and would have had more force had its main beneficiary been at liberty. As it was, the plan was given seeming supernatural weight by another of the current crop of prophecies, this time one predicting the overthrow of the sixth king after John (i.e. Henry) by a triple alliance from the west (Wales), north (Northumberland), and Ireland (where the Mortimers had lands).[32] Despite the poor quality of Irish troops, if Richard and/or French support had continued to hold onto Dublin in 1399–1405 this would have given them extra manpower and confidence to advance. The same effect was possible if Richard had been genuinely hiding in Scotland and had had the aggressive young Prince David, Duke of Rothesay (d. 1402), not the elderly and cautious 'regent' Duke Robert of Albany, available to lend troops. By this date the Welsh rebels had control of most of the crucial castles in Wales and varying amounts of the countryside even in the southeast. Henry's repeated armed invasions with locally invincible English armies from 1400 gained temporary control of his hinterland but no long-term reconquest. As with Henry II, John, and Edward I's invasions, the Welsh rebels could retreat into the forested hills and resort to ambushes, retaking control when the English King ran out of supplies and had to go home. Henry was also hampered by bad luck in the form of atrocious weather, especially in 1402, and on one occasion his tent blew down and nearly killed him; the superstitious could claim that the 'wizard' Glyndwr was summoning up the elements to fight him (as made much of by Shakespeare).[33]

An extra factor to hamper King Henry from June 1405
From 1405 Henry IV's health was a problem and restricted his ability to campaign, as did his shortage of money to fund his troops. His first attack of an apparent skin-inflammation occurred on 8 June 1405 as he was travelling north from York to deal with the second revolt by the Earl of Northumberland, with him suddenly afflicted by a burning sensation and temporarily incapacitated. It soon passed and that autumn he was able to march into South Wales to relieve Glyndwr's siege of Coety Castle, but thereafter his decline was notable.[34] The timing of the first attack during the height of the summer 1405 revolt was crucial, giving a temporary advantage to his foes – though luckily he had managed to reach Yorkshire and dispose of the rebel Archbishop Scrope before his collapse. His incapacity at an earlier date would have given Scrope time to consolidate his position and link up with Northumberland. If this had been the case, the Welsh would have had the opportunity to advance unchecked across the southern Marches into the West Midlands if they could elude or defeat Prince Henry and there was no superior English army blocking their route. A French contingent would add to the 'reach' and confidence of their force. So would the personal presence of a Mortimer, if Roger had been alive after 1398 or his son Edmund had escaped from Henry's custody in February 1405; the Mortimer lands were centred on Ludlow in the central Marches. In 1403, lacking the French or a Mortimer force and wary of frontal confrontation with the King, Glyndwr seems to have hung back cautiously from a quick advance into Shropshire to assist the Percies. (It is uncertain if he was close enough to the battlefield at Shrewsbury to watch it from afar, as alleged by legend.) In 1405 there was no Welsh advance towards the central or northern Marches in June to link up with Scrope or to force the King to turn against the Welsh rather than the Yorkshire rebels. Henry could thus tackle his foes

one by one, with greater ability to concentrate all his main force on one of them at a time.

Would there have been any difference to the 1405 plan had a live and adult Richard not a captive under-age Edmund Mortimer been the intended beneficiary? Or had the rebels had a solid base in Ireland which Richard had held from 1399? Richard was the first English king to visit Ireland in person since John, and duly attracted an unusual degree of loyalty from its lords (some Celtic nobles included as well as Anglo–Norman barons). Given Richard's success in attracting adherents in Ireland by personal attention in the 1390s, he should have received Irish support from the MacMurroughs in Leinster directly across the sea from rebel-held ports in Pembrokeshire. The King would have been distracted by the revolt of the Earl of Northumberland and Archbishop Scrope in Yorkshire, as in real life. The French, Irish, and Welsh army could have been strong enough to reach further east than it did in reality (Worcestershire) and attract more adherents, with or without Richard being present in person, though the King may still have preferred to tackle the Yorkshire rising first. The latter was headed off in time in real life, with Henry's representative, the Neville Earl of Westmorland (the Earl of Northumberland's hereditary foe), arriving quickly to disperse a large but poorly-armed rally of disaffected citizens outside York led by their Archbishop. The latter was then seized, subjected to a brief 'show-trial', and executed, which shocked the disaffected into sullen submission.[35]

Only the firm adherence of the Percies to Henry in 1403–5 – possibly out of fear of Richard – or their complete neutralization would have given him a decided advantage over the Welsh–French invaders and a rebel Mortimer tenant army from the Marches. In this case there would be no major northern revolt, enabling him to concentrate his efforts against the Welsh, French, and Mortimers. In that case he should have been able to link up with Prince Henry and fight another battle like that at Shrewsbury in 1403, with a good chance of victory given that the Welsh rarely won 'set-piece' battles in the lowlands and were lightly armed compared to the King's knights; the French were far from home, and Richard had never commanded in battle. Prince Henry was an increasingly competent and successful commander, usually having the better of the Welsh in direct clashes as at the relief of Coety Castle and at Grosmont in 1405; he and his father together would have been as formidable as at Shrewsbury in 1403, and not facing as skilled opponents as they did then in 'Hotspur' and the Earl of Northumberland. The King might still have faced a plot by and executed Archbishop Scrope without a Percy revolt, the Archbishop probably betraying him out of principle (as a usurping regicide) as much as Percy-instigated ambition. In an age that took oaths seriously, it appears that both Scrope and (in an earlier complaint) Henry's French ex-ally the Duke of Orléans were infuriated that he had gone back on promises not to depose or kill Richard. Scrope's plot would have been less dangerous without Percy participation, although his archiepiscopal rank and his local aristocratic dynasty provided him with substantial sympathy and potential support.

The King's serious illness in June 1405, recurring within months, would have meant that Prince Henry would have had the role of principal commander in the campaigns from then on. This mysterious and still-debated physical collapse[36] (similar to that of the 'Black Prince' at the same age?) would have been an unexpected setback to his cause if he had not achieved a quick victory in 1405. The military skills of the two Henries as opposed to Richard and Glyndwr, the fact that any French commander with the latter would have been far from home in unfamiliar territory, and the extended rebel supply-lines would all have worked in the King's favour for a major victory if it came to battle. The mixture of dissident magnates, (fewer) Welsh rebels, and French mercenaries was to give Henry Tudor victory over the equally insecure usurper Richard III in 1485, but the rebels' chances of success in 1405 would have been slimmer. Henry IV and his eldest son in combination would have been more formidable than Richard III, unless the Percies (loyal to this point?) had treacherously refrained from intervening in the battle as 'Hotspur's great-grandson was to do at Bosworth in 1485. But destroying the Ricardian army would have left the Welsh rebels at large, and as the King's health deteriorated Prince Henry would have had the main role in reconquering Wales from 1406.

Richard and Prince Henry: how the timing of King Henry's collapse could have aided the rebels

What if Richard had been available in exile (France or Ireland) to return to England as the rebel candidate to confront Henry in 1405? Or the young Edmund Mortimer had succeeded in reaching Wales in February and been paraded as a talisman for the invasion? In the case of Richard, his known vindictiveness towards his foes was a potential drawback – at least to the chances of Northumberland, who had betrayed him in 1399, supporting him. Thus if the 1405 plot had been in Richard's name Scrope might have had to rise without Percy support – though in the event the Percy troops were unable to reach him in time to stave off surrender to the advancing King so they had no practical use. The increasing ill-health of Henry IV from his mysterious collapse in 1405 would have curtailed the Lancastrians' main asset in a vigorous leader, though they had Prince Henry (when not absent in Wales) and the King's eldest half-brother John Beaufort (who retrieved Edmund Mortimer in February 1405). Much would have depended on Richard's own (dubious) ability to attract English support and his avoidance of the political follies of the late 1390s.

Prince Henry, the English claimant to be Prince of Wales – in charge of the royal forces in Wales that would have been facing Richard/Edmund, Glyndwr, and the French – had been on good terms with Richard as a 'hostage' at his court in 1398–9 and is supposed to have retained affection for his memory. His antagonism towards his father did not become a political factor until the King's ill-health led to the Prince struggling for dominance at court in the late 1400s, but if Richard and his wife Isabella had still been childless (or without a son, no woman having ever ruled England successfully) he could have been prepared to offer the Prince the heirship in return for abandoning his father. The longer the confrontation between Richard and Henry IV continued, the greater the chance would have been of this occurring – with the King's illness a major opportunity for Richard. If Henry IV had scored a decisive, Shrewsbury-style victory over his enemies while in good health in 1404–5 there would have been no opportunity for this, but a serious royal illness during the war would have stalled his campaigning. So would a successful seizure of York by Archbishop Scrope, backed up by Northumberland and his Scots allies.

Richard, like the similarly-deserted Edward IV in 1470, could with luck and energy have used the narrow base of his supplanters' regime and swift disillusionment with the new order to stage a 'comeback' – with the Welsh manpower of Glyndwr's armies available on the right terms. He had one problem in that he lacked the military skill, charisma, and decisive temperament of his grandfather, father, cousin Henry IV, and the later Edward IV – he had ruled in the mid-late 1390s by fear and intimidation, which put him at a disadvantage in leading the nobility by consent. But senior nobles, his protégés in 1397–9, felt enough personal loyalty to attempt to restore him in January 1400 and the Percies (who had abandoned him in 1399) revolted in 1403 when he was rumoured to be still alive and hiding in Scotland; his conduct in the 1390s had not lost him all noble support and if he had been alive in exile this would have aided his cause. The lack of military competence or calculation shown by Richard before September 1399 would not have mattered so much in the decisive campaign against Henry if Northumberland or 'Hotspur', hardened veterans of border warfare with a private army of tenants, were available to organize strategy for him. Had the rebel candidate been Mortimer, a boy, he would have had to rely on the skill of his senior commanders as the juvenile pretender 'Lambert Simnel' had to do in his attack on Henry VII in 1487. 'Simnel' had to rely on the Earl of Lincoln, Richard III's nephew, a semi-royal noble in his twenties, and on Richard's senior adviser Francis, Lord Lovell; Edmund would have found an experienced French commander like Marshal Jean Boucicaut invaluable.

As with the civil wars of 1470–1, 1483, and 1485, the advantage of surprise would lie with the invader and the crucial question would be who would defect to him. As with Richard III facing Henry Tudor in 1485, the invader would have a coherent French force to assist him against the incumbent King – a man beset by treachery since his accession and unsure of who to rely on. Unlike Tudor, Richard (or Edmund Mortimer) would have a large Welsh force from across the latter nation provided that he came to a satisfactory agreement with Glyndwr; Tudor was only joined by a limited number of gentry and their tenants (led by Rhys ap Thomas of Dinefwr) in 1485.

If Henry IV had not managed to defeat first the Yorkshire rebels and then the disparate French-Welsh-Irish army by superior generalship and more disciplined troops, his chances of victory in a war drawn out over several years would have been reduced by his poor health. The latter apparently struck suddenly in 1405 within days of his execution of Archbishop Scrope (which implied Divine retribution to observers) and incapacitated him for some weeks, returning in 1406. Its nature is unknown, except that the King complained that his skin was on fire and he was unable to continue his travels for weeks. It did not totally incapacitate him again until 1408 when he fell into a coma,[37] but the attack of 1405 would have been perilous to his cause if it had occurred at the height of an undecided campaign. It would paralyse his army's manoeuvrability for vital weeks unless his eldest son was available at or near his headquarters to take over. The leadership of the campaign would have passed to Prince Henry, already commander against the Welsh rebels since he was around sixteen and an experienced general able to call on the landed resources of the Duchies of Lancaster and Cornwall (and Chester as its Earl, if not lost to Ricardian rebels) to add to the Marcher lords aiding him against Glyndwr. But if Henry IV had caused a revulsion of feeling against his rule by the unprecedented execution of Archbishop Scrope in autumn 1405 (at least Becket had been killed by 'unauthorized' royal agents) and then fallen sick within days this would have handed a major psychological boost to the invaders, making it seem to be Divine vengeance. Even if the Prince held the invaders at bay in the West Midlands in autumn 1405, they could easily retreat into Wales and resume the attack next spring with French ships (and Ricardian lords in Ireland?) bringing in reinforcements. English control of the Channel, preventing French meddling in Wales, was not fully restored until Henry V took the Norman ports in 1415.

The sick and incapacitated King Henry, his troops worn down since 1400 and facing battle by a larger Welsh-French-Ricardian/Mortimer army while the exiled Percy Earl of Northumberland struck at the north and with support fading away, could have faced his son and heir coming to terms with Richard in spring 1406 to end a destructive civil war. Prince Henry would still have had a substantial 'bargaining-counter' in the form of his army, and given Richard's political follies of 1397–9 he and other leading armed magnates would have been prudent to insist on a strong political role for the council and some Parliamentary statutes to reinforce just and unpartisan royal rule and prevent a return to the 'autocracy' of 1397. The wise political resolution of the end of the civil wars in 1217 and 1267, winning over most of rather than punishing most of the losing side, were the obvious precedents, and the use of Parliament as the forum for legal/administrative reform in 1397 would have given it the major role in enshrining a peace-settlement. But if the invading army was clearly undefeatable except by a major effort that was beyond the Prince's current capacity, the King's ill-health and unpopularity in 1405–6 makes it more likely that he would have been the claimant who had to give up and flee the country and flee. The rightful sovereign's restoration would have been likely to have included detailed negotiations with distrustful nobles and all sorts of legal promises and requirements for an amnesty 'policed' by senior aristocrats.

A restored Richard II – and Henry and Owain, rival Princes of Wales
Having had to grant Wales – or at any rate those parts of it now held by the rebels, all except parts of the south and east – independence despite the resulting discomfiture of Prince Henry and the loss of lands for infuriated Marcher nobles, Richard would have been in a weak position for dispensing patronage and holding onto power though the death of King Robert III of Scotland and accession of a 12-year-old in 1406 would have meant no threat from that region. (As in real life, James might have been captured by the English en route to France and thus been kept in custody as a 'hold' over the regent, Duke Robert of Albany.) Presumably, Richard would have been able with French help to persuade Glyndwr to abandon claims on any ex-Welsh lands in the Marches now held by lords loyal to Richard, the large Mortimer estates around Ludlow in particular, and to leave the English control of Glamorgan and major southern coastal ports sooner than risk a war over them between Glyndwr's captains and the local Marcher lords. The restored 'Principality of Wales' would have centred on the Crown lands of Ceredigion, Powys, and Gwynedd and whatever extra Marcher lands Glyndwr was holding at the time. Prince Henry would have had to be compensated for this loss of the heartland of his 'power-base', probably with his father's confiscated Duchy of Lancaster.

Richard, restored at the age of around thirty-nine, would not have been in the position to damage his enemies that he was in the 1390s. Humiliatingly restored by French and Welsh soldiers, which would have done his public reputation no good however unpopular Henry IV had become, he would have had to tread warily. Prince Henry, the victor of Shrewsbury against the Percies in 1403 before Richard's invasion and having campaigned with credit against the Welsh, would have been in a powerful position if he had come to terms with Richard – assuming that he had not stayed loyal to his father in the face of massive odds and managed to secure an Agincourt-style victory over Richard, not an experienced commander, and the Welsh and French in 1405/6. Richard might have had to accept Henry as his heir as part of a peace-deal to end the civil war, abandoning the Mortimer claim. It would be interesting to see how long Richard could survive on his throne for a second reign, faced with a vigorous young heir with prestige and troops and the rising demands that England abandon his French alliance and take advantage of the savage in-fighting that broke out at the French court after the Duke of Orléans' murder in 1407.

Richard's queen (in real life married off as a widow to Orléans' son) would have been as much of a factor as Richard's personal 1390s policy of alliance to support the French court, making alliance with the Armagnacs – her mother Queen Isabella's ex-lover Orléans' associates – more likely if it came to a choice. Indeed, Richard's survival would have cast a long shadow on later fifteenth century French politics; her real-life second husband, Duke Charles of Orléans (d. 1465), was widowed without children when she died in 1409 and due to captivity in England after Agincourt (1415–40) could only remarry in 1440. His son Louis, who succeeded to the French throne in 1498, was born in 1462. If Charles had not married Isabella, would he have had a son by another wife by 1415? This boy, or his son, would thus have been the new king of France when Charles VIII was killed in a freak accident (hitting his head on a door-lintel) in 1498. The results of Isabella's freedom to remarry from 1400 thus affected France for a century, with son-less Louis XII (Duke Charles' son by his second wife) being succeeded by his cousin François I on New Year's Eve 1514.

If Richard II had continued his pacific policy of the 1390s, as seems likely due to his gratitude to Charles VI for restoration, he would have been missing a chance to retake Normandy or expand Guienne, and thus infuriated Prince Henry and his brothers. Any requirement in a treaty with Glyndwr that the Marcher lords abandon lands in south and east Wales, especially Brecon and Radnor, would have left a body of restive landless noble warlords in need of new lands and hence keen to attack France, the cause of their expulsion. Richard would have had to make up for the loss of revenue from his Welsh Crown lands with the confiscation of as much land as he could confiscate from Henrician loyalists, while preserving a substantial landed inheritance for Prince Henry and having to make grants to angry magnates evicted from the further Marches by Glyndwr. The weak landed position of the Crown in the later 1400s would have argued in favour of an eventual French war once Prince Henry took the Crown to improve its position, given that Duke Robert's Scotland was an ally and its young king was an English hostage.

Assuming that Henry IV had managed to destroy Richard's half-brothers and their partisans as a factor in politics in 1400 and 'Hotspur' Percy and his uncle Worcester had fallen in battle in 1403, only a pardoned and restored (ageing) Earl of Northumberland and the pardoned Mowbrays would have been rivals to Prince Henry as the leading figure at court. Henry would presumably have been able to win amnesty for the Beauforts as well as his brothers, but Archbishop Arundel – a close ally of Henry IV – if still physically intact would have been lucky to evade another deposition from office and the anti-Lancastrian Archbishop Scrope of York would have been the most powerful cleric if not caught and executed by Henry IV in 1405. Lacking a personal core of support as in 1397–9, Richard would have had to be more astute than his record suggests likely, to have avoided becoming a figurehead for the more dynamic and capable Prince Henry through the 1410s. If he had survived for a number of years, it is probable that tension would have arisen between him and the Prince over the advisability of intervening in faction-torn France after 1412 with the latter as keen to invade as he was in real life 1414–15. The English aristocracy, denied a war against either Scots or Welsh, would have needed a campaign to promote unity and win control of loot and lands and the likelihood is that the Armagnac-Burgundian feud over control of the French court would have enabled Henry to persuade Richard (via his Queen?) to assist one faction or other. An expedition, possibly led by Henry or his brothers John of Bedford or Thomas of Clarence, would have militarily aided Richard's mentally declining father-in-law against one of his unwelcome would-be controllers, probably Duke John of Burgundy on account of the English Queen's closer family links to the Armagnacs. The French court would not have suffered the catastrophic losses of senior aristocrats and the psychological shock that it did in real life at Agincourt, but its weakness would have enabled the English to recover from their weak international position at Richard's restoration and become 'power-brokers' in France.

At some point Henry would have had the chance to win a military conflict with one or other French faction, and thus to become the major politico-military influence over Charles VI. He could well have secured Queen

Isabella's younger sister Catherine as his bride around 1420 as in reality, and as the indispensable prop of Charles' regime demanded the Duchy of Normandy as his fief or in full independence. Following Glyndwr's death (?) without a son in around 1416, he would also have been encouraged by the dispossessed Marcher lords to repossess the Principality of Wales and, a seasoned warrior from his French campaigns and probably with French mercenaries, been able to overcome the leaderless Welsh and restore the English Crown's position in the area. There was no obvious successor for Glyndwr, or a major source of military aid for the Welsh apart from the now ineffective French; the military advantage would have lain with Prince Henry.

Whether or not Richard – only fifty-three in 1420 – was still alive, Henry would have been the dominant military figure in England and as long as Richard had had no son would have been the unchallenged heir. The regained Principality of Wales added to the Duchy of Lancaster (by c.1420?) would in due course have made him as powerful a magnate as Warwick was to be in the 1460s, with the added advantage of being heir to the throne and possibly the grantee of lands in France from the grateful Charles VI. But with Wales to reconquer he would have been too preoccupied around 1420–2 to afford the effort of taking over the kingdom of France when Charles VI died, thus sparing England the long wars with Charles VII until some later dispute arose.

What if it had not been Richard but Edmund Mortimer at the head of the rebel army in 1405?

It is also worth considering that the above scenario of a more serious revolt in 1405 might have occurred without it being Richard who benefited. He was not the only alternative candidate to lead or link up with an invasion from France and Wales, as his chosen heir of 1398–9 could have been available. The grandson of John of Gaunt's elder brother Lionel, his daughter's son Roger Mortimer (born 1374), had died in Ireland as Lord Lieutenant in 1398. Roger's son Edmund (born 1391) was, however, alive and in Henry IV's custody. As satirized by Sellars and Yeatman in *1066 and All That*, the confused dynastic situation in the early 1400s could be claimed to be 'nobody ever really was King but Edmund Mortimer ought to be'.[38] Edmund was probably not a viable candidate for those magnates willing to see the 'tyrant' Richard deposed but not favourable to Henry in September 1399, given that he was only aged eight and his accession would entail a long regency. England had had a poor experience of regency recently under Richard's kingship from 1377, culminating in the 'Peasants' Revolt', and an adult king was a safer bet for stability; in any case Henry of Bolingbroke had not been willing to stand aside in Edmund's favour. Nor did the Percies, who had witnessed and may have suggested Henry's oath, insist on Edmund's rights. It is possible, however, that the apparent promise that Henry gave in Yorkshire soon after his landing that he was not aiming at the throne implied to some deserting royalists that he would back Edmund as the new king, and even that the Earl of Northumberland favoured this scenario. That might have been one reason for the bitterness of the Earl and 'Hotspur' against Henry as of 1403, rather than them cynically pretending to be taken by surprise by Henry demanding the throne.

The initiative lay with Henry in September 1399, and it was unlikely that he would show himself willing to risk the political danger of allowing Edmund to become king. As with Richard of Gloucester in 1483, the only ultimate guarantee of his security from a later disgrace by an untrustworthy boy-king linked to his foes was to take the throne himself. The revolt of New Year 1400 was launched by Richard's former 'duketti' in the ex-king's name not Edmund's, and after Richard's announced death in February he was still rumoured to be alive. A plausible 'lookalike' candidate, the 'Mammet', was at large in Scotland and the public display of Richard's body did not prevent his emergence – though it appears that Henry's main foreign foe, Charles VI, accepted that Richard was dead as he requested the return of his widow, Isabella, to France.[39] Thereafter Edmund Mortimer and his brother Roger were held in custody by Henry IV under close supervision, though this did not prevent their uncle Mortimer reaching an agreement with his captor Glyndwr on his behalf early in 1405. This 'Tripartite Indenture' would divide England between Edmund (ruling the south-east and Midlands), Glyndwr (ruling the lands west of the Severn and Trent with Wales), and Northumberland (ruling north of the Trent and Humber). It was supposed to be prefigured by a current prophecy that the sixth English king from John, i.e. Henry IV, would lose his throne and the kingdom be divided into three – which acted to encourage the superstitious to back the 'inevitable' by supporting the side destined to win, the Mortimers.

The prophecy made the revolt more dangerous, by implying that the King was doomed. Ahead of the summer 1405 revolt, an attempt was duly made to rescue the Mortimer boys from Henry's custody and carry them off to Wales to join their uncle and Glyndwr, allegedly masterminded by the son and daughter of Edward III's fourth surviving son, Edmund, Duke of York (d. 1402). York's son, the new Duke Edward, had been loyal to Richard and, as the adult son of the man trusted by Richard as regent in 1399, may have considered his own chances of the throne as greater than the boy Edmund's if Henry stayed disinherited in exile. He had already been accused by his sister, Constance, Lady Despenser, of one plot to kill Henry in 1404; now in February 1405 Constance changed sides and abandoned Henry (who had executed her husband for his part in the New Year 1400 plot). She arranged for her servants to copy the keys of the Mortimer boys' rooms at Windsor Castle and abduct them in the night of 13–14 February, and she joined the runaways. They were caught near Cheltenham; York was imprisoned as well as Constance for alleged implication, but was freed later in 1405.[40] If the boys had not been seized in time they would have been in the custody of their uncle and Glyndwr in Wales when the revolt occurred and/or a French force landed, and could have been used as its figureheads.

Edmund was now fourteen, so there was less need of a regency if the rebel cause triumphed; Edward III had not had a regent at a similar age in 1327, and the role his eldest male relative (Henry of Lancaster) had held as his 'guardian' in 1327–8 would have gone to Edward of York in 1405. The Mortimer boys had one advantage over Richard as titular leaders of the revolt, as they did not have Richard's controversial reputation for treachery and misrule; some nobles would have been more likely to hang back from aiding the unreliable Richard than from backing Edmund. His legality as rightful king would have been aided by Richard's recognition of the Mortimer claim in 1398–9, which derived from allowing inheritance through the female line as was customary in England. (Legally, it could be pointed out that the whole English claim to France from 1328 rested on this right.) In any case possession was the most powerful argument in any late medieval sovereign's favour. Arguably, the lack of Edmund Mortimer at the head of the rebellion in 1405 was a major bonus for Henry – and it is to Henry's credit that he did not resort to arranging for the boys' convenient deaths in 1400–5 in the manner of John with Prince Arthur or Richard III with Edward V and his brother. If Edmund had later died childless as in real life (1425) his successor would have been his sister Anne or her son by Earl Richard of Cambridge – Richard, Duke of York (born 1411). Henry IV having been deposed, his son Henry V would not have been in a position to execute Cambridge for treason in 1415; would the latter have been regent from 1425?

What if Henry IV had won in 1403–5 and not fallen sick?

A major royal victory over Richard (or Edmund Mortimer?), Glyndwr, and the French in 1405 would have been far likelier if the timing of the campaign had enabled Henry IV to meet his enemies in battle before his illness. His first serious attack occurred in mid-June, so the timing would have been tight. Indeed, the whole question of his mysterious physical collapse overshadowed political developments in 1405–13 even in real life, as he was sporadically incapacitated from the age of 38 or 39 and died at 45 or 46. (The latest assessment of his elusive birth-date, by Ian Mortimer, places it at

Maundy Thursday 1367.)[41] The parallels with the condition of the 'Black Prince' are notable, with both incapacitated from campaigning for five or six years before they died, though the latter's illness was initially centred on dysentery, which had him travelling by litter as early as 1370 (he died in 1376). In Henry's case he could travel at a reasonable pace within weeks of his first attack, though his sickness returned in spring 1406 and after 1408 he seems to have travelled mainly by river, which would imply difficulty riding. He had a chronic skin-condition – called 'leprosy' by contemporaries and blamed on Divine punishment for his execution of Archbishop Scrope[42] – and later it affected his mobility. Various theories have been drawn up to explain the King's illness, though a series of strokes are less likely than a mixture of nervous and physical symptoms given that he staged impressive recoveries throughout 1405–12 and was able to move around the south of England and govern with assistance until early 1413. He had a serious physical collapse in 1408 and was unconscious for several days and not expected to live, but recovered; in 1410–12 he was in a poor physical state, unable to walk far, and reduced to using a litter but his mind was unaffected.[43] Possibly he picked up some progressive skin disease in the Baltic or the eastern Mediterranean during his travels in the early 1390s and it took a decade to manifest itself, though the similar collapse of the 'Black Prince' may suggest a genetic problem in the family. There was a family link already to the Valois dynasty, where serious health-problems manifested themselves in the form of mental disturbance (schizophrenia?) with Charles VI – who thought himself made of glass – from 1392 and these were passed on to Henry VI of England. There are suggestions that Edward II and Richard II were both emotionally unstable, and both were erratic and sporadically violent in their behaviour. Physical violence and uncontrollable rages had been a characteristic of Henry II and his sons, and had recurred in the behaviour of Edward I. But the only evidence for serious physical problems was in the case of King John, who alternated extremes of action with lethargy in possible 'bipolar disorder'. None of the English royal family had been struck down by long-term physical incapacity until the 'Black Prince'. Nor was there any sign of serious long-term incapacity in the family of Edward III's mother, Isabella of France, whose kingly ancestors usually lived to their mid-late fifties in full control of their faculties. Edward II's mother Eleanor of Castile's family were also full of competent and relatively long-lived kings. The family of Edward III's wife Philippa of Hainault did, however, include some cases of mental instability.

Whatever the cause of Henry's incapacity, it meant that once the need for his eldest son to be active in Wales far from court receded the ambitious Prince became a major factor in government. Probably stimulated by problems in receiving adequate financial help to wage war, the Prince was increasingly at odds with his father's leading councillors – most notably the Chancellor, Archbishop Arundel, Henry IV's partner in exile and revolt in 1398–9. The Prince's own 'party' was headed by his Beaufort half-brothers, John (d. 1410), Bishop Henry, and Thomas. The tensions of 1408–13 are usually explained in terms of a Beaufort vs Arundel confrontation, with the Prince's choice of senior ministers for his council in 1410 indicating his preferences; his antagonism to Arundel may have been exaggerated but he removed the Archbishop from office twice as soon as he had the opportunity, in 1410 and 1413. A political confrontation ensued as the Prince came to exercise more power at the end of the Welsh insurgency and could spare time for government; Arundel was removed from office, and the Prince's partisans (led by Thomas Beaufort as Chancellor) took over leading roles on the council in early 1410. The Commons had been active in criticising the current council and erratic royal control of finances in its previous meeting in 1406, a rare example for this era of 'grass-roots' criticism of government that cannot be traced to a faction of ambitious nobles.

This has been played up by some historians as an example of 'democratic' assertion by the ordinary provincial gentry,[44] who in practical terms would have to pay extra taxes if the King's apparent extravagance and/or generosity was not checked. (The King, unlike his predecessors used to operating as a provincial magnate and not brought up to government, had placed his own Duchy of Lancaster household 'trusties' in charge of state finances in 1399.) Most MPs were tenants or other connections of the large Duchy of Lancaster estates and thus of Henry's 'affinity', suggesting that they were probably loyal to him not motivated by political ambition on behalf of his enemies; the King sent word that he was too ill to attend Parliament so they probably stepped – uninvited ? – into a governmental vacuum.[45] Probably able to assert itself due to weak governmental control of proceedings following Henry IV's recent illness, the Commons secured a rare degree of control over membership of senior offices in 1406; previous control of a king's government by a committee (e.g. 1264 and 1310) had been arranged and exercised by magnates incensed at his 'favouritism' and his exclusion of them from the benefits of patronage. The question of finance and too-high taxes was cited as their reason for anxiety, and had already been used by the King's enemies in rebel manifestoes as evidence of his misrule.[46] Had Henry been fully active a more serious clash could have occurred with the Crown, rather than the King being powerless to interfere; the Commons' advice to him to live quietly and cheaply on his estates was implicitly humiliating to his dignity.

The creation of the new 'government' in 1410 is usually regarded as a 'revolution' aimed at replacing the ailing King's men with the Prince's,[47] with the King's decline in health a major factor in his son's ability to 'force' the removal of men loyal to his father (as it had been in the King's inability to face down Parliamentary critics in 1406). The two opposing factions are regarded as identifiable by their contrasting choice of French ally, with the Prince's choice of council sending aid to the Duke of Burgundy in 1411 but the restored 'pro-Henry IV' council aiding their Armagnac foes in 1412.

This neat characterization of two hostile factions is simplistic, and ignores mitigating possibilities such as the mutual co-operation throughout of King and Prince in their principal aims – securing enough taxes from Parliament to pay for their wars, and in France forcing the faction-ridden government of Charles VI to restore Normandy and Maine and carry out the terms of the Treaty of Bretigny (i.e. handing over all Henry II's Aquitaine and paying all John II's ransom). It should be remembered that Henry IV was not 'pro-French' and 'anti-war' compared with his eldest son; after all, the propagandist 'prophecy' promoted along with the use of the sacred anointing oil back in 1399 had spoken of him as the destined reconqueror of Normandy.[48] This was a clear sign of his presentation of himself as more aggressive towards France than the pacific Richard had been. Nor was Archbishop Arundel, a 'hard-line' close intimate of Henry IV, implacably hostile to his son, as the Archbishop's valuable aid to his fellow-exile in 1398–9 had not been followed by any long-term grant of political office until 1407. The Prince was too preoccupied in Wales to aid his father at Westminster until c.1408–9, and not 'excluded' from office by the malice of a faction led by Arundel, though he clearly mistrusted the latter and backed his dismissal; the King may have acquiesced in the decision of early 1410 that new men (led by the Beauforts, his kin as much as his son's) were needed in government. Antagonism between King and Prince, with the Archbishop as the former's closest ally, is only undoubtedly visible in 1412 with the Prince excluded from influence and notoriously roistering in London (as used by Shakespeare). Even then, the Prince's appearance in London at the end of June 1412 with a large escort of retainers (following a public letter from Coventry denying his hostile intent to royal policy) was probably not the 'anti-royal' coup threat as it has been interpreted.[49] More plausibly, it was a specific reaction to the snub and mistrust implicit in the King's reversal of the 'pro-Prince' Council 's 1410–11 policy towards France (by sending aid to the Armagnacs in place of the Prince's ally Burgundy). Given the trouble caused to the political nation's loyalties by one legally dubious coup in 1399, Prince Henry could hardly depose his father without danger of more turmoil, potentially led by the 'sidelined' Prince Thomas and abetted by Archbishop Arundel.

There was undoubtedly tension between King and Prince in 1412, as seen by Henry IV sending his second son Thomas (now created Duke of

Clarence) not his heir as the new lieutenant of Aquitaine, in charge of English military aid to the Armagnacs – a policy humiliatingly halted by the unexpected public reconciliation of all the feuding French ducal magnates in alliance against England in mid-1412. The choice of Thomas as commander implied that his father trusted him more than he did Prince Henry and wanted to snub the latter, but not (as rumoured) that he wished to disinherit the Prince.[50] There is no hint of the Prince distrusting or marginalizing Thomas once he was King, as should have been expected if he feared his brother's ambition or a 'plot' to replace him in 1412. The choice of their younger brother, John, Duke of Bedford, as the King's administrative deputy instead was more likely due to Thomas' rash character (he was killed in an avoidable French trap at Baugé in 1421).

This tension between King Henry IV and his heir over the choice of a French ally cannot be 'down-played' as can the question of their mutual hostility in domestic affairs (at least until 1412). It would have been probable even had the King been in full health, and the King's physical decline did not mean total incapacity and resulting loss of control over government until winter 1412–13 (apart from a couple of serious temporary collapses earlier). As events turned out, the opportunities offered to Henry IV by rising tension between senior French dukes – acute after the murder of the Armagnac leader Louis of Orléans, probably by Burgundian agents, in Paris in 1407 – coincided with the Prince being less preoccupied by the (improving) Welsh situation. At most, the King's declining energies made it easier for him to allow the Prince and his allies a relatively free hand in government in 1410–11 – which he reversed when it suited him, probably with the quarrel over which French faction to back as a catalyst.[51] Even had Henry IV been in full health the end of the Welsh war as a major distraction would have brought the Prince back to London, with the chance that disillusionment with the state of government and finances in 1407–10 (as expressed in an assertive Parliament) led to a change of ministers and royal permission for the Prince to send aid to the Duke of Burgundy. The sharp divergence in interests and mutual mistrust of King and Prince could then have developed in any case, given the latter's restlessness and determination – in a parallel case the adult and war-experienced Prince of Wales of the early 1360s, Edward III's heir, had no obvious political divergence from his father to cause tension. The young Edward II, twenty-three by the time he became king, had had no interests in politics or foreign affairs to threaten his father Edward I and had indulged in 'unmanly' leisure – pursuits and crafts that enraged the King.[52] Edward I, also adult (and militarily active like Prince Henry) under his father's rule, was twenty-five or six in the crisis of 1264–5, and acted independently of his father in overthrowing the de Montfort regime then and overshadowed him in the years 1265–70. Henry III, like Henry IV, was ailing and politically weakening in his final years and his heir dominated politics. But Edward had no occasion to quarrel with his father, as they had a mutual interest in defending the monarchy's powers against the De Montfort party and restoring them thereafter; nor did Henry III have a powerful minister (like Henry IV's Archbishop Arundel) at odds with the heir. The nearest parallel for tension between King and Prince of Wales would have been if the 'Black Prince' had been back in England but physically fit in the mid-1370s and seeking to oust the influence of Alice Perrers and her allies, which the doting and probably senile Edward III would have resisted.

The main difference for political developments if the King had been fit and active in government as of 1410–12 would have come for the future; he was only 45 or 46 when he died and if he had lived for another decade or two the difficulties between Prince and King would have persevered. Henry IV's demands from France – the surrender of Normandy, Maine, and Aquitaine and the payment of all John II's ransom[53] – were the same as his son's; the terms' demands for peace did not suddenly alter in March 1413 as Henry V became king. The potential for using French civil strife to force English demands on King Charles VI was constant from 1407, and continued after March 1413. It was this fratricidal obstinacy and cycle of revenge killings that gave the Lancastrian kings their chance to intervene. Even when Henry V was already overrunning Normandy in 1419 the Armagnacs around the Dauphin preferred to take an opportunity to murder the Duke of Burgundy at Montereau bridge rather than unite with him to attack Henry. Henry IV would have benefited from this French court spiral of hatred and reprisal as his son did. Only the means of achieving the English demands were different from 1413, with Henry V sharply reversing the projected aid to the Armagnacs in favour of renewed approaches to the Duke of Burgundy. The temporary reconciliation of the two factions in 1412 had not lasted – and in 1458 it was to be the turn of Charles VI's grandson Henry VI of England to fail to reconcile his feuding senior lords.

The events of 1413–15: how would they have been different under Henry IV?

Had the Duke of Burgundy's party not been driven out of Paris in an uprising in 1413, he would have been the senior court minister dealing with Henry V's demands and might have been more amenable to his 1411 ally than his rivals were. Alternatively, the Armagnac-led government of 1414 might have been more amenable if it had been Henry IV – prepared to send Clarence to aid them in 1412 – not their foe Henry V making demands on them But the handover of all Aquitaine and/or Normandy would still have been difficult to accept; Henry IV seems to have had more interest in Aquitaine than his eldest son did, given Henry V's neglect of it in 1415–22, and it had been his father's governorship in the 1390s. Logically, the aggressive Henry V was less likely to accept any compromise than his father, with one theory arguing that he needed a French war to unite his fractious nobles in a foreign enterprise and thus 'move on' from the civil wars of his father's reign.[54]

Even so, he faced a murder-attempt by his cousin Richard of Cambridge, Edward of York's brother, who had married the next claimant of Richard II's Mortimer heirs, in July 1415. His forces were assembling for the Agincourt campaign in Southampton, where the plot was betrayed; the French may have been involved but were significantly not blamed (as might have been expected to justify the imminent attack on them). It is questionable how dangerous the plot was; details are confused and it is not clear if Cambridge was acting on his own behalf or, as alleged, that of his late wife's brother Edmund Mortimer. The latter had a stronger claim than Cambridge's infant son, Richard, as the heir of Duke Lionel's claim to the throne, and a grudge against Henry for being fined for an unauthorized marriage. But if he was ever seriously involved he backed out; instead of fleeing to the Welsh borders to raise an army of his tenants (to be joined by the Lollards and the Scots?) he informed the King. He was pardoned, but Cambridge and his stepfather Lord Scrope (an ex-treasurer and seeming Lancastrian loyalist) were executed. The plotters' nebulous plans were wildly optimistic, in imagining that their imaginary forces had the manpower or generalship to hold off Henry and his just-assembled army until foreign help arrived;[55] it was not a credible scenario.

Henry IV had claimed to be planning an attack on France (via Aquitaine not Normandy) in early 1406 when his health caused its postponement;[56] this could have been his preferred target. His father, John of Gaunt, and his esteemed grandfather and exemplar, Duke Henry of Lancaster, had both commanded there. As with his son Henry V and with Edward III, a French war would have served to unite the nation after recent civil strife and had he been in good health intervention would have been tempting. Henry IV would not have been sent the famous and usefully insulting 'gift' of a set of tennis-balls, marginal though this issue was (except as propaganda for Henry V). But a breakdown in talks between Henry IV and his ex-host of 1399, Charles VI, over Aquitaine and/or Normandy in 1414–15 was still possible, with a subsequent English expedition to Aquitaine likelier than one to Normandy. Henry V seems to have been consciously copying Edward III's glorious expedition of 1346 in 1415, particularly in his risky and nearly fatal decision to march across country to Calais without adequate scouts and supplies. This programme is less likely from his father, a veteran warrior who had nothing to 'prove' as a commander or as a knight and had been on 'Crusade' against the pagan Lithuanians in the early 1390s, though the rash Clarence was capable of taking such a risk had Henry IV sent an expedition to take a Norman port. Henry IV, like his uncle the 'Black Prince' and his mother's father Duke Henry of Lancaster in the 1350s, might have concentrated on restoring his ancestral lands in Aquitaine in 1414 or 1415 rather than invading Normandy.

Once the talks failed and the French government would not concede meeting the terms of Bretigny in 1414, invasion of France to secure Normandy by force followed with a campaign of public vilification of the treacherous French treaty-breakers to justify it. The main question at issue is whether a similar snub to Henry IV as king in 1414–15 would have led to the same result; the current regime in Paris was led by his potential Armagnac allies who may have been more cautious about alienating him than they were in real life about alienating his Burgundy-allied son. Ultimately, the demands made by Henry IV were as unmeetable as those made by Henry V but it is uncertain if the former meant them as seriously as his son did – would he have settled for payment of part of the ransom and a handover of part of Aquitaine? Or for the marriage of Princess Catherine to his still-unwed heir in 1414–15 (with more territory as her dowry)? The deaths of Charles VI's two elder sons, leaving the more questionably legitimate Charles (VII) as heir by 1420, would still have presented an opportunity to the latter's husband – the future Henry V as a result of a compromise French treaty with his father? – to meddle in French politics in the 1420s. Arguably, the crucial murder of Duke John ('the Fearless') of Burgundy by the Armagnacs may have occurred as a result of an immediate quarrel and/or opportunism at Montereau but was feasible in any case. Blamed for killing Louis of Orléans, he was a target for retaliation even if Henry V had not been overrunning Normandy at the time. This would have ended any chance of a second 'reconciliation' as in 1412, and forced the Burgundians to seek English aid to avoid destruction – giving either Henry IV or Henry V the inviting prospect of major gains in France and thus making invasion probable.

It should also be noted that if circumstances had allowed the Duke of Burgundy to satisfy the Prince's request for marriage to his sister Anne in the 1411 talks[57] the future Henry V would not have been able to marry Catherine as part of the Anglo-French peace in 1420. It would not have affected Henry V's ability to demand the heirship to France in 1420, as this came via his ancestress Queen Isabella (mother of Edward III) not via Catherine; the latter could have been married to his brother John, Duke of

Bedford (who in real life married Anne of Burgundy). Anne had no children by John, a major factor in subsequent Lancastrian politics in the 1440s and 1450s as that left Henry VI's heir as the Duke of York and stoked the political feuding at court. Would Anne and Henry V have had any children? If they had not done so, then Henry V's heir would have been Bedford (aged 33 in August 1422) not Henry VI (aged eight months). In that case, England would have had an adult king and Bedford would not have been restricted to acting as regent of France; he could have called on more troops to fight in France in 1422–9. Whether he would have secured men or taxes from a war-weary England is another matter. But the problem of a lack of heirs may have lain with Bedford rather than Anne; his next wife, Jacquetta of St Pol, had no children by him either but had at least ten by her second husband Sir Richard Woodville.

Chapter Four

Henry V

1422 – no early death of Henry V at 34/5. What if he had lived to the same sort of age as his brother John, Duke of Bedford, and died around 1435? Would he have been able to conquer and unite all France? Or had he taken on too much?

Agincourt: success due to luck as much as judgement? Due to French feuding and military incompetence as much as to Henry's skills? How nearly did his gamble (the march to Calais) fail, and was he at serious fault himself?

The political and military initiatives seemed to lie with Henry V in the summer of 1422. Son-in-law and designated heir of the feeble Charles VI and allied to the greatest feudatory of the French realm, Duke Philip of Burgundy, he was 'mopping up' the remaining towns in the Isle de France and Champagne that did not accept the new order. The success that he had achieved in seven years of French campaigning was remarkable, even allowing for his crushing victory at Agincourt that had wiped out many of the leading French nobles and demoralized the larger French army. As in 1356, the attacking French had expected an easy victory over a smaller, trapped English army that was exhausted from a long march across their land. The French had demanded surrender but had unexpectedly had the tables turned on them. The English position at Agincourt was probably more perilous than at Poitiers, though then and after the French did their best to play down the difference in numbers, and their victory was duly seen as 'miraculous' and Divinely aided. It was certainly more politically vital to Henry than Poitiers was to Edward III (who unlike him had not been in command at the vital battle) and his son and commander at Poitiers, the 'Black Prince'. It showed that the Lancastrian line's usurpation in 1399 and regicide in 1400 had not brought Divine vengeance on them at their first international battle, and thus gave the lie to the claims of their Mortimer rivals who had tried to overthrow Henry only months previously in the Southampton plot. (Shakespeare duly followed the Lancastrian chroniclers in having Henry praying before battle to ask God to overlook his father's sins.)

Henry's outstanding military reputation at the time and since relied largely on the Agincourt campaign, which humiliated the numerically superior French commander-in-chief, the Dauphin Louis, as effectively as Poitiers had King John II – although at least the Dauphin was not captured and led off for ransom as John had been. He had not been present on the battlefield, unlike John being short of military experience (and probably of bravery too), and had relied on his equally inexperienced cousin Duke Charles of Orléans who spent the next twenty-five years in English captivity. Notably Duke Charles (barely twenty) was politically trustworthy for the embattled French court, as the son and successor of the murdered Duke Louis, the feeble King Charles VI's principal minister in the early 1400s and head of the 'Armagnac' faction (and reputed lover of the Dauphin's promiscuous mother, Queen Isabella). This outweighed his military inexperience – the far more capable military veteran Duke John of Burgundy, aged forty-one, was kept at arms' length by the French court in 1415 as the head of the rival 'Burgundian' faction (and reputed hirer of Duke Louis' murderers), to Henry's benefit. Both King John in 1356 and Dauphin Louis in 1415 anticipated an easy victory over the smaller English force they had been chasing across France and trapped, and attempted to overwhelm the foe by sheer weight of numbers. Instead, the English held up their charge on a narrow front, with the French 'high command' either not anticipating or not fearing what could happen to their army if it was sandwiched into a 'log-jam' by the narrow space available for fighting and could not maintain forward momentum. They seem to have been confident that their momentum would carry them forwards quickly enough to counter-act the inevitable hail of arrows from the English archers. Indeed, if the attackers' charge was fast and thorough enough it could cause serious problems to a defensive position reliant on archers. At Shrewsbury in 1403, for example, the royal army vanguard of Henry IV survived the arrow-storm unleashed by the Percies' Cheshire archers and had to be halted by Percy infantry. And what would happen if the archers ran out of arrows? Both at Shrewsbury and at Poitiers the army most reliant on archers (those of 'Hotspur' and the 'Black Prince') had to beat the enemy back, giving their own archers time to run forward and collect their spent arrows for a second volley. The tactic worked for the archers at Poitiers; it did not work at Shrewsbury, but the Percy archers there were a smaller force than those of the 'Black Prince's at Poitiers. The crucial advantage that Henry V had at

Agincourt was the lack of sustained pressure from the multi-commanded French troops, which gave his men a 'breathing-space' and enabled his archers to re-load. This had also been the case at Poitiers, and he was no doubt aware of this advantage when facing the poorly-led French 'feudal' army whose senior commanders were less amenable to centralized direction than English armies had been at Crécy and Poitiers. But relying on it as his main hope would have been risky.

The attackers at Agincourt faced great danger, due to the combination of a narrow 'field' to fight on between woods and bogs and the recent wet weather. The rain-sodden ground caused the charging French heavy cavalry to slip, and a line of stakes that the English archers set up in front of their position prevented those horsemen who reached them from trampling them underfoot; the front line of the charge ground to a halt and the next line 'piled up' behind it. The result was a bloodbath with the frustrated heavily-armed attackers virtually 'sitting ducks' for the English counter-attack, heavy horses and knights floundering in the mud, and the lightly-armed English able to kill and capture at will. Henry undoubtedly had superior tactics and used the terrain and weather to full advantage; he had instructed his archers to carry stakes with them on their march across northern France so that he could counter a cavalry attack whenever it came.[1] This defensive tactic by the smaller army, halting the enemy charge with infantry and then pushing them back while the enemy rearguard 'piled up' behind their vanguard unable to use their numbers and outflank the defence, had worked at Crécy in 1346. But Henry had not chosen the battlefield unlike Edward III did in 1346 – he had been marching close to the pursuing French since he belatedly crossed the Somme but not seeking them out. Indeed, the English were avoiding battle due to his men's inferior numbers, anxiety over rumour multiplying enemy numbers, recent problems in finding an unguarded ford over the Somme, lack of provisions after spending more time on the road than anticipated, and the demoralizing rain. The French had sought out his exhausted army after the Somme crossing and issued a challenge on 20 October – to ask the intended English route to Calais so they could fight them – with the intention of blocking the road to ensure that they did so. Henry showed public nonchalance but was vague over his route (the 'most direct' one) and clearly had less eagerness to fight than he had before leaving Harfleur for Calais, when he sent a herald to challenge the French at their Rouen headquarters.[2] His hope once he was north of the Somme was clearly to try to avoid his army having to fight a well-provisioned and confident foe in such a poor condition, and to reach Calais without battle instead. But the French succeeded in blocking his route on 24 October, so he had to make the best of the situation.

The site and the weather were to his advantage, but these were factors beyond his control; he was capable of using such matters to his best advantage but that should not obscure the fact that as of the 24th he had led his men into a far worse situation than Edward III had faced on his northwards march from the Seine to Calais in late summer 1346. The 'narrative' produced by the victors tends to obscure the fact that Henry had made bad mistakes in his campaign. For one thing, although precise numbers are unclear and he did have a viable army of c.6,000 men, this was smaller than the army Edward had led in 1346[3] and had been affected by the number of troops who had fallen sick during a recent epidemic of dysentery before they left Harfleur around 6 October. Many officers and men who would normally have been expected to participate in the King's final march of the campaigning season had had to be shipped back to England ill that autumn – and experienced voices were raised at the pre-march council-of-war that Henry should give up the campaign and sail home too.[4] The smaller than expected size of his expeditionary force thus put it at risk. More to the point, he had allowed a French noble then in Harfleur (De Goucourt) to accompany his herald on the journey to Rouen to issue the challenge to the Dauphin before the march so that man could report the epidemic and the small numbers of Englishmen available for the expedition, making attack more likely. Captured French nobles at Harfleur, released on licence to collect their promised ransoms, had been asked to bring the money to Henry at Calais later in October[5] – showing that that was his destination rather than the rumoured Aquitaine. The likelihood that if he headed for Calais he would be intercepted en route was expected by the town's commander, Sir William Bardolf (in a letter) on 7 October,[6] as Henry set out. Short of troops and artillery (too slow to drag by waggon across the countryside) and unable to stop en route to attack any fortified towns such as Dieppe or Boulogne, Henry needed to make haste and set the expected time for the march as eight days, provisioning accordingly.[7] But this depended on the vital Somme ford at Blanche Taque being taken and held for him by troops sent out from Calais, and these men were ambushed and dispersed en route by the part of the French army operating north of the Somme. Thus, Henry arrived at the river on 12 October to find the ford blocked and had to head upstream, short of provisions and uncertain of finding another ford unoccupied.[8] It must raise the question of why he did not anticipate the ambush of the Calais troops – did he think there were too few French troops in the area to challenge them? And why did he have no local scouts ready? (He had to rely on fortuitous help to locate an alternative ford upstream at Nesle.) Is the established heroic 'narrative' of the Agincourt campaign a careful deflection of attention away from Henry's incompetence in being caught out at the Somme?

Henry's battlefield tactics were not unique for that era and should not have taken the French by surprise. Their superior heavy cavalry had been held back from enemy infantry and then deluged with arrows, surrounded, and massacred by the Ottoman Turks at Nicopolis on the Danube during the 'Crusade' of 1396 – an expedition largely arranged and headed by the Duke of Burgundy, current Duke John's father. Veterans of that disaster were in senior command in the French force at Agincourt, including the elderly knightly paragon 'Marshal' Jean Boucicaut who led the initial French force 'shadowing' Henry as he marched north to the Somme in early October. Boucicaut advised against a frontal attack on the English, and was ignored. The combination of a 'surprise' defeat for a cavalry charge by armoured knights and a withering rain of arrows were the main features of Nicopolis as of Agincourt – and many senior French survivors were led off for ransom on both occasions. (The Turkish army at Nicopolis was, however, much larger than Henry's, so more dangerous – and Middle Eastern cavalry archers had terrorized French mounted knights since the First Crusade.) Henry's 'trap', the best use he could make of inferior numbers and his reliance on infantry archers, was thus avoidable if the French nobles had not been so sure that they could ride his men down quickly. It appears that their army – around 36,000 according to the reliable Jean de Wauvrin, but up to 60,000 by some accounts[9] – was so much larger than the English that they had sent some infantry volunteers home. Pikemen and archers would have been invaluable on the muddy battlefield, where the sodden ground affected the French cavalry – but such men were seen as socially inferior and marginal to an expected easy victory.

The success of any reasonably-sized infantry force, backed by archers, in holding back a cavalry attack was not a 'given'. Indeed, the superiority of a well-armed defensive 'bloc' of infantry (with or without archers) over a cavalry charge was a new and unwelcome phenomenon of the late thirteenth century, first seen in the – temporary – success of William Wallace's Scots 'schiltrons' against the English in 1298. The French heavy cavalry had prevailed over defensive infantry at Courtrai in 1302, where the enemy (Flemish) archers had not yet become as formidable as they were to be under Edward III. The main English innovation of the 1330s was the use of concentrated 'firepower' by a large body of archers against cavalry – but that depended on the archers being protected from enemy attack for long enough to destroy them. Here Henry was at a disadvantage in 1415 – as the French knew. The infantry divisions that Edward III mustered at Crécy had been larger than at Agincourt, commanding a wider 'sweep' of level ground and less vulnerable to outflanking. The army that Edward's son the 'Black Prince' had led to unexpected victory at Poitiers in 1356 had also been smaller than that of the French attackers, but able to hold them back for hours in a defensive battle. Even so, Poitiers had been a 'close-run thing' with the French cavalry 'wings' luckily failing to ambush the English archers on the march before the battle commenced. At Agincourt Henry's army was substantially more outnumbered. A quick French cavalry charge could disrupt the English archers before they had time to bring their arrows to bear against the foe. Henry's fear of his men being swept away by an overwhelming charge is shown by his instructions to them to carry stakes on their march – with the stakes substituting for the more usual defence of a line of infantry with pikes, which he did not possess in sufficient numbers. For the final few days' march before Agincourt his men were marching in full battle-armour or mail, evidently prepared to fight at short notice. Given the smaller number of archers – or pikemen to protect them – that he had, than Edward III had had in 1346 or the Sultan had had at Nicopolis in 1396, it was indeed possible that the French cavalry could break up his archers quickly. Had they been able to operate on a large and level plain of firm ground and outflank his infantry, Henry would have been in serious trouble.

This advantage was not present at Agincourt, where the heavy rain on the Artois clay (also a hazard to quick action in the First World War 500 years later) added to a narrow field with woodland on either side. This made a charge by armoured men on heavy horses risky, but the French moved in anyway. Equally dangerous, the multitude of French horsed landowners – semi-autonomous local lords – were unused to fighting together and were thus unwieldy as a 'bloc' of men. Given their strong sense of social superiority, they were not likely to take kindly to orders from social inferiors (or, given faction-feuds, political enemies). The Burgundian force, led by the Duke's brothers, would distrust the Armagnac 'high command' – and were apparently 'dumped' out on the wings. Indeed, it is possible that the over-confident French commanders even sent some infantry volunteers home; they were expecting an easy victory, led by their cavalry, with the outnumbered English running away. (Fires were lit on the night before the battle to detect any English flight.) However the French did have the sense to avoid a 'head-on' charge on the morning of the 25th, and waited in their ranks for several hours, forcing the English to open the battle. (Due to poor provisions and shaky morale, the English needed to clear the route to Calais that day and so to fight.)

The English thus 'closed' quickly with the French front ranks of cavalry, an essential tactic so that the latter had no time or space to launch a charge against them. This manoeuvre also enabled the English to move forward into a narrower part of the field, so they could not be outflanked – though while they were moving the archers had to pull up and carry their defensive stakes, laying themselves open to attack until they were in their new position. Had the French been further away or the ground firm enough for a charge, the French would have been well-advised to charge as soon as they saw the English advancing – and this 'push' at speed could have won the battle. But the cramped confines of the battlefield prevented this, although it appears that at least part of a bloc of aristocratic French cavalry entrusted with the opening charge did perform their duty – inadequately. Whether due to being caught by surprise, not having all their ranks ready to counter-attack, bad leadership, not having the space to build up speed, or the mud, they were held by the English. They then appear to have withdrawn, and it has been noted that most of their leaders survived the battle unscathed and uncaptured (perhaps arguing a lack of zeal). The English advanced, and the front ranks clashed at a walking-pace as the English archers opened fire; the French crossbowmen appear to have been sidelined on the flanks by their 'high command'. Once the English archers were destroying the waiting ranks of the enemy as 'sitting ducks', the French duly tried to push the English back with their cavalry but had not the space to outflank them; a mixture of boggy ground and scrubby bushes protected the English ranks. The nature of the battlefield prevented a flanking charge, so all the French could do was to press onto the narrow 'front' in the centre – where only a limited number of men could come into contact and the English thus faced equal numbers.

The weight of the French rear ranks was useless, and the rearguard indeed never saw action – though a panic about them moving in to attack late in the action apparently led to Henry ordering his prisoners to be killed lest they return to the fray. This has been cited as a 'war crime' and was seen as shocking at the time, breaking the chivalric code, but it was a practical if cold-blooded response to an emergency. Unlike the French nobles, he had trained in the guerrilla warfare of the Welsh insurgency and had no time for knightly gestures with his army threatened by a prisoner-breakout. (The main criticism of Henry's action in contemporary terminology was not so much that he killed prisoners who had surrendered, but that he deprived his men of the fortunes they would earn from ransoming their captives. Nor did he bother to arrange individual burials for the lower-ranking English casualties after the battle.) Henry's main reward to his middle-ranking soldiers seems to have been to allow or turn a blind eye to the widespread assumption of heraldic coats of arms – a sign of 'gentry' status – by Agincourt veterans, rather than financial grants. He showed reluctance or inability to repay loans of money by wealthy troop-raising supporters for the French campaigns, and kept the ransom money for his own prisoners for himself rather than repaying his debts. His acquisitiveness has also been explained as a reason for his bizarre decision to arrest and despoil his stepmother, Joan of Navarre, for alleged 'witchcraft' in 1419 – she was never charged, which suggests a lack of evidence. Only one man ever testified to her alleged crime.[10] The idea of using a 'political' charge against a wealthy and inconvenient queen dowager to seize her estates and use the money was to be repeated by Henry VII, another ruler accused of cold-blooded greed, against Elizabeth Woodville in 1487.

Once the French were proving themselves unable to cut or push their way through the English centre, there was no attempt either to disengage or to send any men from the rear ranks round the outskirts of the battlefield (on foot due to the bogs) to attack Henry's rear and cause panic. There was no co-ordinated French leadership, giving Henry the initiative. The isolated French raid on his camp that did cause panic was probably a private initiative and was a missed opportunity to save the day by a similar but stronger counter-attack. Instead the French were cut down en masse, and lost 3 dukes, 5 counts, 90 lords, around 1,050–2000 knights, and some 5,000 'gentlemen' and 5–6,000 men of lower ranks. The English lost much smaller numbers despite bearing the brunt of the onslaught in the centre, with their own estimates from 22 to 100 killed and the French putting their losses at 300–1,000; it is significant that only two senior nobles (the Duke of York and Earl of Suffolk) fell as these men traditionally 'led from the front'. The disproportionate losses of senior nobles on the two sides were probably not much affected by the massacre of the well-born French prisoners in the panic over a counter-attack late in the battle, the numbers involved in which are unclear. The numbers of French prisoners who survived the massacre and were taken off for ransom were disputed, at between 700 and 1,500 (suggesting that most survived the killing); they included not only Charles of Orléans but Boucicaut (who had suffered a similar fate in 1396 from the Turks), the Duke of Bourbon, and the Duke of Brittany's brother Arthur of Richemont.[11] The English were able to make the most of this in subsequent propaganda and in the King's entry to London, where his prisoners were paraded as at a Roman 'triumph'. In contemporary terminology the overwhelming victory showed that Henry had God on his side, and it was accordingly used to argue that whatever the legal quibbles about allowing inheritance of the French Crown by Henry through a female, God clearly favoured this. The argument that Henry was now the Divinely-favoured candidate for the French Crown – and only he could reunite faction-torn France – was duly put to the council of Constance to impress the new Pope Martin and his cardinals.

French faction-strife: a help to Henry in 1415?
Henry's ability to secure a victory was helped immeasurably by the failure of
the leadership to listen to the few counsels of caution about fighting on the
25th rather than just blockading the English camp and starving the enemy
into attack or flight. The latter would have been sensible but not 'knightly',
and the French underestimated the use Henry could make of his archers even
without a large body of protective infantry. In the absence of the Dauphin,
the highest-ranking royal prince was the 22-year-old Duke Charles of Orléans
– who had no experience but failed to accept the cautious advice of D'Albret
or Boucicaut who did have the necessary experience. The absence of the most
high-ranking survivor of Nicopolis, Duke John of Burgundy, was important
in the muddle and lack of initiative among the commanders. Captured at
Nicopolis and ransomed at great cost, John was a cautious commander who
was unlikely to have been as confident about riding the English down easily
as the less-experienced senior nobles in camp were, and as the King's cousin
he had the rank to be listened to with respect. Would he have been able to
warn Orléans off the folly of attacking Henry on a narrow 'front' of boggy
ground ? But this is unlikely, given recent French politics. His role as leader
of the 'Burgundian' faction and foe of the Count of Armagnac, the senior
Armagnac leader, was compounded by his rumoured role in the 1407 murder
of Orléans' father, Duke Louis. The Dauphin (had he been in command),
Orléans, and many senior nobles distrusted him; in 1412–13 his 'Cabouchon'
faction had been in control of Paris until removed by a coup. Despite the
recent Burgundian-Armagnac truce he did not 'sign up' for the war against
Henry until well into the campaign, holding out for an extension of the
truce's amnesty to more of his arrested Parisian allies.[12] He was suspected of
intending to use his troops to attack Paris again.[13] There were also well-
founded suspicions that he was in contact with the English and might even
prefer to see an Armagnac-led army under the Dauphin defeated; Henry had
an envoy, Philip Morgan, at his court in October 1415.[14] Accordingly, he was
asked to send his men to the Dauphin's camp but stay at home himself, and
never joined the expedition. His son, Philip Count of Charolais, failed to
arrive at Agincourt in time to fight (as did the Duke of Anjou). It is also
possible that the fear of Burgundian plots helped in the catastrophic absence
of clear 'central command' at the battle – due to rank, only enforceable by the
King, Dauphin, or a recognizably senior royal duke. The King was too
mentally feeble to issue orders, but the Dauphin had the rank to order the
nobles to follow one particular course of action and he was not in camp,
having stayed at 'base headquarters'. Possibly he was encouraged to stay away
lest the Burgundians in the army kidnapped him as part of Duke John's
expected coup.

The factional strife at the French court thus served to make Henry's chances of victory at Agincourt greater, and to counter the superior numbers which Henry knew he faced when he set out from Harfleur for Calais around 6 October 1415. It was the unexpected ambush of the Calais 'task-force' at Blanche Taque by 'Constable' D'Albret's force in Artois which made an encounter with the pursuing French army probable, not Henry's plans – he learnt of the fact that D'Albret had barred the ford when he arrived nearby on 13 October. It has to be asked why he had no 'contingency plan' to deal with such an eventuality, or at least local guides to find another ford quickly. Without the failure to secure Blanche Taque he would have been several days ahead of the Dauphin when he crossed the Somme on around 13 October, with a short dash west of Amiens to the border of the English 'Pale'. The Dauphin's army, moving up from Rouen to Abbeville, did not know Henry's precise location until 20 October, even with him delayed for several days while finding a new crossing of the Somme – without the delay they would have been outpaced. The smaller local French contingent waiting in Artois – the men who had ambushed the Calais 'task-force' sent to Blanche Taque – would have found it difficult to hold Henry up in open country, and his lack of interest in halting his men en route to attack any fortified town shows that he was unlikely to have let an assault on Boulogne hold him up. According to plan he should have been in Calais around 16 October.

A battle was thus possible but by no means certain as seen from Harfleur as the English marched out around 6 October – with the risk still considered great enough for some locally-experienced English captains (including Henry's brother Clarence) to oppose the march. Indeed, Clarence reputedly boycotted it and had to be sent home by sea – and he had fought in France before (1412), unlike Henry. If it had not been for the serious outbreaks of dysentery that had afflicted Henry's army at the town of Harfleur since it fell, far fewer men would have had to be shipped home and he would have had a larger force that was at less risk. Crucially, he would have had more men-at-arms to protect his archers – the usual solid blocs of infantry ('battles'), not a force of well under 1,000.

After Agincourt

A victory like Agincourt was not the inevitable precursor of the conquest of Normandy and collapse of France. The 1415 campaign had seen only the loss of one town – Harfleur – to England, albeit the major Seine basin port, and the advances in fortification since 1346 meant that the walls of the other Norman towns were much better able to stand up to sieges than they had been in Edward III's time. Despite the lack of a Castilian fleet to aid the French navy, the latter was able to call in help from Genoa – whose large 'carracks' were taller than English warships – and blockade Harfleur's English garrison by sea in winter 1415–16, causing major efforts to relieve it. The threat of recapture did not end until a major victory by England over the Franco-Genoese fleet on 15 August 1416 (the Feast of the Assumption of the Virgin, so a useful sign of Divine support for the devout Henry).[15] On land, the military loss of the experienced 'Constable' D'Albret at Agincourt and the political loss of the Dauphin Louis (who soon died) were offset by the assumption of military leadership by the Count of Armagnac, head of the eponymous faction, in 1416. (The new Dauphin, John, was younger and even less experienced than Louis, though he had a useful marital alliance to the County of Holland, and he died in 1417.) Nor did the Count's grip on power drive his enemy John of Burgundy irrevocably into the English camp; his 1416 treaty with Henry saw him accept Henry's claim to the French Crown in principle but only promise military aid once Henry had achieved substantial conquests in that country.[16] At best, the second English invasion of France in 1417 could rely on Burgundian neutrality, meaning that the Burgundian-controlled 'bloc' of towns north-east of the Seine could not be used by the Armagnacs to attack Henry's positions south-west of the River around Harfleur (and soon Caen inland). Henry was able to operate south of the Seine without fear of attack from one major direction, and was able to secure first Caen (August 1417) and then Alençon, Belleme, and (February 1418) Falaise, thus taking over all 'Lower Normandy' as far as the Breton border. A truce with Brittany (a traditional English ally from the fourteenth century wars) and Maine followed, and isolated Cherbourg finally surrendered in September 1418.

With his southern and western borders secured Henry could then move in on Rouen, the traditional Norman administrative capital – and the best-defended city in the region. Its size required a massive blockade by most of Henry's army, and its walls made storming it difficult – even with cannons. The inhabitants had had time to prepare, bring in supplies, and burn down houses outside the walls that would give the besiegers shelter, and there was no question of surrender (even with a Burgundian-appointed military governor). Ironically, by the time that the siege opened Duke John of Burgundy had seized control of Paris in yet another coup (29 May 1418), killing the Count of Armagnac and other faction-leaders and forcing the new Dauphin Charles (aged fifteen) into flight. This coup did not lead to any attempt by John to reach terms with Henry despite their meeting and private treaty of 1416; as the new head of the French royal government in anti-English Paris he was publicly expected to and committed to keeping on with his predecessors' campaign. Any slackening of effort would doubtless have led to plots and riots at his lack of patriotism.

A long English siege of Rouen followed before it was starved out, with artillery not yet advanced enough to enable Henry to batter down its walls quickly. Henry had to rely on forcing the city to surrender by showing that resistance would only cause more hardship, and in that cause his brutal refusal to feed those 'non-combatant' citizens expelled by the garrison was a trial of strength with the latter not a deliberate atrocity. Refusing to let the civilians pass through his lines and keeping them penned up without food in front of the walls duly forced the garrison to take the survivors back and feed them, making surrender occur quicker. He allegedly claimed that he had not been the one to turn them out into the ditch,[17] and was clearly determined to show himself immune from moral blackmail – with his tactic usefully encouraging other citizens at future sieges to surrender quickly. As he put the case in all his official proclamations, he was the rightful Duke of Normandy by hereditary descent and his treacherous 'subjects' had violated their duty to their sovereign;[18] indeed, he usually allowed demonstrably well-affected French residents to stay in all the Norman towns as they fell. His goodwill towards his loyal French subjects and good treatment of non-combatants, even those exiled from a fallen town like Caen, was played up by his chroniclers.[19] Rouen was the exception, largely due to the stiffness of its resistance; its size made its long defiance particularly irksome and necessitated reprisals.

The 'end-game' and the advance on Paris, 1419–20. Henry's position compared with Edward III's in 1359–60

Once Rouen surrendered on 19 January 1419 Henry could think about pressing his claim beyond conquered Normandy via the Vexin to Paris and the Crown itself, and play off the mutually hostile Duke John and Dauphin (whose truce of September 1418 never led to any military combination against him). The land grants made at Bretigny in 1360 were a *sine qua non*, and technically Henry could claim that the French had violated their then promise to cede all the old Angevin 'empire' in Aquitaine. Now Normandy (plus other towns taken in the campaign) and the marriage to Princess Catherine were added in line with the previous English demands since 1410, and were required of both French factions. Duke John of Burgundy, the militarily stronger French faction-leader and in physical control of King Charles (and the legal machinery necessary to seal a treaty with the Crown), had done nothing to advance from his base at Amiens to rescue Rouen in winter 1418–19; the more hostile Dauphin lacked the military means to fight Henry. The pair's mutual hostility made a combination to fight the English unlikely, although the failure of the English-Burgundian meeting at Meulan in May 1419 led to a formal *rapprochement* between the two at Pouilly in July.

Henry could advance steadily towards Paris, taking the vital western bastion of Pontoise in July, and blockade the city's Seine supply route while negotiating separately with each French leader in order to keep them apart. His position was thus stronger than Edward III's had been when attacking Paris in 1359–60; Edward had faced a united 'regency' government under a competent, politically experienced, and dynastically secure Dauphin. The latter had managed to regain control of Paris from the Étienne Marcel faction and the treacherous Charles 'the Bad' of Navarre before the English army arrived; by contrast, in 1419 the French factional feuds were unresolved. The crucial years after Agincourt had seen major – and slow – changes in the political and military balance, which are sometimes neglected in a simplistic Shakespeare-derived 'storyline' leading quickly from Agincourt to Henry's marriage to Princess Catherine in 1420. The hesitant but inexorable English advances were sporadically threatened by a French factional reunion, as late as July 1419 by the Burgundian-Dauphinist meeting at Pouilly. Luckily for Henry, the worst French blunder was yet to come.

Edward III and the 'Black Prince' had achieved similar victories at Crécy and Poitiers ahead of the advance on Paris in 1359. They had had the French King captive from 1356 while their 'chevauchées' terrorized the enemy's local leadership and social and civic unrest paralyzed Northern French countryside and towns alike. As in 1415, a smaller army from a smaller state had been able to humiliate the greatest power in Western Europe repeatedly. King John II had anticipated being able to ride down the English by force of numbers at Poitiers as the French nobility was to do at Agincourt, and suffered catastrophic defeat. But on that occasion the walled French capital had resisted the English King's forces that did not have the men, siege-engines, or time to starve it into surrender and the Dauphin Charles was co-ordinating resistance. He had also failed to persuade the Archbishop and townsmen of Rheims, the traditional place for French coronations, to surrender and let him in to be crowned earlier on his march, which would have stiffened Parisian resolve. Edward III, unable to mount a prolonged siege of Paris with no secure supply-lines to the coast (unlike Henry V he did not have Normandy under control) and lacking an overwhelming military advantage, had to move on and grudgingly negotiate a treaty to end the stalemate. He could not retreat to a secure base in an occupied Normandy and mount another attack in the following year, whereas Henry could proceed slowly with a secure supply-route and garrisons to his rear.

Henry had painstakingly overrun Normandy in 1417–19 as a base, concentrating on the major towns. He had restored English control to the situation in 1203 and could threaten Paris long term as no English ruler had done since Richard I. Unlike Edward in 1346, he had methodically invested a substantial portion of his invasion force in holding onto a defensible fortified position on the Norman coast (Harfleur) – which indeed seems to have been the principal intention of the invasion. Most of his senior officers had then recommended him to return home direct by sea, not by way of marching overland to Calais, and Henry's decision to do the latter was an unwelcome surprise to them. Once Henry had destroyed the French army and wiped out much of its leadership, capturing one of their semi-royal generals (the Duke of Orléans) and killing several others, the demoralized French nobility was unwilling to tackle his army again and he could conquer Normandy piecemeal. The most probable figurehead left for the French 'war party', Dauphin Louis, then died and the absence of Orléans in English captivity reduced their coherence further. The French also had to beware the intentions of their Eastern neighbour, 'Holy Roman' Emperor-elect Sigismund of Luxembourg, who visited Henry to secure an alliance in 1416. In 1346 Sigismund's grandfather, the blind King John of Bohemia, had been fighting on the side of his daughter's French husband at Crécy (and was killed). The French in 1415–20 lacked the German allies they had possessed in 1346. Nor did they have the naval aid of Castile, where the Crown was in the hands of a minor (John II) and there was no interest in aiding France; the Castilian navy was not as much of a threat as it had been in the 1340s–1380s. Henry could proceed methodically to overrun Normandy at leisure in 1417–19 without fearing a major counter-attack at sea to cut off his supply routes. King David II of Scotland had been hostile to Edward III (who had helped the Balliol faction to depose him in 1333) and had been restored with the aid of France; he was defeated and captured at Neville's Cross as he invaded in 1346 but Scotland's government remained a problem and had to be punished with the 'Burnt Candlemas' raid in 1357. Henry V did not have this problem to his rear as he was on good terms with the pragmatic elderly Scots regent, the Duke of Albany, and held King James I as a hostage throughout his reign.

The French king was incapacitated in 1419–20 as in 1359, this time by inertia and mental weakness, but there was no united resistance among the French leadership with his two elder sons dead and the youngest, the future Charles VII (born in 1403), young, physically unimposing, and of dubious legitimacy. With Burgundy as his ally, Henry had friendly forces in control of the lands bordering the Isle de France to the north-east, east, and south-east though some towns within the royal domains still held out and had to be reduced one by one. He had granted large strategic counties in Normandy (e.g. Harcourt and Perche) to his principal aristocratic lieutenants, led by his half-uncle the Duke of Exeter, to give them a stake in preserving English rule and even had limited 'colonization' underway within the principal towns.[20] As shown by the amount of looted wealth that ambitious English captains were able to bring home to bolster their family fortunes, a considerable amount of the lesser gentry also had a practical reason for long-term commitment to conquest in France.[21] (Some prominent mid-fifteenth century mansions like Hurstmonceaux Castle were built on the profits of Henry's wars.) Even when Henry was dead and the English in retreat an impressive number of captains fought to defend their gains in France until the early 1450s. Talbot and Fastolf, in particular, were committed to fighting on. Meanwhile, the local Church by and large collaborated, though the end of the papal schism and emergence of one undisputed Pope (Martin V) in 1417 meant that the English could not use political pressure on one of the two rival Popes to secure favourable new Norman bishops. Instead, Henry went along with the new Pope's aggressive appointments to vacant sees of his own Italian nominees.[22]

Murder on the bridge at Montereau, 10 September 1419 – fatal for one cause immediately but for both in the long run?

Crucially, at this point in 1419 the feuds among the two factions of senior nobles over control of the inert King Charles erupted into a spectacularly bloody killing instead of the rivals closing ranks to rally to their sovereign. This factional blood-letting had been present in the 1350s to early 1360s too, with King Charles 'the Bad' of Navarre, a Machiavellian schemer who claimed the French throne as senior descendant in the female line of King Louis X (d. 1316), trying to destabilize the regime of Dauphin Charles (later Charles V) in 1358–64; but the Dauphin had been older and far better supported than his namesake Dauphin Charles was in 1419–20. The latter was the mascot of the Armagnac faction; Charles V had led the 'nationalist' ministers and Estates-General to reject King John's humiliating treaty with Edward III in 1358 and had driven the Navarre and Étienne Marcel factions out of Paris. Henry V was thus in a stronger position than Edward III had been. The failure of the Burgundian-controlled royal government to agree to cede Aquitaine/Poitou (as promised at Bretigny in 1360) and conquered Normandy in full sovereignty at the Meulan talks with Henry in May 1419 were followed by a rapprochement with the Dauphin – but not yet any joint campaign. Long-term alliance was as unlikely as it was to be for the similarly feuding factions at Henry VI's court after 1455, given the bad feeling between their followers and the list of past murders to be avenged (headed by those of the Duke of Orléans in 1407 and Armagnac in 1418). But the spectacular disaster that followed at the second meeting between the Dauphin and Duke John of Burgundy on 10 September was a bonus for Henry. Duke John was cut down on the Seine bridge at Montereau by members of the rival Armagnac faction at a truce-meeting, moments after doing homage to the Dauphin. The murder took place in the presence of the Dauphin, who whether or not he had approved of it in advance was treated by the 'Burgundians' as the instigator.[23] Foolishly, he even expressed no regrets in his first letter to Duke John's son and successor, Philip, instead complaining at the late Duke's past treachery with the English.[24] The incident had far worse consequences than the previous murder of the Armagnac leader Duke Louis of Orléans in Paris in 1407 – a 'mugging' claimed to be Burgundian work – and the resulting blood-feud led to Duke Philip allying with Henry V against the Armagnacs and seizing control of the French court. Henry was at once able to declare to the French court (27 September) that he was no longer prepared to abandon his claim to the Crown in return for the handover of Aquitaine/Poitou and Normandy in full sovereignty, as he had done at Meulan in May. He would, however, do without a dowry for Princess Catherine, which the financially ruined French Crown would have difficulty finding.[25]

The Anglo-Burgundian alliance was not agreed quickly. Initially these heightened English demands led to Burgundian rejection, with the new Duke's party refusing to accept such dishonour for the truncated French Crown and its dominions and rights at English hands. It is possible that the ambitious Philip hoped for the succession to the French throne himself if the Dauphin was disinherited, although he was not the next male heir (his grandfather Duke Philip I had been the youngest son of King John II, and the Anjou line was senior). If Henry married Catherine and came to dominate the French court he could prefer his brother-in-law the Dauphin as a weak king, under his thumb, to backing the powerful Philip as king. In reply, Henry offered landed inducements and offices to the Duke if the latter would back the English claim, and alleged that the proclaimed Burgundian concern for a strong French king would best be met with Henry on the throne; under him, the English and French crowns and administrations would remain separate so France would not be 'swallowed up' by England.[26] This promise of the continuation of the separate identities of the two kingdoms, made by Henry to Duke Philip's envoys at Mantes in November, was probably decisive. The mutual fear of Duke and Dauphin meant that Duke Philip had little option but alliance with Henry, who could menace his lands around Paris and already held disputed towns; Henry's strong military presence close to blockaded Paris and his known ruthlessness implied that his terms would not be modified by waiting. The debate over alliance in the Duke's council at Arras in December seems to have hinged on the practical fact that it was necessary to secure peace with the invader in the war-ravaged country for the welfare of the nation;[27] the abandonment of the Crown to a foreign pretender could be sidelined.

As a result the two allies negotiated the Treaty of Troyes that provided for
Henry to marry Charles VI's younger daughter Catherine – the sister of
Richard II's Queen – and succeed him to the throne, debarring the
'illegitimate' Dauphin. If the latter was the promiscuous Queen Isabella's
son by a lover not the King, the heir under French law should have been
Orléans' son Charles – who since his capture at Agincourt was an English
captive (and remained so until 1440). After him came the families of the
Dukes of Anjou and Berry, Charles VI's late uncles, and then Philip of
Burgundy. The house of Anjou were luckily distracted from French politics
by their own claim to the throne of Naples, but there was an implicit threat
that Henry might back their claim in 1419–20 if the Burgundians did not
ally with him. The 'Salic Law' – as politically interpreted by the French
peers – technically barred female inheritance, thus ruling out Edward III's
mother Isabella's claim when her brothers died without sons and bringing in
the Valois line in 1328. This was duly pointed out by episcopal supporters of
the Dauphin,[28] but was ignored for practical political reasons. Henry's reply
to the legal arguments was that God had shown His favour for the diversion
of the French Crown to Isabella's English descendants by their repeated
military victories – though claiming a crown by conquest was
unprecedented in legalistic France, unlike it had been in England (1066 and,
arguably, 1399). All French kings since the anti-Carolingian coup of 922 by
Duke Robert (the current royal family's ancestor) had succeeded by right of
descent, not by a revolt hastily legitimized afterwards. The powerful French
royal administrative system had even functioned on behalf of an unborn king
– when Louis X and Charles IV had died their pregnant widows had been
allowed to produce their offspring during an interregnum to allow a boy to
succeed at birth, with ambitious uncles politely awaiting the result. This
would have been more difficult in England. 'Legal rights' under Roman law
were thus important if the French governing machine was to back the next
ruler.

**Henry's advantages as of 1420 – and one potential blunder. What of
Aquitaine?**
Henry was Edward III's great-grandson by direct male descent – though not
the head of the eldest line by female descent, that claim having descended
via the Mortimers to the young son of the executed Richard, Earl of
Cambridge. Thus, illegally or not, Henry was poised to succeed Charles VI
as King of France, and had physical control of the French King and capital
from 1420 thanks to John of Burgundy's murder. The French head of
government (Dauphin Charles) and the French capital, in contrast, had both
held out against Edward III in 1359. With the Burgundian armies on

Henry's side, his undefeated army had a military force to outmatch that of the bastardized Dauphin, an untried leader of no military reputation whose main resource was the sheer size of that part of France still loyal to the Valois. One crucial factor was the dominions of the Dukes of Anjou, which controlled the central and lower Loire valley, and the marriage of Duke Louis II's daughter Yolande to the Dauphin (July 1422) was to place them in the latter's camp.

Unlike Edward III, however, Henry did not have a large domain in south-west France to serve as a base for attacks on 'loyalist' areas from the south. This could have been altered by the terms of peace in 1420, which were his to dictate; Burgundy had no rival interest there to satisfy. The return of all previous English territory in Aquitaine had been cited in English demands of the French monarchy since 1399, but Henry did not now press it – perhaps in order to avoid having to send garrisons there from the more important Normandy. It is arguable that his failure to insist on the return of all Aquitaine in 1420 was a serious mistake, as it meant that the nobility and military resources of this area remained in Valois hands; if Henry could not spare the time and men to occupy it himself he could have sent a trustable lieutenant (perhaps one of the Beauforts). Possession of his 'rightful' hereditary dominion, Poitou – taken from King John in 1205 and formally surrendered in 1259 – would have enabled him to threaten the refugee Dauphin's court in Anjou from the rear in 1420–2. Interestingly, his father, Henry IV, had treated Aquitaine as of more importance by proposing to campaign there in 1406 and sending his second son, Thomas, to march there in 1412. Was Henry V's lack of interest due to reaction against their policies, which he had been excluded from influencing at the time? Or did he simply regard Normandy as of far higher strategic value? Aquitaine had been a legal problem after Edward III regained it in 1360, as its autonomist and tax-resisting lords had still been able to launch appeals against 'injustice' to its English Duke's French royal suzerain's courts. Thus even if Henry had been its 'overlord' as King of France after Charles VI died rebel lords could still have appealed to his rival Charles VII's courts. But that problem could have been lessened by transferring it to the legal overlordship of the King of England, and requiring the French legal machinery in Paris to register this.

Even with the adherence of the Burgundian domains, Henry had no military presence south of the Paris area except for the small English duchy of Guienne around Bordeaux (the remnants of Aquitaine). Nor was the adherence of Brittany – which could help him by threatening the mouth of the Loire – secure despite his useful possession of Arthur of Richemont, the Duke's brother, as a prisoner after Agincourt. There was anti-Breton feeling in England in the mid to late 1410s, with complaints about greedy Bretons at the Dowager Queen Joan's court leeching off English revenue and even spying for France, and in 1419 Henry was to arrest Joan for alleged 'witchcraft', place her under house arrest at Leeds Castle, and seize her revenues. Perhaps unsurprisingly, after his ransom Arthur of Richemont gravitated to the Dauphin's court and became his 'Constable' (1424). Henry and his council successors in ruling England thus failed to lure Brittany into friendship, though both its Duke and Duke Louis III of Anjou – controllers of the lower Loire – were drawn towards the Dauphin in any case by 'peer group jealousy' of Henry's ally Duke Philip of Burgundy.

The weakness of the French Crown during the English wars since 1338 had accelerated a degree of informal 'devolution' to the local nobility, with particular local powers for the royal princes in charge of the great appanages. From Charles V's time the principal 'players' in this were his brothers in Anjou, Berry, and Burgundy. Berry died without a son in 1416; the other two were the founders of the semi-royal ducal houses who now had to choose between Henry and the Dauphin. Brittany, originally an independent principality and ruled by an ancient 'native' line of Dukes linked by blood to both Plantagenets and Valois, was even more autonomous (aided by differences of language and culture) and had been fought over by pro-English and pro-French rivals in the 1340s. Fear of the centralizing French monarchy and the latter's crude mishandling of its role as overlord had resulted in a pro-English orientation after 1350; this was not now so certain and Henry's treatment of his stepmother, the Duke's and Arthur's absentee mother, cannot have helped. The change of sovereign in Paris by a legally dubious manoeuvre – in favour of a foreigner with whose nation France had been at bloody war on and off for eighty years – would not necessarily be accepted or enforceable. Anjou (owned by a junior Valois line, next heirs to the Crown if Charles VII was disinherited) blocked Henry's way south after 1420 and he did not have access to the Loire bridges to invade the 'Dauphinist' heartland.

Philip of Burgundy, ruling the lands to the east of the 'Dauphinist' headquarters at Bourges, was never to be persuaded by his English allies to invade the loyalist lands, outflanking the Loire bridges, even during the height of English power in the mid-1420s. But Henry's reputation for invincibility was a major asset, and he seemed likely to be able to improve on his position before or after he succeeded to the French throne despite having to maintain a large garrison-force in Normandy. Crucially, the French were unable to use their principal diplomatic weapon of the mid-fourteenth century – their Scottish ally, the young King James I being an English hostage (since 1406) and his regents (Duke Robert of Albany to 1420 and then his son Murdoch) being unwilling to challenge Henry. There was thus no Scottish invasion of England to assist France, as in 1346. If the regency allied to France Henry could send the now-adult James home to distract them; the potential for a resulting Stewart dynastic bloodbath was to be shown when James did return in 1424 and liquidated Murdoch's family. At most the Scots could permit volunteers to assist the 'Auld Ally' and add to the Dauphin's Scots guardsmen, as the Earl of Douglas' force did in 1424.

As chance would have it, Henry died suddenly at the end of August 1422 and preceded Charles VI. He had already spent most of the campaigning season bogged down in minor sieges aimed at securing full control of the south-eastern approaches to Paris, while the Dauphinist cause remained unchallenged in the Loire valley – and had won a surprise victory at Baugé in 1421 that showed they still had an effective military capacity. That victory had removed the defeated and killed English commander, Henry's next brother Thomas of Clarence, as a factor in English politics – and as a useful and experienced commander to campaign in France. Henry had military reasons for concentrating on the Meaux campaign rather than proceeding straight to the Loire in 1422, and of course had no idea that his health was declining and a quick victory was important. But the way in which the defiance of walled towns was holding up an army unbeaten in the field and negating the English advantages in 1422 was ominously reminiscent of the similar frustration that had met Edward III, the Prince of Wales, and John of Gaunt as their unbeaten armies ravaged their way across France. Lacking the ability to bring sieges to a quick end – which later in the fifteenth century would be provided by improvements in cannons – the advantage lay with the defenders. This would have been so even when Henry had succeeded to the French throne, and could only have been countered by a lack of the will to resist.

Was the war unwinnable? Parallel cases – and the crucial advantages that England possessed over France

The English army in France was, crucially, smaller than the Dauphinist one in the years after 1420 and large numbers of men were tied down garrisoning strongpoints in Normandy (where brigandage and plots to betray towns continued). In the vital 1424 campaign, for example, the Duke of Bedford had around 1,800 men-at-arms and 8,000 archers according to the Burgundian chronicler Wauvrin, even after denuding Norman garrisons for a major offensive – and the reinforcements he could summon from England, under prestigious and enthusiastic captains Oldhall and Lord Scales, only numbered around 1,600. Would even Henry V have had the extra goodwill or prestige to enable his recruiters to acquire many more? After all, technically the Treaty of Troyes kept the two realms separate – England and its Parliament were not legally required to provide men or money to 'France'. The Norman estates-general's (and that of the clergy assembly) tax-raising were thus to be the financial mainstay of the local English regime and army, and granted the anxious Bedford 50,000, then 60,000, and then 200,000 'livres' in three meetings in 1423. But this was to defend Normandy, not for expansion. A 'national' French meeting of a full 'estates general' for those areas under English control in Paris was possible, but would only show how limited such support was – and taxing still 'debateable', ravaged areas like Champagne would encourage defections. That applied to Paris too. (The 1428 Bedfordian 'estates-general' was to grant a mere 60,000 'livres' for the war.) The English regime, under Henry or Bedford, would need to have shown that it was winning and was establishing security to gain even grudging backing – and how would it win without much larger funding and armies?

Against them the Dauphin could call on a mercenary force of 2,000 Scots knights and 6,000 men-at-arms in 1424 – and his *parlement* at Bourges had granted him an impressive 'war-chest' of 58 million 'livres'. The recruits summoned from England were only on short-term contracts (six months for the 1424 campaign) so had to be used quickly, not 'bogged-down' at sieges, and there was fierce resistance to any notion of longer contracts than was normal. Once the contracts expired, desertions were likely by men standing on their rights – even from the King. But it should not be assumed that the English failure to destroy their larger and better-resourced enemy was inevitable – and by implication that Henry V set himself an impossible task. (In the late twentieth century some fashionable historians even adopted contemporary not fifteenth century standards of conduct to call him a bloodthirsty 'war criminal' who launched an unwinnable war.[29]) A smaller power can overwhelm a larger one, given military superiority, a lethal concentration of force, and the psychological advantage of being believed invincible. Destruction or co-option of the enemy leadership is also vital. The lack of a competent enemy leader can paralyse resistance, and as of 1420–2 the Dauphin lacked any military experience and showed no keenness to leave his residence at Chinon Castle (once the birthplace of Henry II of England) to inspire his troops. (The experienced Scottish commanders who were then recruited to fight for him, the Earls of Buchan and Douglas, were neutralized by the English at the battle of Verneuil in 1424.) His best commanders were those experienced at 'hit-and-run' ambushes, minor clashes, and sieges like the 'Bastard of Orléans' (Dunois) and the mercenary La Hire.

All these factors were present on the most impressive occasions of the conquest of a much larger power by a smaller one, which could provide a template for an English victory over the larger and better-resourced power of Valois France. One example was the conquest of the massively larger Persian empire by Alexander 'the Great', where a relentless application of force, tactical superiority by a brilliant and ruthless commander, an endless round of victories, and the destruction of the defenders' small 'high command' combined. In recent history as seen from 1420, the application of a sizeable 'bloc' of skilled archers – adequately protected from cavalry charges – had enabled Edward III and his eldest son to defeat the larger French royal army time after time and to range at will across France in 1346–60, a feat repeated by independent bands of mercenary companies. A skilled and highly mobile smaller army with superior weaponry, morale, and generalship was to enable successive Swedish armies under Gustavus Adolphus, Charles X, and Charles XII to rampage across Europe (particularly Poland) through the seventeenth century. Their enemies, the Catholic forces of the Holy Roman Empire in the first two cases and the Polish kingdom and Russian empire in the third, were aided by size and the possession of larger armies, which like that of Valois France in 1420–2 could withdraw into safe territory after a defeat and regroup. The marches of Edward III into Champagne and Burgundy in 1360 (before his attack on Paris) and of John of Gaunt across the whole of south-central France to Aquitaine in 1373 were as impressive signs of the defence's fearful, battle-avoiding retreat as when Charles XII crossed Belorussia into the Ukraine in 1708–9. The same tactic of avoiding battle and waiting for the enemy's supply-lines to become overstretched was used by Kutuzov against Napoleon in Russia in 1812. None of these invading commanders was able to use their local superiority to win a long war far from home; and the adherence of impressed or calculating vassals of the invaded regime and seizure of towns and supplies was crucial. (Charles, unlike the others, managed to secure local – Ukrainian Cossack – help, against Czar Peter of Russia, but was defeated anyway.) Would a victorious Henry V moving across the Loire into Berry or the Massif Central in the mid-1420s have ended up like Charles XII did in 1709 in Russia if he could not secure towns or defecting Armagnac lords? This fate might have awaited Henry V or, later, Bedford in an invasion south of the Loire in the mid-late 1420s even had they had control of Orléans or another bridge. Smaller English armies met this fate south of Normandy time and again, as at Baugé in 1421 and when John de la Pole was captured on a raid in 1423.

All these aggressors had an effective administrative 'machine' behind them to organize a regular 'input' of men and weaponry, plus adequate supplies. It has been argued persuasively that the superior organization of resources by the English Crown in the fourteenth and fifteenth century gave Edward III and Henry V major advantages in 'war-readiness' plus training, equipment, and supplies. This factor therefore applied to England by 1420–2 and gave it a distinct advantage over France – the Dauphin was unable to use a smoothly-operating administrative machine, which all were used to obeying, to call a mass-levy of his vassals south of the Loire. Indeed, when a large force of skilled French aristocratic cavalry had been assembled last – for the Agincourt campaign – they had little experience of fighting together and proved ineffective in battle. The status-conscious lords were also chary of obeying social inferiors in battle, meaning that it had to be a royal prince of impeccable lineage who commanded them – and at Agincourt the genealogically-qualified commander, Duke Charles of Orléans, lacked any serious military experience as he faced the veteran Henry V. The English captains, fewer of whom were 'touchy' and autonomous great aristocrats who rarely came into contact with the state, were more used to fighting together cohesively and obeying orders. (The only great English lords with semi-autonomous domains and usual freedom of action were arguably the Marcher lords; the Percies of Northumberland had had this status until destroyed by Henry IV in 1403.) Again, England had the advantage on this issue in 1420–2. Bedford's 1424 army was heavily weighted in favour of their 'knock-out' arm, archers, as Gustavus Adolphus' was to be in favour of cavalry and artillery. The danger lay in the enemy over-running the archers before they had time to fire – as La Hire was to do at Patay in 1429.

To a certain degree, the advantages of mobility, concentrated and lethally-armed force, and reputation were in play as late as Rommel's campaigns in 1941–2 in North Africa. The idea of delivering a swift 'knockout punch' against a demoralized, retreating foe by using mobility and concentrated force was also present in Montgomery's abandoned plan to smash through the German 'left wing' in Holland into Northern Germany in late autumn 1944. (The Iraq campaigns of 1991 and 2003 were based on mobility and lethal force too but were less equal.) The advantages that Alexander, Gustavus Adolphus, Charles XII and Henry shared included superior generalship (verging on rashness), a towering reputation to demoralize their foes, and neutralization of the enemy leadership. The English in the late 1410s, the seventeenth century Swedish armies, and the French revolutionary armies shared well-motivated, trained, and disciplined forces with superior 'punching-force' – flexible infantry phalanxes and armed cavalry for Alexander, artillery for the others (archers in Henry's case, muskets and cannons for the Swedes and French). All could devastate their larger but less lethally-armed enemies with what the Americans attacking Iraq in 2003 would call 'shock and awe'.

But Henry lacked one crucial advantage, as had Edward III – the ability to seize and retain large areas of territory quickly. The nature of the defenders' terrain, covered by walled towns that artillery could not yet overwhelm, assisted his enemies. One destructive battle that wiped out the enemy leadership (using archers as well as cavalry) had won Duke William of Normandy all England in 1066, but that had been before the era of stone walls round towns; Agincourt could not win Henry all France, and neither could Verneuil in 1424. This could arguably be countered by overwhelming towns' captains' will to resist, for which mobility and an unbroken run of success were vital; and the murder of Duke John of Burgundy in the Dauphin's presence in 1419 blackened his 'faction' as especially faithless to potential waverers. Baugé was therefore an ominous indicator for the future – it showed that the English were not invincible. Baugé was also a reminder that archers lacked lethal force if there were not enough of them at the battlefield to effectively cripple and demoralize the enemy, or there was no enemy obligingly charging along a narrow 'front' that could be 'raked' with arrows; it was a forerunner of the disaster at Patay. The lethal effect of English (or Welsh) longbows had repeatedly worked against armoured knights since Halidon Hill in 1333, and was to work against a slow-moving mass of infantry as late as Flodden in 1513. (It was not a new tactic to use archers against well-armed and superior numbers; the Parthian cavalry had used it against Crassus' Romans at Carrhae in 53 BC.) But archers were not decisive if they were unable to bring lethal fire to bear for long enough, and they needed a suitable battlefield; a closely-packed mass of slow-moving cavalry, as at Halidon Hill or Agincourt, was an ideal target. Mud (as at Agincourt) or a steep hillslope (as at Halidon Hill) could enable them to pick off either infantry or cavalry. Archers that lacked these advantages were not able to keep the revived French from victories after 1429 – and the French victories at Patay (1429) and Formigny (1450) both took place in the 'open field'. The need for the English to garrison conquered towns indeed meant that after the acquisition of Normandy in 1417–19 some archers were bound to be absent from the 'field army', serving in garrisons – and the supply from England was not inexhaustible. The new army that the Earl of Salisbury was contracted to raise for what was to become the Orléans campaign in March 1428 consisted of only 600 men-at-arms and 1,800 (mounted) archers – and only for a six-month campaign. They did, however, receive a grant, equivalent to one 'subsidy', from Parliament – the first such English taxation for the French war since 1422.

Another major English victory, destroying the Dauphinist army and avenging Baugé, would have helped but the physical elimination of the enemy leadership – particularly of 'Charles VII' – would have been far more crucial. If the French nobles had no candidate to rally around, resistance would be pointless; any subsequent revival of national feeling against a foreign king would need a leader. The Dauphinists had far greater potential resources if less willpower in concentrating them, so Henry would have had to prove quickly that resisting him was futile. He had to neutralize the Dauphin, who was at a disadvantage as a national symbol of resistance over his disputed legitimacy, and then ensure that no new French pretender emerged claiming to be the rightful king. The next heir if 'Charles VII' was dealt with was Duke Charles of Orléans, who was in English hands from 1415–40, and then the next male line of the Valois, that of Charles V's brother Duke Louis of Anjou (d. 1384) – represented in 1417–34 by Duke Louis (III). After the Anjou line came the Burgundians, who may indeed have had hopes of securing the French Crown by the Dauphin's removal from the line of succession after 1417. The English Crown never secured the allegiance of the Anjou line, and the alliance with Burgundy after 1420 was built on mutual convenience rather than trust. But even if this removal of rival French heirs did not occur, Henry's remaining alive and in command through the mid-1420s would have given the English extra advantages over the 'Regent' Bedford's position in real life. Henry would have been less distracted by quarrels among the ruling council in England after 1422. Bedford, though regent of France, was only head of the council in England when he was there and could not send orders home from France with an expectation of unquestioning obedience, as could a king. In his absence, his ambitious brother Duke Humphrey of Gloucester was senior councillor – and Humphrey was to embarrass his Burgundian alliance by seeking to 'cut out' Duke Philip in the contest to secure the heiress of Holland, Jacqueline, in 1426–7. Humphrey would not have defied Henry in that manner. The senior minister in the English regency council, Bedford's half-uncle (Chancellor) Bishop Henry Beaufort, was subject to intrigue and eventual removal by his rivals – which he would not have faced as the appointee of a vigorous adult king rather than of a regency. All this distracted Bedford from his work in France in the mid-1420s. But the round of sieges north of the Loire could have been expected to continue under Henry as it did under Bedford from 1422 – at risk of a sudden French counter-attack and morale-boosting victory such as that achieved at Montargis in 1428 by Charles' new captain, Dunois. The latter, a bastard of the murdered Duke Louis of Orléans and half-brother of the captive Duke Charles, and the 'Dauphinist' mercenary-commander La Hire were to show that the English did not have a monopoly in effective leadership by the late 1420s. The new French leaders were also 'professionals' from a middling social background, not the ducal amateurs who had ruined the Agincourt campaign. They showed more loyalty to their king than the intriguing royal and aristocratic commanders had in the 1410s, even with Charles rarely seen on the battlefield and evidently lacking in 'elan' or confidence. Dunois was a competent soldier and a worthy foe of the English commanders – and he was not hampered in command in the field by his social superiors, unlike the 'professionals' (Constable D'Albret and Marshal Boucicaut) had been at Agincourt. This was a serious danger for the English. The potential kindling of a 'nationalist' spark of enthusiasm for the Dauphinist cause was duly lit by Joan of Arc – backed by Dunois in 1429. Recent research has also reminded us of the role played behind the scenes in this by Charles' mother-in-law, Yolande of Anjou, a princess of Aragon.

A question of leadership after 1422. Was the war unwinnable by Henry as it was in real life by his brother Bedford?

The main question is whether Henry had the ability or resources to press the war to a conclusion. If not, his presence at the head of the Anglo-Burgundian alliance after 1422 as an adult sovereign would have provided their cause with a more effective leader than the regent, his brother John, Duke of Bedford, could be for the infant Henry VI. For all his skills and leadership, Bedford lacked the final legal legitimacy of being the sovereign whose decisions could not be reversed at the end of his regency – and he had to interrupt his French campaigns to deal with his disgruntled brother Humphrey of Gloucester in England. But he was able to continue the war, albeit more sporadically than Henry would have done – he had to deal with crises in England from December 1425 to March 1427, chiefly due to Humphrey who would have been unlikely to challenge Henry with his full royal powers. He had worryingly low numbers of fresh English recruits for his 1424 and 1428 campaigns which may testify to 'war-weariness'.[30] Would Henry have done any better? He would have had full power in England but still might have been ignored by disgruntled local leaders; the barons had refused to back belligerent Edward I, as forceful and popular as Henry, in 1294.

Bedford was able to cement the Burgundian alliance through good personal relations with Duke Philip, his brother-in-law (who noticeably did not abandon the alliance until Bedford was dead), and as a competent general he won another major victory over Charles VII's army at Verneuil in 1424. This destroyed the large and coherent body of experienced Scots warriors (c. 8,000 men?) that had reinforced the Dauphinist cause under the militarily experienced Earls of Buchan, a cadet of the ruling house of Stewart who had fought at Harlaw in 1411, and Douglas. It ended the threat to Normandy that had existed since Baugé, and in 1425 Bedford occupied Maine. But it did not open the way to a quick occupation of the crucial Loire valley and Charles' main bases at Chinon (ironically formerly a major stronghold of the English Angevin kings, as Henry II's birthplace) and Bourges, though it led to Brittany's defection to the English cause in 1427 and provided a recruiting boost for the new army raised in England in 1428.[31] It would have been more useful if Bedford had not had to return to England in the interim, giving the Dauphinist cause time to recover from Verneuil. But although the council clash between Humphrey and Bishop Beaufort was the main cause of this pause in the war in France, the accompanying lack of troops would have affected Henry too. And Verneuil did not prevent the 'fence-sitting' Duke of Brittany agreeing a truce with the Dauphin in 1425–7, freeing the latter to concentrate on Maine where a major success against Fastolf at Ambrières in 1427 countered the Breton return to Bedford's side. Another Dauphinist success at Montargis, south of Paris, preceded the new English campaign in 1428.

The military resources available to Bedford when he belatedly planned his southern advance for 1428 were not much smaller than those that Henry V would have been able to command. Probably the King, glamorous victor of Agincourt, would have had more of a success in attracting recruits from England than Bedford. His status as king not regent and his thoroughness and determination in organization would have led to more forceful orders for levying men by his vassals than Bedford could give – the latter faced challenges from his younger brother Humphrey and English court rivals. The war duly became bogged down again in the years to 1429, with no major advances and the worrying betrayal of Le Mans to La Hire even with a competent and well-supported local English commander (Sir John Talbot) nearby. It was recovered, but could any French officers be trusted? Bedford did not lead the Orléans campaign of 1428 in person. This was arguably a mistake in making the campaign look less vital by its lacking personal royal leadership, though the Earl of Salisbury was a militarily adequate substitute. Orléans, with its vital Loire bridge, was a more controversial choice for the Loire crossing than downstream Angers (Bedford's own choice, changed by Salisbury) on account of it being the fief of the captive Duke Charles rather than a stronghold of the pro-Dauphinist Duke of Anjou – thus not a 'legitimate' target by contemporary custom. Also, Philip of Burgundy coveted it for himself and thus refused to take part in the siege without a promise of it being handed over to him. Orléans' determined and experienced commander, Raoul de Gaucourt, would not have been available if Henry had been alive – the late King had forbidden this former captive's release as he was too dangerous a foe.

An attack downstream on Angers would have been risky due to the extended communication-lines south-west from Normandy or Paris, even with Brittany now an ally to provide support from the north-west, and a flanking force would have had to protect the supply-line from a sally by Dunois from Orléans. But it would have enabled the English to claim that Anjou was a legitimate target, its Duke being a 'Dauphinist' ally defying the English King's claim to rule France. The English commander, the competent Earl of Salisbury, died at the start of the attack on Orléans. Bedford did not bother to press the siege in person, and the town remained untaken when Joan of Arc appeared on the scene in 1429. Would Henry have fared any better? And did Henry understand the need for mobility, given his willingness to tie himself down in minor campaigning in Champagne in 1422 instead of leaving it to a lieutenant and heading straight for the Loire then? The argument that Henry did not have the troops to deal with the strategic threats to Paris (e.g. Meaux) and to attack the Loire in 1422 has some weight, but he could still have shown signs of preparations for a Loire campaign at this point – and sought Burgundian troops' support with a promise of Orléans to Duke Philip? Even with Burgundian military support, Henry did not have the troops available to hold down garrisons across a much wider area than that held by the English in 1422. Garrisoning extra areas in strength would have been impossible, so local co-operation was essential – and Henry was a foreign conqueror unlikely to attract sincere French backing unless the leading French nobles had no alternative Valois king to support. The frequent plots to hand over Norman and Maine towns to the Valois show how dangerous it was to rely on French co-operation. An overwhelming military superiority would have helped, but he did not have the legal powers under English law to call up massive levies for an indefinite war. Royal tenants-in-chief and other noble 'contractors' were supposed to produce a fixed number of levies for a defined period, usually a year, with a royal 'fiat' on the numbers but excessive demands likely to lead to protests in the next Parliament. Alternatively, Parliament could vote the money for the King in taxes to hire mercenaries, professional troops who would serve for longer. 'War-weariness' was not a major threat by Henry's death, but was likely to rise if he was unable to bring the conflict to a quick conclusion. The rejoicing at the Treaty of Troyes was likely to turn sour as it became apparent that it had not ended the war, and Baugé had already served as an indication of that in 1421. Bedford – though hampered by his political problems as regent – was unable to raise the major forces needed for a firm 'push' southwards when Vernueil provided the opportunity in 1424–5 and only made a major effort in 1428. Henry had more forcefulness and an established reputation as a victor, but even he could have faced difficulties in raising large armies and regular taxes for a prolonged war that would seem to have no easily-attainable objective. The longer the war went on, the greater the likely resistance in England.

A major victory over the forces of Charles VII and the death or comprehensive defeat of the latter could however have provided a chance for a break in the stalemate of the mid- to late 1420s. It would have broken up the Valois cause and left anti-English resentment without a focus, on the assumption that Henry could have added to the capture or exile of Charles's son Louis (born 1423) by bribing the next Valois line – of Anjou – into acquiescing with his claim not taking up the Valois cause. In a parallel case of civil war and a foreign-born clamant in possession of the capital, in England in 1216, the 'native' cause had indeed benefited from the death of its controversial adult leader – King John. Distrusted and largely deserted by his barons in favour of his niece Blanche's husband, Prince Louis of France, John had been reduced to operating in his outer provinces as the Dauphin was in France in 1422; however when he died many nobles rallied to his under-age son's cause. The death of the controversial Dauphin, blamed for the murder of Duke John of Burgundy, might have rallied sentimental support to his 'innocent' son Louis as a figurehead king free from blame for his father's mistakes, with Dunois as his 'regent' as William Marshal was regent for John's son Henry in 1216–19; a boy-king named after the national hero, St Louis, was a potential focus for patriotism. Joan of Arc and/or Dunois would have had greater ease in rallying public opinion to him, with an inspiring coronation at Rheims, than to the physically unattractive and withdrawn Dauphin Charles. But the parallel is not exact; Louis's father, unlike Henry III's, could have been denounced as illegitimate. The removal of Charles could also have brought the Duke of Anjou into the field as the new centre of the Valois cause,

Given the proximity of the Duchy of Anjou's lands to Henry's troops on the Loire and their alternative dynastic interests in the Kingdom of Naples, his greater military strength should have enabled him to reach an agreement with Duke Louis. This would have been contingent on their support in return for keeping the Duchy unplundered and English support to their claim on the kingdom of Naples, which Louis' father had occupied in the 1390s before its reconquest by their rivals under King Ladislas. Ladislas, like the Valois in France from 1328, relied on the predominance of 'male descent only' legal theory; his father King Charles III had been the descendant of a younger brother of King Robert (r. 1309–49) whereas the Angevins depended on a more distant genealogical link that was cemented by the support of Robert's grand-daughter Queen Joanna I, deposed and killed by Charles' faction. As of the 1420s, Ladislas' sister Joanna II was in possession of Naples. As in real life in the 1440s, Henry V's son was an obvious candidate for an Angevin bride in any treaty between the English kings and the Angevins – Duke Louis III's niece Margaret, born in 1429. With the throne of Naples in the hands of a woman, Joanna II, the Angevins were to launch repeated attacks through the second third of the fifteenth century – and although Naples was to fall instead to its other enemy Aragon in 1442 the Angevin line kept up their attempts to regain it until the 1650s. As seen by his choice of residence even when France was free from the English, the cultured and luxury-loving 'Good King René' (Duke from 1434) preferred Provence to Anjou. The Angevins were thus unlikely to make a sustained struggle for the French throne against Henry if the senior Valois line had been neutralized in the mid-1420s.

There was, however, one major practical difficulty in neutralizing Charles VII, as he rarely campaigned in person and resided safely south of the Loire at Chinon. He was known for his timidity and unmilitary nature, which according to the Joan of Arc legend was reversed (temporarily) in 1429 by Joan's inspiration and apparent role as a messenger from God promising him his throne. She was supposed to have ended his fears that he was not the real son of Charles VI and rightful king by giving him a 'sign' in a private encounter, and the effects of his military revival could be played up as showing Divine approval. He was unlikely to be accessible to capture if his cause in the Loire valley collapsed after 1424; nor was his son Louis. A major defeat of his army north of the Loire – and even Henry's quick advance to seize demoralized Orléans or Angers – would have given him time to escape south-east towards the Auvergne. In practical terms, Henry would have been well-advised to make a plan with some bribeable commanders at the court of Chinon to have Charles kidnapped and handed over to him. Charles' army was dominated by mercenary commanders who fought for the highest bidder rather than feudal vassals, men like La Hire who were potentially bribeable – at least if the war seemed lost and they needed to protect themselves. (The one block to this was Charles' regiment of Scots troops under the Earl of Buchan in 1421–4, who were implacably anti-English and could protect him. The Scots notably refused their own captive King James' order to surrender one town to Henry and some were still Charles' bodyguards after 1424.) If Charles was still at large, the fall of Orléans – or even Bourges and Chinon – would not end the war.

Conversely, a victory and conquest of the Loire valley would have led to English hopes that the war was over and as a result new royal demands for men or money for garrison-work would have been resisted. Assuming success at the siege of Meaux and other minor but time-consuming sieges around the area east of Paris in the course of 1422–3, but no major victory, Henry as the new King 'Henri II' of France from October 1422 would have been keen to bring the war to an end and overcome resistance that was concentrated south of the Loire. Unlike Bedford, he would not have had to spend time dealing with making arrangements for the government of England with a near-equal brother and ministers in London in 1422–4. He would have been able to continue issuing orders from Paris or his current camp, and as the crowned adult King of France would have had the authority and dynamism to recruit men and demand money from his vassals for a larger French army than Bedford could raise. Some major armed clash with the Dauphinists could be expected for 1423 or 1424, with the upper Loire an obvious target. But troops would have had to be detached to deal with two dangerous enemy strongholds on the borders of Normandy – Le Crotoy on the Somme, which Bedford's regime tackled in 1423–4, and Mont-St-Michel. The first held out for six months; the latter, impregnable from cannon on an island, never surrendered although there were attempts to suborn some of its garrison. These would have held Henry up too, unless he had reversed his cautious 1422 strategy.

Was Henry adaptable enough to win the French war? Is his generalship over-rated? And how reliable were his French allies?

The 1420s – Henry and central France
The problems of the post-Troyes campaigns in central France were legion. Crucially, the resistance in areas of France backing the Dauphin was aided by the defensibility of walled towns and castles – which had improved during the fourteenth century. Henry could hardly besiege and starve out every well-fortified town and castle from Orléans to Guienne or the Rhône valley, many of them in the southern French mountains with better natural defences than the places that had held him up for so long in Normandy. Nor did he have the men available from England to garrison them once they had fallen or the reliable officers to command them. The grant of lands and loot to his own countrymen was not sufficient to entice enough of them over to France to form the sort of network of occupying landowners that had cemented the equally alien hold of William 'the Conqueror' on Anglo-Saxon England by the 1080s. Ambitious English landowners, captains, and soldiers were far from a majority even in occupied Normandy by the 1430s, with titles and estates to lure them into the province and no immediate threat of a French reconquest to deter them. The implication is that if Henry had physically secured the lands to the Loire, and all its castles from Sully to the river-mouth, in the mid-1420s he would not have had enough English volunteers to hold them – and thus would have had to rely on his French allies. Orléans would have had to be given to Duke Philip of Burgundy as he demanded in real life, and probably the Breton ducal house would similarly have coveted their nearest Loire strongholds – Nantes and Angers.

Depending on French nobles would have run the risk of them defecting if there was ever a 'Dauphinist' revival or, assuming Charles VII and his heir to be dead or imprisoned, a claim to the throne by another Valois prince (probably once Henry was dead).

The largest invading English armies that Henry and Bedford commanded in their major campaigns of the 1415–25 period were probably no more than 7–8,000 strong,[32] and not particularly mobile at that as their preponderance of infantry and their baggage and siege-trains required them to proceed at walking pace. The army had to move at the pace of its slowest members, on poor roads. As shown in French tactics towards the 'chevauchées' after the crushing English victories of 1346 and 1359, the defeated enemy – unwilling to fight in open country – could always hold each town individually and force the victorious English to contest them one by one. That would result in a military stalemate, with the advantage lying with the defenders. Cannons were not yet sufficiently developed to enable easy razing of a town's walls, as seen at Harfleur; at best they could open breaches and assist an attack provide that the defenders were given no time to carry out repairs. Edward III had tried to counter that problem by heading straight for Paris, the 'nerve centre' of resistance, in 1359 but had been unable to storm it or starve it out. Also, his lines of communication to the Channel coast had been dangerously extended and he had had to live off local supplies, which became exhausted within weeks; once his camp was wrecked by a vicious hailstorm he had to move on south towards Chartres. The same problems would have faced Henry or Bedford had they taken Orléans or Angers and headed south for the Dauphin's base at Bourges, in the well-fortified middle Loire valley (still renowned for its impressive chateaux).

Henry's future success from 1422, even had he been in good health and now the crowned adult King of France, required the co-operation of the majority of his future subjects in the unconquered region of France. A piecemeal conquest would have been too costly, time-consuming, and impossible to carry out; he would have been bogged-down south of Paris as surely as Salisbury was in 1428. For this success, a decisive shift of the campaign in his favour was essential with him appearing to most senior French nobles as the inevitable victor so that they were induced to make terms and profess loyalty (whatever their private thoughts about the illegitimacy of his claim on their throne). The adherence of leading nobles in possession of local fiefs, particularly the Dukes of Brittany and Anjou for Northern France, was crucial although Brittany's ruler, not a Valois prince as were the Angevins, was likely to back the victor. (In real life he abandoned Charles VII in 1427 despite his own brother Arthur of Richemont being the latter's constable.) The Dukes of Brittany were always wary of threats to their independence from Paris, their duchy having been independent until the ninth century – and Celtic not Frankish in ethnic origin. It had indeed been an English ally under Edward III, though with a pro-French faction that led to civil war in the 1340s; the kings of France could not count on its loyalty though logically the dukes would be as wary of an over-powerful king of England. The military advantage lay with the defenders of the 'loyalist' towns and castles in tying down an opposing army in the Loire valley, even with the Duke of Burgundy to their east able to add his resources to Henry's armies and move against them in co-ordination with Henry provided that they remained on good terms. In real life Philip of Burgundy was alienated from full co-operation in 1424–6 by Duke Humphrey of Gloucester's attempt to take over Holland in his place by marrying its duchess Jacqueline. This problem would have faced Henry V too had Humphrey been unmarried then. In 1428–9 Philip was demanding Orléans from Bedford as his price for co-operation.

The 'legitimist' French strategy of not meeting the English in the field but retiring behind walls to sit it out and let them burn the countryside had served the Valois cause well against Edward III's marauding armies in the 1350s – the French government and nobles did not care what happened to the rural populace in the process. Edward III had had to come to the best available agreement and settle for a treaty that did not give him the French crown in 1360 due to these tactics, and the French could have done the same to Henry V in 1419–20 despite the added English advantage this time round that they had conquered all Normandy instead of just Calais. But the fratricidal disputes of the Armagnac and Burgundian factions in the1410s were a danger to French unity that had not existed in the 1350s, when the incompetent John II had had an able – and legitimate – eldest son and no treacherous brothers ready to aid England. His main dynastic enemy, Charles 'the Bad' of Navarre, had been checkmated by the Dauphin in 1358–9 and was never a secure English ally – he and Edward III both wanted the same throne. Crucially Duke John of Burgundy's murder at Montereau in 1419 by the Dauphinists caused his son Duke Philip to ally with Henry and turn the weight of his own faction to forcing the French court into agreement with Henry in 1420. Even a victorious Henry V would have been dependant on Burgundian co-operation for any joint 'pincer-movement' against Charles VII in the Loire valley in 1423–8, and at risk of losing much of his support and lands if the Duke ever decided that he would get better terms from his father's murderers than from the national enemy. If Henry ever ended his succession of victories or became immobilized by ill-health the risks of this happening would be magnified. There were also inevitable dangers of a dispute over the spoils of war causing this sort of breakdown in co-operation, particularly given Philip's territorial acquisitiveness and relentless collection of new territories for his family.

Technically still the vassal of the French King not an independent sovereign and a Valois prince by blood with a claim on the throne that Henry had seized, Philip's relationship with Henry as King of France from 1422 would have been wary and potentially increasingly hostile. Henry was keen on enforcing his legal rights and capable of keeping the adult Scots King – a 'guest' when captured en route to France as a boy in 1406 – a prisoner/hostage for years sooner than risk him returning home and becoming an enemy. Similar high-handedness as 'King Henri II' of France towards an errant and potentially treacherous vassal could well have led to a violent quarrel if not armed clashes if Philip sought conquered lands of Charles VII's on his western borders (Berry or Orléans?) that Henry had already been promising to his own English or French adherents. Nor could Henry hope to make up the deficit in men due to limited French support from English sources for more than one or two campaigns. Even a forceful, administratively thorough, domineering, and ruthless king who had the full loyalty of his major vassals could face a potential 'strike' over an endless stream of demands for men and money for a Continental war, as had happened to Edward I in the 1290s. If Henry had been calling on his countrymen for troops and/or finance every year through the early and mid-1420s without producing a war-winning battle, his support might well have been ebbing by 1429. His personal absence in France would not help matters, with the inevitable rumours that he was neglecting his countrymen in pursuit of personal glory or was taxing the English more than the French.

The English would have been outnumbered and on the defensive again once Armagnac/Valois and Burgundians came to an agreement to expel them, as happened in 1435. In retrospect, Henry might have been wiser not to insist on overturning French law and custom and securing the throne for himself, and to settle for the Duchy of Normandy and all Aquitaine in full sovereignty with defensible borders. That at least would have preserved him from an endless series of campaigns south of the region that he held by armed force, and enabled him to consolidate his position within French regions that had historic ties to his dynasty and easy sea-routes for reinforcements to use. In that sense, the opportunities opened for him by the killing of Duke John of Burgundy at Montereau were ultimately disastrous for his cause.

One possibility for developments after the fall of Normandy. Henry as Duke of Normandy after 1420? The results of avoiding the murderous clash on the bridge at Montereau in 1419

The slowness of the conquest of Normandy in 1417–19 was a warning of the difficulties ahead, and it is probable that if Duke John of Burgundy had not been murdered – throwing his son into enforced alliance with Henry – Henry would not have regarded the achievement of the French Crown as practicable. His much- emulated predecessor Edward III (model for many of his actions)[33] had been prepared to negotiate away his claim to the French Crown for peace in 1360 – would Henry have done so too? And did the murder of Duke John radically alter matters in England's favour?

Before the murder the talks between Duke John, in control of the French court in Paris, and Henry centred on the secession of Normandy and Aquitaine, probably in full sovereignty (see above.) This was a continuation of the basic English terms from those demanded by Henry IV in 1410–13 – Agincourt did not lead to Henry V demanding the French Crown. The simplistic notion of the victory opening the way to an inevitable demand for the French crown, played up by Shakespeare, denies the reality of French politics in 1415–20 – and of Henry's own conception of what was possible. These terms could have been the basis of a settlement if the Duke had not been killed, with Henry willing to concentrate on securing Normandy and unable to gamble for higher stakes in 1419–20 using the revulsion against the Dauphin Charles that followed the murder. Indeed, as of 1417–19 Duke John was maintaining an uneasy balancing-act between Henry and the French court, and (as seen above) at times when he was in control of the French government he was officially 'tied' to their hostility to Henry's invasion. When he had power over the French King and his administrative 'machine' in 1418–19 he had failed to relieve Henry's siege of Rouen, thus aiding him indirectly – but he had not hastened to reach agreement with him either. There was also the factor of the strongly anti-English mood in Paris, which would go over to the Dauphinist/Armagnac cause and be lost to the Burgundians if the Duke was openly pro-English. As Henry demanded the Duke's backing for his claim to the Valois Crown from 1417, the best John would offer was that a substantial English conquest within France would show him which cause God preferred.[34] As the misery of war intensified, reaching peace with Henry was also given practical weight as the responsible and realistic way for the Duke to aid the suffering French public.[35] But as of summer 1419 no agreement had been reached with Henry, and talks had been held with the Dauphin resulting in a formal (if unimplemented) move towards military alliance. This led to the meeting at Montereau – and to the resulting Burgundian return to negotiations with Henry and the Treaty of Troyes. But it should be noted that these talks were slow and hesitant on the Burgundian side, and that it appears that the new Duke Philip toyed with the idea of using the Dauphin's 'illegitimacy' to claim the French Crown for himself.[36] Henry continued his military advance, to put pressure on his unreliable negotiating-partners. Nor did Duke Philip immediately break off all contact with the Dauphinists after his father's murder, and the Dauphin's high-handed refusal to apologize for it (and complaint at Duke John's past treachery) may have been as vital as the murder in souring relations.[37] The Anglo-Burgundian alliance was thus probable but not inevitable once the Dauphin's supporters irrevocably alienated the Burgundians. But was the scuffle on the bridge at Montereau as fatal to the English cause – albeit not until 1429–30 – as it was for French unity in the 1420s?

The turning-point in the war: Montereau, not Agincourt?

It is uncertain if the murder of Duke John was premeditated or the result of a momentary panic among the Dauphin's men that they were about to be attacked. Both sides were nervous as they met on the bridge, and any unexpected gesture could be misinterpreted as a sign of imminent attack – in 1475, with Montereau in mind, the equally suspicious Edward IV and Louis XI met on a bridge at Picquigny behind a fenced barrier so that they could talk without risk of a clash.[38] What if a practical Burgundian or Armagnac noble had suggested that sensible solution in 1419 and the two sides had talked successfully? Or did the 16-year-old, inexperienced Dauphin fail to realize the risk of an argument turning into a violent confrontation? (It may be remarked here that this insecure young ruler showed no ability to control his lords at his court in Bourges and Chinon during the 1420s either.) Possibly one of his elder brothers, the two Dauphins who had died in 1415 and 1417, would have handled the meeting better.

If Dauphin Charles had been more in control of his senior lords at that meeting and ordered them to be more careful France might well have been spared thirty years of war, with Henry not confident of a permanent Burgundian alliance and so settling for his current possessions plus some more ancestral lands in a peace treaty. As of summer 1419 he did not possess Paris or physical control of the French government, both of which were opened to him by the Burgundian alliance. His military position was stronger than Edward III's had been in 1359–60, but not strong enough for him to insist on securing the Crown as a *sine qua non*. That peace term only emerged after Montereau, and as of spring 1419 Henry's demands centred on recognition of his conquests and the return of the 'Angevin empire' – in full sovereignty so he did not have to pay homage to the Valois king. That infuriated French opinion as a humiliating loss of territory and was resisted by Burgundians as well as Armagnacs,[39] but would it have proved unsurmountable? A settlement reached without the Anglo-Burgundian alliance would have entailed a weak, dubiously legitimate Charles VII being allowed to succeed his father as king in Paris in 1422, with Henry holding Normandy and Aquitaine (and Maine?) in full sovereignty and as such not vulnerable to the French legal requirements of vassalage that hampered his ancestors. Securing the English royal house's ancestral lands in full sovereignty would restore the power that English kings had held in France until 1204, thus vindicating the all-important matter of ancestral honour, and prevent a confident French king from using his courts to receive complaints from restive English vassals in Aquitaine as Charles V had done in 1369–70. This seems to have been what Henry IV required, and without the opportunity to have permanent Armagnac support and possession of Charles VI's person Henry V would have been faced with years more war to obtain more than this.

Henry had a better position in 1419 than Edward III had had in 1360, with Normandy now under his control so he could threaten Paris at will. (Edward had held the person of the French king, but had been defied by John II's able heir and had not been able to starve Paris out for fear for his own long supply-route up the Seine.) Henry could have used the threat of renewed war or a Burgundian alliance to induce Charles VI to grant him the full lands that Richard I had held in 1199 to make Guienne more defensible, added to Normandy and Maine. As this would entail handing over lordships that had been French vassals for nearly two centuries in an area remote from the control of Paris, it would have led to years of local warfare as Henry sought to enforce English control over refractory vassals. The latter would have been likely recipients of unofficial aid from anti-English ministers at the French court and the Valois dukes, in order to keep Henry occupied. But an active and forceful commander such as Henry – or his brother Bedford as his deputy, in the manner in which Aquitaine had been entrusted to the 'Black Prince' under Edward III and to John of Gaunt in the 1390s – would have been able to reassert English control in due course. Local revenues (e.g. from the complete control of the south-west's wine-trade) would aid the English Crown's financial position in paying for defensive constructions in Normandy. If the lands were held in full sovereignty Henry would not have been at risk of legal appeals to their overlord in Paris causing Anglo-French antagonism, and his control of Normandy made the French government less eager to risk his wrath than Charles V's regime had been to aid Aquitaine rebels in 1369–70.

There would have been serious potential for a French attack on the Norman frontier in due course, certainly if Henry had then died young from the effects of his warfare. Though he would not have been besieging Meaux in 1422, he would still have had to deal with recalcitrant towns and castles in the lands allotted to him by treaty and back up his nominees to strategic posts. The unwarlike Charles is unlikely to have risked renewed war in Henry's lifetime, and the terms of a treaty would have not stopped England from using Burgundy as an ally if the French King defaulted on his agreements. Henry would have had to pour money and men into Normandy to build up secure defences, probably giving important lordships to his captains to give them a stake in the area's defence. He would probably also have had to fight the Bretons if he was allotted Maine by the Treaty of Troyes, with the Duke's brother Arthur a Valois loyalist, leading to an advance on Brittany (as in real life in 1427) to force the latter's ruler to accept Henry – as Duke of Normandy – as his overlord and recognition of the new frontiers. But protecting only Normandy and Maine would have been more within English means than the attempt to conquer the upper Loire proved to be. As the victor of Agincourt and the Normandy sieges, Henry would have had the prestige to avoid major military challenges for some years – and he should have been able to reduce his demands on England for men and money by c.1426. Luckily, with James I in his hands and the Scots regency regime wary of a hostile Henry returning him to Scotland he need not have feared major Scots' aid to the Valois government – Bedford was able to contain the limited Scots aid to them in 1424 in real life.

As a vigorous war-leader with a reputation for invincibility, Henry would have presented a far more appealing and useful overlord for French provincial lords seeking the 'winning side' than the hesitant, timorous, and unmilitary Charles with his court (as in real life) prone to factional conflict. There was no great rush of French lords to aid Charles' court at Chinon in 1422–9 even with Henry V safely dead; the army of Dunois defending Orléans in 1429 had to wait for the inspiration offered by Joan, not for spontaneous support from patriotic central French lords loyal to their king. (Some speculation since the 1860s has suggested that Dunois and his 'war-party' 'stage-managed' Joan's appearance to inspire Charles, or even that Joan was an illegitimate offspring of the ducal house of Orléans, Dunois' half-sister.[40]) The mobile and effective French mercenary companies mostly only returned to allegiance to Charles VII in 1435, once he was clearly winning the war; as of the 1420s Charles only had the support of a few capable 'warlords' such as La Hire. A victorious and advancing Henry V would have been likely to win their support. Given time and health to add to his English and local French support, Henry would have been capable of adapting existing and constructing new, well-armed frontier castles as defences for Normandy if not for the more exposed Maine. The securing of Maine (and Anjou?) and defeat of Brittany would have been the major military action of the early 1420s, though money and troops would have been needed thereafter for garrisons.

Henry could even have spent some time in England to reassure his subjects, probably connected to a definitive agreement with Scotland over the restoration of James I to rule there as his vassal. In this scenario the years from 1424(?) to 1430 would not have seen the English army in France exposed to long campaigns and defeats on the upper Loire, but all quartered within Henry's own lands which would have been at peace (apart from illegal local mercenary-raids and other minor disorder). The cost of garrisons and construction work would have been large and been resented by the English Parliament, with Normandy impoverished by the war of 1417–19 and unable to contribute much to the cost of defence. But Henry's prestige as the victor who had regained his dynasty's ancient lands would have acted in his favour in reducing English discontent for years. It helped that his main potential dynastic rival, Richard, Earl of Cambridge – married to the heiress of the Mortimer claim as Richard II's heirs – had been exposed for a plot and executed in 1415. Henry could raise extra money from forcing a 'contribution' out of Scotland in any formal agreement to allow James I to return home – or even cynically allowed the regent Murdoch Stewart to pay him to keep James away in England. Serious questioning of the cost of defending the Norman-Aquitaine principality might have been delayed until his son's reign.

The danger is that local conflict over the allegiance of lordships in disputed border-areas and assorted minor raids would be blamed on Charles VII's sustained malevolence by Henry, and vice versa. The weakness of the French Crown in controlling its local feudatories would have stimulated disorder. Impatient captains such as Dunois and La Hire could have been raiding Normandy or Maine/Anjou to assess the extent of English resistance, with the French court ready to disavow them if they failed and take up their cause if they succeeded. As the peace of Bretigny in 1360 did not prevent an escalation of incidents and French hopes of success leading to a second war in 1369, peace in 1420/1 might have only lasted for a decade or so. If Henry had not been available to lead the English campaign, the conflict would then have proceeded on a parallel with what really happened in the 1440s once the English had lost their lands around Paris and been reduced to Normandy and Maine. The main advantage to England should have been a powerful military position in Aquitaine, enabling attacks on the French King's lands from the south by militarily futile but psychologically damaging 'chevauchées'. A competent commander would have been needed to keep the restive lords of Aquitaine in line and to lead raids north, and if Henry had been succeeded in Normandy by Bedford – who died in real life in 1435 – and the Duke of Exeter and Earl of Salisbury been dead (1426 and 1428) Richard Beauchamp, Earl of Warwick, and then the young Duke of York were the obvious choices. Both were highly competent defenders of the English domains in France in real life, and able to inspire loyalty from their followers. The Duke of Somerset (d. 1444), head of the next senior Lancastrian royal line of Beaufort so a probable prominent courtier, was in real life inadequate at defending Normandy and would have been no better in Aquitaine.

And if the murder at Montereau had led to an Anglo-Burgundian treaty but Henry had lived through the 1420s...?

Henry as king of France from October 1422. The need for a quick victory. The 1424 campaign and the battle of Verneuil
Henry, as the new king of France in 1422–3, would have been safe as long as he held the Burgundian alliance and Duke Philip perceived that he was winning. A successful invasion of Maine and then the Loire valley, and defeat of Charles VII there, was within the capabilities of his army in 1423/4 provided that he had used his authority and prestige to raise a larger force of English troops than Bedford could do and did not allow himself to be held up by a succession of sieges. Probably securing Normandy's eastern flank by taking Le Crotoy (Picardy) would have caused delay during 1423, as Meaux did in 1422 – with a blockade as cannons were not advanced enough to wreck the walls quickly. But the only way that the war could have been won quickly – and perhaps at all – was by a 'war of movement' with another psychological as well as battlefield triumph and then a speedy advance south in strength. A 'war of movement' had been attempted unsuccessfully by Edward III in his attack on Paris in 1360, but he had lacked a solid base in Normandy and once the French capital had decided to hold out there was not much that he could do with his supplies running out. Henry, by contrast, had a safe supply-line behind him had he advanced south in 1424. Using his governmental machinery in England to call for reinforcements and with more troops from his Burgundian allies, could he have achieved a victory more crushing than Verneuil over the 'loyalists' and their Scots allies?

Henry would have needed a substantially larger army than Bedford had in real life – perhaps 10,000 men – and the luck to account for as many senior French nobles as he had at Agincourt to demoralize the resistance. The *esprit de corps* of the battle-hardened Scots at Verneuil also made the Valois army a tougher challenge than the over-confident nobles at Agincourt who had blithely proposed to ride down the English infantry. One Scots commander, the Earl of Douglas, was used to border warfare against the English (and their archers). The other, the Earl of Buchan, was a veteran of a major battle against invading Hebrideans under the 'Lord of the Isles' at Harlaw in 1411. The battle of Verneuil was quite closely-fought with the Scots putting up a fierce fight and mercenary Milanese cavalry trying to ride down the archers

– tactics that would have been the same against any English commander, Henry included. The Scots also dominated the casualty-list.[41] The French never repeated their suicidal charge at Agincourt and the undisciplined Milanese wasted time after initial success by pillaging the unprotected English baggage-waggons. But it is possible that a larger force of English and Welsh archers at Verneuil, summoned in their thousands by a determined king for the 1424 campaign, would have destroyed the enemy at a distance as effectively as at Crécy and Agincourt and made the battle a far less equal affair. The loss of most of the enemy leadership, local landed magnates, would have neutralized their lands from providing recruits to the Dauphinist cause as Henry handed those estates within his sphere of influence to his own loyalists.

Even had Verneuil turned out to be as hard-fought as in real life, Henry would have been unlikely to be distracted by English politics over the next few years as Bedford was. He could thus have advanced further than Bedford was able to do. His personal willingness to take risks was certainly greater, as shown by his bold march to Calais with a smaller-than-expected army in October 1415 over his officers' protests; in 1424 Bedford did not gamble on a bold advance to the Loire after Verneuil and his caution meant that England failed to exploit a major opportunity. His triumphal entry to Paris was no substitute for an advance to Angers. With around 7,200 French casualties at Verneuil (plus their two best Scottish commanders and a senior French general, the Count of Aumale, killed), it is possible that the timid Dauphin/Charles VII would have fled Bourges if attacked. The opportunity offered by the destruction of the Scots 'war party' leadership on the battlefield would logically have suggested restoring James I as resident king of Scotland as Henry's client, entailing a treaty and possibly a royal marital alliance as in real life in 1424.[42] In real life, the Bedford regency sought to tie James to an English alliance by marrying him off to one of the royal semi-legitimate Beaufort kin, Bishop Henry's niece Joan; and James was too preoccupied regaining control of Scotland to assist the French. A strong but controversial ruler, he showed his priority by executing the ex-regent, his cousin Murdoch Stewart, and some of his kin in 1425 – probably holding a grudge that they had failed to negotiate his return home earlier. (Had he died heirless, Murdoch was his closest male heir; wiping out his family thus better secured James' position. But another relative was to murder him in 1437.)

But a Henrician settlement with Scotland need not have entailed more than a winter visit to London between campaigning seasons in 1424–5, assuming that Henry did not carry out the negotiations in Paris instead. The King of Scots could have been compelled to supply a mercenary force to

Henry as part of the terms of his release, and this army then been used for a second 'push' southwards in 1425 or 1426 to cross the Loire. (Why did Bedford's government not insist on this? Presumably because the Duke had to return to England to deal with Duke Humphrey in 1425–6, after armed clashes between Humphrey's and Bishop Beaufort's men in London in October 1425.) Logically James would have seen the advantages of sending potential enemies within turbulent Scotland abroad so they could not challenge him; his reign from 1424–37 was a constant struggle to dominate the nobility and his return home led to a reign of terror on Murdoch Stewart's family to demoralize resistance. He thus had every reason to aid Henry by ordering potential challengers out of Scotland to fight for Henry – though killing them had the advantage that he could confiscate their estates too. Another decisive battle would then have followed against the 'Dauphinists'.

Taking the Loire valley – a vital military objective
Assuming a complete victory with his men suffering no serious losses, Henry would have had to march south quickly into the Loire valley while the enemy did not have a viable army to oppose him, and secure the surrender of Angers and Blois with the main bridges over the river. One siege of a strong castle would have been enough to hold him up while the French regrouped, so he would have needed enough men to leave an adequate force to surround any places whose commanders held out and press on while he still had the initiative. Ideally, a force of knightly cavalry should have hurried ahead of the English infantry to enter Blois and/or Angers before the defenders had time to prepare for them, if necessary using the old ruse of pretending to be fleeing Frenchmen or else using fake civilian 'waggoneers' to block the open gates with their carts. This was how the Scots had famously regained the impregnable Edinburgh Castle from Edward III's men in 1341. But it should be noted that Henry's previous campaign of conquest of a province – Normandy in 1417–19 – had been methodical with slow progress from one siege of a major town to another, not a quick campaign of movement. Had he repeated these tactics in 1424 or 1425, advancing to take each town and major castle one by one, he would quickly have lost the advantage of momentum after his victory as the enemy regrouped. With a large and confident army and the lack of an opposing force he could well have secured Blois, Angers, and Orléans – though the lure of reconstituting his ancestors' County of Anjou as part of his domains would have argued against a prudent halt at the defensible Loire. Chinon, Henry II's birthplace and Charles VII's main residence in the late 1420s, and the south of Anjou 'belonged' with the rest of Anjou – and that would land

Henry with as indefensible a frontier as the nebulous 'frontier' between English and French south of Paris was in the real-life 1420s. All these towns and castles would need garrisons, and once Henry was dead or incapacitated the enemy would have had the chance to attack. Any quarrel with Burgundy would open Anjou and Blois/Orléans to attack from the east, and the 1430s or 1440s would have been probable years of French reconquest in any circumstances.

The vital breakthrough for the English would occur if Henry could win the surrender of the main Loire castles and the city of Bourges while the forces of Charles VII were in disarray. The important factor was not to be held up by sieges, and if the 'Dauphinist' army had been destroyed the commanders of the local castles would not have had the prospect of relief and would thus have been likely to surrender. Each military advance and conquest of a town or castle would have added to the demoralization of the enemy, and a swift advance could have secured the entire area provided that one or more well-fortified castles did not delay Henry and counter the advantage a victory had given him. Psychological advantage, as would have been given by the destruction of the Valois army and the death, capture, or ignominious flight of Charles VII some time during the course of the campaign, would have been crucial in preventing Henry getting 'bogged down' in the Loire valley and reducing the war to a round of sieges.

As Charles virtually never fought in person at battles, killing or capturing him would have been less likely than sending him fleeing into the Auvergne as the English advanced on Chinon or Bourges. The deaths or captures of the ablest Valois generals, Dunois and Arthur of Richemont, would have not been enough to secure victory in the long term if Charles – and his young son Louis – had remained at large as a focus for rebellion and the Dukes of Anjou, next in line as Valois 'pretenders', had not been won over. The logical way to win over the Anjou dynasty would have been an offer of aid to assist their claims to Naples, where usefully the competent adult King Ladislas had died in 1414 leaving a female ruler, Joanna II. Duke Louis III's brother and (1434) successor René of Anjou was married to the heiress of Lorraine, making him a major threat even before he became duke, but he had interests in Lorraine and Provence to distract him: could he have been bought off?

Without a rapid 'war of movement' even a crushing military victory in Maine or the upper Loire region and/or the fall of major riverine strongholds would not have secured an overwhelming advantage. There were plenty of fortresses in Berry and Poitou to hold out even if Henry had taken the Loire crossings – provided that there was still a will to resist. Once Henry had achieved a breakthrough, he would have had the probable adherence of most of the southern French lords who now had no Valois army to defend them and would have had to seek terms. The English could have marched right to Bordeaux, and Henry re-constituted the old Duchy of Aquitaine (as an appanage for one of his brothers, probably John, Duke of Bedford?). If Charles VII had been dead or missing and his son Louis in English custody, the lords of Poitou and Aquitaine would have been more likely to back the perceived winner and come to pay homage – if only to save their estates from plunder and with every intention of deserting to a Valois pretender later. Henry could also rely on his Beaufort kinsmen for total loyalty, with his uncle Thomas, Duke of Exeter, the most experienced commander available to take on an appanage in southern France until he died in 1426.

The sheer scale of geography would, however, aid the Valois cause – even if now nominally in the hands of Charles' infant son Louis (XI) as the next surviving 'legitimate' heir – in preserving a foothold in southern France. The refugee Valois court would have been able to rally in the south if Henry's army was not strong enough after the adherence of the local lords in Berry to risk a march right to Toulouse or (perhaps through friendly Burgundy) to Lyons in 1425 or 1426. Without a major military 'demonstration' in these areas, Henry is unlikely to have received the adherence of their landowners even if he had destroyed the Valois army in the Loire area in 1424/5 and secured the grudging support of all lowland western France.

The isolated castles and towns of the Massif Central and the geographically-remote areas of Languedoc and the Rhone valley would have been likely to remain out of his control if an alternative Valois candidate as king had remained at large. Lacking the manpower to garrison the areas he had conquered south of the Loire, Henry would have been even more dependent on the support of opportunistic ex-'loyalist' and Burgundian allies than he had been to win and keep Paris and Champagne. He did not have the men to enforce obedience except when he and his army were personally present, and would have had to make extensive concessions to the local lords and promise a continuance of the 'status quo' to secure their adherence (perhaps making examples of a few 'die-hards' and giving their lands to the likeliest potential allies). As long as Henry had the momentum of victory he was unlikely to be directly challenged on the battlefield, provided that he had the adherence or neutrality of the adult Valois males of the Anjou line.

As king of England as well as of France, and overlord of Ireland (and hopefully Scotland), Henry could not have stayed in south or central France long even if he had not been opposed in a march as far as the Mediterranean or the Rhone – or return often. This area was therefore at most risk of eventual revolt should the surviving 'legitimist' heir – Dauphin Louis? – secure enough troops to mount a campaign there or some oppressive or incompetent 'Henrician' governor touch off a revolt. Valued captains such as the Earls of Salisbury and Warwick would have been crucial royal lieutenants in this region, probably as holders of local counties taken from 'die-hard' Valois partisans – but with mainly French vassals. The Valois princes of the House of Anjou, who would have lost their lands in the Loire valley for opposing Henry, were a crucial factor here as they also owned the Duchy of Provence – safe across the lower Rhone from Henry's army. Had Charles and Louis been captured or killed, they had the next claim to France, and Duke Louis (d. 1434) and his brother René would have been claiming the throne. From 1431 René was also Duke of Lorraine by marriage, throwing extra resources into the potential Valois 'legitimist' cause in eastern France. It would have strained Henry's resources, even as adult king of France and victor in the west, to march an army all the way to the lower Rhone to force – temporary? – adherence out of Louis and René. He would have needed the aid of foreign rulers such as his long-term ally Emperor Sigismund – whose main concern at this time was the revolt in Bohemia. At best, Henry might have forced the Angevin princes to accept him as king of France for his lifetime by a risky march to Lyons and Avignon around 1427 and handed back Anjou to them as the price of their support. It is possible that Henry's son Henry VI's real-life bride of 1445, Margaret of Anjou (born 1429), would in due course have been considered as a suitable focus for a marital alliance to keep the Anjou dynasty loyal to Henry's cause.

The reign of 'Henri II' after military victory – and the succession

The prior demands of the French campaigns would have kept Henry in France for most of the 1420s, and probably mainly resident there thereafter. It was the larger of his realms and the adherence of its nobility was more problematic and in need of reinforcement by his personal presence and his demonstrations of military power and a firm Burgundian alliance. Probably his youngest brother Humphrey, Duke of Gloucester, and/or Cardinal Henry Beaufort would have been effective deputies in ruling England except during his infrequent visits, as they were for the minority government of Henry VI in the 1420s, with Duke John of Bedford deputizing for Henry in France during his absences in England. Humphrey had been chosen by Henry as his deputy in England in 1421–2, so this role was likely to continue. The Cardinal had been Henry's choice as chancellor in 1410–12 and had more administrative experience than Humphrey, so his return to a senior position in 1423-4 would have been likely anyway. His exclusion from any special role in the English regency by Henry in 1422[43] was not an indication that Henry backed his 'foe' Humphrey in their confrontation, not yet an issue, but to keep full semi-royal powers with the intended regent Humphrey. Without Humphrey resenting his exclusion from full regency powers by the council, led by Beaufort, in 1422 the confrontation between Duke and Cardinal[44] might well not have developed.

As in real life, there would have been strains between Humphrey and his political rivals in England, though not necessarily Beaufort – and strains are likely to have developed between Humphrey and Henry. The issue of Humphrey's restless ambitions may still have led to him considering marriage to Jacqueline of Holland, exiled in England in 1424, as he did in real life. This match was intended to acquire him untrammelled political power over his own principality and thus to make up for his marginalization in England. This would lead to his challenging the validity of Jacqueline's disputed marriage to her estranged husband, the Duke of Brabant (a Burgundian candidate), and thus putting the English alliance with Duke Philip in danger. The probability is that he would have married her and invaded Holland before the definitive papal ruling of 1428 that she and Brabant had been legally married.

As in real life, this would have led to Humphrey being at war by proxy with the Burgundians and thus have infuriated Duke Philip – reducing his co-operation with the English in France at a crucial moment. Henry V would have been as angry with Humphrey for ruining his French strategy as Bedford was in real life. But would Humphrey have been less likely to defy Henry – in possession of full royal powers – than he was to defy Bedford in 1424–6? Certainly, Humphrey would have been in a weaker position to impose terms for reconciliation on Henry than he was on Bedford in real-life 1426; he could not have insisted that Beaufort be removed as chancellor as the price for this.[45] But Henry, like Bedford, may well have looked favourably on the papal idea of using Beaufort – removed from English politics to decrease faction (as in real life in 1426), if not by Humphrey's insistence – as a 'crusader' papal legate against the Hussites in Bohemia. Henry was not as bloodthirsty about killing heretics as Archbishop Arundel, the sponsor of the pioneering statute 'De Heretico Comburendo', as shown by his famous intervention to try to save one of the victims (John Badby) from the stake in 1410. (One argument has it that Arundel, and Henry IV, were only responding to insistent 'grass-roots' pressure to punish heretics; but they never made public personal efforts to halt an execution as Henry V did.) But he was a conventional Catholic and the point about Badby's execution is that Henry wanted to save his life if he repented at the last minute, not in any case.[46] Henry had no discernible sympathy for heretics, and indeed his stern willingness to accept brutality in a good cause suggests that he would have persecuted 'Lollards' if that was necessary to show his devoutness to the papacy for political reasons. He expressed support for the notion of his going on Crusade – though this had a political reason, in protesting to Pope Martin V (a would-be mediator) that he really wanted to shed 'infidel' not French blood.[47] Sending Bishop Beaufort or another 'crusader' with troops to attack 'heretic' Bohemia would aid his ally Emperor Sigismund, that country's titular but excluded sovereign.

To avoid the strain of a constant watch on the Scots border, Henry would eventually have seen the counter-productive nature of forever keeping the now-adult Scots King James I as a hostage at his court and agreed some form of treaty of close alliance, sending him home to act as his vassal. It could have involved the same sort of marital alliance that the regency government formed with James in reality in 1424. James could also have been forced to supply regular troops to his ally to garrison French strongholds – there would be little danger of them deserting if there was no rival candidate as King of France to attract their support. As mentioned earlier, it would have suited him to use this excuse to remove distrusted nobles from Scotland and thus bolster his power. Without any potential Valois support for a challenge to Henry, James would have had to concentrate on reasserting his authority in Scotland as a reluctantly loyal ally – at least until Henry's death gave him an opportunity to assert more independence.

Henry VI showed no physical symptoms of taking after his Valois grandfather until 1453, and as a young adult king from 1437 was at worst lacking in his father's skills. Not excessively pious or at all feeble-minded as far as can be judged, he was prone to the influence of the Duke of Suffolk's faction at court, interested in religion and building, and not as enthusiastic for military matters as his father or uncles. According to reports he was also unusually prudish and unworldly. His real-life reign until 1450 showed at worst that he was unskilled in balancing political factions or standing up to flatterers and lacked the forcefulness of his father and his paternal grandfather.[48] Like Richard II, Edward II, and Henry III, he was unaware of the dangers of relying on a narrow group of personal favourites – or the danger to his own position that they would not tell him the truth about political matters. In all these cases but Edward II's, the nature of their early accession and thus position at the ceremonial centre of court life was an important factor – they did not have a 'normal' aristocratic childhood. None took to the aristocratic 'norms' of energetic chivalric sport, and Henry VI showed signs of attracting adverse comment as Edward II, fond of 'lower-class' pursuits such as crafts and rowing, had done. In his case, his prudish nature and religious fervour were noted in well-known tales by the 1440s.[49] Henry VI clearly rejected the lifestyle and 'mores' of his 'governor' from

1428, the aristocratic military hero Richard Beauchamp, Earl of Warwick – and he showed no eagerness to campaign in France to save his dominions. Richard II had showed far more forcefulness in political initiatives from his teens than Henry VI did, though both came to fear and distrust the uncle who was their next heir (John of Gaunt and Humphrey of Gloucester).

The likelihood is that Henry V would have been encouraging his son to take to warfare and chivalric sports as Warwick was attempting to do in real life, with equal failure. But there was no rumour of Henry VI's mental incapacity at this stage, although the records do recount occasional public jibes at his naivety.[50] The danger of a 'mad king' to succeed Henry V would not have been apparent in the conduct of his son in the 1430s or 1440s, though the Prince could have proved as much of an exasperating disappointment to his father as Edward II did to his father.

A division of England and France back into two realms under Henry's sons?

Henry V had not produced any known bastards in the years of his warfare in Wales, or from his roistering in Eastcheap. But he had made Catherine pregnant early in their marriage, and she was to produce at least three sons by Owen Tudor after c.1428.[51] None of his brothers had children, but his father had four sons. What if Henry and Catherine had had more children during the 1420s? If they had had more sons there could have been talk of dividing up Henry V's realm after him – one son to rule England, one to rule France. Ironically, it would be a repeat of the arrangements made by England's Viking-French conqueror Duke William in 1087 – the eldest son to have his father's ancestral lands, the next to have those lands taken by conquest. The idea of one son ruling both England and France was theoretically possible and had precedents, as it had been considered – in reverse – by Philip Augustus of France in 1216 when his son Louis (husband to King John's niece) had been offered the throne of England by John's enemies. Importantly, dividing two kingdoms ruled by the same dynasty between two princes was a well-known European royal method of reassuring opponents of any 'threat' of a permanent union. In Spain, for example, the extinction of the royal house of Aragon in 1410 gave the throne to their closest relatives, the royal family of Castile – a hereditary rival, as England was to France. A union of the two kingdoms under King John II of Castile was thus too politically dangerous, and the throne of Aragon went to his uncle Ferdinand 'of Antequera' instead. Could Henry V have divided the two kingdoms under his sovereignty between two sons?

Technically, if Edward III had succeeded in enforcing the surrender of Paris and possession of the Dauphin as captive in 1360 he could have ruled both kingdoms and passed them on to the 'Black Prince', Edward of Woodstock. The latter was to have two sons, Edward (who died young) and Richard (II), who could thus have taken one kingdom each had both survived to adulthood. Nor was it suggested in 1216 – when rebel English nobles invited Louis, heir of France, to claim the English Crown and depose John – that Louis could not rule both kingdoms. There was no insistence on separating the two kingdoms as a condition of the nobles accepting union in either 1216 or 1360, even if circumstances had made this a wise outcome of such a union. But there were already complaints at Henry V neglecting England by the amount of time he spent in France by 1421,[52] and these would have escalated if his need to conciliate his new subjects made him concentrate on France after 1422. The nobles of neither kingdom would appreciate the amount of time that Henry V/II spent in their rivals' realm, and English grumbling at the amount of taxes and men raised for the French wars would have been more acute in the 1420s than in 1415–20 if the French war had dragged on with annual campaigns. Even if Henry V had achieved major victories, the elimination of Charles VII, and control of most of France in 1422–6, he would still have needed a personal army and garrisons and England would have had to find money to fund his projects.

Ultimately, a division of Henry's kingdom into two would have been probable in the next generation if he had more than one son – as happened to other 'unions of crowns' in the Mediterranean area in the late mediaeval period. Practice among other royal houses in Europe in the 1430s and 1440s is instructive. Ferdinand of Aragon's son Alfonso overran Naples after the extinction of its royal house in 1435, securing it from the Angevin claimant King René in 1442, but on his death in 1458 Naples passed to his illegitimate son Ferrante not to his brother and heir to Aragon, John. The union of Norway and Denmark (plus temporarily Sweden) under Queen Margaret passed to her great-nephew and heir Erik (husband of Henry V's sister Philippa) in 1412 and on to his heirs in 1439–40, but Sweden broke away. In Eastern Europe, the dynastic union of Poland and Lithuania – a smallish but more civilized kingdom and a larger but recently pagan Grand Duchy, so of unequal status – by marriage in the 1380s proved permanent, but with a semi-autonomous Lithuania being insistent on its own Grand Duke for the next century. The agglomeration of duchies in the Low Countries (Flanders, Brabant, Holland, and Luxembourg being the most prominent) in the hands of the House of Burgundy from 1384 to the 1430s was permanent, but not without problems – as when Duke Humphrey endeavoured to prise Holland away from it. Permanent dynastic unions were thus problematic. If one son of Henry V had succeeded to both kingdoms after Henry V and a younger brother been without a crown, a local aristocratic revolt on the latter's behalf in one of the kingdoms was a possibility.

Given Henry VI's lack of political skill or a forceful character, he could not have held both kingdoms together by personal charisma and a masterly balance of factions like his father. He would have been as open to capture by one court faction, and the resentment of those excluded from power, as he was in real-life England in the 1440s. Arguably, he repeated the failings of the previous two English kings to lose their crowns, Edward II and Richard II, in being seen as the exclusive 'property' and puppet of one noble faction and blocking advancement to its rivals. Given the probable choice of Margaret of Anjou as his wife, as in real life, the House of Anjou would have been prominent at his French court. Due to Margaret's father René's eviction from Naples by Alfonso of Aragon in 1442, his main dynastic interests now lay in France. Indeed, had Henry been mainly resident in France the estrangement of him and his uncle Humphrey (as principal councillor in England) was a possibility. The manipulation of the young King by the dominant Beaufort faction into arresting Humphrey in 1447 could thus have occurred as in reality, with the Beauforts having been leading pillars of the Plantagenet regime in France since the 1420s.

Alternatively, the personal bonds that had tied the French nobility – and the Dukes of Burgundy – to the successful warrior Henry V would have lapsed and they would have had to weigh up the chances of his son surviving as king. If Henry V had lived to the age of his grandfather John of Gaunt (58/9), he would have died around 1445–6; his father had had some unusual health-problems and Henry was likely to have lived longer than him (45/6). Bedford, worn out by campaigning in France, died at 46; Humphrey died at 57, possibly of a seizure induced by fury at his arrest at Bury St Edmunds (though rumour had it that he was murdered).[53] Henry VI or a brother was likely to have been ruling France by the mid-1440s. If the new English ruler in Paris had been visibly not up to the challenge, Charles VII or his son Louis (XI), born in 1423, would have seemed to stand a chance of regaining the throne, with or without some nationalist 'Joan of Arc' figure rallying popular opinion among the French gentry and peasantry for an uprising. One theory had it that Joan was an illegitimate daughter of Charles VII's mother Isabelle and/or a 'figurehead' chosen by anti-English nobles at Charles' court, e.g. Dunois, to spark off a patriotic revival which Charles was incapable of doing; some such plan could have been arranged to expel an unwanted 'foreign' king. The limited military strength available to the government of the new, Paris-based Lancastrian King of France would have tempted the Valois 'legitimist' claimant to invade with the possible assistance of the Angevins from Provence. The presence of an under-age or militarily inexperienced new king would have been another inducement.

The task of keeping a largely French political and military coalition of supporters loyal would have taxed even an energetic and capable administrator like Bedford, or if he had died in 1435 as in reality some other senior English figure. Only a man of royal blood would be acceptable to the French nobles as regent or chief minister to the young Lancastrian King of France, so if Bedford was dead the Beaufort John, Duke of Somerset was the obvious choice. (The younger Richard, Duke of York, born in 1411, was an able commander in 1440s France but might still be tainted by his father Cambridge's treason.) The conflicting demands of satisfying rivals for particular offices and commands in Paris under the new King would encourage the unsuccessful French contenders to join the rebels, and by the late 1430s Salisbury (killed earlier in real life) and Warwick the English generals would be ageing. Somerset was not noted for his success as a general, and York might well have been undermined at court by being the Beauforts' rival (as in real life) and a potential contender for the English or French crowns. The Duke of Burgundy, still Philip until 1467, would have been quick to auction his support to whichever rival offered him the best terms.

The English position in France could have collapsed quickly once their generals started to lose battles and the rebels had seemed to stand a chance of winning, and after the deaths of Salisbury, Bedford, and (1439) Warwick the English did not have capable or committed generals unless their Paris government had trusted York. The latter proved the most able of the English commanders in France, holding onto Normandy through the early-mid 1440s, but was sidelined by the Beauforts with his role as childless Henry's probable heir causing court jealousy of him. The English would have needed to keep their trusted officers and men north of the Loire to protect Paris, Maine, and Normandy and would have been seriously over-stretched even there without major trustable French support. The task of preserving a vast and hostile realm south of the Loire is likely to have been beyond them, with the ministers in London (or, had the crowns been split, the English king) unwilling or unable to send large-scale reinforcements of men and money to a losing cause. The French war could still have been lost by 1453 – with even more catastrophic suddenness as the English claimant had such a vast realm to defend with so little resources – and seen a humiliatingly quick defeat of a seemingly mighty edifice like John's loss of the Angevin realm in 1203–4. Once the nobility had decided that a king was a 'loser' he could be deserted with remarkable ease and lose a large domain quickly, as King Eric of Denmark, Norway and Sweden found in 1439.

If one son of Henry V had been ruling France and another son ruling England, the expelled King of France would have been seeking assistance from his brother and/or ending up as his unwilling pensioner with a crowd of exiled Henrician landowners and commanders from France. The King of England would be a likely target for their resentment for not lending them enough support, even if that had proved impossible for him to force through Parliament. If it had been the by-now mentally feeble Henry VI ruling England his throne would have seemed a tempting target to a dispossessed younger brother and his lords. (His uncle Duke Humphrey, born in 1390, is likely to have been politically eclipsed by ambitious younger lords such as Suffolk by this point.) If Henry VI had been the expelled King of France, he would still have had a claim on England as the late King's elder son and his wife – Margaret of Anjou as in real life, as a result of a Lancastrian-Anjou/Provence alliance? – would have been capable of intriguing on his behalf. Violent recriminations and civil war would have followed in England as in real-life 1450–61.

Chapter Five

Henry VI

A hopeless war? After Henry V: why was the French war not abandoned once the tide turned? Or halted with England still possessing Normandy?

The situation before the French revival in 1429

The position of Bedford as French regent for Henry VI ('II' of France, though subsequently airbrushed out of French history) was weaker than that of his late brother would have been as king. As seen previously, there were limits to English enthusiasm for the long-lasting war in the 1420s and no great rush of volunteers for new expeditions in France.[1] The delay caused by Henry V's death from August 1422 to early 1424 was not crucial, in that the war was already 'bogged down' in sieges east of Paris and the refugee Dauphin Charles did not have enough men, money, or co-ordination to mount an offensive; his new body of Scots recruits under the Earl of Buchan were better-experienced and motivated than the French loyalists but not enough to change the course of the war. The next English expedition of 1424, and the victory at Verneuil, could not be followed up, although Bedford was suspiciously sluggish in his choice of targets in the aftermath. Unlike Henry, he had no record of taking bold decisions and running risks; a swift march to the Loire in autumn 1424 might conceivably have won his small army a vital bridgehead. In addition, Bedford faced the problem that his receipts from the combined revenues of Normandy (c. £25,000 p.a.) and the French royal exchequer (c. £21,000 p.a.) in the mid-1420s did not match up to the size of the demands his brother had forced on the Norman 'estates' for the war in 1421 (£75,000). This restricted his ability to hire troops until he had secured more funds from the English regency a few years later; and the position of a reigning king (e.g. Henry V) to make large demands on his subjects was easier than that of a regent.

Worse, Bedford was required to return to Engand in 1425–6 to sort out feuds among the governing council. Bedford was constrained from demanding more recruits or money from England by the fact that he was not in full legal control of both realms as Henry would have been, Henry having bequeathed control of his French domains alone to him by his dispositions of August 1422 – though Bedford had the right of precedence in the council in England when he was there.[2] In his absence, the role of principal councillor – but no more than *primus inter pares*, and without the quasi-royal powers of regency – went to Duke Humphrey. The latter then proceeded to wrangle over leadership of the council with Bishop Beaufort, an escalating feud that Bedford had to return to sort out in 1425; there was no lasting settlement until Beaufort was induced to leave the country on a papal 'crusade' against the Hussites. Humphrey alleged that Beaufort was plotting a coup to become regent, and Beaufort's huge financial resources made his goodwill essential; in 1429 he could pay for an army. The English Parliaments continued to insist on only paying for any new expedition to France for the first six months; after that the troops sent from England would have to be financed out of the hard-pressed exchequer of occupied Normandy (weakened by Henry's 1415–19 ravaging), revenue from Paris where the war had restricted trade-income, or loans. The captured French royal treasury was reduced by decades of embezzlement and extravagance, and Bedford was endeavouring to win over not fleece his infant nephew's Parisian subjects.[3] The latter showed no spirit to resist the English, with no prospect of rescue by a French 'Dauphinist' army in case of revolt – by contrast, there was a serious plot in Rouen but the citizens of Paris had a fiercely independent civic tradition, a history of sudden riots (e.g. in 1412) and could not be taken for granted. They had been resolute in opposing the advancing English in 1419 after the fall of Normandy, arguably adding to pressure on Dukes John and Philip of Burgundy not to ally with Henry as this would lose them Parisian support.

In military terms, the campaign to occupy more of France was bound to enter stalemate unless a major success boosted either side. Neither Bedford in Paris, drawing on the revenues of Paris and Normandy, nor 'Charles VII' in Chinon, drawing on what he could bargain from his largely autonomous subjects in the provinces of southern France, had the money for a large army and a major campaign. This Agincourt-level clash was desirable for the English, but they lacked the resources; it was not so desirable for Charles' group of discordant commanders, demoralized from recent military disaster. The six months that Parliament would pay for an English expedition to back up Bedford's army was too short a timescale for the sustained campaign needed to deal with the resistance in the upper Loire valley; in a countryside dotted with defensible positions long sieges were the norm and the English could only advance slowly. Crucially, Duke Philip of Burgundy failed to come to their aid from his lands to the East of Charles VII's upper Loire garrisons, and thus to outflank the 'Dauphinist' defences from the rear. In the mid-1420s, he was at loggerheads with Bedford over the plans of Humphrey to take over Holland as Duchess Jacqueline's new husband, in place of his own candidate.

Thus what clashes occurred in 1424–9 were small-scale, centring on a steady English advance through the region between Normandy/Paris and the upper Loire, with Bedford's victory of Verneuil opening the way to the occupation of Maine in 1425, victory over the pro-Dauphinist commander Arthur of Richemont in Brittany, and the defection of Arthur's brother Duke Francis of Brittany to the English side in 1427. Luckily, Richemont – the best general available at Chinon until the emergence of Dunois, a survivor and prisoner at Agincourt, and resolutely anti-English – was at odds with a powerful court rival who had Charles' favour, La Tremoille. He was marginalized from command at Chinon in the years 1424–5 and driven to take his anti-English struggle back to his native Brittany; had he been in Charles' confidence he had the ability to weld the disparate 'Dauphinist' troops together into one army. Commanding only in Brittany instead, he was containable by Bedford's lieutenants and his defeat over Maine in 1425 led to the leadership of his brother's duchy defecting to Bedford to preserve Breton security. Le Mans, capital of Maine, was lost to La Hire and recovered. A planned English advance on Angers and the lower Loire in 1428 was cancelled in favour of the attack on Orléans further up-river, which Bedford had opposed;[4] arguably Bedford's lack of power to constrain his deputy, Salisbury, on this issue was disastrous in this instance. Henry V would have faced no such veto. Salisbury, a bolder commander than Bedford, proposed the Orléans campaign as providing a more direct route to Charles' 'capital' of Bourges. As suggested above, this was legally dubious in a law-conscious age. It was dubiously legal to attack the lands of a captive lord who could not defend them, and the Duke of Orléans had been an English prisoner since Agincourt. Attacking it also annoyed Duke Philip, who had a claim to it.

In the meantime, the equally competent Lord Talbot – a veteran of the guerrilla wars against the Welsh, and used to such 'hit-and-run' activities as the lord of a Marcher estate at Goodrich Castle, Herefordshire – took over as governor of Maine in 1427. His flexible new tactics of sudden raids on concentrations of enemy troops or attackable garrisons gave the English added boosts in psychological reputation, terrorizing resistance, and a few extra acquisitions of garrisons. It also made up for lack of troops by making the few he had seem invincible – though it was no long-term substitute for the conquest of major towns and one defeat could easily ruin a hard-won reputation for military success. Most dangerously, the proportion of archers in the English recruits to the French campaigns seems to have diminished in the mid-late 1420s, from around 1 in 3 to 1 in 10 – and been accepted by the English council as necessary due to the small number of extra archers coming forward to fight.

A vital mistake? Attacking Orléans rather than Angers – and the French revival of 1429

Angers had the advantage of being the possession of the pro-Charles Dukes of Anjou (and a former English possession of many of Henry VI's ancestors). Smaller than Orléans, it was probably easier to capture, was within easy reach of occupied Maine and friendly Brittany, and would open the way for an advance south via Poitou to Aquitaine. The English fleets could bring supplies, and men if funded for a campaign by Parliament, up-river from Nantes and England (weather permitting). Instead, the English army was diverted in autumn 1428 to besiege Orléans with desertions already a problem,[5] and did not have enough men to completely surround the town. It suffered the blow to morale of the death of its commander Salisbury after a 'fluke' cannon-shot days into the siege, and was still encamped outside the walls when Jeanne/Joan 'of Arc' arrived with reinforcements from Chinon and rallied the French in April 1429. The arrival of her reinforcements with a convoy of food-waggons (apparently with a 'miraculous' change in the wind), their successful penetration of the English blockade to cross the river, and the following successful sortie against the English siege-lines, served to inspire and unite the French even if she did not bring many men or any military experience. The question of her practical value, as opposed to being a useful talisman supposed to fulfil a 1398 prophecy by Marie Robine, is still debated. She may indeed have been used – or selected? – by aristocratic proponents of a more aggressive resistance to force the Dauphin's hand; her first sponsor, local castellan Robert de Baudricourt near her home at Domremy, was a partisan of Duke René. René, titular King of Naples and heir to the head of the House of Anjou, was a 'hard-liner' in terms of resisting the English, possibly with hopes of the French Crown if the Dauphin Charles should die or be overthrown as an alleged bastard. The Dauphin could still have turned Joan down, as an embarrassing potential heretic inspired by 'voices' and dressed as a man; he had clerics question her carefully. She had French and European parallels in her role as a female admonitory visionary, e.g. Marie Robine and St Catherine of Siena, but none as a warrior. The famous scene where Charles hid among his courtiers in the Chinon throne-room and let a friend sit on his throne, thus challenging Joan (who had never seen him) to prove her Divine support by locating him in the crowd and denouncing the 'fake', may have impressed him but the Church's approval of Joan was more politically vital. But even when she was allowed to accompany the army to Orléans, success was lucky. The English were careless in their siege tactics, as a (feasible) barricade of boats across the Loire would have added to the hazards the relief-force faced and might even have repulsed them. If the current broke up a barrier, patrols were feasible. But it should be remembered that even had Orléans fallen, the smallish and exhausted English force might well not have ventured further south in 1429 as too risky. Did the relief of Orléans really make a serious difference?

Dunois provided the necessary military strategy and Joan the 'elan' for the defence, and the English had no inspiring leader to counter the two of them acting together in the crucial encounters outside Orléans and further North in May 1429. It does not appear that the English kept adequate scouts to their rear as they retreated,as Dunois and Joan could surprise their main army later at Jargeau; no effort was made to anticipate what the French might do next. What is not clear is why Bedford, supposedly bringing reinforcements to the siege from Paris, halted his advance at Chartres; his personal appearance to lead the besiegers would have rallied their spirits even if the French refused battle by staying inside the walls. Instead, the cautious and inexperienced commander who had taken over at Orléans, Henry VI's future minister the Earl of Suffolk, chose to withdraw north in early May and to split up his army; the latter left the initiative and easier odds to the emboldened French. The French were able to trick the isolated English Loire garrison at Beaugency into surrendering, then take on and defeat his separated forces piecemeal, which they did at Jargeau (capturing Suffolk) and Patay. At Patay, the French rode down the English archers before they could open fire. This was luck as much as skill – the same tactic had failed earlier at the 'Battle of the Herrings', an attack on a food convoy. This opened the way to a French advance on Paris or into Champagne – and towns in the latter (held by Burgundians, not English) surrendered to the Dauphin with suspicious alacrity. The lack of English archers was a constant threat to Bedford's forces, and it may be asked why he had not had the flexibility to send urgent orders to the council in England to train some more – hired – men if volunteers were not coming forward. The English government had the money to hire men, although Bedford did not; but did it have the will? And were many useful soldiers sent off to fight the Hussites with Beaufort's expedition, or taken to Holland by Duke Humphrey earlier?

The reverses were not unprecedented, as even Henry V had suffered the defeat and death of his next brother, Thomas of Clarence, at Baugé in 1421, but eight years on the English were without his leadership and weary of providing more men and money for France. Henry, heroic victor of Agincourt and unquestioned political leader of England as well as France, could have fought a bold campaign against superior French numbers in 1429–30 as he had done in 1415, and had an eye for a battlefield, though Dunois was a skilled general who had won minor skirmishes even in 1428 and was likely to avoid a trap. Henry could also have appealed to his English subjects for men and money with more charisma and authority than Bedford had. Instead, Bedford followed the French royal tactics of 1359–60 and 1415–20 and avoided battle, sitting behind the walls of Paris while the French army marched on and mopped up isolated garrisons en route to a morale-boosting coronation for Charles VII at Rheims on 18 July. The town of Rheims had refused to admit the previous importunate arrival demanding coronation there (Edward III) in 1359; it did admit the Dauphin. This was a 'public relations disaster' for England, as until then Charles could not claim to be a crowned king and was thus more at risk of 'fence-sitting' nobles or foreign powers ignoring his legal claims on the throne. From now on Charles could claim to be the anointed King of France not just a pretender who might even be illegitimate due to Queen Isabella's noted promiscuity, as alleged by the English occupation-authorities. His coronation also gave Philip of Burgundy a legal excuse for defecting back to him, as the crowned King of France, once it was convenient – though he did not attend the coronation.

The combination of the coronation and the English military paralysis led to the defection of most of the provinces and garrisons around Paris and Rheims. The loss of Rheims, Troyes, Laon, Sens, Senlis, Beauvais, and most of Brie and Picardy cut English-held Paris off from Calais and reduced the English possessions south and east of Normandy to the capital and a few outlying garrisons. Bedford was caught off guard again, being away collecting reinforcements in Normandy, as Joan arrived outside Paris earlier than expected. It was lucky for the English that her quick assault on the walls on 8 September was defeated with herself being wounded, the end of her myth of invincibility and the first failure of one of her 'prophecies'. But the French maintained the pressure, and only the arrival of Bishop Beaufort with an English expedition supposedly en route to Bohemia saved Paris from probable capture in 1429–30 as Bedford lacked enough men to hold the large city's walls for a sustained period.[6] But there was no sign of any patriotic Parisian enthusiasm for evicting the English garrison by force, even when Joan was outside the gates.

The English reaction to Charles' coronation: was Henry VI's coronation as King of France unwise in blocking a potential settlement?

From now on the momentum lay with the newly-crowned Charles VII, even when the charismatic Joan was luckily captured by Duke Philip's men on a private venture to assist the town of Compiègne in May 1430. (It had been regained from the English by Charles VII's forces, but the region was promised by England to Duke Philip in return for his aid; thus Charles and his generals did not want to offend the Duke by keeping it from them. Joan saw things more simply.) She was handed over to the English for trial and execution for heresy – which Charles did not endeavour to halt by demanding a 'prisoner exchange' or endeavouring to put ecclesiastical pressure on the Church official in charge, Bishop Cauchon of Beauvais. Did he fear being thought 'soft' on 'heretics' or antagonizing her (Burgundian nominee) Church prosecutor Cauchon? He did not order Cauchon's archbishop (Rheims) to intervene or appeal to the new Pope Eugenius.

Notably Charles had refused to let her join any new official campaign in 1429–30, effectively marginalizing her once her usefulness decreased – a sign of eclipse for Dunois' 'war party'? One French courtier observed cynically that Charles had now been hailed as the nation's divinely-aided saviour by another mystical talisman, a holy shepherd boy, so he had no need of Joan. In military terms, the English had been put on the 'back foot' by the loss of Chateau Gaillard, a vital fortress controlling the Seine 'corridor' up-river to Paris, and the southern frontier town of Louviers to La Hire early in 1431. As a result, when Henry VI arrived in France (Calais, 23 April 1430) there was much to do before he could be escorted to Rouen, let alone Paris – and besieging Rheims to force a coronation there was out of the question. In political terms, the renewed ascendancy of Joan's critic La Tremoille – jealous of 'dangerous' French military leaders as a threat to his power, as Henry VI's civilian minister Suffolk was to oppose Duke Humphrey and York having military resources in London – delayed a further French military advance. This ended with Arthur of Richemont's coup in 1433.

For the moment, Bedford showed a vigour he had lacked in 1429 as he successfully defended the remaining English positions around Paris. The army sent with Henry to France in 1430 was the largest since the 1417 expedition – 3,199 men crossed to Calais before Henry and a further 4,792 were contracted to accompany him. They were actually contracted to stay for twelve months, a vast improvement on the usual six months and thus could be used for a longer campaign – though after their initial six months' advance pay ran out their payments became so irregular that many returned home early. Chateau Gaillard and other places were retaken in 1430 and

Louviers in 1431, clearing the way for Henry to be escorted to Paris to be crowned, though in military terms this was merely a 'holding operation'. In 1433 Bedford secured new troops from England, and at this point he had around 6,000 men serving in garrisons in France plus 1,600 besieging St Valery, 1,200 in lower Normandy and 900 in Alençon and Maine. He managed to organize the administration and finance within his regency lands to raise a viable, if small, army to defend Normandy (based on the Calais garrison) in 1433–4.[7] It can be argued that his lack of long-term strategic understanding was shown by his blaming Joan's successes on black magic rather than any improved French capability.[8] Was he in 'denial' about his long-term chances of holding out? The resort to allegations of 'witchcraft' was commonly used against powerful women for political purposes in the period, e.g. to politically neutralize and seize the property of Dowager Queen Joan and the Duchess of Gloucester. Joan of Arc wearing male attire to travel and fight – almost unique for the period – laid her open to charges of 'unnatural' behaviour. In psychological terms explaining her away as an agent of the Devil would reassure the English commanders and troops that her success was due to malign forces not their military weakness. The use of this explanation would suggest that Bedford was too conventional a thinker to react imaginatively to the French military challenge – a charge reinforced by his insistence on crowning Henry VI as King of France. Having failed to regain Rheims so Henry could be crowned in the traditional place, he resorted to using Paris, although this meant a long wait for the royal party in Rouen until the route there was secure. On 25 October 1431 Louviers fell; on 2 December the royal entourage arrived in Paris and on the 16th Henry was crowned at Notre Dame. But did Bedford seriously think that the worst of the crisis was over once Joan was burnt at the stake and the Burgundian truce with Charles of 1429–30 was over? Lacking enough English troops or money, he resorted to supernatural reasons for Joan's success – though his explanation would reassure potential English or Burgundian recruits that the main threat was supernatural not military and had now ended. 'Disengagement' from England's exposed position around Paris was the last thing he contemplated in 1429–35, even if this would save well-defended Normandy from attack for decades. His truculent determination not to waver was shown by his speech to the English Parliament in 1433, challenging his critics to a duel and implying attacks were a slur on his honour.

In military terms, the position of the hard-pressed English was probably untenable outside Normandy in the long run given the relentless pressure to be expected on Paris and the lack of will, money, or men to defend it. (The current level of commitment to Normandy, Alençon and Maine was a total of 3,936 men in garrisons in the year from Michaelmas 1433 to Michaelmas 1434; the English told Burgundian envoy Lannoy in summer 1433 that they had around 9,700 men in France, around 6,000 in garrisons.[9]) The garrisons around Paris were a drain on resources and not defensible in the long term – and neither was Paris. Normandy was the priority, not least as some commanders were defending their own land-grants there but had no personal links in Paris. New help from England would be limited – only around 1,200 men joined Lords Camoys and Hungerford's 1432 expedition, and Bishop (now Cardinal) Beaufort had to pay them himself. Geography would seem to indicate that Paris was doomed and a waste of a garrison after Charles' gains of 1429 – but abandoning it was politically impossible.

The sheer size of Paris meant that defending its walls was a logistical problem, quite apart from the fear of a 'nationalist' rising in this always turbulent city with a history of swift and violent changing political allegiances in the 1410s. Once the outlying garrisons were lost it would be vulnerable to blockade and could only be reinforced up the Seine – a temporary expedient if the starving populace were hostile to a small English garrison. Once Charles VII had been crowned, and Duke Philip had failed to turn up at Henry VI's coronation to do homage, the eventual defection of Burgundy was to be expected. He failed to meet Bedford again after 1429, arousing English suspicions – as the Earl of Warwick told Lannoy. Logically, the losses of 1429 and the lack of English military resources should have given the English commanders the excuse needed to open negotiations on the basis of the terms that Henry V had been able to abandon in 1419 – accepting that they had the military means only to hold Normandy and Aquitaine, if that. But this would mean abandoning Henry's cherished claim on the French Crown, which had been recognized as legal by the French court in 1420 and implemented for his son in October 1422. This was too great a loss of 'face' to be contemplated easily, especially by a regency rather than an adult king. (In legal terms, a guardian for a young feudal lord was supposed to hand over his inheritance intact on his majority.) It was unrealistic to expect the English 'high command' to accept military reality so swiftly, given their past history of successes over the French, which they could hope would soon resume. Indeed, Bedford's only potential challenger of equal rank, Duke Humphrey, was equally 'hard-line' militarily as he showed in 1436–7; he did not form a 'common front' with the more amenable Beaufort but continued to feud with him over power. (In 1431 he tried to indict him for treason.) And even Beaufort was not as 'pacifist' as some have assumed, merely more realistic about concessions. Initial exploratory Anglo-Valois contacts in 1433 thus got nowhere, although the Valois government was as determined not to moderate its position as was Bedford (even when Cardinal Albergati attempted a papal mediation in 1431).

Retreating from a seemingly 'hard-line' position on a claim to the French throne was not new. Edward III had accepted terms of territorial aggrandisement short of the French Crown in 1360 (without ever explicitly renouncing the latter), but he had never been recognized as King of France in Paris as Henry VI had. In territorial terms, he had held far less of France in 1360 than Henry VI and Bedford did in 1430–5. The French would not now accept any terms short of recognizing Charles VII, duly crowned and anointed, as rightful King of France – though it would have been different had Henry VI been crowned on accession in 1422 (when he had been an infant of ten months old). There was an excuse for not doing this, quite apart from the logistics of transporting an infant across the Channel from his residences around London. French kings were not necessarily crowned (always at Rheims) immediately on accession, though the fact that there was only one under-age accession between 923 and 1422 – a remarkable run of luck – meant that there was no precedent of an infant king who had not been crowned swiftly. The previous youngest English king, Henry III in 1216 (aged nine), had not been crowned in the usual Westminster Abbey on accession due to civil war, but had been crowned once he regained his capital; Richard II had been quickly crowned aged ten in 1377.

Why had Bedford not thought of crowning Henry before 1429, or did he see no need to hurry the ceremony? Legally, crowning him as King of France would put him in a superior position to the uncrowned 'Charles VII'. It might still have been feasible to crown Henry VI at the age of six or seven in the late 1420s, with a quick journey from Calais to Rheims; the young King does not appear to have been physically fragile. But there was another problem to any settlement with the Valois involving the uncrowned Henry VI abandoning the French Crown. Technically the English king would have to renounce his claim in person, which an 'under-age' king (aged eight as of December 1429) subject to administrative and legal tutelage could have later claimed was illegally forced on him and was thus invalid. A full, indisputably legal renunciation would have had to wait for Henry VI's majority, which in terms of the conclusion of the authority over his person of his royal 'governor' (the Earl of Warwick) was to be in 1437. Until then the renunciation's legality could be challenged later if Anglo-French relations deteriorated again. Accordingly, when a papal peace-mission finally brought both sides to the negotiating table at Arras in 1435 the English would not consider any alteration of the legal situation of their claim until Henry VI was fully adult and could unquestionably act of his free will in renouncing it.[10]

It was thus dubiously legal if Henry's French 'regent' Bedford renounced the claim on his behalf. As of 1430–5 the English still had some cards in their favour, not least the uneasy adherence of Duke Philip and the Burgundian army; and a French siege of Paris could be long and costly. Nor was Charles a bold military leader ready to risk a premature attack on his intended capital; it was only recaptured after Burgundy returned to his side in 1435. Until Tremoille's fall in 1433, Charles hardly undertook any new offensives – aggression thereafter was probably due to Richemont's influence. Bedford was able to hold Paris for his lifetime, and would not have abandoned his late brother's great prize except in extremity; and it was more vital for the French cause that Paris be regained than to press doggedly for the return of Normandy or Maine. Their terms in 1435, when England still held Paris, would only concede Normandy and Guienne to Henry – and then only as Charles' vassal, on the same terms as English kings had held French lands until Edward III's claim to their throne.[11] Any firm and binding Anglo-French settlement by treaty, dealing with the English cession of isolated Paris and the recognition of Charles as king in return for the continued occupation of Normandy and Bordeaux, was thus likely to be delayed for years.

But there was initially one legal loophole for the question of Henry's claim – that which the papal lawyers used to help Duke Philip back out of his oath to Henry V as rightful king of France in 1420. A claim and an oath could be cancelled out, and its swearers absolved, if it was legally invalid – and in 1435 Philip was able to use this excuse for backing out of his English alliance with the papal lawyers agreeing that his oath to Henry V had been illegal.[12] The same could apply to Henry VI's claim to France, assuming that he and Bedford would accept a ruling by Rome that their legal grounds for the claim were incorrect. It had been Henry V, not Henry VI, who had insisted on the French Crown and had signed the terms at Troyes in 1420 – could the new King renege on his father's claims?

But this potential resolution to the problem was not followed; it assumed an English willingness to accept that the gamble of occupying all of France had failed. Bedford's response to the disasters of 1429 made a settlement even less likely, as he proceeded to shore up his nephew Henry VI's shaky position by persuading the English council to send him to France for his coronation. Having been given precedence over his brother Humphrey and all of the council when he was in England in August 1422 by Henry V, he could not be defied. The usual site of a French coronation, Rheims, was now back in Charles' hands and Paris, the substitute site, was so unsafe that Henry had to wait in Rouen for nearly a year until Bedford judged it safe to bring him to the city with an army. The largest English grants of taxation since 1418 and an army of several thousand men had been collected for the enterprise, which served no military purpose except to make the royal expedition to Paris and back safe for its duration, and the cost of the coronation-festivities further impoverished the English treasury for military spending in the mid-1430s.[13] Moreover, the coronation at Notre Dame on 16 December 1431 served to complicate future Anglo-French talks unnecessarily and make any voluntary abdication of Henry's rights virtually impossible; like Charles, he was now a crowned king. It is probable that Bedford naively over-estimated the importance of a legal oath to a crowned king in inhibiting future French desertions. The complexities of English royal family quarrels also saw a temporary breach between Bedford and his main financial supporter, Bishop Beaufort, in 1431 which could have had serious consequences. Beaufort, based in Rouen and Paris during Henry VI's visit and unable to return home due to Humphrey's intrigues, sought to shore up his power-base as (civilian) president of the French regency council by securing the limitation of Bedford's patent of regency from 'by dynastic right' status to a personal grant by King Henry, i.e. revocable at any time (October 1431). This infuriated Bedford, who was now technically in the same *primus inter pares* position on his regency council as Humphrey had been forced to accept in England – by him among others. But it had little effect on the war, as Beaufort was not radically more inclined to peace with the Valois than Bedford was and in any case Charles VII's government made no serious efforts for talks in 1431–5 except on a brief truce.

The coronation of Henry 'II' of France was no doubt intended as a sign that the English position in France was not hopeless, and as a defiance of defeatist counsels. It was an act of loyalty by Bedford to his late brother's plans and evidence of his chivalric fidelity, but it made little political sense given that the Henrician regime lacked the means to hold out indefinitely. It created a legal impasse – although it did not prevent pragmatic French noble allies who had accepted Henry as rightful king, led by Duke Philip, deserting him and recognizing Charles instead when that was politically convenient. (Burgundy did not attend Henry's coronation in person, which was ominous.) The military impasse created by the petering out of the French offensive of 1429 was to be partially broken by Burgundy's defection in 1435 and the loss of Paris to Richemont. But Paris had always been an isolated outpost once the 1429 campaign lost the major garrisons of the region and most of neighbouring Champagne and Picardy to Charles VII; its loss simplified the English lines of defence. Its populace notably jeered the English garrison as, taking refuge in the Bastille, they were allowed to leave for Normandy by the conquerors. From then on the English were reduced to defending Normandy and Maine, and were able to hold the French back from the vital Vexin fortress of Gisors in 1436. But one serious and insoluble problem involved discontent and potential defection within Normandy, exacerbated by pillaging and arbitrary killings by out-of-control English soldiers (some unpaid, some opportunists). There was a particularly serious massacre of civilians who resisted this at Vicques in August 1434.[14] The English no longer guaranteeed local order, and this would encourage local Normans – soldiers in the garrisons included – to think that only French reconquest would end the pillaging.

As the French mercenary companies rallied to Richemont's expanding army after 1435, Charles VII was provided with an 'in-built' advantage in numbers – perhaps around 15,000 regular troops to around 6,000 English troops facing him in Normandy and Maine. He was also able to secure valuable grants of direct taxation from the French Estates enabling him to lure more 'waverers' back to his side and to afford to develop artillery to batter down the walls of English-held towns.[15] In the absence of a vigorous and warlike young English king – one major drawback for their leadership's motivation – an adequate commander had to be appointed and supplied with men and money to hold the Norman frontier. This man also had to be able to rely on unwavering political and financial support from England. Crucially, this was lacking – the three English supreme commanders after 1435, Duke Humphrey, Richard of York, and Edmund Beaufort, all had enemies at court. Beaufort, the most secure in royal support, suffered the most from lack of finance, which negated his potential in the late 1440s. As Charles' generals had been undermined by jealous court rivals like La Tremoille before 1433, so Henry's were to be undermined by their English court rivals.

Slide to inevitable disaster? England in France after 1431

The vagaries of court politics in England meant that a steady and concentrated effort in France could not be guaranteed. The death of Bedford at Rouen on 14 September 1435, aged forty-six, was a crucial blow, though the recent Valois–Burgundian reconciliation at Arras had crippled his strategy anyway. His negotiators at this alleged 'peace congress', led by Archbishop Kemp of York not by the more influential Cardinal Beaufort (so as not to expose the latter to criticism from the expected failure?), had been hoping for a twenty-year truce, but were not empowered to accept revision of the Treaty of Troyes. The Valois delegation, by contrast, was not empowered to accept any terms that did not involve the abandonment of the Treaty and of Henry VI 's claim to France; all it would offer was the Duchy of Normandy plus part of Picardy, to be held as a feudal vassal of Charles VII. The only hope the English thus had at Arras was to prevent a Valois-

Burgundian reconciliation, and Charles had been secretly subsidizing Duke Philip's chief ministers and wife Isabella to ensure their goodwill. The papal legates, Cardinals Albergati and Lusignan, were empowered to absolve Duke Philip from his oath to the Treaty of Troyes, which they obligingly did at the formal Valois-Burgundian reconciliation ceremony at Arras cathedral a week after Bedford's death. Accordingly, with the legates as well as Philip's leading advisers taking a pro-Charles 'line' Bedford's only hope at Arras would have been to promise on oath that his nephew Henry would abandon his French Crown as soon as he reached his majority and could legally do so, and hand back Paris – logical, but too much of a humiliation for it to be acceptable to such a proud prince.

On a personal level, would Duke Philip have deserted so quickly had his sister Anne, Bedford's first wife, not died in 1433? Bedford's second wife, Jacquetta of St Pol, was niece of his Anglophile Chancellor, Bishop Louis of Thérouanne, but the Duke disliked her family. Bedford was personally respected as being honest, well-intentioned, and committed to his brother's French kingdom – even by Parisians.[16] As seen before his final illness in 1435, his position was not desperate in the short term. In 1433 he secured a stable and amenable council on his trip to England, balancing Humphrey against Cardinal Beaufort; the two men would never combine against him given their long-term hatred and Humphrey's recent (1431) attempt to indict his clerical uncle for treason and seize his treasury. He issued wide-ranging military reforms to improve effectiveness and discipline in Normany in 1434, showing that he recognized the problem of lawlessness.[17] (Whether they achieved much in reality is dubious; rules were often ignored by local captains.) He also imposed a capable new treasurer in England in the person of Ralph, Lord Cromwell, opening the possibility that the English regime in France could in due course be subsidized by the English regency instead of having to rely on handouts from Bishop Beaufort. (As of summer 1433 Cromwell reckoned that the regency's revenues were £35,000 smaller than its outgoings so this would take some time.[18]) His zeal and capability were undoubted, and he endeavoured to ban misbehaviour by his soldiers, which did much to add to Norman civilian resentment. In 1435 he revived the post of Seneschal of Normandy providing an empowered military deputy (the veteran Lord Scales) if he was absent or ill.[19] He regained full control of Calais by taking over as its lieutenant from Humphrey. But would all this have only delayed disaster had he lived – by two to five years? The balance of resources was tipping inexorably in Charles VII's favour – though Charles, as seen by his reaction to Joan, was a very cautious man and the new ascendancy of the 'war party' under Arthur of Richemont from 1433 scared Philip of Burgundy into reviving his close links with Bedford via the embassy of Lannoy.

The survival of Bedford for another decade could well have put the final 'showdown' between the English and the cautious Charles into 'cold storage', with Philip unwilling to abandon his English alliance and Bedford's new wife from 1433, Jacquetta of Luxembourg, as their link. The ending of Bedford's authority as full regent of France on Henry VI's majority in 1437 would have opened the possibility of scheming English courtiers – the Beauforts? – endeavouring to persuade the King to dismiss him from his presumed new post, that of royal lieutenant in France. But there is no evidence of any tension between Henry and Bedford, and in case of a crisis between Duke Humphrey and the Beauforts over power in London, Bedford was likely to back Humphrey. Bedford's survival could thus have delayed crisis in both kingdoms, well into the 1440s. The reasonable size of the new English army raised in 1436 (see below) indicates what could have been achieved in terms of reinforcements, probably by a visit by Bedford to London on Henry achieving his majority to confirm his new role as royal lieutenant in France.

Duke Humphrey was able to make only a brief – and successful – intervention in the Calais area (with an impressive 8,000 men) in 1436[20] and the ablest of his successors, the young Duke Richard of York in 1437 and the early 1440s, faced political difficulties at home. Neither had their King's undisputed confidence. Both men showed what could be done with a determined effort, and the English Parliament could raise 2,000 men-at-arms and 9,000 archers in the crisis of 1436. In 1435 the veteran commander Sir John Fastolf had submitted a coherent memorandum requesting a return to aggressive annual 'chevauchées' in Artois and Anjou to intimidate the French into 'backing off', which was ignored – though he was too optimistic about English recruits.[21] In 1437–9 the lieutenancy of the Norman-Maine 'realm' was given to the capable veteran Warwick, trusted by the young King (his ex-ward) more than Humphrey was and uncontentious; he could have lived longer rather than dying in office in his late fifties. In 1441 the larger and recently successful French army – now joined by Richemont again – deliberately retreated after the loss of Pontoise sooner than fight York and Lord Talbot. In 1436 Humphrey saved Calais and raided Artois but failed to catch Duke Philip, while York arrived at Honfleur (with 4,500 not the promised 11,000 men) too late to save the East Norman ports, having delayed sailing while he vainly demanded full regency powers like those of Bedford.[22] Ironically, in view of his future, self-proclaimed reputation as the competent 'hard man' who would have saved Normandy if it were not for treacherous courtiers at home, York proved as problematic for the Duchy's defence by his delay in 1436 as his rival John Beaufort was to do in 1443. Any chance of a two-pronged offensive timed to coincide with Humphrey's was lost, though either or both of them were unlikely to have saved Paris from capture as this would have required a larger army arriving much sooner.

Once York was in Normandy, he co-ordinated a strong and partially successful attempt to restore the frontier. In 1436 Talbot and Lord Scales defeated Charles' mercenary commander La Hire at Ry; in 1437 Talbot recaptured Pontoise; in 1440 Talbot defeated Richemont at Avranches; and in 1441 York and Talbot relieved Pontoise. The 'outer glacis' of Normandy, dominated by the Vexin and frontier towns, remained safe or if lost was swiftly recaptured e.g. Dieppe (lost in 1435); Louviers was lost permanently (1440).[23] In the long term, Richemont's creation of a standing army for France and the development of the French royal artillery made Normandy's safety dubious; the towns could be battered into submission one by one unless an English army came to their rescue. In 1443 the new English expedition under John Beaufort, Marquis of Somerset failed to co-ordinate with York for political reasons (see below), but as of 1437–44 England was able to hold onto Normandy while Charles' offensives were under threat again, this time from his own turbulent subjects. Henry VI was not the only king afflicted by unpopular court favourites and rebellion by marginalized magnates, coalescing around the heir to the throne; in 1440 the Dukes of Bourbon and Orléans and Dunois joined the Dauphin Louis in the abortive 'Praguerie' revolt. The renewal of French internal conflict thus served to threaten a renewal of the fatal French weaknesses of 1415–20 – but Charles VII, unlike Charles VI, was both mentally alert and politically capable and saw off the revolt. Had he been overthrown the resulting weakness of his teenage son's new government would have given the English regime in Normandy a valuable 'breathing space'.

After 1435, the will of the English government to fight or negotiate suffered from additional problems in that there was no continuation of the firm and capable government that Bedford had presented. In any case the lapsing of the regency arrangements on Henry VI's majority would have denuded the power of Bedford, and the King could be expected to develop his own policies. But there were two extra factors – Duke Humphrey was a divisive figure, the centre of intrigue against the regency council in the 1420s, and the King was not a strong personality. The route lay open to a revival of faction at court, with effects on French policy. The intervention by Humphrey in France in 1436 was his sole expedition there, strategically marginal and aimed at his old enemy Duke Philip not at Charles VII, and he had his position at court in England to defend from increasingly successful rivals. The latter were logically behind his failure to secure any new command in France after 1437; the appointment of the King's ex-'governor' Warwick was a politically satisfactory compromise but in 1438 Maine and

Anjou were granted for seven years to Edmund Beaufort, no doubt at the Cardinal's request. He had inherited lands there from Bedford and had a legal claim on them; but sending him (with 346 men-at-arms, 1,450 archers, and £7,333-6-8d funding from the Cardinal[24]) was a considerable distraction of men and money from Normandy. After Warwick's death on 30 April 1439 there was no 'neutral' supreme commander available, except the lower-ranking Talbot and Scales who clearly lacked court patrons.

Henry VI, like Richard II, seems to have been ready to listen to jealous courtiers' whispers about his uncle's ultimate political threat to his throne, and Humphrey was an isolated and hot-headed figure never known for his political wisdom. He had been putting his own advancement above national unity when he undermined the council and asserted his claim on Holland – both to Bedford's detriment – back in the mid-1420s and had made exaggerated claims about and violent threats to his rival Bishop Beaufort. He was Bedford's heir to a 'no surrender' policy, as seen by his objections to releasing the Duke of Orléans to negotiate with the French in 1435–40, but he was not able to assert influence over his unmilitary nephew Henry VI and lead a sustained and effective campaign to rally support for the English domains in France after Bedford died and Burgundy deserted. He faced problems from ambitious, mainly 'civilian', courtiers who coveted his estates and offices and were more personally appealing to the King – especially the emergent Earl/Marquis of Suffolk, ironically a descendant of Richard II's civilian 'favourite' Michael de la Pole. One de la Pole had challenged Richard's male relatives' influence at court in the early-mid 1380s; his heir now challenged the latest teenage King's uncle. But his adherence to what could loosely be called a 'peace party' over the French issue did at least derive from personal experience of the war, as he had been fighting in Normandy from 1417–29 and been captured at Jargeau. It is noticeable that there was no concerted effort by other courtiers to save Humphrey's (unpopular?) wife Eleanor Cobham from a charge of sorcery in the early 1440s, after she had been caught asking an astrologer how long the King would live.[25] (The English sovereigns could be as touchy about the 'treason' of ambitious courtiers dabbling in astrology as Roman emperors.) Humphrey's political isolation cannot be ascribed solely to a toadying desire among senior figures to rally to his successful rivals Somerset and Suffolk; he had aroused antagonism since 1422. He was still accusing Cardinal Beaufort of corruption in 1440.

Nor was Humphrey's successor in France, Richard, Duke of York (born 1411), secure in his position at court and thus able to command a viable, well-financed army for a long period in France. Like John of Gaunt, he was an heir to a suspicious king who was being encouraged against him by his domestic rivals – and his position may have been easier had he not faced a rival dynastic 'bloc', the Beauforts. Crucially, if Bedford or Humphrey had had sons York would not have been the King's heir and so a magnet for the 'reversionary interest' of alienated nobles and the suspicions of his sovereign. Like Humphrey, he was as committed to advancing his political powers as to military duty, as he showed in 1436 by trying to insist on extra authority. (The availability of money was dubious in any case; in 1433 the government was so short of cash that Henry had to 'close down' his expensive court and spend several months as the guest of the Abbot of Bury St Edmunds).[26] The son of the executed Earl Richard of Cambridge and grandson of the Duke of York left as regent by Richard II in England in 1399, he was also the son of the Mortimer heiress Anne (Richard's 'heir' Edmund's sister) and so laid claim to the direct heirship of Edward III's second surviving son Lionel. Lionel's descendants were regarded in some quarters as rightful possessors of the English throne, as shown in the chapter on Richard II; the Duke could thus be portrayed by his enemies at court, led by the Beaufort family, as a potential rebel and so too dangerous to be allowed a military command. The Beauforts, descended from John of Gaunt's third marriage, were technically barred from the throne but this could be reversed by Act of Parliament. Like Duke Charles of Orléans with Charles VII, York's role as potential heir could be used against him.

Until 1447 the childless young King's heir was Humphrey, already the long-term rival of Bishop Henry Beaufort, who thus bore the brunt of Beaufort enmity. His sudden death followed his surprise arrest at the early 1447 Parliament at Bury St Edmunds, probably engineered by the Beauforts and their ally the Marquis of Suffolk (powerful and acquisitive Steward of the Royal Household) after careful playing on the King's fears that Humphrey planned to overthrow him. Abbot Wheathampstead of St Albans recorded that by the mid-1440s Henry believed that Humphrey intended regicide. Given Henry's suggestible nature, he was presumably encouraged to fear Humphrey by Suffolk and the Beauforts. Thereafter York was the nearest lineal heir to the throne and the object of Beaufort-Suffolk enmity, with similar rumours of his malevolent intentions towards the King. The apparent 'Mortimer' links (or false claims) of the 1450 rebel leader Jack Cade increased suspicion, York being the Mortimer heir, though the absent York's support for the rebels was only rumour.[27]

York was at odds with John Beaufort (d. 1444), Earl/Marquis of Somerset and nephew of Bishop Henry, over the defence of Normandy, with Somerset having enough influence at court to be appointed as governor (nominally subject to *in absentia* Humphrey) in 1439. One other potential commander without such a problematic political role as a dynastic rival of York, the young Earl of Arundel, had been mortally wounded in Normandy in 1435. Could a surviving Arundel have been a useful 'safe' commander in France? Unlike his two predecessors as commander, York and the veteran Earl of Warwick, Somerset – a French captive for seventeen years after a previous military disaster – was neither experienced nor competent at war; this mattered less to the King than his loyalty. His appointment was probably also a 'pay-off' to his uncle Cardinal Beaufort, a major war-funder (who could not be repaid in cash), who had insisted on his ransoming from the French. He was seeking to carve out his own reputation and new domains while York was commanding in Rouen from 1441, and he achieved an independent command on the southern frontier in 1443. This was intended as a bold 'forward policy' to reach the Loire valley, as in 1428, but lacked either the resources or the dynamic leadership and it is possible that Somerset's poor health was already an issue, which would have alerted a more competent king to the lack of wisdom of choosing him.[28] Whether from illness, confused objectives, hesitation, or timidity, Somerset's grand campaign of 1443 fizzled out and he died in 1444. His younger brother Edmund had acquired control of Maine and was also a rival of York. The commitment of both Beaufort brothers to the war was thus reliable, unlike Suffolk's, and lack of troops rather than incompetence may have been their main problem; but defending both Normandy and Maine long term was a risky strategy. It might have been better strategically to abandon Maine to the French in the 1439 peace talks (see below); but that would have been seen as dishonourable and enraged its English defenders and Duke Humphrey. The rivalries of York's supporters – from 1447 apparently joined by Humphrey's faction – against the Suffolk faction at court aided the difficulty the English leadership had in a coherent and militarily effective policy as France resumed the attack on Normandy and Aquitaine after 1437. It all added to the difficulty the English armies had in a coherent long-term defence.

Given their lack of natural frontiers to defend and the preponderance of troops and money for the French Crown, the chances of long-term English survival in Normandy decreased year by year. The Crown's financial difficulties in the early 1440s were another ominous sign, although Henry had the advantage over other recent kings of a small and diminishing royal family in need of grants and appanages. (He inherited Bedford's substantial landed assets in 1435, his mother Catherine's and step-grandmother Joan's in 1437, and Humphrey's and Cardinal Beaufort's in 1447; until 1445 he had no queen.[29]) It would appear that this potential for spending resources on the French war was thrown away by Henry's reckless and incoherent prodigality, mostly in favour of his household intimates and their friends, relations, and clients.[30] His spending on his new foundations at Eton College and King's College Cambridge were less dangerous, though unwise in wartime, as they served to boost royal prestige. Arguably, the importance of court faction in the 1440s encouraged rising but insecure ministers like Suffolk to promote royal prodigality rather than parsimony – the more money they were granted by the King, the more clients they could buy. Thus fewer soldiers could be afforded, under-strength campaigns (e.g. Maine) fizzled out, and the French were emboldened to press on with the war – though the French Crown's greater resources gave them a major advantage anyway.

At best, a competent and administratively interested king raising larger armies could have held up the French advance for a decade or so – unless the French state fell into factional war again, which the defeat of the 'Praguerie' in 1440 prevented. But the French rebels, led by the belligerent Duke of Bourbon and his indisciplined mercenary allies who Charles sought to restrain (the 'ecorcheurs'), were more hostile to entering talks with England than Charles was; their victory would have solved nothing. The English weakness encouraged the French to press on with regular campaigns and to accept at best short-term, tactical truces – with the English insistence on retaining Henry's rights as crowned King of France meaning that a viable treaty was hard to agree even for the short term. In any case, the evident English weakness in military and financial resources, their King's lack of military interests, and the divisions among his senior courtiers would have encouraged Charles VII to break any agreement and resume the 'final push' to reconquer Normandy and Aquitaine within a few years of any treaty that denied him all his demands for his 'rightful' territories.

Missed opportunity? The conference of Gravelines, 1439
Despite these 'caveats' for a long-term truce, the English made some efforts to secure a truce once Henry had attained his majority and could legally agree to irreversible Government decisions. Usefully, the newly revitalized Church in Rome under the reunited papacy was able to put pressure on the French leadership for talks, aided by prestigious international politician and ex-'crusader' Cardinal Beaufort. The international situation in the late 1430s saw the reunion of the Eastern and Western Churches at a major Church council in Florence and moves towards a new crusade against the advancing Ottoman Turks, and English and French military efforts could be usefully diverted towards that. (Noticeably, despite his piety Henry VI showed no interest in crusading – personally or by his militant nobles.) The efforts of Pope Eugenius were to bear fruit in the Balkans expedition of 1444 – though it had to be led by the young King of Hungary and Poland, Wladyslaw,

rather than by a Western European ruler. French involvement was minimal. Had Henry V been alive, aged 51 in 1437–8, would he have led it?

In 1439 a conference met at Gravelines near Calais, with the official English position of not giving up Henry's claim possibly open to negotiation in his 'secret' instructions to Beaufort's negotiators.[31] The Cardinal's idea was to get the French to accept that having two kings within one French realm did have a – Carolingian – precedent. The last French ruler to have a co-king possessing a distinct territory (as opposed to a crowned heir) had been Charles 'the Bald' (d. 876), with his sons ruling Aquitaine; technically the entire Carolingian realm, which split into France, Germany and 'Lotharingia' in 843, had been one kingdom ruled by several kings. (Louis III and Carloman, brothers, had ruled French territory jointly in 879–82.) The flexible, clerical-led English team under Cardinal Kemp suggested that a long truce obviate the potentially humiliating demand for a peace-treaty, which the obstinate noble commanders on both sides might resist or sabotage. Henry would refrain from using his French title and Charles would refrain from claiming suzerain rights over those lands that Henry still held in France. That would prevent annoying legal appeals from disaffected English vassals in France to Charles' court, a potential opportunity for the Valois royal legal machine to stoke up a dispute as in Aquitaine in 1369–70.

As far as the account of Beaufort's assistant Bishop Beckington can be assessed, the Duchess of Burgundy (Beaufort's Portuguese niece), acting for France, and Beaufort reached a tentative agreement on this basis, with truce rather than peace, no precise delineation of the frontier yet, and any resumption of the war to be advertised by the aggrieved party a year in advance. Permanent peace would require Henry to renounce the French Crown and pay homage for his remaining French lands – a return to the pre-1415 'status quo'.[32] This was similar to the terms Burgundy had suggested to Henry's ministers after he returned to Charles' side in autumn 1435 – and which they had rejected. It had to be submitted back to Henry and the council in England for agreement in August 1439, and this was not forthcoming – apparently with Cardinal-Archbishop Kemp, the leading proponent of acceptance, and Humphrey denouncing it, successfully. The King, absent from decision-making in 1435, had the power to overrule the 'war party' but did not – an ironic missed opportunity for the allegedly holy pacifist Henry VI.[33] But in any case the lack of Anglo-French agreement over the precise limits of English occupation in Normandy, the Vexin, Maine, and Guienne would have made implementation of a truce difficult without determination to co-operate on both sides. Kemp's clever suggestion of 'two kings in one realm' would have saved English 'face' – but Charles VII was never interested in it.

Missed chances? The English fight-back, 1440–3

The long-delayed release of the most notable Agincourt prisoner, the Duke of Orléans, to press for a truce at the French court had been suggested by Bedford years before but was finally implemented in 1440. Unfortunately, Charles refused to receive Orléans, who he had been suspiciously hesitant in helping return home (as a potential plotter?) and who gravitated disgruntled towards the French 'opposition' peers involved in the 'Praguerie'. The defeat of the latter showed that France would not return to the factional chaos and weak monarchy of the 1410s, and thus a united military 'machine' would face the English defences. Several mercenary captains were executed. But even before this a diplomatic solution to the long-running Anglo-French crisis was advisable for England once the firm leadership of Bedford in 1422–35 ended. Although there was no clear indication yet that their newly-adult king would prove unmilitary and politically incompetent, the fissiparous nature of politics at court made a united and determined 'war policy' unlikely. Duke Humphrey's temporary ascendancy after 1435, securing the decision and supplies for a major campaign in 1436, was a 'false dawn'; his large army was strategically wasted after it had rescued Calais. He was never more than *primus inter pares* among an adult King's Council, unlike Bedford. Nor had his political neutralization of the Cardinal in 1431 been forgotten by the latter's family. The decision of the government to aim for a peace-conference in 1439 was politically wise and probably determined by the King – although Humphrey was likely to oppose it from a mixture of loyalty to Bedford's uncompromising policy and dislike of the main promoter of peace, Cardinal Beaufort. Despite Humphrey's lurid claims, it is unlikely that the King was cozened into either the Gravelines conference or this over-optimistic personal diplomatic mission by an unpatriotically pro-French Beaufort.[34] Humphrey had taken the worst possible opinions of Beaufort's intentions towards him (as usual) and the government and had not learnt discretion – but now there was a technically adult king and Humphrey acted as if nothing had changed.

Hopes of success at Gravelines rested to a large extent on the goodwill of the Duke of Orléans, whose help to the English mission was to be rewarded by his release. But as might have been expected, despite his position as the 'second-in-line' to the French throne after Dauphin Louis and his impressive hereditary appanage the Duke had little influence in Paris after twenty-five years in captivity. As a result, the war resumed after the defeat of the 'Praguerie', with the English having to show Charles VII that they were too strong to be evicted from Normandy so he should resume talks. Most usefully, Harfleur – Henry V's first conquest – was besieged during the 'Praguerie' and forced to surrender; the highly capable Talbot became its governor. This freed English shipping from harassment as they took supplies up the Seine. However, on the southern frontier the French now retook war-damaged Louviers.[35] Overall command now fell to the young Duke Richard of York, who lacked Humphrey's long-standing enemies at court but was a potential focus for suspicion by his position as second heir to the King (after Humphrey). His genealogical rival, to make matters worse, was the 'peace party' leader Cardinal Beaufort's nephew John Beaufort, Marquis of Somerset – eldest heir of the Beaufort line, and son of Henry IV's half-brother John. The family were technically debarred from the throne by Act of Parliament dating from the time that John's father, John of Gaunt, had married his mother, Katherine Swynford – but Acts could be reversed. Somerset was both York's dynastic and military rival, though he was also committed to aggressive defence of Normandy, unlike the Cardinal.

The success York achieved with his expedition of 30 knights, 2,700 archers and 900 men-at-arms in Normandy in 1441–2 could not hide the fact that his action was only a delaying one, particularly with the £20,000 he needed to pay his troops siphoned off to pay for his rival Somerset's independent command in the south. Even so, York was only able to relieve the vital south-eastern border town of Pontoise from its French siege; the besiegers refused battle and hid behind their entrenchments so he could not defeat them in battle and drive them off. Once he had left, the assault was renewed – with cannons to blast holes in the wall – and Pontoise was stormed on 16 September 1441. Evreux was also taken, in a surprise attack by pretend 'fishermen' on the adjoining river who were really French troops under Robert Floques, captain of Conches, and who put scaling-ladders up the wall while nobody was looking.[36] In this war of gruelling sieges and sudden attacks, the initiative lay with the army with most time and resources to use – the French. Moreover, in England there was marked reluctance to serve in the new army, which the short-term nature of military contracting obliged York to raise for the 1442 campaign. He sent Talbot to appeal to Parliament and a contract was drawn up in March 1442 for an army of 2,550 men, but the army that was raised was short of both men-at-arms and archers – only 300 of the latter were mounted, so they would not be much use in a mobile campaign. The King had to pawn the Crown jewels to pay for the expedition,[37] a sign of his shortage of money even before his 1445 marriage (which is often blamed for his financial problems). But giving York more men and money, had Parliament and the local gentry been more enthusiastic, and not sending Somerset into Maine with a separate expedition would not have altered matters much given Charles VII's determination to avoid battle.

Somerset's campaign of 1443 had its own political as well as military advantages for the English council – in 1442 Charles VII, absent from the war in Normandy, had been campaigning inconclusively in Guienne but had local military superiority over the under-funded English defence and might easily prevail in 1443. Were the cash-strapped council to try to save the heartland of the Duchy of Aquitaine, English since 1152, from conquest or divert resources to aid York, whose Norman campaign was grinding to a halt? (Talbot, with his own English reinforcements' time-limit for campaigning running out, had had no time to complete his assault on Dieppe in autumn 1442.) The Treasurer, Lord Cromwell, confirmed that the government could not afford to send armies to both Normandy and Guienne.[38] Accordingly, it was decided to deal with both problems in one campaign – Somerset would take an army to southern Normandy and then march south into Maine and over the Loire to attack Charles in the rear, forcing him to pull back from Guienne. If Somerset was lucky, he could even conduct a 'chevauchée' all the way to Guienne, as John of Gaunt had done in 1373. The instructions given to Garter Herald on 5 April of what he was to tell York about Somerset's intentions made it clear that a march this far, and bringing Charles to battle, were on the agenda. This bold move was intended to impress the French into accepting English resolve ahead of any more negotiations, as well as to pay for itself by 'living off the land' and possibly winning a new clash on the scale of Verneuil, 1424 – but it needed competence, luck, timing, and a large army. Somerset lacked all of them except possibly the last. He made the most of his position, by requiring full power independent of York's command – technically only in those areas where York was not currently operating, i.e. Normandy – and the right to dispose of captured towns and castles as he wished, plus a dukedom, some of the late Earl of Bedford's lands, and 1,000 marks (£360,000), which was reduced by bargaining to 600 marks (£210,000).[39] His greed and blatant haggling did not do his reputation any good, and probably exacerbated the ease with which York's faction were able to blame him and his brother Edmund for coming disasters. When York sent a delegation to London to discover if Somerset's command encroached on his authority (and if so to object) the council could not pay him the £20,000 outstanding for his men's pay as the money had gone to Somerset's army.[40]

But the expedition was not inevitably a disastrous 'side-show' – Somerset had a coherent if risky plan and a valuably large army of around 8,000 men, and the Cardinal paid their wages for six months to save on royal finances.[41] The most disturbing fact was that Somerset did not land in Cherbourg until early August – the intended rendezvous date for sailing of 23 April (the patriotically inspiring St George's Day) was perhaps too ambitious and some 'slippage' in timing from troops and supplies arriving late was inevitable, but even the lackadaisical Henrician government was complaining at his not sailing by the new date set for 17 June. Somerset was warned that every day's delay cost the government £500 and the cost of billeting and feeding them in England was more than a Parliamentary subsidy and only benefited France. When he eventually arrived in Normandy he achieved nothing in terms of gaining territory. Somerset's 'razzia' through Maine to the Loire petered out in late August 1443 and he made no attempt to cross the Loire, pulling back to attack the town of Pouancé further north (possibly to lure the nearby Duke of Alençon out of his base to a battle, but if so it failed). Having acquired useful loot but annoying the new Duke of Brittany by attacking Alençon's garrison in the Breton town of La Guerche, Somerset withdrew – though technically the truce with Brittany had expired and it was not supposed to allow French garrisons in its territory so his retaliatory action was not illegal.[42] The resources that Henry had been prepared to give him showed that the King's adherence to peace at all costs was not secure; only after Somerset's failure did peace efforts resume.

The contemporary accusation that Somerset unnecessarily infuriated the wavering Duke of Brittany by his assault on La Guerche on the Breton frontier was thus inaccurate, but Somerset unnecessarily blackmailed the Duke into paying ransom for the captured La Guerche (and pocketed the ransom). It led to a furious Breton embassy to Henry, led by the King's friend Gilles (the Duke's brother). This compromised the Duke's goodwill as potential mediator with Charles VII and boosted the anti-English Arthur of Richemont's influence at the Ducal court. More seriously for the 1443 campaign, Somerset ignored York and frittered away time on unsuccessful sieges and his demands drew away men from Talbot's siege of the important Dieppe (which the Dauphin Louis relieved on 14 August).[43] The English garrison of the blockading fortress erected outside Dieppe was overrun by Charles VII's army, which York or Talbot could have prevented had they had the troops. Again, no attempt was made to concentrate all resources on a defensible – Norman – perimeter by regaining lost fortresses first. The English refused to give up on Maine after 1442 – partly due to court rivalry, as its defence gave Somerset politico-military status and kept him as a viable rival to York in France. On his return he was disgraced, and died a few months later (May 1444). His title and his role in France passed to his brother Edmund as he had no son, though his infant daughter Margaret was to end up as the Beaufort heiress and the mother of King Henry VII.

The main impression given of Henry's French policy in 1439–43 was instability, as he considered a marital link to one of the leaders of the 'Praguerie', the Count of Armagnac, in 1442 but went back on this plan.[44] Backed by the anti-Charles Dukes of Orléans and Brittany and the Count of Alençon, Armagnac had the military capacity and personal links to lead a rebel French noble coalition to hold up Charles' already dangerous threats to overrun all Guienne (shown in an offensive of 1442 where the King reached the outskirts of Bordeaux). Instead, he was abandoned and was duly arrested and neutralized by Charles; the Somerset expedition of 1443 was meant to break through the Loire barrier to rescue Guienne from French pressure but never reached the river. In both cases, the fault lay with the King for not deciding on a firm policy and pursuing it coherently; a dilatory general like Somerset would never have dared to defy Henry V.

The French renewed requests for negotiation in autumn 1442, possibly stimulated by York's successful efforts to lure Burgundy out of an active part in the French royal army (which secured an Anglo-Burgundian truce in April 1443).[45] As long as the disruption to French military unity from restive provincial magnates continued, the capacity of Charles VII to overrun Normandy or Guienne was limited. Indeed, Henry owed his future wife – and the nature of domestic English politics in the 1450s – to these internal French disputes. Margaret of Anjou, who he was to marry in 1445, was originally intended by her father René as the bride of the Duke of Burgundy's nephew, the Count of Nevers, but in 1443 a suspicious Charles VII vetoed the proposal.[46] Without this, Charles was more likely to have had good relations with and troops from Burgundy in the mid-1440s – perhaps leading to an attack on Normandy. But if Margaret had been unavailable, Charles' daughter Jeanne (born 1435) was Henry's likeliest bride and an Anglo-French *rapprochement* was still possible with Charles as Henry's father-in-law. However, the real-life pressure that Charles put on Henry for territorial concessions suggests that Charles would still have pursued this course – whoever Henry's French bride was, she was intended as a tool of French diplomatic aggression not a goodwill gesture signifying a permanent truce. The impact of Henry marrying Charles' daughter, six years younger than Margaret of Anjou – an older girl, Catherine, who was Margaret's age, married the Duke of Burgundy's son in 1440 – would have been that she was not as dynamic and controversial a queen as Margaret was in the 1450s. Could she have been more acceptable to the anti-Beaufort faction in the English nobility, and so blunted the danger of civil war?

The new Queen and the Truce of Tours, 1444–5: a missed chance?
Margaret was still available as a bride for Henry as Anglo-French talks resumed in 1443, though one source claimed that she was a substitute for the original expected bride, one of Charles' young daughters. The latter had also been suggested as a bride for the future Edward IV, then the baby son of 'third-in-line' Duke Richard of York. This match would have made him unavailable for Elizabeth Woodville in 1465 and so had a major effect on

English history, but was unlikely to succeed given the long 'time-lapse' before the partners could marry and the probability of Anglo-French war breaking off the match. The chances of either a Henry-Jeanne or Edward-Jeanne marriage improving Anglo-French relations in 1445–50 would have depended heavily on Charles' attitude to forcing a quick handover of Maine or retaking Normandy. Charles' intention seems to have been only for a short truce, cemented by the marriage-alliance, rather than a permanent settlement as in 1439. For a start, continuing war enabled him to serve as a focus for national unity as the 'heroic' recoverer of his patrimony – and to raise troops and taxes to the benefit of royal centralization. His commitment to unrelenting warfare had not exactly been noticeable in the 1420s, when he had stayed immobile at Chinon, and in 1430–1 he had failed to demand that the English released his 'saviour' Joan of Arc; a militant policy in the 1440s thus served to bolster his reputation after the 1440 rebellion. He was only politically confident enough to have Joan's conviction by the Church as a heretic and witch reversed after the fall of Normandy in 1450.

If the great magnates and semi-royal dukes (in possession of private armies of retainers) were part of or sending troops to the royal army against England, they were less free to revolt (as they did in 1440). This implies that it was French obstinacy that prevented the possibility of a permanent settlement in 1439; English agreement to hold Normandy and Aquitaine as a vassal might not have brought a stable peace. Possibly Charles was already confident enough to contemplate the final attack on Normandy for the near future.[47] In any case, the continuing English obstinacy over retaining Henry's title to France and the question of the extent of English 'vassal' lands in France would have rendered any long-term settlement unlikely unless major provincial revolts had shaken Charles' throne and forced him to seek a compromise.

The English efforts for a truce were opposed by a suspicious York and were led, successfully, by a Beaufort ally, the new Marquis of Suffolk, Steward of the Royal Household, major target for and dispenser of royal patronage, and an ally of the Beaufort clan against Duke Humphrey and later York. The dramatic rise in household expenditure in the 1440s would show that Suffolk, the King's chief adviser, had other priorities than securing money to fight wars – primarily his own acquisition of power at court as a conduit for patronage.[48] As condemned in Parliament in 1449–50, this undermined military effectiveness.[49] It undermined his own political ally as governor of Normandy, Edmund Beaufort, in 1448–9 as well as his enemy York, and contributed to anger in Parliament. In June to July 1449, just before the final French assault on Normandy, the MPs were refusing to send any money to Normandy unless Henry 'resumed' all his grants of land made since his majority, i.e. cancelled those seen as given to Suffolk and his cronies. The popular resentment of Suffolk's greed thus damaged the defence of Normandy. But he has been unfairly written up as a 'peace at any price' man, interested solely in his own position and pocket; he was reluctant to lead the talks in case they failed and he was blamed.[50] Major French 'actors' advising Charles also had their own private priorities. The intention of Duke René of Anjou, Lord of Anjou and Provence and claimant to Lorraine (and the titular King of Jerusalem), was to regain Maine for its 'rightful' lord, his brother Charles, who was also high in Charles VII's favour. The French King and René, his Queen's brother, duly made that the centrepiece of the negotiations with England in 1444 and Henry was induced to agree by his leading negotiator, Suffolk (who Charles VII had asked for as negotiator, a sign of his expected willingness to co-operate).[51] The French were intending to grant Henry only Calais and Guienne, the lands held before 1415, as a French vassal; the English negotiators required the cession of Normandy too but were prepared to abandon Henry's claim to the French throne.[52] The 21-month truce agreed at Tours in May 1444 left the question of Normandy open, but in return for the Henry–Margaret match Henry tacitly abandoned Maine to its Angevin claimant (or so the French alleged) and transferred the allegiance of the Duke of Brittany, still an English ally recognizing Henry as King of France, to Charles.[53] At the very least, Suffolk failed to set out any open English claims to Maine or Brittany. (The later beneficiary of his disgrace, York, may have been seduced by the promise of Charles' daughter for his son into keeping quiet.) Negotiations now proceeded with Charles' envoys in England in July 1445 to follow up the truce agreed at Tours – but with no softening of the French position.

Suffolk was duly accused when his critics impeached him of incompetence and Francophile sympathies, having privately agreed to hand over Maine to no good purpose. More pressure was put on the government by the new Queen who Henry secured through the 1444 talks, René's daughter Margaret of Anjou, whose private letters home show politically naïve encouragement for the English to hand over more territory.[54] This was clearly her role, as hoped for by Charles. In June 1445 Suffolk warned Parliament to be prepared to pay for war if the talks failed – was he just excusing himself in advance, or being realistic?[55] With the stalled negotiations in 1445 holding up the handover of Maine, it was Henry not Suffolk who made a secret written promise to the French on 22 December 1445 to hand over Maine to his father-in-law, René, before a treaty was agreed, regardless of progress.[56] The original date for handover was April 1446, but it was repeatedly put back. Thereafter Charles could justly claim that the delay in doing this was a sign of breach of faith, and threaten war unless Maine was surrendered at once. The English council, York as nominal governor of Normandy and his successor Edmund Beaufort, and the English commanders in the field had no idea of the promise and the naïve King was clearly worked upon by his wife and her visiting compatriots. In practical terms, Henry's Chancellor, Archbishop Stafford, did secure Parliamentary permission in 1446 to revoke the Treaty of Troyes without their approval – a royal preparation for an unpopular surrender?

End game? 1447–50
Charles eventually invaded Maine to take it back by force in spring 1448, with a mere 2,500 or so English troops defending Le Mans and no prospect of relief; unlike Charles, Henry had not used the truce of 1444–8 to build up his armed forces. Indeed, the increased expenditure at court under Suffolk's leadership – and the cost of the new Queen's household – pushed the government further into the 'red'. The garrison at Calais, for example, was owed substantial arrears of wages and York had faced serious difficulties before he left Normandy. New troops could not be sent to reinforce the King's overseas dominions. The capital of invaded Maine duly had to surrender to avoid the sack.[57] Suffolk and his episcopal allies in the council, who had prevailed with Henry over the more distrustful Humphrey in accepting the Anjou marriage and its terms, were prepared to gamble on the hope that Henry's willingness to come to terms over the claim to the Crown, Henry's new position as Charles' nephew-in-law, and the good offices of René with Charles would make the French King more accommodating over Normandy and/or doing homage. But the weak English military position made this a risk worth taking to preserve Henry's inheritance, as the failure of Somerset's 1443 campaign had ended hope of taking the military initiative. A stronger English military reaction would have entailed securing drastic cuts in domestic revenue – which the King was too feeble to do and which was not in Suffolk's political interests. Duke Humphrey was too isolated and feared by the King (and allegedly the Queen too)[58] to have any influence over his nephew, who at the very least consented to his arrest in February. Parliament was summoned to Bury St Edmund's, in Suffolk's 'powerbase' county and safe from pressure from London crowds. A treason charge was pre-empted by Humphrey's death in custody (probably natural) on 23 February;[59] his disgraced wife was declared legally dead so Henry could inherit his assets. The money was not used where it was needed – for troops. Once Humphrey was dead, the only possible political combination that could have forced Henry to dismiss Suffolk and secure a grip on his expenditure was the highly unlikely reconciliation of the two dynastic rivals to be Henry's heir, York and Edmund Beaufort.

Once it was clear that the French terms in two successive embassies in 1445 were not altered from those before 1444, the choice was to surrender or fight. The latter would entail financial difficulty in providing enough troops to defend Normandy and Maine, though not inevitably relying on York as commander as Edmund Beaufort had shown himself an adequate general while serving in France since 1440. Henry also had some military support within nearby Brittany, led by his militarily able personal friend Count Gilles (the new Duke's brother) whose small appanage was close to the Normandy border. If Henry was to endeavour to save his French lands he would have had to abandon his prodigality with his resources at home, and to embark on an effective policy of raising revenue and troops, as Charles was doing during the early 1440s. Charles took the opportunity of his Lorraine campaign of 1445, backing up René's claim there, to regularize his army in fifteen new regiments, ending reliance on unwieldy, indisciplined, disloyal, and rapacious *ad hoc* mercenary companies. Henry, who made much of his affection for his French uncle in their mid-1440s correspondence,[60] had every reason to follow this example – or, given his unmilitary nature, a minister such as Suffolk or the Sussex magnate Lord Saye and Sele (whose lands might be raided if France won the war) should have suggested it. The current Lord Treasurer, Bishop Moleyns of Chichester, was a cleric and diplomat so unlikely to be competent in military matters. Talbot, the best commander in Normandy in the 1440s, had been sent off to Ireland in 1445.

As events in the 1450s were to show, there were plenty of armed and pugnacious noble retainers at large in England with military capability – or still in Normandy until eviction in 1450, if serving a noble commanding there. Such commanders included Talbot, Lord Scales, and Henry Bourchier (a descendant of Edward III's youngest son, Thomas, Duke of Gloucester), Count of Eu. When these men returned to England after the loss of Normandy they formed the core of the marauding 'affinities' of the feuding noble dynasts, especially following York and the Nevilles. As in France with its entrenched provincial nobility and their loyal retainers who followed them to war (against the King if so commanded by their lords), these men needed to be welded into an effective and loyal military force by the monarch or his representatives. Failing that, Henry needed a coherent and competent resident commander in Normandy who the troops would follow and who Charles feared. The obvious person with appropriate rank was York, or failing him Edmund Beaufort; but after York returned to England for the autumn 1445 Parliament, his term of office about to expire, he was not replaced by Beaufort for many months and it was early 1448 before the latter set foot in Normandy. The military force there (2,100 men in garrisons in 1448)[61] was not augmented either, with Henry probably over-confident of achieving a lasting peace by means of the current plans for a personal meeting between him and Charles (which foundered). The King did order that 1,000 archers be raised to accompany Beaufort to Normandy in January 1448, with the £20,000 per annum that he was supposed to receive from England in wartime, although technically there was still a truce – which indicates some degree of anxiety.[62] Some 2,000 more archers were added, and on 9 May Beaufort finally arrived at Rouen. But this was 'too little too late'; he and his men and money would have been of more use in autumn 1447, before Charles struck at Maine.

The intended peace conference of 1446 or 1447 was delayed and later abandoned, and the time gained by a renewed truce through 1446–7 was not used for quick rearmament either. Instead, the English government allowed matters to drift as Henry failed to own up to his secret promise to Charles and the latter menaced him with the renewal of war unless French terms for peace were met. This incoherence and dithering could plausibly be ascribed to Suffolk as well as Henry, as he had the governmental experience and knowledge of Norman affairs (and ability as a decision-maker?) that the King lacked – and had the latter's confidence, which 'war party' leaders Humphrey and York did not. Or did he lack the nerve to risk Henry's displeasure by pointing out military and financial reality to him?

When his army was ready, Charles invaded Maine in February 1448 – and Henry's commissioners who were supposed to have handed it over by 15 January, military veterans Matthew Gough and Fulk Eythin, were caught out without the ability to defend it adequately. Given the size of Charles' army and the number of his cannons, they stood no chance – and there was no senior English commander currently in Rouen to march to their rescue. Indeed, Henry's personal representatives sent from England, Bishop Moleyns and Lord Roos, hastened to Charles' army to try to avert bloodshed by speeding up the surrender. The 'sticking point' for the commanders in Maine in winter 1447–8 appears to have been the question of proper compensation for those officers holding lands in Maine (e.g. Gough and Osbern Mundford, 'bailli-general' of the province and captain of Le Mans) who had to be evicted on the French takeover. How much money were they to receive, and should it be paid by Henry or by Charles? Mundford was particularly obstreperous, refusing to hand over his commission as governor of Le Mans to anyone but his appointer, Edmund Beaufort.[63] Charles could have made a generous offer of money as he was currently better-resourced than Henry, instead of haggling. At the crucial Anglo-French discussions of the handover of Maine at Le Mans on 1 November 1447 the English 'contrôleur général' of Normandy's treasury, Sir Thomas Molyneux, complained that the terms for its surrender included reasonable provision for those to be expropriated, which meant French compensation, but was ignored by the French envoys.[64] Charles may thus have hoped to drive the English into breaching the agreement to give him an excuse for aggression. But the blame at least partly lies with Beaufort – he was not hurrying to take up his new post in Normandy in winter 1447–8 but haggling for full compensation for himself for lands he would lose in Maine, for which Henry's council duly granted him £10,000 per annum on 13 November.[65] He was more concerned with lining his own pockets than putting Normandy in a position to defend itself quickly, let alone assisting Maine.

Gough and Eyton were not solely to blame for delaying the handover of Maine and provoking Charles – captains like Mundford were in a state of truculent near-mutiny and could easily have refused orders to surrender without full compensation; Henry did not have the money, and Charles would not pay it. So the French royal army attacked in February, and they had to ignominiously surrender Le Mans to prevent a siege (16 March 1448) after annoying Charles by delaying to no good purpose.[66] Once Maine had been conquered, Normandy was next – as Charles told the men of Rheims in autumn 1448.[67] He also extended his concept of a national army further, creating a systematic levy of crossbowmen – the so-called 'franc-archers' – from across the country and so involving local communities in all his provinces in the royal-directed reconquest.[68] The attack followed, with a number of increasingly bold unofficial attacks on isolated border towns in summer 1449 (Verneuil in July and Mantes in August) being followed by outright invasion in September. In October Charles himself marched into Normandy to lead the siege of Rouen.[69] The French were clearly the aggressors, and were joined by local Norman garrison-commanders who changed sides (probably by prior arrangement);[70] but the English had staged an unwise provocation by the seizure of Fougères on the Breton border by a mercenary captain, François de Surienne, in March 1449. This was apparently arranged by Suffolk, who had hired de Surienne and paid him off with the Order of the Garter and a Norman castle, as a means of blackmailing Duke François of Brittany into releasing his arrested Anglophile brother, Gilles, King Henry's old friend – or so de Surienne later claimed.[71] Doubtless Charles would have used any English 'provocation' as an excuse, but Suffolk was insufficiently alert to the risk. His use of de Surienne for a minor success that would give Charles an excuse to retaliate indicates 'short-termism' and an inability to assess the likely consequences.

The corruption, incompetence, and favouritism of Henry's ministers paralysed England with revolt. But even before the revolt broke out the ominous warning sent by the attack on Maine had failed to stimulate much-needed investment in Normandy's defences. The fact that unpaid local Norman captains were living off the land and alienating the local population was not remedied,[72] though this would only encourage the locals to defect to Charles VII at the first opportunity. The February 1449 Parliament ignored testimony by Abbot Reginald Boulers of Gloucester, a member of Edmund Beaufort's governing council in Rouen, that the estates of Normandy could or would not raise any money for new soldiers, meaning that England must supply them, and that the French commanders on the Norman border were consistently and contemptuously violating the truce there. (The estates had refused a government request to raise 100,000 livres in taxes in spring 1447, and only granted 30,000.[73]) Charles VII had issued orders for all his feudal vassals to arm and train their levies ready for a new war, which could be expected soon.[74] The assault on Verneuil in July 1449 duly opened the attack, and when Charles arrived at Rouen with his main army in October Beaufort swiftly opened negotiations. He could not hold the city due to the rebellious townsfolk rioting in favour of surrender, and had had to retreat into the castle. As his surrender (29 October) preceded any bombardment of his defences he could be accused of cowardice, and was certainly keen to save himself from being held to ransom; he and his garrison were allowed to leave.[75] The piecemeal conquest of the rest of Normandy followed – and the English could not even send ships to relieve well-defended Cherbourg on the coast. Notably, the crucial losses of autumn 1449 preceded the meeting of Parliament in London; the ignominious failings of the defence and its suppliers in government made the backlash worse and on 9 January Bishop Moleyns was lynched in a riot in Portsmouth where a relief force was mustering.[76] Apparently, he confessed to his killers that Suffolk was to blame for handing over Maine in an attempt to save himself – though in any case York had already been clashing with the two of them over their alleged guilt in this issue before he left for Ireland in summer 1449.[77]

The King had refused to allow Parliament to continue sitting in July 1449 as it was demanding that he 'resume' all his grants of land made since his majority before it would grant him any money for Normandy.[78] This indicates irritation and distrust among the local county political elites over his unwise prodigality, especially in Suffolk's favour, and – in desperation? – attempted blackmail of their sovereign. Without this clash and Henry's refusal to give in, would he have had the money to equip a proper rescue-force in late summer or autumn 1449 and save Rouen? (War-weariness makes it likely that the expedition would have been small.) As it was, now – like Charles I in 1640 – he had to call a new Parliament in unpropitious circumstances in winter 1449–50, with his armies humiliated and his chief minister likely to be made the scapegoat. Suffolk's arrest and impeachment in January–February 1450 followed, apparently by virtually unanimous demand among the angry Commons, though one claim has been made that his eclipsed court rival Lord Cromwell put them up to it.[79] The accusations centred on 'his' foreign policy, which was in effect indicting the King whose naïve wishes over Maine he had been carrying out, and he was accused of conspiring with the French envoys in 1447 to arrange an invasion and of intending his son John (betrothed to the late Marquis of Somerset's daughter Margaret Beaufort) to be the next King of England.[80] Paranoia and distortion apart, the more logical and provable charges of abuse of office and amassing lands and offices were tantamount to accusing the unwise King who had granted them. He was able to point out that other councillors had known as much of secret talks with the French and that the handover of Maine had been carried out by Moleyns, not him. In March Henry absolved him of the greater charges, without risking a trial, but banished him for the lesser ones.[81] His flight abroad before he could be rearrested, and arrest off the Kent coast and execution by a shipload of vigilantes, followed.[82] There was no royal leadership for the paralysed and faction-ridden government in London or aid to the last garrisons on the Norman coast, but given past actions Henry was incapable of decisive action anyway.

Harfleur, which had a garrison of 1,200 plus some 400 more refugee soldiers from elsewhere,[83] surrendered at the New Year. It should have held out for longer if English shipping had been sent to supply it. Sir Thomas Kyriell, sent with a small force from England to reinforce Beaufort at Caen, only arrived – at Cherbourg – in March 1450. He was unlikely to have stopped the momentum of conquest had he arrived earlier (which the chaos in Portsmouth and Moleyns' lynching partly prevented) and gone directly to join Somerset at Caen from a landing place nearby, but made matters worse by his surprise choice of landing place. As might have been expected, he was ambushed en route to Caen and defeated at Formigny (15 April) – though he apparently had a larger force than the attackers and managed to hold them back until Arthur of Richemont arrived with Breton reinforcements.[84] After that, the loss of the remaining towns was inevitable and on 1 July Somerset surrendered Caen. All that could have been saved was Cherbourg, which the English had held against a hostile Normandy in the 1370s but was now vulnerable to cannons – if adequate reinforcements had been sent, which did not occur. Isolated Bordeaux fell too, was reconquered by Talbot (now Earl of Shrewsbury) with a final effort, and was conquered a second time. The English 'empire' in France was lost after nearly four centuries.

Somerset's inaction at Caen in early 1450 can be particularly criticized, given that he made no effort to link up with Kyriell before Formigny and seems to have sat waiting for an inevitable attack. He gave the impression of sitting on a sandcastle in an incoming tide, knowing he had no chance but unwilling to take any action to save himself. Around 4,000 English troops at most were to be evacuated from the surrendered towns and castles in coastal Normandy,[85] and if about half of these had linked up with Kyriell's force (c. 2500?) they could have won at Formigny. Even so, it was a closer battle than the 'narrative' of inevitable English collapse has it, with the English ensconced behind a palisade of stakes holding back wave after wave of French attackers, and the decisive event was Richemont's arrival to outflank them as the defence was becoming exhausted. But given Charles VII's greater numbers, cannon, and determination, in the long run the best they could have hoped for was to save Cherbourg and keep it as a Norman equivalent of Calais. It was the distraction of the English political elite and the potentially fund-raising Parliament with the indictment of Suffolk in winter 1449–50 that prevented any useful expedition to France – the blame for which lay with the King's incompetence and favouritism. If Henry had sacrificed Suffolk to Parliament in summer 1449 in return for a grant of money, he could have had a larger expedition ready to defend the Norman coastal towns that winter – but this would still not have prevented the fall of Rouen and the hinterland. Given Charles' determination and Henry's bankruptcy, Normandy was lost by 1448.

Long-term effects of Henry V's early death: a note on the Tudors
One significant result of Henry V living into the 1430s would only have been felt in the long term. As a result of his death, his widow, Queen Catherine, was able to conduct a liaison with her attendant Owen Tudor (related to two of the leaders of the Glyndwr revolt, and descended from Llywelyn 'Fawr' of Gwynedd's steward Ednyfed and the royal house of Dyfed). As far as English noble conceptions of royal blood went, Owen was far below his mistress in status and the idea of a marriage with him demeaning to her. The liaison was evidently discreet as its timing and the dates of the birth of their four (?) children are unclear. Their secret marriage probably occurred once Henry VI received a separate household around 1428 and her affairs were not so closely involved with her son's; the Parliamentary statute of 1428 against unlicensed marriage to a queen dowager was presumably due to rumours of the relationship.[86] Owen was imprisoned in Newgate when the marriage was revealed and escaped back to Wales; the Queen's 'retirement' to the royal apartments at Bermondsey Abbey may or may not have been under coercion to keep her separate from him, illness being an alternative possibility. (She died in January 1437 aged 35/6.[87])

Had her first husband, the King, still been alive the relationship would have been unlikely, given that her French royal blood and Valois court connections would have made her a crucial asset to Henry in his years holding court in France and her presence with him there would have been more essential than it was in 1421 (when she stayed in England to give birth to her first son). Had her second son by Henry been intended to inherit France – a possible resolution to Parliamentary complaints in the 1420s at England being bled dry by taxes to pay for a union with France – the boy would probably have been brought up in Paris as a focus for Valois loyalty, with or without his mother in attendance. It is possible that Henry's long absence on campaigns would have enabled the Queen to become involved romantically with Owen, if she had showed no more political sense than her promiscuous mother, Isabelle of Bavaria, did in the 1400s (when her louche court was notorious and she was widely presumed to be her brother-in-law Orléans' mistress). Henry could not divorce her for adultery, given that his claim to France through the Troyes settlement partly rested on her. But the secret birth of children to a reigning queen would have been impossible, and if a relationship between the Queen and her 'squire' had proceeded so far it would have been after Henry's death. There would have been no time for the birth of more than one child had Henry died in 1435 and Catherine in January 1437.

Without the birth of Edmund Tudor, Henry VI's half-brother, he would not have been available to marry the Beaufort heiress Margaret (daughter of John, d. 1444, the older brother of the Duke of Somerset killed in 1455). Edmund was made Earl of Richmond by his half-brother and used as a royal deputy in South Wales in the mid-1450s, along with his brother Jasper (Earl of Pembroke). Controlling Aberystwyth and Carmarthen for the King, he was captured by his local political rivals – York's partisan Sir Walter Devereux and his son-in-law Sir William Herbert, later to be Edward IV's principal Welsh supporter – in a private war in summer 1456. He died in prison before his posthumous son Henry (VII) was born on 28 January 1457, though Jasper survived to lead the South Wales 'Lancastrians' against the Yorkists at Mortimer's Cross in 1461 and held out against the victor Edward IV at Harlech for years.

Had Edmund, and thus Henry VII, never been born the Lancastrian claim would have passed on Henry VI's death (21 May 1471) to whomever Margaret Beaufort had married instead of Edmund. Her real-life second husband was Henry Stafford, a relative of the Dukes of Buckingham (1450s Lancastrian magnates, descended from Edward III's youngest son Thomas), and her third was Thomas Stanley, principal magnate in Lancashire and later Richard III's betrayer at Bosworth. Given that she gave birth to Henry VII at the age of thirteen, it is possible that her subsequent lack of children by her later marriages was due to forcing her to procreate too early in a political eagerness for Beaufort/Tudor heirs. A later marriage could have enabled Margaret to have more than one child, possibly by Henry Stafford (a younger son so the children would not have affected the prior claims to the Buckingham title of his older brother's family).

Henry V had been accused of wild living as Prince of Wales, at least in the year-and-a-quarter of political frustration after his father's partial recovery ended his direction of government in December 1411. The stories about debauchery with his social inferiors at taverns in Eastcheap that inspired the Shakespeare version of 'Prince Hal' and Falstaff cannot be verified, although his alleged 'contempt of court' in striking Justice Gascoigne and other incidents (such as trying on the crown when he thought his father was dead) may be true.[88] But although he remained unmarried until the age of 32 or 33 no mistress or bastard child was ever named, unlike with other vigorous (some married) and equally religious kings like Edward I. It is thus difficult to say if it was conceivable that the King could have taken a mistress during years of campaigning away from Catherine in France and provided alternative Lancastrian 'heirs of the half-blood' to the Tudor brothers in the late 1420s or early 1430s. But any such boys would have had as much potential to assist Henry VI in the 1450s as Edmund and Jasper did, and unlike them had a blood claim on the English throne – technically debarred by illegitimacy, like the Beaufort offspring of John of Gaunt and Katherine Swynford who had been born in his previous wife's lifetime. Had one of these boys been married off to Margaret Beaufort and served as Henry VI's choice as lieutenant of South Wales in the mid-1450s, they and any sons would have been in a stronger position than the Tudors (who were only descended from Queen Catherine and the Valois dynasty in the female line). Indeed, as Henry V had campaigned in Wales against Owain Glyndwr for years in the 1400s and then had Welsh feudatories from his principality in his army in France it is not impossible that he could have had a Welsh mistress, thus providing his illegitimate son(s) with kinsfolk back home to assist their role governing for Henry VI there in the 1450s.

Notes

Chapter One

1. Ian Mortimer, *The Greatest Traitor: the Life of Roger Mortimer, Ruler of England 1327–30* (Pimlico 2000), pp. 185–95, 197–9, 244–52, 256–63; Mortimer, 'The death of Edward II in Berkeley Castle', in *English Historical Review*, cxx (2005) pp. 1175–1214; Mortimer, *The Perfect King: the Life of Edward III, Father of the English Nation* (Pimlico 2006) pp. 64–5, 82, 152–3, 405–18; Paul Doherty, *Isabella and the Strange Death of Edward II* (London 2003).
2. Mary McKisack, *The Fourteenth Century: 1307–1399* (Oxford 1959) p.112.
3. Mortimer, *The Perfect King*, pp. 134–6.
4. Ibid, p. 127.
5. Ibid, pp. 140–1.
6. Ibid, pp. 134–5; *The Poems of Laurence Minot, 1313–52*, ed. T B James and J Simon (Exeter 1989), pp. 69–82; B J Whiting, 'The Vow of the Heron', *Speculum* xx (1945) pp. 261–78.
7. Mortimer, *The Perfect King*, p. 151; Adam Murrimuth, *Chronicon Chronicorum*, E M Thompson (ed.) (1889) pp. 84–5.
8. Mortimer, *The Perfect King*, pp. 164–5, 167–8.
9. See W M Ormerod, *Edward III* (Yale UP 2011) pp. 195–6, 212–14 for discussion. The issue of the 'Salic Law' as the reason for Edward's losing out to Philip VI was only formally cited later in the century; see C Taylor 'The Salic Law and the Valois Succession to the French Throne' in *French History* vol xv (2001) pp. 358–77.
10. Ibid, pp. 166–7; W M Ormerod, 'A Problem of Precedents: Edward III, the Double Monarchy and the Royal Style' in J S Bothwell (ed.), *The Age of Edward IIII* (Boydell 2001) pp. 133–54.
11. Randall Nicholson, *Edward III and the Scots: the Formative Years of a Military Career, 1327–1335* (Oxford 1965).
12. Mortimer, *The Perfect King*, pp. 243-4; H G Hewitt, *The Organization of War under Edward III* (Manchester 1966).
13. Finance: Edwin Hunt, 'A New Look at the dealings of the Bardi and Peruzzi with Edward III', *Journal of Economic History*, vol l, pt 1 (1990), pp. 149–62. Size of English army in the 1346 campaign: Sir James Ramsay, 'The Strength of English Armies in the Middle Ages', *EHR*, ccix (1914), pp. 221–7; Alfred Burne, *The Crécy War: A Military History of the Hundred Years' War from 1346 to the Peace of Bretigny 1360* (London 1955). Battle of Crécy : F Dragomanni (ed.), *Chronica de Giovanni Villani* (Florence 1845) vol iv, pp. 110–11; *Chronicon Galfridi Le Baker de Swynbroke*, E M Thompson

(ed.) (Oxford 1889) pp. 83–4; Gilles Le Musset, *Chronique et Annales*, H Le Maistre (ed.) (Paris 1906) p. 162; J A Buchan, *Collection des Chroniques Nationales Françaises: chronique de Froissart* (Paris 1826) vol xiv p. 90; Jules Viard, 'la campaigne de juillet – aout 1346 et las bataille de Crécy ', *Le Moyen Age*, series 2, vol xxviii (1926) pp. 1–84; Burne, *The Crécy War*, pp. 193–203.

14. Dragomanni, Le Baker, Le Musset: ibid.

15. Jean Le Bel, *Chronique*, J Viard and E Depree (eds) (Paris 1904–5) vol ii p. 167; Dragomanni, iv, p. 146; Mortimer, *The Perfect King*, pp. 246–53; Jules Viard, 'La siege de Calais' in *Le Moyen Age*, series ii, vol xxx (1929) pp. 128–89; Jean le Patourel, 'L'occupation Anglaise de Calais au XIV siècle', in *Revue de Nord*, vol xxxiii (1955) pp. 228–41.

16. Mortimer, *The Perfect King*, pp. 273–4; Burne, *The Calais War*, pp. 234–43.

17. *Chronique Galfridi le Baker*, pp. 109–11; *Chronicles by Sir John Froissart*, T. Johnes (ed.) (London 1848, 2 vols) p. 199; Thomas Rymer, *Foedera* (1869) vol iii, pp. 202–3; Robert Avebury, *De Gestis Mirabilis Edwardi Tertii*, E M Thompson (ed.) (Oxford 1889) pp. 408–9, 412; Jonathan Sumption, *Trial By Fire* (London/Philadelphia 1996) pp, 66–7.

18. Kenneth Fowler (ed.), *The Hundred Years War* (London 1971) pp. 96–146.

19. Sumption, *Trial By Fire*, pp. 128–30; Kenneth Fowler, *The King's Lieutenant: Henry of Grosmont, First Duke of Lancaster, 1310–1361* (London 1961) pp. 122–6.

20. Fowler, p. 126; Mortimer, *The Perfect King*, pp. 310–12.

21. Henry Knighton, *Chronicon*, vol ii, Joseph Lumby (ed.) (London 1895) p. 107; R Delachanel, *Histoire de Charles V* (Paris 1909–31) vol ii, pp. 155–7, 160; H Moranville, 'Le Siege de Rheims 1359–0', *BEC*, vol lvi (1895) pp. 90–8.

22. Rymer, *Foedera*, vol iii, p. 126; Murrimuth (1889 edition), p. 203; Jonathan Sumption, *The Hundred Years' War: Trial By Battle* (London/Philadelphia 1990) p. 510.

23. Galfridi le Baker, pp. 204–5.

24. Richard Barber, *Edward, Prince of Wales and Aquitaine: A Biography of the Black Prince* (Boydell 1978) p. 139.

25. *Eulogium Historiarum sive Tempus*, F Scott Haydon (ed.) (London 1863), vol iii, pp. 220–1; Delachanel vol I pp. 202–3.

26. Delachanel, pp. 202–3; *Eulogium*, vol iii, pp. 220–1; Rhymer, *Foedera*, vol iii, pt 1, pp. 33–4.

27. *Eulogium*, vol iii, p. 223; C Douet d'Arcq, 'Petite Chronique Francaise de l'An 1270 a l'An 1356', in *Mélanges de la Société des Bibliophiles* (London 1867) pp. 27–8.

28. Delachanel, vol I, p. 228; H T Riley, *Memorials of London and London Life* (London 1868) p. 286.

29. Galfridi le Baker, pp. 146–53; Chandos Herald (Le Chartier), *Life of the Black Prince*, Mildred Pope and Eleanor Lodge (eds) (Oxford 1910) vol ii, pp. 1103 ff; Delachanel, vol I, pp. 237–8 and 242–3; C. Douet de l'Arcq p. 28; V H Galbraith, 'The Battle of Poitiers', *EHR* (1938) pp. 473–5.

30. Delachanel, vol ii, pp. 59–68; Jonathan Sumption, *The Hundred Years War vol ii: Trial by Fire*, pp. 290–1.

31. Delachanel, vol ii, pp. 47–67; *Chronica de Joannis de Reading et Anonymi Cantuarensis 1346–67*, J. Tait (ed.) (Manchester 1914) pp. 207–8; Knighton, vol ii, pp. 94–5.

32. Delachanel, ibid.

33. Delachanel, vol i, pp. 251–2; Delachanel, vol ii, p. 157; Knighton, vol ii, pp. 107–8; Moranville, 'Le Siege de Rheims', pp. 94–7.

34. Delachanel, vol I, pp. 254, 257; Sir Thomas Gray, *Scalachronica*, Sir Herbert Maxwell (ed.) (Glasgow 1907) pp. 153, 156; Knighton, ii, pp. 107–8; Rymer, vol iii, p. 473; *Chronicle of Jean le Venette*, tr. Jean Birdsall, R Newball (ed.) (New York 1953) pp. 98–101; Jean le Patourel, 'The Treaty of Bretigny 1360' in *Trans. Royal Historical Society*, series 5, vol x (1960) pp. 19–39 especially pp. 31–3.

35. Kenneth Fowler, *The Hundred Years War* p. 209.

36. Delachanel, vol ii, pp. 155, 160; Knighton, ii, p. 107.

37. Delachanel, vol iii, pp. 428–9 n. and vol iv, pp. 153–6; Gabriel Loisette, '*Armand Amanieu, Sieur d' Albret et ses rapports avec la monarchie française pendent la régime de Charles V*' in *Melanges Histoire Offerts à Charles Bemont* (Paris 1933).

38. Barber, *Edward Prince of Wales and Aquitaine*, p. 242.

39. Delachanel, vol iv, p. 23; Thomas Walsingham, *Chronicon Angliae ab anno domini 1328 usque ad 1388*, E M Thompson (ed.) (1874) pp. 88–9. For tributes to the Prince at his death, see: Walsingham, p. 91; Knighton p.124; *The Sermons of Thomas Brinton, Bishop of Rochester 1373–1389*, Mary Aquinas Devlin (ed.), vol ii, Camden Series, vol lxxxv (London 1954) pp. 355–6.

40. Barber, pp. 213–14.

41. J R Maddicott, *Simon de Montfort* (Cambridge UP 1994) pp. 106–24.

42. Delachanel, vol iv, pp. 281–6; Chandos Herald, *Life of the Black Prince*, p. 404–9; Walsingham, p. 67; Alfred Leroux, '*Le sac de la cité de Limoges et son relèvement, 1370 – 1464*' in *Bulletin de la Société Archaeologique et Historique de Limousin*, vol lvi, pp. 155–233 especially pp. 167–73 and 175–95.

43. Walsingham, pp. 68–93; Anonimalle, *The Anonimalle Chronicle 1338–1381*, V H Galbraith (ed.) (Manchester 1927) pp. 79–95.

44. See *The Peasants' Revolt*, R B Dobson (ed.) (London 1983) pp. 183–4.

45. Walsingham, pp. 118–21; *Anonimalle Chronicle*, pp. 103–4; Anthony Goodman, *John of Gaunt* (Longmans 1992) pp. 54–9.

46. Barber, pp. 232–3; G Holmes, *The Good Parliament 1376* (OUP 1975) pp. 51–2; for French opinion see E Perroy, *L'Angleterre et la Grande Schisme* (Paris 1933) p. 60.

47. J Sherborne, 'The Cost of English Warfare with France in the Later Fourteenth Century', *Bulletin of the Institute of Historical Research*, vol I (1977) pp. 66–9.

48. Walsingham, p. 200.

49. Walsingham, pp. 118–21; *Anonimalle Chronicle*, pp. 103–4; Anthony Goodman, *John of Gaunt* (Longmans 1992) pp. 54–9.

50. *Calendar of Patent Rolls*, vol iii, p. 258; *The Perfect King*, p. 365.

51. Foedera, vol ii, p. 497.

52. Michael Bennett, 'Edward III's Entail and the Succession to the Crown, 1376 – 1471', in *EHR*, vol xiii (1998) pp. 580-609 especially p. 591.

53. Nigel Saul, *The Three Richards* (London 2005) pp. 153-6 discusses this; it is disputed if an explicit public recognition was made.

54. Barber, pp. 208–9.

55. Ibid, pp. 209, 213.

56. Quoted in Barber p. 250 – and the theory that Froissart believed the Prince's character deteriorated in the 1360s.

57. P E Russell, 'The English Intervention in Spain and Portugal in the Time of Edward III and Richard II' (London 1955) pp. 64–9; Barber pp. 89–90.

58. J Moisset, *Le Prince Noir en Aquitaine* (Paris 1894) pp. 103–4; Rymer, vol iii, pp. 809–11; Jules Delpit, *Collection Générale des Documents Françaises qui se trouvent en Angleterre* (Paris 1847) pp. 175–6.

59. Delpit, pp. 173–5.
60. P E Russell, pp. 109–14; Barber, pp. 204–5.
61. Barber, pp. 166–8.
62. Loirette, pp. 31–7; Moissant, p. 211.
63. Walsingham, pp. 192–3.
64. James Sherborne, 'The Battle of La Rochelle and the War at Sea, 1372–5' in *BIHR*, vol xlii (1969) pp. 22–5.
65. *Calendar of Patent Rolls 1385–9*, entry for 20 October 1385.
66. Walsingham, p. 74.
67. Barber, pp. 232–3.
68. Sherborne, pp. 66–9; Nigel Saul, *Richard II* (Yale UP 1997) pp. 54–5.
69. *Rotuli Parliamentorum* (6 vols, 1767–77), vol iii, pp. 88–90; Saul, p. 54.
70. R B Dobson (ed.), *The Peasants' Revolt of 1381* (London 1983) pp. 163–6, 177, 185–6, 194–7, 204. On the necessity of a conciliatory approach by the regime, see B Wilkinson, 'The Peasants' Revolt of 1381' in *Speculum*, xv (1940) pp. 20–4.
71. N Housley, 'The Bishop of Norwich's Crusade, May 1383' in *History Today*, vol xxxiii (1983), pp. 15–20; Saul, pp. 103–5.
72. Mortimer, *The Perfect King*, p. 353.

Chapter Two

1. *Chronicle of Adam of Usk*, E M Thompson (ed.) (London 1904) p. 190; *Kirkstall Abbey Chronicles*, J. Taylor (ed.), Thoresby Society, vol xii (1952) p. 83; *Chronicles of the Revolution 1397–1400*, C Given-Wilson (ed.) (Manchester 1993) p. 242; *The Complete Works of John Gower*, G Macaulay (ed.) (Oxford 1902) vol iv, pp. 362–4; *Three Prose Versions of the Secrtea Secretorum*, R Steele (ed.), E.E.T.S. extra series, vol lxxiv (1898) pp. 136–7.
2. Nigel Saul, *Richard II*, p. 380; *Knighton's Chronicle 1327–1396*, G. Martin (ed.) (Oxford 1995) pp. 424–6; Walsingham, vol ii (1863–4 Rolls Series edition, ed. H T Riley), p. 172.
3. J L Gillespie, 'Thomas Mortimer and Thomas Molineux: Radcot Bridge and the Appeal of 1397', *Albion*, vol vii (1975) pp. 61–73.
4. *Chronicles of the Revolution*, pp. 14–15, 79–83, 211–12, 219–23; Sir John Froissart, *Chronicles*, T. Johnes (ed.), vol ii, p. 665. On the murder of Gloucester: A E Stamp, 'Richard II and the Murder of the Duke of Gloucester, *EHR*, vol xxxvii (1923) pp. 249–51, J Tait 'Did Richard II Murder the Duke of Gloucester?' in *Historical Essays by Members of the Owens College, Manchester*, J Tout and J Tait (eds) (Manchester 1902) pp. 193–216.
5. K B McFarlane, *Lancastrian Kings and Lollard Knights* (Oxford 1972), pp. 44–6; Saul, *Richard II*, pp. 395–7; C Given-Wilson, 'Richard II, Edward II and the Lancastrian Inheritance', *EHR* vol cix (1994).
6. Froissart, vol ii, pp. 685–8; *Rotuli Parlianmentarum*, vol iii, p. 353.
7. On 1326 numbers: Ian Mortimer, *The Greatest Traitor*, pp. 149, 163; on 1399 numbers, *Chronicles of the Revolution*, p. 126.
8. *Chronicles of the Revolution*, pp. 116 ff.
9. Saul, pp. 397, 419; Ian Mortimer, *The Fears of Henry IV: the Life of England's Self-Made King* (Vintage 2008), p. 185.
10. *The St Albans Chronicle: the Chronica Majora of Thomas Walsingham 1376–94*, J Taylor, Wendy Childs, and Leslie Watkiss (eds) (Oxford 2003) pp. 39–41; the fact that in 1376 Gaunt petitioned Parliament to make inheritance of the Crown via a female illegal in England implies that it could be considered legal then.

11. BL Harleian Mss. 3600.
12. *Chronicles of the Revolution*, pp. 192–7, for differing versions.
13. Saul, p. 396.
14. A Tuck, *Richard II and the Nobility* (London 1973) p. 214.
15. *Historie of the Arrivall of King Edward IV*, J. Bruce (ed.), (Camden Society 1838) pp. 3–6.
16. *Rotuli Parliamentarum*, vol iii, p. 372.
17. Ibid, p. 355.
18. Saul, pp. 384–6; see also *Chronicles of the Revolution*, p. 68, on Richard's grandeur.
19. Saul, pp. 385–7; English Historical Documents, A N Myres (ed.) (1969) pp. 374–5.
20. *Chronicles of the Revolution*, pp. 58–9.
21. Saul, pp. 389–90.
22. National Archives: DL 28/1/6, f. 22v.
23. C Given-Wilson, 'Richard II, Edward II and the Lancastrian Inheritance', p. 563; *Chronicles of London*, H. Kingsford (ed.) (Oxford 1905) p. 54. For Bagot's central role, see Saul, pp. 395–6 and 398.
24. Mortimer, Fears of Henry IV, pp. 103–4.
25. Gerald of Wales, *De Principe Instructione, in Workd*, J. Brewer, J. Dimmock, and F. Warner (eds) (London 1861–91) p. 301.
26. John of Salisbury to Bishop Bartholomew of Exeter, in John's *Materials for the History of Thomas a Becket: Epistolae*, vol v, J C Robertson (ed.), p. 381.
27. *Nicholae Triveti Annales*, T Hog (ed.) (London 1845) pp. 281–3 and 300; National Archives: C 47/4/5, f. 47v; BL Additional Mss. 7965, ff, 15v, 18.
28. *Chronicle Anonimalle*, p. 364; *The Westminster Chronicle 1381–94*, L C Hector and B F Harvey (ed.) (Clarendon Press 1982), pp. 112–15.
29. Saul, pp. 175–6 and 183–4.
30. *The Westminster Chronicle*, pp. 112–14.
31. *Rotlui Parliamentarum*, vol iii, pp. 379–80; Adam of Usk p. 161.
32. H T Riley (ed.) *Johannis de Trokelowe et Henrici de Blaneford, chronici et annales*, vol 28 (Rolls Series 1861), p. 219.
33. M Clarke and V Galbraith, 'The deposition of Richard II' in *Bulletin of the John Rylands Library*, vol xiv (1930) pp. 170, 172.
34. *Chronicles of the Revolution*, pp. 128, 133–4.
35. On 1330: C Crump, 'The arrest of Roger Mortimer and Queen Isabel' in *EHR*, vol xxvi (1911) pp. 331–2. Naval battle off Winchelsea, 1350: Galfridi le Baker, p. 111; Froissart, vol I, p. 99. Infiltration of Calais 1350: *The Perfect King*, pp. 272–3.
36. Ibid, p. 199.
37. M McKisack, *The Fourteenth Century*, pp. 231–3.
38. A Tuck, 'Anglo-Irish Relations 1382–93', *Proceedings of the Royal Irish Academy*, vol lxix (1970) p. 28.
39. Saul, p. 274.
40. *Anglo-Norman Letters and Petitions*, M D Legge (ed.) (Anglo-Norman Text Society 1941), no. 3.
41. *Historiae Vitae et Regni Ricardi Secundi*, G B Stow (ed.), (Philadelphia 1977) p. 134.
42. E Curtis, *Richard II in Ireland 1394–5 and the Submission of the Irish Chiefs* (Oxford 1927) pp. 80–5.
43. D B Johnston, 'Richard II and the Submission of Gaelic Ireland', *Irish Historical Studies*, vol xii (1980) pp. 6–7.

44. Saul, pp. 386–7.
45. Ibid, p. 288.
46. A J Otway-Ruthven, *Medieval Ireland* (London 1968) pp. 335–6.
47. Saul, p. 407.
48. *Chronicles of the Revolution*, p. 106.
49. Froissart, vol ii, pp. 365–8.
50. *Chronicles of the Revolution*, pp. 110–11.
51. Ibid, pp. 40, 192–7.
52. Ibid; Michael Bennett, *Richard II and the Revolution of 1399* (Sutton 1999) p. 192; James Sherborne, 'Perjury and the Lancastrian Revolution of 1399', *Welsh History Review*, vol xiv (1988).
53. Adam of Usk, pp. 182–4; Mortimer, *Fears of Henry IV*, pp. 183–4. For the legal position, i.e. Edmund Mortimer was legitimate heir under canon law, see G E Caspary, 'The deposition of Richard II and the Canon Law' in *Proceedings of the Second International Congress of Medieval Law*, (Boston 1965) pp. 189–201. See also C Given-Wilson, 'The Manner of Richard II's Renunciation: a Lancastrian "Narrative"?' in *EHR* vol cviii (1993) pp. 65–70.
54. *Chronicles of the Revolution*, pp. 187, 190–1; see also G Sayles 'The deposition of Richard II: Three Lancastrian Narratives' in *BIHR*, vol liv (1981) pp. 257–70.
55. Adam of Usk, p. 177; *Chronicles of the Revolution*, pp. 135–7.
56. *The Complete Works of John Gower*, Macaulay (ed.) (Oxford 1902), pp. 362–4; Saul, pp. 388–9. C B Stowe, 'Richard II in Walsingham's Chronicles' in *Speculum*, vol lix (1984) p. 83.
57. *Calendar of Patent Rolls 1396–9*, pp. 200–10, 213–16, 224, 280–1; analysis in Saul, pp. 382–3.
58. *The History of Parliament: the House of Commons 1386–1421*, J Roskell, I Clark, C Rawcliffe (eds), appendix C3 (HMSO 1992); Rymer, *Foedera*, vol viii, p. 14; Adam of Usk p. 154 on the use of Cheshire archers for intimidation.
59. See Saul, pp. 366–7, 380.
60. See also Saul, pp. 340–3; Mortimer, p. 195.
61. T A Sandquist, 'The Holy Oil of St Thomas of Canterbury' in *Essays in Medieval History Presented to Bertie Wilkinson*, T Sandquist and M Powicke (eds), (University of Toronto Press 1969) pp. 330–44. On Henry IV's use of the oil: *Chronicles of the Revolution*, p. 201.
62. M V Clarke, 'The Wilton Diptych' in *Fourteenth Century Studies*, (Oxford Clarendon Press, 1937)pp. 272–92; J H Harvey, 'The Wilton Diptych: a Re-Examination' in *Archaeologia*, vol xcviii (1961) p. 19; D Gorden, *The Court of Richard II and the Artistic World of the Wilton Diptych* (London 1996).
63. *Chronicles of the Revolution*, p. 122.
64. Ibid, pp. 122, 154.
65. Ibid, pp. 106, 121–2, 131–2, 139–40, 154, 222.
66. Ibid, pp. 146–51. On Richard's death: Froissart, vol ii, p. 178 (regarded it as mystery), *Eulogium*, vol iii, p. 387; *Historiae Vitae et Regni Ricardi Secundi*, in *Chronicles of the Revolution*, p. 241 (either hunger-strike or deliberate starvation); Brut, vol ii, p. 360 (deliberate starvation); French observer Jean Creton (hunger-strike supposed) in *Chronicles of the Revolution*, p. 344. Also J H Wylie, *The History of England under Henry IV*, 4 vols (1884) vol I, p. 229; *Gower's Triperita: the Major Works of John Gower*, G Stockton (ed.) (Seattle 1962) pp. 324–5.

67. *Chronicles of the Revolution*, pp. 144–5 and 155.
68. Ibid, pp. 146–51, 155, 159.
69. Quoted in Saul, p. 415.

Chapter Three
1. The potential backers of any genuine 'Richard', France, did not take the Welsh stories seriously. They only bothered to check out the main Scottish contender, the 'Mammet', in 1402.
2. E Owen, ' Owain Lawgoch – Yeuain de Galles – Some Facts and Suggestions' in *Transactions of the Cymmrodorion Society* (1899–1900) pp. 6–105.
3. Adam of Usk, p. 72.
4. R R Davies, *The Revolt of Owain Glyndwr* (Oxford 1995) pp. 167–9.
5. R R Davies, *Wales 1063–1415: Conquest, Co-Existence and Change* (OUP 1987) p. 442.
6. Ibid, pp. 450–1.
7. Adam of Usk, pp. 161 ff; Mortimer, *Fears of Henry IV*, pp. 252–3.
8. Davies, *Revolt of Owain Glyndwr*, pp. 107 ff.
9. Trans. by Sir James Ferguson, (Edinburgh 1970).
10. *The Brut*, F de Brie (ed.) (2 vols, Oxford 1906–8) vol ii, p. 360; *The Fears of Henry IV*, pp. 206–7.
11. Ibid.
12. Ibid, pp. 249–51; for the prophecy, see Brut, vol I, pp. 75–6.
13. J D Griffiths Davies (ed.), *An English Chronicle of the Reigns of Richard II, Henry IV, Henry V and Henry VI*, Camden Society, Old Series, vol lxiv (1856) pp. 24–9; Walsingham p. 341.
14. *Historiae Vitae et Regni Ricardi Secundi*, p. 159; *Chronicles of the Revolution*, p. 155; H Wright, 'The Protestation of Richard II in the Tower in September 1399' in *BJRL*, vol xxiii (1943) pp. 151–66. On Edward II's abdication: C Valente, 'Deposition and Abdication of Edward II' in *EHR*, vol cxiii (1998) pp. 880–1 and *Calendar of Close Rolls 1327–30*, p.1.
15. W Bower, *Scotichronicon*, M. Watt (ed.) (Aberdeen 1987),vol viii, p. 65.
16. Ibid, pp. 41 and 65.
17. A Boardman, *Hotspur: Henry Percy, Medieval Rebel* (Sutton 2003) p. 149; *Calendar of the Patent Rolls 1401–5*, p. 213; *The Brut*, vol ii, p. 548; National Archives: CHES 2/74, m 7; Alexander Rose, *Kings in the North: the House of Percy in British History* (Phoenix 2005) pp. 425–6; *Fears of Henry IV*, p. 264.
18. Rose, ibid; *Proceedings and Ordinances of the Privy Council of England*, Sir Harris Nicholas (ed.) (London 1834–7) pp. 203–5; *Fears of Henry IV*, pp. 266–7.
19. R R Davies, *Wales 1063–1415: Conquest, Co-Existence and Change*, p. 446.
20. *English Historical Documents 1327–1485*, ed. A N Myres vol iv (1969), p 201.
21. *Eulogium*, p. 387; *Historiae Vitae et Regni Ricardi Secundi*, p. 166.
22. *Westminster Chronicle*, p. 450 (Richard did take part in tournament in 1390); Froissart, vol ii p. 477 (ambiguous) and Saul, p. 353 (analysis).
23. J Capgrave, *The Chronicle of England* (London 1858) p. 282; M Clarke and V Galbraith, 'The Deposition of Richard II', *BJRL*, vol xiv (1930) p. 178; *Fears of Henry IV*, pp. 266–7 and 378–9.
24. Capgrave, p. 282; *Walsingham*, Riley (ed.), vol ii, p. 257; Wauvrin account in Sir William and Edward Hardy (eds), *A Collection of the Chronicles of Ancient History... by John de Wauvrin, Lord of Forestal 1399 – 1422* (1887) p. 61. See also *Fears of Henry IV*, p. 268.

25. *Eulogium*, vol iii, p. 397; Adam of Usk, p. 171; Walsingham, p. 367; Wauvrin, Hardy (ed.), pp. 61-2.
26. Walsingham, vol ii, p. 258; Christopher Allemand, *Henry V* (Yale UP 1992) p. 53.
27. *Fears of Henry IV*, pp. 327–8, 343.
28. Philip Morgan, 'Henry IV and the Shadow of Richard II' in R E Archer (ed.), *Crown, Government and People in the Fifteenth Century* (Sutton 1995) p. 21.
29. Morgan, pp. 19–22; James Wylie, *History of England under Henry the Fourth*, vol i (London 1884), pp. 417–28.
30. *Eulogium*, vol iii p. 402; J A Griffiths Davies (ed.), *An English Chronicle* ... p. 30.
31. Wylie, vol ii, p. 41.
32. T M Smallwood, 'Prophecy of the Six Kings' in *Speculum*, vol lx (1985) pp. 571–92.
33. *King Henry the Fourth, Part One*: Act Three, Scene 1.
34. Wylie, pp. 246–52.
35. *Eulogium*, vol iii p. 407; Peter McNiven, *Heresy and Politics in the Reign of Henry IV: the Execution of John Badby* (Boydell 1987) pp. 123–4; *Fears of Henry IV*, pp. 295–7.
36. Ibid, pp. 300–03; Peter McNiven, 'The Problem of Henry IV's Health, 1405–13' in *EHR*, vol c (1985) pp. 747–59.
37. McNiven, p. 761.
38. See Sellars and Yeatman, *1066 And All That* (Penguin, 1967 edition), p. 254.
39. *Fears of Henry IV*, pp. 215–16.
40. Ibid, p. 289.
41. Ibid, pp. 364–5.
42. Wylie, p. 246.
43. *The Chronica Maiora of Thomas Walsingham 1376–1422*, D Prest and J. Clarke (ed.) (Boydell 2005) p. 385.
44. Gwilym Dodd, 'Conflict or Consensus? Henry IV and Parliament 1399–1406' in T Thomson (ed.), *Social Attitudes and Political Structures in the Fifteenth Century* (Sutton 2000) pp. 118–49; D Biggs 'The Politics of Health: Henry IV and the Long Parliament of 1406' in *Establishment*, pp. 185–206.
45. Biggs, ibid; Dodd, ibid; *Fears of Henry IV*, pp. 306–7.
46. M. Ormerod, 'The Rebellion of Archbishop Scrope and the tradition of clerical opposition to royal taxation' in G Dodd and D Biggs (eds), *Rebellion and Survival*, (York Medieval Press 2008) pp. 162–79.
47. Allemand, *Henry V*, pp. 43–7.
48. Ibid p. 65.
49. A N Myres, English Historical Documents vol iv p. 306; P Mc Niven, 'Prince Henry and the English political crisis of 1412' in *History*, vol lxv (1980) pp. 7 ff; *The St. Albans Chronicle*, V Galbraith (ed.) (1937), pp. 65–7.
50. McNiven p. 15; K McFarlane, *Lancastrian Kings and Lollard Knights*, p. 110.
51. Allemand, pp, 55–8; *Fears of Henry IV*, pp. 329–30, 338, 343–5.
52. Michael Prestwich, *Edward I* (Methuen 1988), pp. 126, 549.
53. Allemand, p. 48.
54. *Henry V: The Practice of Kingship*, G Harriss (ed.), (Oxford UP 1985), pp. 53 ff.
55. T B Pugh, 'The Southampton Plot of 1415' in R A Griffiths and J Sherborne (eds), *Kings and Nobles in the Later Middle Ages* (Gloucester 1986) pp. 62–89; Pugh, 'Henry V and the Southampton Plot of 1415' in *Southampton Record Series*, vol xxx (1988).
56. *Fears of Henry IV*, pp. 305–6.
57. *Chronicle of London from 1189 to 1483*, N H Nicholas and E Tyrrell (eds) (London 1827) p. 39; *The Brut*, F Brie (ed.), vol ii p. 371.

Chapter Four
1. See Anne Curry, *The Battle of Agincourt: Sources and Interpretations* (Boydell 2000); A Curry, *Agincourt: a New History* (Sutton 2000) pp. 150–200; Ian Mortimer, *1415: Henry V's Year of Glory* (Vintage 2010) pp. 427–53. *Gesta Henrici Quinti*, F Taylor and J Roskell (eds and tr.) (Oxford 1975) pp. 68–71 on the order to carry stakes.
2. *Foedera*, vol ix, p. 313.
3. Mortimer, 1415, pp. 380, 389, 565–6; Allemand, *Henry V*, p. 88.
4. *Gesta Henrici Quinti*, p. 61. On the King's strategy: Clifford Rogers, 'Henry V's Military Strategy in 1415' in A. Villalon and D. Kagy (eds), *The Hundred Years War* (London 2004) pp. 399–428.
5. Mortimer, 1415, p. 384.
6. *Foedera*, vol ix, pp. 314–15.
7. *Gesta Henrici Quinti*, p. 61.
8. *The Chronicle of Enguerr and de Monstrelet*, T. Johnes (ed.) (2 vols, 1857) vol I, p. 337. *Gesta Henrici Quinti*, pp. 65–6; Mortimer, 1415 pp. 400–02.
9. Mortimer, pp. 421–3.
10. A N Myres, 'The captivity of a royal witch: the Household accounts of Joan of Navarre 1419–21', in *BJRL*, vol x (1940) pp. 262–84; Allemand, *Henry V*, p. 397.
11. On the prisoners: Mary Ambuhl, 'A Fair Share of the Profit? The ransoms at Agincourt 1415' in *Nottingham Medieval; Studies*, vol 1 (2006) pp. 129–50. Casualties: Curry, *Agincourt: Sources and Interpretation*, pp. 11, 53, 93, 110, 123, 134, 168, 182; Barker, *Agincourt*, pp. 324–5; Allemand, p. 96. Massacre of prisoners: Vita, p. 68; Curry, *Agincourt: Sources and Interpretation*, pp. 47, 62, 108, 125, 163; Mortimer, pp. 446–50; Jerome Taylor, 'The Battle of Agincourt: Once More into the Breach', *The Independent*, 1 November 2008.
12. Juliet Barker, *Agincourt*, pp. 272–7; Mortimer, pp. 428–31.
13. Mortimer, pp. 376–7.
14. Ibid, pp. 393, 396.
15. Gesta, p. 69; St Albans Chronicle, vol ii, pp. 100–01.
16. *Foedera*, vol iv, pt 2, pp. 171–3.
17. Caen: *The Brut*, pp. 383–4; *St Albans Chronicle*, pp. 111–12. Belleme: Allemand, p. 119. Rouen: Morosini, *Chronique*, pp. 175–81; *The Brut*, vol ii, pp. 387–424; *The historical collections of a citizen of London in the Fifteenth Century*, J. Gairdner (ed.), (Camden Society 1876), pp. 1–46. Henry's denials of callousness to citizens: *The Brut*, vol ii, p. 410: Gairdner, p. 425.
18. Allemand, pp. 116, 186–9.
19. *The Brut*, vol ii, pp. 419–22.
20. Meulan 'summit': *Monstrelet*, vol iii, pp. 321–2; B Vaughan, *John the Fearless, Duke of Burgundy* (London 1966) pp. 170–2; B L Cotton Mss. Tiberius b xii, f. 99 and Harleian Mss. 4763 ff. 130v, 151. Pouilly 'summit': Vaughan, p. 273. Pontoise: *St Albans Chronicle*, pp. 122–3; *Monstrelet*, vol iii, pp. 322–34.
21. Arguably it gave long-term military experience to the gentry too, aiding their military capability for participating in the 1450s civil wars.
22. Allemand, pp. 261–2.
23. *Monstrelet*, vol iii, pp. 338–45; Janet Shirley (ed.), *A Parisian Journal, 1405-49*, translated from the *Anonyme Journal d'un Bourgeois de Paris* (Oxford 1968) pp. 139–41.
24. Allemand p. 136.
25. Ibid, p. 137.

26. Ibid.
27. Ibid, pp. 139–40.
28. Monstrelet, vol iii, pp. 393–4; P Bonenfant, *Du Meurtre de Montereaus* (Brussels 1938) pp. 221–7; National Archives: E 30/408 and 409.
29. Rev. Joseph Stevenson, *Letters and Papers Illustrative of the Wars of the English in France During the Reign of King Henry the Sixth* (London 1864) vol ii, p. 24–8. Norman financial grants: Charles Beaurepaire, *Les Etats de Normandie sous la Domination Angloise* (Evreux 1859) pp. 19–20. French army size 1424: Stevenson, vol ii, pp. 15–20; B Chevalier 'Les Ecossais dans les Armees de Charles VII', in *Jeanne d'Arc: un Epoque, un Rayonnement: Colloque d'Histoire Medieval 1979* (Paris 1980), pp. 88–9. The modern criticism of Henry as a 'war criminal' starting unnecessary campaigns for glory or personal prestige started with the *DNB* article, in vol ix, p. 505.
30. Baugé: Juliet Barker, *Conquest: The English Kingdom of France during the Hundred Years War* (Abacus 2009) pp. 37–8. Patay: *Chronique de Charles VII, Roi de France, par Jean Chartier*, Vallet de Viriville (ed.) (Paris 1858) vol ii, pp. 192–9; *Monstrelet*, vol iv, pp. 329–33; J de Wauvrin, *Anchiennes Chroniques d'Angleterre*, Mlle Dupont (ed.) (Paris 1858) vol I, pp. 293–5. Bedford vs Duke Humphrey: Bertram Wolffe, *Henry VI* (Methuen 1981) pp. 32–3, 38–41. Recruitment of English troops: Stevenson, vol I, pp. 403–21; Anne Curry, 'English Armies in the Fifteenth Century' in Curry and M Hughes (eds), *Arms, Armies and Fortifications in the Hundred Years War* (Boydell 1994) p. 43.
31. Verneuil: *Monstrelet*, vol iv, pp. 192–6; Chartier, pp. 41–3. Brittany 1427: Roger Little, *The Parliament of Poitiers; War, Government and Finances in France 1418–36* (London 1984), pp. 187–8.
32. Montargis: Chartier, vol i, pp. 54–5. Ambrieres: ibid, pp. 55–6. Le Mans: Bourgeois, pp. 223–4. Orléans: *Monstrelet* iv, pp. 300, 301, 310–14; Stevenson, ii, pp. 76–8; Beaurepaire, p. 30. Plots to hand over towns to the French: J Barker, 'The Foe Within: Treason in Lancastrian Normandy' in P Coss and C Tyerman (eds), *Soldiers, Nobles and Gentlemen* (Oxford 2001) p. 306. Joan at Chinon: Craig Taylor, *Joan of Arc; La Pucelle: Selected Sources* (Manchester and New York 2006) pp. 73–4, 271–2, 274, 275–8; Barker, *Conquest*, pp. 103–9; Little, pp. 99–105. Jan van Heerwarden, 'The Appearance of Joan of Arc' in his *Joan of Arc: Reality and Myth* (Hilversum 1998).
33. See Mortimer, 1415, p. 155.
34. Allemand, pp. 110–11.
35. Ibid, pp. 138–40.
36. *Monstrelet*, iv, pp. 17–20.
37. Allemand, p. 136.
38. *Philippe de Commynes, Memoirs*, J Calmette and G Dunville (ed.), 3 vols (Paris 1924–5), vol ii pp. 63–7.
39. Bonenfant pp. 191–7.
40. See Nancy Goldstone, *The Maid and the Queen: the Secret History of Joan of Arc and Queen Yolande of Aragon* (Weidenfeld and Nicolson 2011) on the 'stage- managing' of Joan by the Queen and her 'war party'. The theory that Joan was Louis of Orléans' secret daughter (by Queen Isabelle?) was first put forward in 1804 but is unlikely as she would have had to be born before his murder in 1407, not her official birth-date of 1412; the Queen had another, attested male baby in late 1407.
41. Barker, *Conquest*, p. 80.
42. See E Balfour-Melville, *James I, King of Scots 1406–37* (London 1936).
43. Wolffe, *Henry VI*, pp. 28–30; *Proceedings and Ordinances of the Privy Council*, vol iii, pp. 247–8.

44. S B Chrimes, 'The Pretensions of the Duke of Gloucester in 1422', in *EHR*, vol xlv (1930); Wolffe, pp. 39–41.
45. *A London Chronicle*, N. Nicholas (ed.) (1827) p. 114; *Chronicles of London*, C L Kingsford (ed) (London 1905) pp. 76–94; *Proceedings and Ordinances of the Privy Council*, vol iii, pp. 183–4, 185–6.
46. Allemand, pp. 290–1; Mortimer, *Fears of Henry IV*, pp. 331–2.
47. Henry did send a Burgundian, Gilbert de Lannoy, to Eastern Europe to sound out aid for a crusade in 1421 – though Duke Philip was probably more interested than him in a crusade.
48. Wolffe, pp. 106–14; also pp. 121–5 and 128–31 on the King's inability to deal with local disorder.
49. BL Cotton Mss. Vespasian, A xii: 'Compilation of the Meekness and Good Life of King Henry the Sixth'. See also Wolffe pp. 8–9. For the theory that this trait was exaggerated in the later fifteenth century accounts to bolster Henry's claims to be a saint, see Wolffe pp. 6–7.
50. National Archives KB 9/262/1; KB 9/262/78 and 122/28; Wolffe, pp. 16–17. KB 9/273/103 for the 1453 slander that Henry was 'but a sheep' who had lost his father's conquests.
51. Wolffe, p. 90.
52. *Rotuli Parliamentorum*, iv, p. 127.
53. J A Giles, *Chronicon Angliae de Regni Henrici IV, Henrici V et Henrici VI* (London 1848), p. 33–4; *Gregory's Chronicle 1189–1469*, J Gairdner (ed.), (Camden Society 1876) pp. 187–8; *Three Fifteenth Century Chronicles*, J Gairdner (ed.) p. 65; *The Brut*, pp. 512–13. See also Wolffe, pp. 129–31.

Chapter Five

1. See Anne Curry, 'English Armies in the Fifteenth Century', as Ch. 4 n. 30.
2. Barker, *Conquest*, pp. 64–5; Beaurepaire, pp. 10–15; Wolffe, p. 31.
3. See Barker, p. 250 for assessment of Bedford's conciliatory record.
4. Beaurepaire, p. 30.
5. James H Ramsay, *Lancaster and York: a Century of English History (1399–1485)*, 2 vols (Oxford 1892), vol I, pp. 382–3; *Proceedings and Ordinances of the Privy Council*, vol iii, p. 322.
6. Chinon: Taylor, pp. 73–4, 144, 317–18. Relief of Orléans: ibid, pp. 279–80, 295–6, 312–13, 340–1, 343–4, 356–7. Jargeau: Kelly Devries, *Joan of Arc: a Military Leader* (Sutton 2003) p. 96–101, Taylor, pp. 306–8, Stevenson, vol ii, pp. 95–100. Battle of the Herrings: *Journal d'un Bourgeois de Paris*, A Tuetey (ed.) (Paris 1881) pp. 327–30. Patay: *Monstrelet*, vol iv, pp. 329–33, Chartier, vol I, pp. 85–7; de Wauvrin, vol I, pp. 293–5. Charles' coronation: Chartier, vol I, pp. 96–8; Taylor, p. 203. Joan's attack on Paris: Regine Pernaud, *Joan of Arc: by Herself and Her Contemporaries*, (tr.) E Hyams (New York 1982) pp. 124–8. Bishop Beaufort's expedition: Ramsay, vol I, pp. 401–4; Bourgeois, p. 238; C Williams, *My Lord of Bedford 1389–1435* (London 1963) p. 176.
7. Joan's capture: Taylor, p. 175–6; Pernaud, pp. 149–53; Monstrelet, vol iv, p. 388; De Vries, pp. 169–74. Chateau Gaillard: Barker, p. 142. Louviers: Chartier, i, pp. 114–15. Henry VI at Calais: Stevenson, ii, pp, 140–1; Anne Curry, 'The "Coronation Expedition" and Henry VI's Court in France 1430 to 1432' in Jenny Stafford (ed.), *The Lancastrian Court* (Donington 2003) pp. 30–5. Bedford's army and campaign: Bourgeois, pp. 254—67; Curry, ibid; Barker, *Conquest*, p. 144. Size of army and garrisons in 1433: Stevenson, ii, pp. 531–2, 540–6.

8. Wolffe, p. 55.
9. Louviers: Bourgeois, pp. 265–6. Henry's coronation: *The Brut*, pp. 458–61; Monstrelet, vol v, p. 1–7; Bourgeois, pp. 274–9; Jules Delpit, pp. 239–4. Lannoy's mission and the English army size: Stevenson, ii, pp. 250, 257–8.
10. Barker, *Conquest*, pp. 189, 225–6.
11. Stevenson, ii, pp. 51–64.
12. Ramsay, vol I, p. 473; G L Harriss, *Cardinal Beaufort: a Study of Lancastrian Ascendancy and Decline* (Oxford 1988) p. 250; Richard Vaughan, *Philip the Good, Duke of Burgundy* (Boydell 2002) pp. 99–101.
13. Barker, *Conquest*, p. 177.
14. Barker, *Conquest*, pp. 195, 221, 244 (Paris); p. 178 (Bedford's regency). Vicques massacre: *Monstrelet*, iv, pp. 104–5; Bourgeois pp. 290, 292: C B Rowe, 'Discipline in the Norman Garrisons under Bedford, 1422–35' in *EHR*, vol xlvi (1931) pp. 194–208.
15. Barker, *Conquest*, p. 76.
16. Barker, *Conquest*, pp. 225–8; Jocelyne Gledhill Dickinson, *The Congress of Arras 1435* (Oxford 195) pp. 174–6; (death of Anne of Burgundy) Bourgeois, p. 282; (Bedford's second marriage) *Monstrelet* pp. 55–6; (Parisians respect Bedford) Bourgeois p. 307.
17. Barker, *Conquest*, pp 213–14.
18. Harriss, pp. 232–7.
19. Barker, *Conquest*, p. 234.
20. Ibid, pp. 233–4.
21. Ibid, p. 235. Stevenson, vol ii, part 2, pp. 431–3; Stephen Cooper, *The Real Falstaff* (Pen and Sword 2010) pp. 71–2.
22. Barker, *Conquest*, pp. 247–9, 260–1.
23. Chartier, ii, pp. 7–8, 181–2; Beaurepaire, pp. 73–4.
24. Barker, pp. 266–7; Harriss, pp. 281–3.
25. Harriss, pp. 321–3.
26. Wolffe, *Henry VI*, p. 305.
27. Ibid, p. 130 n; *Giles' Chronicle*, p. 39; *The Brut*, p. 517.
28. Wolffe, pp. 164–5; Barker, pp. 305–8; Harriss, pp. 334–6.
29. Stevenson, ii, pp. 439–41; Michael Jones, 'John Beaufort, Duke of Somerset, and the French Expedition of 1443' in Ralph Griffiths (ed.), *Patronage, the Crown and the Provinces in Later Medieval England* (Glucester 1981) pp 79–102. Finances: Wolffe, p. 100.
30. Wolffe, pp. 109–15.
31. Ralph Griffiths, *The Reign of Henry VI* (Stroud 2004), pp. 447–51; C T Allemand (ed.), 'Documents Relating to the Anglo-French Negotiations of 1439' in *Camden Miscellany*, vol xxiv, 4th series, pt ix, pp. 79–141.
32. Harriss, pp. 296–304; Griffiths, ibid; *Proceedings and Ordinances of the Privy Council*, vol v, pp. 334–407.
33. Barker, *Conquest*, p. 272.
34. *Proceedings of the Privy Council*, vol v, p. 91; Harriss, pp. 308–11; Stevenson, vol ii, pp. 440–51.
35. Ramsay, ii, pp. 46–7; Harriss, pp. 308–11; Stevenson, ii, pp. 440–51.
36. Ibid, pp. 585–91; *Proceedings and Ordinances...*, vol iv, pp. 259–63. Pontoise: Chartier, ii, pp. 25–7. Evreux: Ibid, pp. 17–18; *Monstrelet*, vi, pp. 21–4.
37. Ramsay, ii, p. 42; Stevenson, I, pp. 431–2; Barker, *Conquest*, p. 299.
38. Barker, *Conquest*, pp. 301–2, 309; Wolffe, p 166; Harriss, pp. 333–4.

39. Wolffe, pp. 163–4; *Proceedings and Ordinances...*, vol iv, p. 281.

40. Ibid, pp. 259–63.

41. Barker, *Conquest*, p. 305.

42. Jones, 'John Beaufort...', p. 95.

43. Chartier, ii, pp. 37–42.

44. Wolffe, pp. 159–61.

45. Beaucourt, vol iii, p. 262.

46. Vaughan, *Philip the Good*, pp. 113–18.

47. T. Basin, *Histoire des regnes de Charles VII et Louis XI*, J Quicheret (ed.), 4 vols (Paris 1855–9) vol I, pp. 154–6; comments in Wolffe, p. 170. Charles VII's plans: Stevenson, vol I, pp. 119, 243–4.

48. Wolffe, pp. 109–15.

49. *Rotuli Parliamentarum*, vol v, pp. 147–8.

50. Barker, *Conquest*, p. 377; *The Parliament Rolls of Medieval England 1275–1504*, C Given-Wilson (ed.) (Boydell 2004) vol xii, pp. 36–7.

51. Wolffe, p. 170.

52. Stevenson, vol I, pp. 131–3, 157.

53. Beaucourt, vol iii, pp. 26–7; *Monstrelet*, vol vi, pp. 96–107; Wolffe, pp. 174–7.

54. Stevenson, vol I, pp. 164–7.

55. *Parliamentary Rolls of Medieval England...* vol xi, p. 412.

56. Stevenson, vol ii, pt 2, pp. 639–42.

57. Ibid, pp. 710–18; Barker, *Conquest*, pp. 356–8.

58. Accounts of Gloucester's confrontation with the King and Queen at Bury St Edmunds in February 1447 say that Suffolk accused him of spreading rumours that Margaret was Somerset's lover, and that Margaret told him the King knew what he deserved.

59. *Giles' Chronicle*, pp. 33–4; *Gregory's Chronicle*, pp. 187–8; *The Brut*, pp. 512–13; *Benet's Chronicle*, pp. 192–3.

60. See Stevenson, vol I, p. 116.

61. Barker, *Conquest*, pp. 360–1.

62. Stevenson, ii, pp. 479–83.

63. Ibid, pp. 704–10; Barker, *Conquest*, pp. 349–50.

64. Ibid, pp. 351–2.

65. Stevenson, vol ii p. 685.

66. *Foedera*, vol v, pt 1, p. 189.

67. Auguste Vallet de Viriville, *Historie de Charles VII, Roi de France et son Epoque* (Paris 1865) vol iii, p. 144.

68. Barker, *Conquest*, p. 359.

69. Ibid, pp. 388–90; Chartier, vol ii, pp. 94–101; A Bossuat, *Perrinet Gressart et François de Surienne* (Paris 1936) pp. 339–41.

70. Barker, *Conquest*, pp. 375 and 381.

71. Chartier, vol ii, pp. 280–2; Stevenson, ii, pp. 189–94 and 283–9; C D Taylor, 'Brittany and the French Crown: the Legacy of the English Attack on Fougeres (1449)' in J R Maddicott and D Palliser (eds), *The Medieval State: Essays Presented to James Campbell* (London 2000) pp. 245, 252–3; M H Keen and M Daniel, 'English Diplomacy and the Sack of Fougeres in 1449' in *History*, vol lix (1974), pp. 388–91.

72. Barker, *Conquest*, pp. 361–2.

73. *Parliamentary Rolls*, Given-Wilson (ed.), vol xii, pp. 54–5: Beaurepaire, pp. 93–5.

74. Barker, *Conquest*, pp. 358–9.

75. Stevenson, ii, pt 2, pp. 609–17; Chartier, ii, pp. 152–4.
76. Wolffe, p. 221.
77. B L Harleian Mss. 543, ff. 161r – 163r.
78. *Rotuli Parliamentorum*, vol v, pp. 147–8.
79. Wolffe, pp. 221–2; Stevenson, vol iim pt 2, p. 766.
80. *Parliamentary Rolls*, vol xii, pp. 92–106.
81. *Rotuli Parliamntorum*, vol v, pp. 182–3.
82. Wolffe, p. 228.
83. Chartier, vol ii, pp. 174–80; Robert Blandel, 'De Reductione Normanniae' in Rev. J Stevenson, *The Expulsion of the English From Normandy* (London 1863) pp. 119–20.
84. Chartier, vol ii, pp. 192–9; Blondel, pp. 170–6.
85. Simeon Luce (ed.), *Chronique de Mont-St-Michel (1343-1468)* , 2 vols (Paris 1879–83), vol ii, pp. 237–9. Fall of Guienne: Chartier, pp. 468–77. Size of English evacuation: Chartier, pp. 452–6, Wolffe, p. 211.
86. *Law Quarterly Review*, vol xciii (1977) pp. 248–83.
87. Wolffe, p. 90.
88. C Kingsford, *The First English Life of King Henry the Fifth* (London 1911) pp. 87–91; discussion in Allemand, p. 58. The 'trying on the crown' story comes from *Monstrelet*, vol iii.

Bibliography

Allemand, C, 'Documents Relating to the Anglo–French Negotiations of 1439' in C Allemand, *Camden Miscellany*, vol xxiv, 4th series, no. ix pp. 79–149.

Allemand, C, 'Henry IV', *New Dict. Of National Biography*, article: vol 26, pp. 487–97 (Oxford University Press 2003).

Allemand, C, *Henry V* (Yale UP, 1992).

Allemand, C , *Lancastrian Normandy, 1415–1450: the History of an Occupation* (Oxford 1983).

Ambuhl, Mary, 'A Fair Share of the Profits: the Ransoms of Agincourt 1415' in *Nottingham Medieval Studies*, vol l (2006) pp. 129–50.

Anonimalle: the Anonimalle Chronicle 1338–1381, (ed.) V H Galbraith (Manchester 1927).

Aston, M, *Thomas Arundel* (London 1967).

Atkinson, R L, 'Richard II and the Death of the Duke of Gloucester', *EHR* xxxviii (1923).

Avebury, Robert, *De Gestis Mirabilis Edwardi Tertii*, (ed.) E M Thompson (Clarendon Press, Oxford 1889).

Balfour-Melville, E W, *James I, King of Scots 1406–37* (London 1936).

Balfour-Melville, E W, *Edward III and David II* (Edinburgh 1954).

Barber, Richard, *Edward, Prince of Wales and Aquitaine: a Biography of the Black Prince* (Boydell 1978).

Barker, Juliet, *Conquest: the English Kingdom of France in the Hundred Years War* (Abacus 2009)

Barker, Juliet, 'The Foe Within: Treason in Lancastrian Normandy' in P Coss and C Tyerman, *Soldiers, Nobles and Gentlemen* (Oxford 2009).

Barron, C M, 'Richard II: Image and Reality', in *Making and Remaking: the Wilton Diptych* (London 1993).

Barron, C M, 'The Tyranny of Richard II', *BIHR*, xli (1968).

Basin, T, *Histoire des Regnes de Charles VII et Louis XI*, J Quichent (ed.), 4 vols (Paris 1855–9).

Beaurepaire, C, *Les Etats de Normandie sous la Domination Angloise* (Evreux 1859).

Bennett, Michael, 'Edward III's Entail and the Succession to the Crown 1376–1471' in *EHR*, vol cxiii (1998) pp. 580–609.

Bennett, Michael, *Richard II and the Revolution of 1399* (Sutton 1999).

Biggs, D, 'The Politics of Health: Henry IV and the Long Parliament of 1406', in *Henry IV: The Establishment of the Regime* , G Dodd and D Biggs (eds), pp. 185–206 (Woodbridge, Boydell 2003).

Bonenfant, P, *Du Meurtre de Montereau* (Brussels 1958).

Bossuat, A, *Perrinet Gressart et Francois de Surienne* (Paris 1936).

Bower, Walter, *Scotichronicon*, edited and translated by DER Watt et al., 9 vols, (Edinburgh 1987–98).

Brie, F W (ed.), *The Brut*, 2 vols (Oxford 1906–8).

Briggs, D R, 'A Wrong whom Conscience and Kindred bid me to right: a Reassessment of Edmund of Langley, Duke of York, and the Usurpation of Henry IV', *Albion*, vol xxvi (1994).

Brinton, Thomas *The Sermons of Thomas Brinton, Bishop of Rochester 1373-1389*, (ed.). Mary Aquinas Devlin, Camden Series, vol lxxxv (London 1954).

Broome, Dorothy M, 'The Ransom of John II, King of France, 1360–70' in *Camden Miscellany*, vol xiv (1926).

Brown, A L and Summerson, H, 'Henry V', *New Dict. Of Nat. Biography*, article: vol 26 pp. 472–87 (Oxford University Press 2003).

Buchan, J A (ed.), *Collection des Chroniques Nationales Françaises: Chronique de Froissart* (Paris 1826).

Burne, Alfred, 'The Battle of Poitiers' in *EHR*, 1938 , pp. 21–51.

Burne, Alfred, *The Crécy War: A Military history of the Hundred Years' War from 1346 to the Peace of Bretigny 1360* (London 1955).

Capgrave, J, *Liber de Illustribus Henricis*, F Hingston (ed.), Rolls Series vol 7 (1858).

Calendar of Patent Rolls Preserved in the Public Record Office: Edward I, Edward II, Edward III (25 vols), (London, HMSO 1891–1916).

Calendar of Signet Letters of Henry IV and Henry V, J L Kirby (ed.) (1978).

Capgrave, John *The Chronicle of England by* , F Hingeston (ed.) (London 1858).

Caspary, J E, 'The deposition of Richard II and the Canon Law' in *Proceedings of the Second International Congress of Medieval Law* (Boston 1965).

Chandos Herald (Chartier), Life of the Black Prince, (eds) Mildred Pope and Eleanor Lodge (Oxford 1910).

Chronica de Joannis de Reading et Anonymi Cantuarensis 1346–67, J Tait (ed.) (Manchester 1914).

The Chronicle of Adam of Usk, E M Thompson (ed.) (London 1904)

Chronicle of Jean le Venette, tr. Jean Birdsall, R Newball (ed.) (New York 1953).

Chronicles of London, (ed.) H Kingsford (Oxford 1905).

The Chronicles of Enguerrand de Monstrelet, T Johnes (ed.), 2 vols (London, Historical Society 1857).

Chronicles of the Revolution, Chris Given-Wilson (ed.) (Manchester 1992).

Chevalier, B, 'Les Ecossais dans l'Armee de Charles VII' in *Jeanne d'Arc: Un Epoque, un Rayonnement: Colloque d'Histoire Medieval 1979* (Paris 1980).

Chrimes, S B, 'The Pretensions of the Duke of Gloucester in 1422' in *EHR* vol xlv (1930).

A Chronicle of London from 1089 to 1483, N H Nicholas and E Tyrrell (eds) (London 1827).

Chronicle de Charles VII, Roi de France, par Jean Chartier, Vallet de Viriville (ed.) (Paris 1858).

Chronicon Galfridi Le Baker de Swynbroke, (ed.) E M Thompson (Clarendon Press, Oxford 1889).

Clark, M and Galbraith, V, 'The deposition of Richard II' in *Bulletin of the John Rylands Library*, vol xiv (1930).

Clarke, M V, 'The Wilton Diptych' in *Fourteenth Century Studies*. L Sutherland and Mary McKisack (eds) (Oxford Clarendon Press, 1937).

Cooper, Stephen, *The Real Falstaff: Sir John Fastolf and the Hundred Years War* (Pen and Sword 2010).

Philippe de Commignes, Memoirs, J Calmette and G Durville (eds), 3 vols (Paris 1924).

Crump, C, 'The arrest of Roger Mortimer and Queen Isabel' in *EHR* vol xxvi (1911).

Curry, Anne, *Agincourt: a New History* (Boydell 2006).

Curry, Anne, *The Battle of Agincourt: Sources and Interpretation* (Boydell 2000).

Curry, Anne, 'The "Coronation Expedition" and Henry VI's Court in France, 1430 to 1432' in Jenny Stafford (ed.), *The Lancastrian Court* (Donnington 2003).

Curry, Anne, 'English Armies in the Fifteenth Century' in A Curry and A Hughes (eds), *Arms, Armies and Fortifications in the Hundred Years War* (Boydell 1994).

Curry, Anne, 'Lancastrian Normandy: the Jewel in the Crown?' in A Curry and D Bates (eds), *England and Normandy in the Middle Ages* (London, Hambledon/Rio Grande 1994) pp. 234–52.

Curtis, E, *Richard II in Ireland 1394–5 and the Submission of the Irish Chiefs* (Oxford 1927).

Cuttino, G P, 'Historical Revision: the Causes of the Hundred Years' War' in *Speculum*, vol xxxi (1956) pp. 463–77.

Davies, R R, 'Owain Glyn Dwr and the Welsh Squirearchy' in *Transactions of the Cymmrodorion Society* (1968), pp. 150–69.

Davies, R R, *Wales 1063–1415: Conquest, Co-Existence and Change* (OUP 1987).

Davies, R R, *The Revolt of Owain Glyn Dwr* (Oxford 1995).

Delachanel, R, *Histoire de Charles V* (Paris 1909–31).

Delpit, Jules, *Collection Generales des Documents Francaises qui se trouvent en Angleterre* (Paris 1847).

De Vries, Kelly, *Joan of Arc: A Military Leader* (Sutton 2003).

De Vries, Kelly, 'Hunger, Flemish Participation and the Flight of Philip VI: Contemporary Accounts of the Siege of Calais 1346–7', in *Studies in Medieval and Renaissance History*, new series, vol xii (1991) pp. 131–81.

Dobson, R B (ed.), *The Peasants' Revolt of 1381* (London, Macmillan 1983).

Dodd, G, 'Conflict or Consnesus? Henry IV's Parliaments 1399–1406' in T Thornton (ed.), *Social Attitudes and Political Structures in the Fifteenth Century* (Sutton 2000).

Dodd, G and Bigg, D, *Henry IV; the Establishment of the Regime, 1399–1405* (Boydell 2003).

Doherty, Paul, *Isabella and the Strange Death of Edward II* (London, Basic Books 2003).

Douet de l'Arcq, C, 'Petite Chronique Française de l'An 1270 à l'An 1356' in *Melanges de las Société des Bibliophiles* (London 1867).

Dragomanni, F (ed.), *Chronica de Giovanni Villani* (Florence 1845), vol iv.

Dunn, A, 'Henry IV and the Politics of Resistance in Early Lancastrian England, 1399–1413' in *Authority and Subversion*, Linda Clark (ed.), pp. 5–24, (Woodbridge, Boydell 2003).

Eulogium Historiarum sive Tempus, F Scott Haydon (ed.) (London 1863).

Fowler, Kenneth, (ed.), *The King's Lieutenant: Henry of Grosmont, First Duke of Lancaster, 1310–1361* (London, Harper Collins 1961).

Fowler, Kenneth, (ed.), *The Hundred Years War* (London 1971).

Froissart, Sir John, *Chronicles by Sir John Froissart,* (ed.) T Johnes , 2 vols (London 1848).

Galbraith, V H, 'The Battle of Poitiers' *EHR* (1938).

Gairdner, J (ed.), *The Historical Collections of a Citizen of London in the Fifteenth Century*, (Camden Society 1876).

Gerald of Wales, Works, J Brewer, J Dimmock, F Warner (eds) (London, Rolls Series 61–91).

Gesta Henrici Quinti, F Taylor and J Roskell (eds) (Oxford 1975).

Giles, J A, *Chronicon Angliae de Regali Henrici Quarti, Henrici Quinti et Henrici Sexti* (London 1848).

Given-Wilson, C, 'Richard II and his Grandfather's Will' in *EHR*, vol xciii (1978).

Given-Wilson, C, 'The Manner of Richard II's Renunciation: a Lancastrian "Narrative"?', *EHR*, vol cviii (1993) pp. 65–70.

Given-Wilson, C, 'Richard II, Edward II and the Lancastrian Inheritance' in *EHR* vol cix (1994).

Gledwill Dickinson, Joycelyne, *The Congress of Arras 1435* (Oxford 1955).

Goldstone, Nancy, *The Maid and the Queen: the Secret History of Joan of Arc and Queen Yolande of Aragon* (Weidenfeld and Nicolson 2011).

Goodman, A, *John of Gaunt: the Exercise of Princely Power in Fourteenth Century Europe* (Longmans 1992).

Goodman, A, 'Owain Glyn Dwr before 1400' in *Welsh History Review*, vol v (1970–1) pp. 67–70.

Gorden, D, *The Court of Richard II and the Artistic World of the Wilton Diptych* (London 1996).

Gower, John, *The Complete Works of John Gower*, G Macaulay (ed.) (Oxford 1902).

Gower, John, *The Major Works of John Gower*, G Stockton (ed.) (Seattle 1962).

Gray, Sir Thomas, *Scalachronica*, (ed.) Sir Herbert Maxwell (Glasgow 1907).

Gregory's Chronicle, J Gairdner (ed.), (Camden Society 1876).

Griffiths Davies, J (ed.), *An English Chronicle of the Reigns of Richard II, Henry IV, Henry V and Henry VI*, Camden Society, Old Series, vol 64 (1856).

Griffiths, Ralph, 'Henry VI', *New Dict. of Nat. Biography*, article: vol 26 pp. 497–510 (Oxford University Press 2003).

Griffiths, Ralph, *The Reign of Henry VI: the Exercise of Royal Authority* (London 1981).

Griffiths, W R, 'Prince Henry and Wales 1400–08' in M Hicks (ed.), *Profit, Piety and the Professions in Later Medieval England* (Gloucester 1990).

Harriss, G, 'Cardinal Beaufort: Patriot or Usurer?' in *TRHS*, 5th series, vol xx (1978) pp. 129–48.

Harriss, G L, *Henry V: the Practice of Kingship* (Oxford 1985).

Harriss, G L, *Cardinal Beaufort: a Study of Lancastrian Ascendancy and Decline* (Oxford 1988).

Harvey, J H, 'The Wilton Diptych: a Re-Examination' in *Archaeologia*, vol xcviii (1961).

The History of Parliament: House of Commons vol I, 1386–1421, J Roskell, I Clark, C Rawcliffe (eds) (HMSO 1992).

Historie of the Arrivall of Edward IV,' (ed.) J Bruce, (Camden Society 1838).

Historiae Vitae et Regni Ricardi Secundi, G B Stow (ed.) (Philadelphia 1977).

Hewitt, H J, *The Black Prince's Expedition of 1355–1357* (Manchester 1958).

Hewitt, H J, *The Organisation of War under Edward III* (Manchester and New York 1962).

Holmes, G, *The Good Parliament 1376* (OUP 1976).

Housley, Norman, 'The Bishop of Norwich's Crusade, May 1383' in *History Today*, vol xxxiii (1983) pp. 15–20.

Hunt, Edwin, 'A New Look at the dealings of the Bardi and Peruzzi with Edward III', *Journal of Economic History*, vol I, pt 1 (199) pp. 149–62.

Jacobs, E, 'The Collapse of France in 1419-20' in *BJRL*, vol xxvi (1941–2).

John of Salisbury, *Materials for the History of Thomas a Becket: Epistolae*, J C Robertson (ed.) (unknown).

Johnson, P, *Duke Richard of York* (Oxford 1988).

Johnston, D B, 'Richard II and the Submission of Gaelic Ireland' in *Irish Historical Studies*, vol xii (1980).

Johnston , D B, 'The Departure of Richard II from Ireland in July 1399' in *EHR* vol xcviii (1983).

Jones, Michael, 'John Beaufort, Duke of Somerset, and the French Expedition of 1443' in Ralph Griffiths (ed.), *Patronage, the Crown and the Provinces in Later Medieval England* (Gloucester 1981).

Jones, R H, *The Royal Policy of Richard II: Absolutism in the Later Middle Ages* (Oxford 1968).

Kingsford, C, *The First English Life of King Henry the Fifth* (Oxford, Clarendon Press 1911).

Kirby, J L, *Henry IV of England* (London 1970).

Kirkstall Abbey Chronicles, J Taylor (ed.) (Thoresby Society, vol xii, 1952).

Knighton's Chronicle, 1327–1396, G Martin (ed.) (Oxford 1995).

Knighton, Henry, *Chronicon*, (ed.) Joseph Lumby (London 1895).

Le Bel, Jean, *Chronique*, (ed.). J Viard and E Depree (Paris 1904–5).

Legge, M D (ed.), *Anglo-Norman Letters and Petitions* (Anglo-Norman Society 1941).

Leroux, Alfred, 'Le sac de la cité de Limoges et son relevement, 1370–1464' in *Bulletin de la Société Archaeologique et Historique de Limousin*, vol lvi (Limoges, 1906).

Little, Roger, *The Parliament of Poitiers: War, Government and Finance in France 1418–36* (London 1984).

Lloyd, J, *Owain Glendower* (Oxford 1931).

Lodge, Eleanor, *Gascony under English Rule* (London 1926).

Loiseau, Gabriel, 'Armand Amanieu, Sieur d'Albret et ses rapports avec la monarchie française pendant la regime de Charles V' in *Melanges Histoires Offerts à Charles Bemont* (Paris 1933).

Luce, Simeon (ed.), *Chronique de Mont-St-Michel (1343–1468)* , 2 vols (Paris 1879–83).

Macfarlane, K, *Lancastrian Kings and Lollard Knights* (Oxford, Clarendon Press 1972).

MacFarlane, K B, *Lancastrian Kings and Lollard Knights* (Oxford 1972).

MacNiven, Peter, 'The Betrayal of Archbishop Scrope' in *BJRL*, vol lii (1971) pp. 172–213.

MacNiven, Peter, 'Prince Henry and the English political Crisis of 1412' in *History* vol cv (1980), pp. 7 ff.

MacNiven, Peter, *Heresy and Politics in the Reign of Henry IV: the Execution of John Badby* (Boydell 1987).

MacNiven, Peter, 'The Problem of Henry IV's Health 1405–13' in *EHR* vol c (1985) pp. 747–59.

McKisack, Mary, *The Fourteenth Century: 1307–1399* (Oxford 1959).

Mathew, G, *The Court of Richard II* (London 1968).

Minot, Laurence, *The Poems of Laurence Minot, 1313–52*, TB James and J Simon (eds) (Exeter 1989).

Moisset, J, *Le Prince Noir en Aquitaine* (Paris 1894).

Moranville, H, 'Le Siege de Rheims 1359–60', in *BEC*, vol lvi (1895).

Morgan, D A L, 'The political after-life of Edward III: the apotheosis of a warmonger', *EHR*, vol cxii (1997) pp. 856–81.

Morgan, Philip, 'Henry IV and the Shadow of Richard II', in R Archer (ed.), *Crown, Government and People in the Fifteenth Century* (Sutton 1995).

Morosini, Antonio, *Chronique*, G Lefevre-Pontalis and G Dorez (eds), (Paris 1899).

Mortimer, Ian, 'The death of Edward Ii in Berkeley Castle' in *English Historical Review*, cxx (2000), pp. 1175–1214.

Mortimer, Ian, *The Fears of Henry IV: the Life of England's Self-Made King* (Vintage 2008).

Mortimer, Ian, *The Greatest Traitor: The Life of Roger Mortimer, Ruler of England 1327–1330* (Pimlico 2000).

Mortimer, Ian, *The Perfect King: the Life of Edward III, Father of the English Nation* (Pimlico 2006).

Le Musset, Giles, *Chroniques et Annales*, H Le Maistre (ed.) (Paris 1906).

Myres, A N, 'The captivity of a royal witch: the household accounts of Joan of Navarre, 1419–21' in *BJRL* (1940) pp. 262–84.

Myres, A N (ed.), *English Historical Documents* (London, HMSO 1969).

Newhall, R A,*The English Conquest of Normandy 1416–24: a Study in Fifteenth-Century Warfare* (Yale 1924).

Nicholson, Randall, *Edward III and the Scots: the Formative Years of a Military Career, 1327–1355* (Oxford 1965).

Ormerod, M, 'The Rebellion of Archbishop Scrope and the tradition of clerical opposition to royal taxation' in G Dodd and D Biggs (eds), *The Reign of Henry IV : Rebellion and Survival, 1403–1413*, pp. 862–79, (York Medieval Press 2008).

Ormerod, W M, 'A Problem of Precedents: Edward III, the Dual Monarchy and the Royal Style' in J S Bothwell (ed.), *The Age of Edward III* (Boydell 2001).

Ormerod, W M, *Edward III* (Yale UP 2011).

Otway-Ruthven, A J, *Medieval Ireland* (London 1968).

Owens, E, 'Owain Lawgoch – Yvain de Galles – Some Facts and Suggestions', *Transactions of the Cymmrodorion Society* (1899–1900) pp. 6–105.

Palmer, J J N, 'The Anglo-French Peace Negotiations, 1390–6' in *TRHS*, series 5, vol xvi (1986).

Palmer, J J N, 'The Background to Richard II's marriage to Isabel of France (1396)', in *BRHS*, vol xliv (1971).

The Parliament Rolls of Medieval England, 1275–1504, C Given-Wilson (ed.) (Boydell 2004).

Le Patourel, Jean, 'l'occupation Anglaise de Calais au XIV Siecle' in *Revue de Nord*, vol xxxiii (1955) pp. 228–41.

Le Patourel, Jean, 'The Treaty of Bretigny 1360' in *Transactions of the Royal Historical Society*, series 5, vol x (1960) pp. 19–39.

Perneul, Regine, *Joan of Arc; By Herself and Her Contemporaries*, tr. E Hyams (London and New York 1982).

Perroy, E, *Angleterre et le Grand Schism* (Paris 1933).

Polychronicon Ranulphi Higden, (ed.) J Lumby (London, Rolls Series 1882).

Prestwich, M, *Edward I* (Methuen 1988).

Prestwich, M, *The Three Edwards: War and State in England 1327–1377* (London, Routledge 1980).

Prince, A E, 'The strength of English armies in the reign of Edward III' in *EHR* vol clxxxiii (1931) pp. 353–71.

Proceedings and Ordinances of the Privy Council of England, Sir Harris Nicholas (ed.) (London 1834–7).

Pugh, T B, *Henry V and the Southampton Plot of 1415*, Southampton Record Series vol xxx (Stroud, Sutton Press 1988).

Pugh, T B, 'The Southampton Plot of 1415' in R Griffiths and J Sherborne (eds), *Kings and Nobles in the Later Middle Ages* (Gloucester 1986).

Ramsay, J, *Lancaster and York: a Century of English History (1377–1483)*, 2 vols (Oxford 1892).

Ramsay, J, 'The Strength of English Armies in the Middle Ages' in *EHR* ccix (1914), pp. 221–7.

Riley, H T, *Memorials of London and London Life* (London 1868).

Rogers, A, 'Henry IV, the Commons and Taxation' in *Medieval Studies*, vol xxxi (1969) pp. 44–70.

Rogers, A, 'The Political Crisis of 1401' in *Nottingham Medieval Studies*, vol xii (1968) pp. 85–96.

Rogers, Clifford, 'The Anglo-French Peace Negotiations of 1354–60 Reconsidered' in J S Bothwell (ed.), *The Age of Edward III* (Boydell 2001).

Rogers, Clifford, 'Henry V's Military Strategy in 1415' in A Villalon and D Kagay (eds), *The Hundred Years' War* (London 2004).

Rogers, Clifford (ed.), *The Wars of Edward III; Sources and Interpretations* (Boydell 1999).

Rose, Alexander, *Kings in the North: The House of Percy in British History* (Phoenix 2005).

Rotuli Parliamentorum ... AD 1278–1503, J Strachey, J Pridden, E Upham (eds) (6 vols), (London 1767–77).

Rowe, C B, 'Discipline in the English Garrisons in Normandy under Bedford, 1422-35' in *EHR* xlvi (1931) pp. 194–208.

Russell, P E, *The English Intervention in Spain and Portugal in the Time of Edward III and Richard II*, (London 1955).

Sandquist, T A, 'The Holy Oil of St Thomas of Canterbury' in *Essays in Medieval History Presented to Bertie Wilkinson*, T Sandquist and M Powicke (eds) (University of Toronto Press 1969).

Stecche, John, 'The Chronicle of John Strecche for the reign of Henry V', in F Taylor (ed.) *Bulletin of the John Rylands Library*, vol xvi (1932) pp. 137–87.

Stevenson, Rev. Joseph, *Letters and Papers Illustrative of the Wars of the English in France during the Reign of King Henry the Sixth of England* (London 1864).

Saul, Nigel, *Richard II* (Yale UP 1997).

Saul, Nigel, *The Three Richards* (London, Continuum 2005).

Sayles, G, 'Richard II in 1381 and 1399', *EHR*, vol xciv (1979).

Sayles, G, 'The deposition of Richard II: Three Lancastrian Narratives' in *BIHR*, vol liv (1981) pp. 257–70.

Sherborne, J, 'The Battle of La Rochelle and the War at Sea, 1372-5' in *BIHR*, vol xlii (1969) pp. 22–5.

Sherborne, J, 'The Cost of English Warfare with France in the Later Fourteenth Century' in *Bulletin of the Institute of Historical Research*, vol I (1977) pp. 66–9.

Sherborne, J, 'Perjury and the Lancastrian Revolution of 1399' in *Welsh History Review* vol xiv (1988).

Smallwood, T M, 'Prophecy of the Six Kings' in *Speculum*, vol lx (1985).

Smith, J B, 'The Last Phase of the Glyn Dwr Rebellion' in *Bulletin of the Board of Celtic Studies*, vol xxii (1966–8) pp. 250–60.

Stamp, A E, 'Richard II and the Murder of the Duke of Gloucester', *EHR* vol xxxvii (1923) pp. 249–51.

Stevenson, Joseph, *The Expulsion of the English From Normandy*, (London 1863).

Stowe, C B, 'Richard II in Walsingham' s Chronicles' in *Speculum* vol lix (1984).

Sumption, Jonathan, *The Hundred Years' War, vol i: Trial by Battle* (London, Faber and Faber/Philadelphia, University of Pennsylvania Press 1990).

Sumption, Jonathan, *The Hundred Years' War, vol ii: Trial by Fire* (London, Faber and Faber/Philadelphia, University of Pennsylvania Press 1996).

Tait, J, 'Did Richard II Murder the Duke of Gloucester?' in *Historical Essays by Members of Owens College Manchester*, J Tout and J Tait (eds) (Manchester 1902).

Taylor, C, 'Brittany and the French Crown: the Legacy of the English Attack on Fougeres (1449)' in J R Maddicott and D Palliser (eds), *The Medieval State: Essays Presented to James Campbell* (London 2000).

Taylor, C, 'Edward III and the Plantagenet Claim to the French Throne' in J S Bothwell (ed.), *The Age of Edward III* (Boydell 2001).

Taylor, C, *Joan of Arc: La Pucelle: Selected Sources* (Manchester and New York 2006).

Taylor, C, 'The Salic Law and the Succession to the French throne', in *French History* xv (2001) pp. 338–77.

Taylor, J, 'The Battle of Agincourt: Once More Into The Breach', *The Independent*, 1 November 2008.

Taylor, J, 'Richard II's Views on Kingship', *Proceedings of the Leeds Philosophical and Historical Society*, vol xiv (1971).

Thomae Walsingham Quondae Monachi S. Albanis, Historia Anglicana, H T Riley (ed.) (London, Rolls Society 1864).

Johannis de Trokelowe et Henrici de Blaneford, chronici et annals, H T Riley (ed.) (Rolls Series, vol 28, 1861).

Thomas Rymer, *Foedera* (London, Records Commission 1869 edition).

Three Prose Versions of the Secreta Secretorum, R Steele (ed.) (EETS, extra series, vol lxxiv, 1898).

Triveti, Nicolae, *Annales*, T Hog (ed.) (London, English Historical Society 1845).

Tuetey, A (ed.), *A Parisian Journal 1405–49: translated from the Anonyme Journal d'un Bourgeois de Paris*, tr. Janet Shirley (Oxford 1968).

Tuck, A, 'Anglo–Irish Relations 1382–93' in *Proceedings of the Royal Irish Academy*, vol xlix (1970).

Tuck, A, *Richard II and the Nobility* (London 1973).

Tuck, N, 'Richard II', in *New Dict. Of Nat. Biography*, article: vol 46 pp. 724–46 (Oxford University Press 2003).

Vale, M G, *Charles VII* (London 1974).

Valente, C, 'The Deposition and Abdication of Edward II', *EHR* vol cxiii (1998).

Vallet de Viriville, A, *Histoire de Charles VII, Roi de France, et Son Epoque* (Paris 1865).

van Heerwarden, Jan, *Joan of Arc: Reality and Myth* (Hilversum 1998).

Vaughan, B, *John the Fearless, Duke of Burgundy* (London 1966).

Vaughan, B, *Philip the Good, Duke of Burgundy* (London 1970, repr. Boydell 2002).

Viard, Jules, 'La Campaigne de Juillet – Aout `346 et la bataille de Crécy', in *Le Moyen Age*, series 2, vol xxviii (1926) pp. 1–84.

Viard, Jules, 'Le Siege de Calais' in *Le Moyen Age*, series ii, vol 30 (1929) pp. 128–89.

Walsingham, Thomas, *Chronicon Angliae ab anno domini 1328 usque ad 1388*, E M Thompson (ed.) (Oxford, Clarendon Press 1874).

Walsingham, Thomas, *The St Albans Chronicle: the Chronica Majora of Thomas Walsingham, 1376–94*, J Taylor, Wendy Childs, Leslie Watkiss (eds) (Oxford 2003).

Watts, J, *Henry VI and the Politics of Kingship* (Cambridge University Press 1996).

de Wauvrin, Jean, *Jean de Wauvrin: A Collection of the Chronicles and Ancient Histories by J de W, 1399– 1422*, Sir William and Edward Hardy (eds) (London, Rolls Society 1887).

The Westminster Chronicle, 1381–94, L C Hector and B F Harvey (eds) (Clarendon Press 1982).

Williams, Glanmor, *Owen Glendower* (London, Clarendon Press 1966).

Wright, H G, 'The Protestation of Richard II in the Tower in September 1399' in *BJRL*, vol xxxii (1939).

Wylie, J H, *History of England under Henry IV*, 4 vols (London 1884).

Whiting, B J, 'The Vow of the Heron', *Speculum*, xx (1945) pp. 261–78.

Wilkinson, B, 'The Peasants' Revolt of 1381' in *Speculum*, vol xv (1940) pp. 20–4.

Williams, C, *My Lord of Bedford 1389–1435* (London 1963).

Wolffe, Bertram, *Henry VI* (Methuen 1981).

Index

TO ORDER THE
OTHER INSTALLMENTS IN THE
ALTERNATIVE HISTORY OF BRITAIN SERIES
AT **20% OFF** THE COVER PRICE
PLEASE CALL 01226 734222

OR PRE-ORDER ONLINE VIA OUR WEBSITE:
WWW.PEN-AND-SWORD.CO.UK

Dr Timothy Venning starts with an outline of the process by which much of Britain came to be settled by Germanic tribes after the end of Roman rule, so far as it can be determined from the sparse and fragmentary sources. He then moves on to discuss a series of scenarios which might have altered the course of subsequent history dramatically. For example, was a reconquest by the native British ever a possibility (under 'Arthur' or someone else)? Which of the Anglo-Saxon kingdoms might have united England sooner and would this have kept the Danes out? And, of course, what if Harold Godwinson had won at Hastings?

9781781591253 •
240 pages • HB • £19.99 •
Available Now

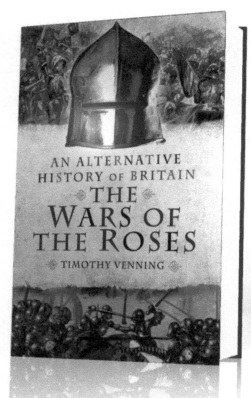

Timothy Venning's exploration of the alternative paths that British history might easily have taken moves on to the Wars of the Roses. What if Richard of York had not given battle in vain? How would a victory for Warwick the Kingmaker at the Battle of Barnet changed the course of the struggle for power? What if the Princes had escaped from the tower or the Stanleys had not betrayed their king at Bosworth? These are just a few of the fascinating questions posed by this book.

9781781591277 •
240 pages • HB • £19.99 •
Available April 2013